THE
HARDER
THEY
COME

ALSO BY T. CORAGHESSAN BOYLE

NOVELS

Water Music (1982)

Budding Prospects (1984)

World's End (1987)

East Is East (1990)

The Road to Wellville (1993)

The Tortilla Curtain (1995)

Riven Rock (1998)

A Friend of the Earth (2000)

Drop City (2003)

The Inner Circle (2004)

Talk Talk (2006)

The Women (2009)

When the Killing's Done (2011)

San Miguel (2012)

SHORT STORIES

Descent of Man (1979)

Greasy Lake & Other Stories (1985)

If the River Was Whiskey (1989)

Without a Hero (1994)

T.C. Boyle Stories (1998)

After the Plague (2001)

Tooth and Claw (2005)

The Human Fly (2005)

Wild Child & Other Stories (2010)

T.C. Boyle Stories II (2013)

ANTHOLOGIES

DoubleTakes (2004) co-edited with K. Kvashay-Boyle

THE
HARDER
THEY
COME

T. Coraghessan Boyle

BLOOMSBURY

LONDON · NEW DELHI · NEW YORK · SYDNEY

Bloomsbury Publishing
An imprint of Bloomsbury Publishing Plc

50 Bedford Square   1385 Broadway
London   New York
WC1B 3DP   NY 10018
UK   USA

www.bloomsbury.com

BLOOMSBURY and the Diana logo are trademarks of Bloomsbury Publishing Plc

First published in Great Britain 2015

British Library Cataloguing-in-Publication Data
A catalogue record for this book is available from the British Library.

ISBN: HB: 978-1-4088-5992-6
       TPB: 978-1-4088-5993-3
       PB: 978-1-4088-5995-7
       ePub: 978-1-4088-5994-0

2 4 6 8 10 9 7 5 3 1

Designed by Mary Austin Speaker

To find out more about our authors and books visit www.bloomsbury.
com. Here you will find extracts, author interviews, details of forthcoming
events and the option to sign up for our newsletters.

For Scott and Nicky, Chuck and Donna,
from Quintara Street to Lion Loop

The essential American soul is hard, isolate, stoic, and a killer.
It has never yet melted.

D. H. LAWRENCE
Studies in Classic American Literature

PART I

Puerto Limón

I.

THERE WAS NO SLANT to the sun—it was just there, overhead, burning, making him sweat, making his underwear bind and the shirt stick to his back as if it had been glued on, and why he'd ever let Carolee talk him into this he'd never know. The bus lurched. There was a stink of diesel. Gears ratcheted beneath the floorboards, metal on metal, as if they were going to fuse or maybe explode into a thousand pieces at any moment. He looked beyond Carolee, out the window, feeling ever so slightly queasy, though everyone assured him the water was good here—*potable,* that was the word on everybody's lips, as if they were trying to convince themselves. Plus, the food was held to the highest standards and the glasses out of which they'd sipped their rum punch and rum cokes and rum tonics scrupulously washed in hot sudsing pristine well water, because this wasn't like Mexico or Guatemala or Belize, this was special, orderly, clean, a kind of tourist paradise. And cheap. Cheap too.

On top of it all, he had a headache. Or the beginnings of one. But that was understandable, because he'd gulped down three rum punches with lunch, so thirsty he could have drained the whole pitcher the waiter had set in the middle of the table, and no, he wasn't going to drink the water, no matter what anybody said—not unless it came from a bottle with an unbroken seal. He rubbed his eyes. He had aspirin in his kit back on the ship. Cipro too. But that didn't do him a whole lot of good now, did it? Anonymous streets rolled by, shops, people, dogs, ratty-looking birds infesting the trees and an armed guard out front of every store—or *tienda,* as his guidebook had it—and what did that tell you about the level of orderliness here? *Bienvenidos.* Welcome. *Mi casa es su casa.*

The bus slammed through one of the million and a half pot-holes cratering the street and Carolee grabbed for his arm. The man in the seat across from him—Bill, or was it Phil?—let out a curse. "I wish he'd slow down," Carolee said, and he shot a look at the driver, at the back of his head that had been shaved to stubble, the white annealed scar in the shape of a fishhook at the hairline, ears too big, neck too thin, and then he was gazing out the smeared window to where the ship lay fixed in the har-bor behind them like a great shining edifice built by a vanished civilization—or a vanishing one, anyway. "I don't know," he said, his voice crackling through its filter of phlegm as if he'd been transformed into Louis Armstrong in his old age—everything, even his laugh, coming out in an airless rasp—"I kind of wish he'd speed up so we can get this over with. *Nature walk*," he said. "In this heat? Give me a break."

"Oh, come on, Sten, lighten up." Carolee was giving him a look he knew from long experience, her eyes wide and her head tilted just a fraction to the right, as if what you'd just said had thrown her off balance. She was enjoying this. If it wasn't the birds and monkeys, it was the trinket shops and the little out-of-the-way restaurants everyone assured her the tourists hadn't dis-covered yet in spite of the fact that they were listed in the back of all the guidebooks and the waiters practically erupted from their shoes when the tour bus pulled up out front. She didn't speak the language, beyond "*¿Cuánto?*" and "*Demasiado*," but it didn't stop her. She wanted things. She wanted life, new experience, a change in the routine. *What good's retirement if you're just going to sit there and rot?* That was her line. He'd heard it all day, every day, until finally he'd given in, though privately he figured that since you were going to rot anyway you might as well do it at home, where at least you could drink the water.

"Didn't you just tell me this morning how you need some real exercise instead of what, shuffleboard and bending your elbow at the bar?" She canted her head a degree more so that her hair, which she still wore long, swept across the right side of her face, and in that moment he felt the thing he'd always felt for her, the thing that had tugged at him now for forty years and more. "Or am I wrong? Did I mishear you? Huh, mister? Was that it?" She poked him for emphasis, but playfully, copacetically, one stiff finger right in the ribs, and he couldn't help smiling despite himself.

Soon they were winding their way along the seashore, the road getting progressively worse, the houses sparser, everything so green it ached. It was one in the afternoon. The sun baked the roof of the bus. People dozed, their heads thrown back or cradled in their arms. Though the windows were open, the air hardly seemed to move, as if it were another medium altogether, solid, heavy, like sludge. Lunch had been at an authentic café, *Ticos* (that was what the locals were called) all around them, going through the motions of fork to mouth like anybody you'd see anywhere. That these people, this place, existed independently of him and everything he knew had astonished him all over again, as if he'd gone outside himself, a ghost drifting through another reality. He tried to capture it with his camera, snapping dutifully away, but the photos themselves were ephemeral, images flashing by on a computer screen, attached to nothing, and no one would ever see them, he knew that. The waiter had brought plates of rice and beans. Some sort of fried fish. And rum punch, thank god for that, though if he stopped to think about it he'd have to wonder about the ice cubes clacking away in the depths of the pitcher and where exactly they'd come from, as if he didn't already know.

The driver jerked at the wheel, shifted down, then up, then down again. He felt his stomach clench. They passed a scatter of houses, a grocery, a school, and suddenly both shoulders of the road were thronged with boys in white shirts and dark trousers and girls in matching blouses and skirts marching through the ochre mud either to or from school, he couldn't say which, half of them going one way and half the other. Maybe it was double sessions, maybe that was it. Or siesta. Did they have siesta here?

Someone had told him education was compulsory for everybody in the country, grades one through eight, after which it fell off to practically nothing. But that was all right. At least they were literate, at least they could do sums, and what more did you need for a tourist economy? Language skills, maybe. Their waiter at lunch spoke a hopped-up Jamaican dialect, a kind of reggae English, but you could hardly understand what he was saying. Still, just about everybody had at least some English, thanks to Imperial America and the consumer fever that kept spiraling outward till the buy-now/pay-later message was practically a tribal chant from every outpost of the earth. What a gulf there was between needs and wants, he was thinking, all these *things,* these appliances, these handheld devices . . . but what he wanted now— needed, urgently—was a rest stop. And something to wet his throat, bottled water, a soda, gum, did anybody have any gum?

Carolee was dozing, her head pinned beneath his left arm, sweating there, his sweat and hers, conjoined. He tried not to jostle her as he reached for her bag, for the water in the plastic bottle with the screw cap she'd remembered to bring along and he hadn't. The bag—one of those black over-the-shoulder things she insisted on wearing looped across her chest so the street punks couldn't make off with it—was on the floor at her feet. He leaned into her, bracing her, and felt the muscles in his lower right side grab as he reached down for it, just a pinch there, a reminder of the intermittent back pain he'd been having and the exercises the therapist had given him to keep limber, exercises he'd been neglecting because he was on vacation, on a cruise ship, and all that seemed to matter on a cruise ship was eating and drinking— you weren't getting your money's worth unless you put on twenty pounds and calcified your liver.

He managed to extract the bottle without waking his wife, using her slack form as a counterweight as he leaned forward, and now he was unscrewing the cap and rinsing his mouth before taking a single long swallow. It seemed as if he was always thirsty lately, thirsty back at home, thirsty on the ship, thirsty under this sun, and he wondered vaguely if it was age-related, the first sign of some as yet undiagnosed syndrome—the dreaded acronym—that would bring him down in a dark bloom of imploding cells. The tires screeched. There was a bump. Another bump. Carolee jolted awake on a ragged intake of breath. "What?" she gasped, her eyes straining to focus.

"You were dozing."

He gave her a minute to come back to the world, the bus, the rank invasive odor of the overheated sea and the sodden jungle. She'd been into the rum at lunch too, rum black as oil, in a smudged glass two-thirds filled with Diet Coke, no ice. Neither of them was used to drinking this early in the day, but then why not, they were on vacation, weren't they? And he was retired—or *pre-dead,* as he preferred to call it. Party on. Everybody else was.

"I was dreaming," she said.

"Me too, but I was awake. You got any gum?"

She shook her head. "Water?" she said, making a question of it, and she bent to reach for her bag before she saw the bottle clamped there in his sweating hand. "Which I see you already found."

He handed her the bottle and she unscrewed the cap and took a sip herself. "Ugh," she said, making a face, "it tastes awful."

"Hot enough to put a tea bag in. And I'll give you even money they fill it from a tap someplace, like in that movie, what was the name of it, in India?"

"No," she said, "no. This came from the ship."

He glanced out the window. More children, more school uniforms, a *tienda* with a wide-open door and maybe drinks inside, Coca-Cola, *Naranja Croosh.* He saw tethered goats, palms, bananas, clothes on a line, a squadron of white-haired men playing cards at a table set up in the courtyard between whitewashed houses, the whole business flitting by so fast it was like a movie in the wrong speed. And then, without warning, the bus veered left at a fork in the road and they shot down a narrow tunnel of vegetation, branches snatching at the roof, dogs and chickens scattering before them. Carolee slammed into his shoulder, loose as a puppet, and there went the water, the bottle hitting the floor with a soft liquid thump before vanishing under the seat and then reappearing an instant later as if it were some magic trick. "Jesus," he said, "what's this guy trying to do, kill us?"

In the next moment he was on his feet, making his way up the aisle toward the front of the bus, bracing himself against the seatbacks. He was a big man, six-three and two hundred twenty pounds, most of it still in the right places, and he filled the aisle. People turned to look at him—the ones who weren't lost in a rum haze, that is—but he focused on the back of the driver's head and tried to keep his balance. There were eighteen or twenty passengers, couples mostly and mostly around his age, and he knew the majority of them by sight, if not by name. The cruise had originated in San Diego and they'd already made stops at Cabo San Lucas, Puerto Vallarta, Puerto Quetzal, Puntarenas, the Panama Canal and Colón, and while there were nearly two thousand passengers aboard, you got to know—or at least recognize—the ones who tended to go on expeditions like this one.

"Excuse me," he said, leaning over the driver, "but I wonder if you couldn't slow down a bit?" The windshield held an image and then snatched it away, dodging like a Brahma bull. The engine labored. The driver shifted down, shot an impatient glance over one shoulder and then turned his back on him. "Excuse me?" he repeated. "People are getting upset back there—*I'm* getting upset."

The driver didn't seem to hear him. And why? Sten noticed now that the man was wearing one of those iPod hookups, the buds fixed inside his ears like decorations, like the black wooden plugs his son's friend Cody wore in his stretched-out earlobes. The bus kept moving, but time slowed. Sten studied the man from above, the shining mahogany crown of his head, the ears like knobs you could take hold of and twist, the sparse bloom of stringy hairs snaking out of his chin. The music was so loud you could hear it even over the noise of the engine. Reggae. The eternal reggae they played everywhere on this side of the country as if it were vital to body function. He hated reggae. Hated this jerk who wouldn't slow down or think to stop someplace so people could relieve themselves. And he hated to be ignored. So what he did, as tenderly as he could, was jerk the cord so the buds popped out of the man's ears, and now the bus slowed, and now the driver—what was he, thirty, thirty-five?—was paying attention to him, all right.

"Go sit," the man said, glaring over his shoulder. He made a motion with one hand, as if shooing a fly, then dug a pair of opaque black sunglasses out of his shirt pocket and clamped them over his eyes.

"I said, could you slow down, is all. You got old people on this bus. What's the hurry?"

The driver ignored him, fixing his gaze back on the road. The buds dangled at his throat, the music released now to a metallic thump and roll and the thin nasal complaint of a voice lost in the mix. The bus accelerated. "You sit," he said without turning his head. "No person is permitted up front." And he pointed to a sign, faded and sun-blasted, that read *Stay Behind Line.*

Sten didn't move. He just stood there, looming over the driver like a statue, one hand gripping the overhead rack, the other braced against the seatback. "And how about a pit stop? Any restrooms out here?" Even as he posed the question he realized how foolish he sounded. He could only imagine what the driver must have thought of him, of all of them, privileged white people demanding this and that, here today, gone tomorrow. What did this guy care? There'd be another boat tomorrow and the next day and the day after that.

Finally, the tension tightening like a cord between them, the driver whipped his head round, his eyes visible as two indistinct drifting spheres behind the black plastic lenses. "Five minutes," he said, the reggae pulsing at his throat, radiating up from the neck of his bright print shirt. Reggae. *Thump-thump, boom. Thump-thump, boom.* "Five minutes and we are there. You sit. *Now.*"

Five minutes? It was more like fifteen—and you can bet he was checking his watch all the way, his stomach doing backflips and his bladder sending urgent messages up his nervous system to his brain, which by now had burned itself clear of any lingering after-effects of the rum so he could focus on what was important. Like escaping this sweatbox. Like pissing. Wetting his throat. Getting all this over with so he could go back to the boat, take a shower and stretch out on the bed, shut his eyes and dream of absolutely nothing.

The driver finally slowed down, but only because the road was barely passable here, so trenched and riddled it looked as if it had been shelled. As it was, they were jolted from side to side as the bus dipped tentatively into one hole after another, the wheels grabbing for purchase, the chassis shuddering and the transmission crying out with a grating whine that had Sten wondering if they were going to wind up walking back. "All we need," he rasped at Carolee as she rocked into him. "You think triple A makes calls out here?"

The nature walk wasn't sponsored by the cruise line, but the concierge or fun director or whatever you wanted to call her—a short grinning wide-faced woman in clopping heels and skirts that rode up her thighs—had pushed the brochure on them, along with brochures for a dozen other activities, ranging from kayaking in the harbor to visiting working potters and silversmiths to a self-guided tour of the local rum distilleries, map included. The brochure had featured a sleek two-tone modern van, silver above, blue below, and a light-skinned Tico driver with a conventional haircut, a welcoming smile and a chauffeur's cap, not that Sten cared whether the man behind the wheel was a Swede or a Man-dingo, but the reality was something else. Here you had this surly thug for a driver and a shabby decommissioned school bus that had been painted over so many times it looked as if it had grown a hide. Nobody had been particularly happy about it ("No air-conditioning? You kidding me?"), but they all climbed aboard and squeezed into the seats designed for children in some other place altogether, Lubbock or Yuma or King City, and told them-selves *At least it's cheap.*

He was staring gloomily out the window, getting more irri-tated by the minute, when they came to a shallow stream that seemed to be incorporated into the road along with the blistered rocks and scum-filled potholes, except that it was flowing, fanning out in front of them in a broad rippling pan. The tires eased into the water with a soft *shush,* spray leapt up and fell back again, and all at once he was thinking of the fish that must have lived there in the deep pools, tropical fish, the characins and Jack Dempseys and brick-red platys he'd introduced to his aquarium as a boy. Sud-denly he was lost in reverie, picturing the glowing wall of tanks in the pet shop he'd haunted after school each day, remembering the pleasure of selecting the fish and paying for them with his own money, of setting up his first aquarium, arranging the rocks, digging in the gravel to plant the—what was it?—elodea. Yes, *elodea.* And the Amazon sword plant that looked like a miniature avocado tree. And what else? The little dwarf catfish, the albino ones, and what were they called?

He hadn't thought about that in years. Or his mother—the way she recoiled in mock horror from the tubifex worms he kept in a Dixie cup in the refrigerator to preserve them. Fish food. The thread-like worms, the smell of them, the smell of the aquarium itself when you lifted the top and the world you'd cre-ated breathed back in your face. He began to feel his mood lift. Carolee was right. This *was* an adventure, something to break the routine, get him outside his comfort zone. The brochure had promised all four types of monkey, as well as agoutis, sloths, peccaries, maybe even an ocelot or jaguar, and here he was getting worked up over taking a leak. He almost felt ashamed of himself, but then he lifted his eyes to where the driver sat block-like at the wheel and felt all the outrage rush back into him. The guy was a clod. An idiot. No more sensible than a stone. He was about to get up again, about to lean over the man and hiss *You did say five minutes, right?*, when the bus emerged on a muddy clearing scored with tire ruts and the driver pulled over to one side and applied the brakes. Everybody looked up.

"Now we have arrived," the driver said in his textbook English, swiveling in his seat to project his voice down the aisle. "Now you must debark." The buds were back in his ears. The dark glasses caught the light. Outside was the jungle. "Two hours," he said, and the door wheezed open.

They were all rising now, fumbling with cameras, purses, daypacks. One of the women—Sheila, sixtyish, traveling alone with what must have been a gallon of perfume and the pink sneakers and turquoise capris she'd worn every day on the cruise, breakfast, lunch, high tea, cocktails and dinner—raised her voice to ask, "Do you meet us back here or what?"

"I am here," the driver said, bringing two fingers to the wisps of hair at his chin. He stretched, cracked his knuckles. "Two hours," he repeated.

Sten peered out the window. There was, of course, no restroom, no Porta-Potty, nothing, just half a dozen mud-spattered vehicles nosed in around the trailhead, where a sign read *Nature Preserve,* in Spanish and English. Across the lot, in the shade of the trees, there was a *palapa* and in the *palapa* a single titanic woman in a red head scarf. She would have something to drink—a soda, that was all he needed—and behind the *palapa,* in the undergrowth, he would find a tree trunk to decorate and all would be well.

They disembarked in a storm of chatter, Phil leading the way—or no, Bill, his name was definitely Bill, because Sten recalled distinctly that there had been two Bills at their table for lunch, and this was the bald-headed one. Not that it mattered. Once the ship docked in Miami he'd never see the guy again— and what he had seen of him so far didn't go much deeper than *How about those Giants?* and *Pass the salt.*

There was a momentary holdup, because Sheila, who was next in line, couldn't resist leaning in to ask the driver where their best chance to see scarlet macaws was and they all had to wait as the driver removed the buds from his ears and asked her to repeat herself. They watched the man frown over the question, his eyebrows rising like twin smudges above the rim of the sunglasses. "*No sé,*" he said finally, waving at the lot, the jungle, the trail. "I have never—" and he broke off, searching for the word.

Sheila looked at him in astonishment. "You mean you just drop people off and you've never even been up there? In your own country? Aren't you curious?"

The driver shrugged. He was doing a job, that was all. Why muddy his shoes? Why feed the mosquitoes? He'd leave that to the gringos with their cameras and purses and black cloth bags, their fanny packs and preposterous turquoise pants and the dummy wallets with the expired credit cards to throw off the pickpockets while everybody knew their real wallets were tucked down the front of their pants.

"Come on," Sten heard himself say. "You're holding up the line."

Outside, in the lot, the sun hammered down on him all over again. He waited a moment, gathering himself while Carolee tried simultaneously to tighten the cord of her floppy straw hat and loop the strap of the black bag over her head, and then he was striding across the lot toward the *palapa* and the woman there. "I'm getting a soda," he called over his shoulder. "You want anything?"

She didn't. She had her water. And no matter the taste, it had come from the ship.

When the woman in the *palapa* saw him coming, she pushed herself laboriously up from the stool she was sitting on and rested her arms on the makeshift counter. She must have weighed two-fifty, maybe more. Her skin shone black with sweat. Like the waiter at the café, she was West Indian, one of the Jamaicans who'd settled in Limón—there was a whole section called Jamaica Town, or so the guidebook had it. Very colorful. Plenty of rum. Plenty of reggae. Trinkets galore. "Good afternoon," she said, treating him to a broad full-lipped smile. "And how may I be helping you?"

There was a plastic cooler set on the ground behind the counter in a spill of green coconuts. Above it, nailed to the crossbeam, was a board displaying various packages of nuts, potato chips and candy. A paperback book—*El Amor Furioso*—lay facedown on the counter.

"You got any sodas back there?" Sten asked, and he'd almost asked for a *cerveza,* but thought better of it—he was already dehydrated. And he had to piss. Badly.

"Cola, Cola Lite, *agua mineral, pipas, carambola, naranja, limón,*" she recited, holding her smile.

"Cola Lite," he said, reaching for his wallet, and then he had the can, lukewarm, in his hand, and he was wading through the trash-studded undergrowth in back of the stall, his fly already open.

At first his water wouldn't come, another trick of old age—your bladder feels like a hot-air balloon and then you stand over the toilet for ten minutes before the first burning dribble releases itself—but he employed the countermeasure of clearing his mind, of thinking of anything but the matter at hand, of the boat and his berth and the way Carolee had looked in the new negligee she'd bought expressly for the trip and what he'd been able to do about it, and then, finally, the relief came. He took his time, christening a tree that was alive with ants, tropical ants, ants of a kind he'd never seen before and would likely never see again. If he was lucky.

A long suspended moment drifted by, the ants piling up and colliding over the cascade of this rank new element in their midst, insects throbbing, birds calling, everything alive all around him. The sun barely penetrated here, and where it did the leaves gave off a dull underwater sheen, the air so dense he half expected to see sharks cruising through the trees. There was a smell of rot, of fragile earth. Something hooted and then another something took it up and hooted back. He might have stood there forever if it weren't for the mosquitoes—here they came, rising up out of nowhere to remind him of where he was. He shook and zipped up, and only then did he rediscover the can of soda in his left hand, an amazing thing really, an artifact, an object of manufactured beauty transported all the way out here to quench his thirst and pump aspartame into his bloodstream.

He cracked the tab and wet his lips. Cola Lite. It tasted awful, like the amalgam the dentist put in his teeth. No matter. It was wet. He took a swallow and started back around the fat woman's stall, the shade of the trees giving way to a blast of naked sun so that the headache came up on him all over again and he couldn't help wishing, for at least the tenth time since they'd left the boat, that he'd remembered his baseball cap.

That was when things changed, changed radically. He was standing there blinking in the light and feeling in his shirt pocket for his sunglasses when a noise—the slamming of a car door—made him look up. There was another car in the lot now, an old American car—what was it, a Chevy?—and it was pulled up right beside the bus. The car was a faded yellow, the finish worn through to rusted metal in so many places it might have been spotted, like one of the big cats that were purportedly roaming the jungle behind them. He saw three men, Ticos, their heads shaved like the driver's, two with goatees, one without, and they seemed to be dancing, flailing their arms and jumping from one foot to the other as if the ground had caught fire.

"*Todo!*" one was shouting, the one without the goatee. "Empty *sus bolsillos,* wallet, cellphone, *todo!*" There was a flash of light, two flashes: the goatees had knives. And the one without, the one doing all the shouting, he had a handgun.

The one with the gun saw him then and pointed it at him, though he was a hundred feet away. "You," the man shouted, his voice so shrill with the rush of adrenaline it was almost a shriek, almost girlish. "You come over here!"

Sten could feel his heart going, accelerating like a flight of ducks beating up off the surface of a pond, *flap, flap, flap.* It was an old feeling, a feeling that took him back to another time and place, a seething green overgrown rot-stinking place like this one all the way across the ocean on the far side of the world. There were tropical fish there too. Monkeys. Men with guns. He dropped the can and raised his hands in the air. "Don't shoot."

The man with the gun was careless—*man,* he was a boy, all three of them were boys, nineteen, twenty years old, their limbs like broomsticks poking out of their baggy shorts and oversized T-shirts and their faces ablaze with excitement and maybe something else, maybe drugs. The weapon was just an object to him, Sten could see that in an instant, like a plate of food he was carrying from one table to another. A shoe. A book. A used CD he'd found in a bin at the record shop. He didn't respect it. He didn't know it. He didn't even know how to take a stance and aim. "You," the man repeated. "Right here, *ahora!*"

Sten shuffled forward, his feet gone heavy suddenly, so heavy he could barely lift them. He saw Carolee there with the others, her face rinsed with fear, the brim of her hat askew. Everybody was tightly bunched, purses, cameras and backpacks dropping at their feet while the goatees prodded them with their knives. There was a blanket there, he saw that now, spread out in the sun-blasted mud to receive the loot. It was one of those Indian blankets they sold in the tourist shops up and down the coast, the colors garish in the harsh hot light.

When he was there, when he'd reached the one with the gun and allowed himself to be shepherded into the group with a quick hot punch of the barrel in his ribs, he was startled by the faces around him. These were the faces of dead people, drained of animation, their eyes fixed on the ground as they gave up what they had, dropping change, wallets, bracelets and wristwatches into the pile as if they were tossing coins in a fountain. Sheila was murmuring "Oh god, oh god," over and over. Another woman was crying. The man with the gun prodded him again and said, "Empty it, *todo lo que tiene—ahora mismo!*"

He exchanged a look with Carolee, then pulled his pockets inside out and dropped the contents on the pile, card key, dummy wallet, a pack of matches, his cell. He was thinking there was no sense in getting shot over nothing, no sense in getting excited, but then the one with the gun nudged him again and he went cold all over. They were amateurs, children playing at cops and robbers, infants, punks, too stupid even to be scared. Why would they be? This was easy pickings, old people, seniors so frightened and hopeless they could barely twist the watches off their wrists, let alone defend themselves. "*Todo!*" the man repeated.

Everything came into focus suddenly, the two goatees with their hands in people's pockets and down the front of their shorts, Sheila whimpering *Please, no, not my passport,* the driver shut inside the bus and the fat woman vanished altogether—in on it, both of them, he was sure of it—and the carelessness, the unforgiveable carelessness of the one with the gun who barely came up to his shoulder for Christ's sake, who'd turned away from him, turned his back on him as if he were nothing, less than nothing, just old and weak and useless. What he'd learned as a nineteen-year-old himself, a recruit, green as an apple, wasn't about self-defense, it was about killing, and does anybody ever forget that? Mount a bicycle, lace up a pair of skates, shoot the rapids: here it was. In the next instant he hit the man so hard from behind he felt the shock of it surge through his own body even as he locked his right forearm across the man's throat and brought his left hand up to tighten the vise, simplest maneuver in the book, first thing they teach you, *Choke off the air and don't let up no matter what.*

The gun dropped away at the moment of impact and it wasn't as if he was merely applying pressure to the man flailing in his arms—he wasn't doing that, no, he was immobilizing him, because that was what he'd been trained to do and he had no choice in the matter. It was beyond reason now, autonomous, dial it up, semper fi. Everyone froze. The two with the knives looked as if they'd been transported to another planet, helpless, stupefied, scared. And then Bill, his bald crown raking at the light, bent to pick up the gun as if it were some pedestrian thing somebody had dropped in the street, an umbrella, a checkbook, a pair of glasses, his face gratified and composed, almost as if he meant to hand it back to the man kicking in Sten's arms. Somebody screamed. The man kicked. Sten held tight, tighter, even as he watched the other two drop their knives in the mud and scramble for the car.

The engine sucked fuel, the wheels spun in the mud and then the car was fishtailing across the lot, spewing exhaust and fighting for purchase. Sten watched it go—they all watched—as it threw up clods of earth and sheared through the puddles till it plunged into the tunnel of the road where the deep holes gathered and the stream sank into its pools and the brick-red platys darted and hovered. Then it was quiet. The man in his arms had gone limp, like an exhausted dance partner, and the only thing Sten could think to do was move back a step and lower him to the ground.

Sheila started up again, invoking God, and then Carolee was in his arms and they were all gathered round, staring down at the man in the mud. He was on his back, where Sten had dropped him, eyes open and staring at nothing. He looked shrunken, shorter even than the five-eight or -nine he must have been, no girth to him at all, his oversized shorts and new spotless white

T-shirt hanging off him like flour sacks. And his ankles—you could have wrapped two fingers around his ankles.

"Is he—?" somebody said, and now somebody else, a boxy officious-looking man with a pencil mustache Sten could have sworn he'd never seen before in his life, was bending over the body checking for vital signs, ear to chest, finger to wrist. This man— certainly he'd been on the bus—looked up and announced, "I'm a paramedic," and began alternately kneading the supine man's chest and blowing into his mouth.

This was something new, something the guidebook hadn't advertised, a curiosity under the sun that beat down steadily on the ochre mud of the lot, and everybody just stood there taking it in, minutes slipping away, the heat exacting its price in sweat, the fat woman emerging from her stall and the bus driver step- ping tentatively down from the bus as if the ground were rolling under him like a treadmill. The main attraction, the man on his back on the ground, never stirred. Oh, there was movement, but it was only the resistance of the inanimate to a moving force, the paramedic thanklessly riding the compression of his two stacked palms, then breaking off to pinch the nostrils and force his own breath past the dry lips, the ruptured trachea and down into the deflated lungs. This was a man, this paramedic, who didn't give up easily. His mustache glistened with saliva and the crown of his head humped up and down as if at the climax of some insistent sexual act. He kept at it, kept at it, kept at it.

Carolee's voice was very soft and at first he didn't know if she was speaking to him or the paramedic. What she said was, "Is he going to make it?"

He didn't know about that—he didn't even know what he'd done. The only man he'd ever killed in his life, or might have killed, nothing confirmed, was a dink two hundred yards away on a moonless night when the flares strobed out over the world and he was in something very much like a panic, his rifle on full automatic.

"We should get him to a hospital," Bill said, still holding on to the gun—a revolver, Sten saw that now, .357 Magnum, six shots—as if he didn't know what to do with it. "I mean, is there a hospital here? In Limón, I mean?"

"There must be," somebody said.

"But where is it?" Bill wondered. "And if we—I mean, should we move him? Maybe there's damage there, a neck injury"—and here he raised his eyes to Sten's—"like in football, you know? Where they bring out the stretcher?"

Up and down the paramedic went, up and down, and now the fat woman was there, peering over Sheila's shoulder as if to make some sort of positive identification of the body on the ground— and it *was* a body, a corpse, not a living thing, not anymore, Sten was sure of it—and here was the driver too, his eyes masked behind the sunglasses, the lower portion of his face locked up like a strongbox.

"Driver," Bill said, and he seemed to be panting, like a dog that had run a long way up a steep hill, "we need to take this man to the hospital. Where—*dónde*—is the hospital?"

The paramedic, without breaking his rhythm, looked up and said something in Spanish to the driver, something that had the cognate *os-pee-tal* in it, but the driver just shook his head and turned away to spit in the dirt. "You don't want," he said finally, shaking his head very slowly. "You want *el córoner.*"

"*Os-pee-tal,*" the paramedic insisted, and Bill joined him, aping his pronunciation: "*Os-pee-tal.*"

The fat woman emitted a pinched labial noise as if she were unstoppering a bottle, then turned—fat ankles, splayed feet in a pair of huaraches that sank into the ochre mud as if it were dough—and started back across the lot. Sten could still feel the blood thudding in his ears, though he was calming now, what was done was done, already thinking of the repercussions. Certainly he'd acted in self-defense, and here were the witnesses to prove it, but who knew what the laws were like in this country, what kind of flaming hoops they'd make him jump through—and lawyers, would he need a lawyer? He scanned the group—they were still milling there, clueless—but no one would look him in the eye. He wasn't one of them, not anymore—he was something else now.

Sheila came up to him then, to where he was standing with his arm around Carolee still, and pressed his hand. "Thank you," she murmured. "You're a hero, a real hero." Then she bent to the tangle of things scattered on the blanket to reclaim her purse and passport—her precious passport—and as if a spell had been broken, they all came forward now, one after another, to sift through the pile and take back what belonged to them.

2.

THE RED CROSS CLINIC (*La Clínica de la Cruz Roja*) was where they wound up, the whole tour group, as if this were part of the package. The driver had retraced their route at the same breakneck speed he'd employed on the way out—or no, he'd seen this as an excuse to go even faster, pedal to the metal all the way, as if the bus had been scaled down and transformed into an ambulance, though as far as Sten could see there was no need for hurry, not on the gunman's account. He hoped he was wrong. Hoped the guy was only unconscious, in a coma maybe, deep sleep, dreaming. They'd give him oxygen at the hospital, defibrillation, adrenaline, something to kick-start his heart and wake him up . . . but what if he didn't wake up? Was that manslaughter? A term came to him then: *justifiable homicide*. That was what this was. He'd acted instinctively, in self-defense, in defense of his wife and all the others too—he'd neutralized a threat, that was all, and who could blame him? But what if the man was paralyzed, alive still, but dead from the neck down, what then? Who'd pay for the nurse to spoon-feed him and change his diapers? There was no health care down here, no insurance, no nothing. Would there be a lawsuit? They had lawsuits everywhere. And jails. They had jails everywhere too.

He tried not to think about it, tried to wipe his mind clean. The whole way back he'd held tight to Carolee's hand, his eyes locked straight ahead, the bus rattling till every nut and bolt down the length of it began to sing. Time compressed. The jungle slashed by on either side and the potholes exploded under the wheels. He felt sick. There was a kind of buzzing in his skull, as if a swarm of insects had got trapped inside. His knees were cramped. He felt thirsty all over again. Three rows up, laid out in the middle of the aisle, was the foreshortened form of the gunman, the paramedic hovering over him, but all he could make out were the soles of the man's feet, jutting up like parentheses enclosing a phrase he didn't want to decipher.

At first, there'd been some question about where to put the man. No one wanted him inside the bus, but what were they going to do, strap him to the roof? Leave him there in the mud for the police? The buzzards? The dogs? He was a human being, no matter what he'd done, or tried to do, and there wasn't much debate about it—he was going with them. That was the consensus, at any rate, people wringing their hands, their voices shaky still. Bill's wife—processed hair, low-cut blouse—held out, her teeth clamped as if she'd bitten into something gone bad. "I don't want him near me," she insisted. "I don't want—" and she'd broken off, fighting back a sob.

It turned out they couldn't fit the man lengthwise across any of the seats, so Bill and the paramedic, who'd hauled him up the steps by his shoulders and feet, laid him out in the aisle, the back of his head bisected by the scuffed white line on the floor, the one you were advised to stay behind. Most people were already on the bus at that point, their faces blanched and reduced, eyes staring straight ahead, but the final few, Sten and Carolee amongst them, had to step over him to make their way down the aisle. Sten took his wife by the arm and tried not to look down at the glazed eyes and the teeth glinting in the open mouth, and if he missed his step and one foot wound up coming down on the man's sprawled wrist, so much the worse. The guy was feeling no pain, and besides, he'd asked for it, hadn't he?

Last to board was the driver, who removed his dark glasses to squint down the length of the bus, counting heads, and then, bending awkwardly to dig under the seat—he had a belly, Sten saw now, the belly of a man who sat for a living—he produced a neon-orange rain slicker, unfurling it with a flourish to make sure everybody was watching. Was he going to drape it over the man's face? Was that it then, was it all over, forget the charade? But no, he folded the slicker into a makeshift pillow, plumped it two or three times, then bent again, all the way down now, and slipped it under the man's head. No one said a word. Flies buzzed. Sten's throat was so dry he couldn't swallow, and yet he didn't reach for Carolee's water bottle because he didn't want to call attention to himself—or any more attention, that is.

For a moment—too long, because this was an emergency, wasn't it?—the driver simply stood there looking down on his handiwork, shaking his head slowly. Did he know the man? Had they been in collusion? It was hard to judge from his expression, but when he sank into his seat and pulled the door closed, he shot a withering look down the aisle and repeated his mantra—"You sit"—though everybody was already seated. Incredibly, he was glaring, actually glaring at them, no mistaking the severity of that look, the reprobation, the censure, as if they'd all gone so far beyond the bounds of propriety it wasn't worth mentioning, as if they were in fact children and had behaved badly, as if they hadn't been attacked and he hadn't been in on it or at least complicit. Sten was sure he was. Lure the tourists out here in the middle of nowhere, call the gang, split the proceeds, what could be simpler? The man—the driver, the hypocrite—held that look a beat, then he fished out his sunglasses, and as if performing a delicate operation, fitted them carefully over his ears, adding superfluously, "We go now."

When they reached the outskirts of the city and the harbor came into view, the bus swung off the main road and hurtled down a series of surface streets, one careening turn after another, until suddenly, without warning, right in the middle of a nondescript block of *tiendas,* market stalls and apartments, the driver hit the brakes hard, and they lurched to a stop in front of a low concrete-block building that might have been a warehouse or machine shop but for the Red Cross emblem over the door.

Caught off guard, Sten was violently pitched forward, and if he hadn't been holding on to Carolee—protecting her—he might have slammed face-first into the seatback in front of him. As it was, he just managed to tuck his shoulder and soften the blow as the chassis recoiled and a rain of purses, cameras and water bottles spilled from the overhead racks and skittered across the floor, seeking equilibrium. The paramedic wasn't as fortunate. All this time he'd been on the edge of his seat, leaning over the gunman and bracing him against the bumps and dips and wild looping turns, but he lost his grip at the final moment and the body rucked forward, sliding partially down the stairwell and shedding the rain slicker in the process.

People looked to Sten, as if it was his responsibility, but he was having none of it. It was the paramedic's problem now—he'd taken it upon himself, hadn't he? He was the professional. Let him deal with it. For one stunned instant, people just stared, and then, cursing, the paramedic—short, square-shouldered, too heavy in the butt and with a face as round as the moon—sprang up out of his seat to wedge himself in the stairwell and prop up the man's head, but he was clearly having trouble, the body having come to rest on one shoulder, canting the neck at a spastic angle. "Give me a hand here, will you, somebody?" he gasped, but nobody moved, or at least not expeditiously enough—they were old, all of them, old people—so he slid his hands in under the man's arms, cradling his head as best he could, and began easing him down the steps.

At this point, Bill—the other Bill, the one with hair—pushed himself up to help, ducking into the stairwell in a shuffling stoop to catch hold of the patient's feet at the door, but at the last second they slipped from his grasp, flopping down on the hot pavement like fish on a stringer. The sound of it was nothing, barely audible, the small dull thump of dissociated flesh striking an unyielding surface, but it reverberated through the bus like a thunderclap. Sten could feel Carolee tense beside him. Nobody breathed.

The paramedic—he'd seen worse—just seemed to shrug it off, dragging his patient up over the curb even as Bill, fumbling forward, managed to take hold of the abraded heels and lift them from the pavement. "Set him down," they heard the paramedic say. "No, not in the dirt—right here, right on the walk." Awkwardly, in a stoop that had him bent over double, Bill swung the man's legs into alignment as the paramedic eased him down—waist, shoulders, one hand to protect the head, easy does it, and there was their collective burden, harmless enough now, laid out on his back like a sunbather on a glittering gum-spotted beach. Satisfied, the paramedic straightened up and threw a quick glance at the bus before hurrying up the walk and disappearing into the building, leaving Bill there to stand watch.

That was the scene: the man called Bill, skinny, sunburned, his shoulders slumped and his waxen hair flattened to his head as if it had been dripped in place one hot strand at a time, standing there over the man who wasn't breathing and whose throat was discolored under the point of his up-thrust chin—dark there, too dark, as if he'd decided to grow a goatee after all. Bill shifted in place, put his hands on his hips, dropped them. There was a smell of the sea, tepid and redolent of small deaths. Someone was revving a motorbike in the alley next to the clinic. A car rolled slowly up the street, its windshield molten under the sun.

And then the paramedic (his name was Oscar, Sten would later learn, Oscar Ruiz, of Oakland, California, sixty-two years old and in his first month of retirement) emerged from the building, an attendant in pale green scrubs hustling along beside him, pushing a gurney. Everyone leaned forward to watch as the attendant bent to the motionless form, checking for vital signs—futilely, as far as Sten could see, though one woman kept insisting there was no reason to give up hope because the electroshock machine, the defibrillator, was a real miracle and it had saved her husband, *twice*. "The guy's gone, can't you see that?" the man behind her put in, and a whole sotto voce debate started up. Sten ignored it. He sat there with the rest of them, sweating, thirsty, wanting only to be back on the ship. The police would be coming now, he knew that. At the very least he'd be required to give a statement, they all would. But what then? Would they charge him? Would he and Carolee have to stay here in this reeking excuse for a city for days on end—weeks, even—while all the others climbed back aboard the ship and cruised away into the sunset?

His eyes shot to the driver. The man had swung his legs out into the aisle to get comfortable. He had a cellphone to his ear now, speaking his whipcrack Spanish into the receiver, and who was he contacting if not the authorities? Sten looked to Carolee and she breathed his name, twice, in a kind of moan: "Oh, Sten, Sten." She fidgeted in the seat, and whether consciously or not, she pulled her hand away from his and rubbed her palm, the moisture there, on her shorts. She spoke in a whisper: "You think they'll let us go back now?"

He shrugged. He wasn't exactly in a talkative mood. All he felt was tired. Sleep, that was what he wanted, another realm, a way out of this. He watched dispassionately as the paramedic helped the attendant load the limp body onto the gurney and wheel it up the walk and into the yawning double doors of the clinic. Everybody saw it, the retreating feet, the wheels of the gurney, the doors snapping shut like a set of jaws, and as if at a signal, people began stirring. Here came Bill, the good Samaritan, to lead it off, mounting the steps of the bus and sliding into the front seat beside his wife. A man Sten couldn't place stood and started sorting through the daypack he'd stowed overhead. There was a rustle of bags and papers, as if a stiff internal wind had started up to whip through the bus. Bottles of water appeared. Power bars. Cellphones. The unpleasantness was over now and it was as if nothing had happened: they were tourists deprived of a nature walk and thinking only to get back to the boat, to their cabins and staterooms, to privacy, air-conditioning, cocktails, dinner at the captain's table. They'd had an experience, all right, something to text home about, but it was over now.

"Driver?" It was Bill, the first Bill, the bald-headed one, who seemed to have become their spokesman. He was seated two rows up from Sten and Carolee, his shirt soaked through with sweat and a baseball cap pulled low over his eyes. His wife was there beside him, her brittle hair set aflame by a shaft of sun slanting through the window.

The driver was in no hurry to respond. He pursed his mouth. Tapped the cellphone at his ear. "Driver?" Bill repeated, and finally the man swiveled round in his seat and lifted his eyebrows as if to say *What now?*

"We just wanted to know what the holdup is."

The driver said something into the phone, then pulled it away from his ear and held it up like an exhibit in a courtroom. "I am talking," he said, "to *la Fuerza Pública,* the police. You will need to make a testimony for the facts of this"—he couldn't find the word—"today. *A la reserva.* The crime. You must make a testimony of the crime."

"Yes, all right, fine," Bill said, waving a hand in dismissal. "But can't we do that back aboard ship? We've been through a lot here, I'm talking trauma, real trauma, and it's not doing anybody any good to sit here sweltering for no reason . . ."

"Take us back," a voice boomed from the rear of the bus.

"Yeah, let's get this thing moving," somebody else put in.

As if awaiting her cue, Sheila cried out suddenly, her voice stretched to the breaking point: "We need a restroom. We haven't—I mean, I haven't—" She was two seats up, on the left, sitting beside the woman whose husband had been revived twice (but not, apparently, a third time). Sheila's makeup had gone gummy in the heat and from this angle, Sten's angle, it looked as if the skin were peeling away from her face. "We're hot. Thirsty. I don't know about anybody else, but I for one could use a cold shower."

The driver slowly shook his head. "This is not possible," he said, before returning the cell to his ear. "Not at the moment."

"What is this," Sten heard himself say, "a debating society?" He'd had enough. Who was this supercilious jerk to hold them here? He had no authority over them, he was nothing, less than nothing. "Hell," he said, pulling himself up from the seat, "we can walk from here. Or get a taxi. There's got to be taxis."

Everyone was in motion now, people clambering to their feet, pulling down bags, looping packs over their shoulders, white hair, trembling hands, a shuffle of sneakered and sandaled feet. In the same moment the driver came up out of his seat, as if to block their way, and what Sten was thinking was *Just let him try*. It might have been a standoff, might have gotten out of hand—people were scared, angry, impatient—but then the doors to the clinic swung open and the paramedic, one of their own, was hurrying up the walk to them, bringing the news.

Sten watched the man duck into the shadow of the bus, then reappear in the stairwell, his face neutral. He was saying something in Spanish to the driver, something detailed, but nobody could fathom what it was. Sten felt his stomach clench. But then the first Bill, who was standing in the aisle now with the others, called out, "So, Oscar, what's the deal, is the guy going to be okay or what? And when are we going to get out of here?"

The paramedic turned and blinked up at the faces ranged above him as if he couldn't quite place them.

"Well?" Bill demanded.

"They're going to need a statement."

Sheila let out a groan. "What sort of statement, what do they want? We didn't do anything."

The paramedic—Oscar—held up a hand for silence. "But they say they can do that on the ship." *On the ship:* those were the incantatory words, the words they'd all been waiting to hear, the spell broken, relief at hand. Everyone exhaled simultaneously. "For the witnesses, that is, and I guess that includes all of us." His eyes settled on Sten. "Except you—they're saying you're going to have to wait here till the police arrive."

He didn't know whether to grin or grimace. His face felt hot. His back ached, low down, where he must have tweaked something out there in the mud lot, one of the tight lateral muscles that didn't get enough use, one of his killing muscles.

"But don't worry," Oscar went on, "I'll stay with you, in case you need an interpreter."

"Yes, okay," Sten said, barely conscious of what he was assenting to, and then he was moving forward—dehydrated, light-headed, unsteady on his feet—and Carolee, the bag looped over her chest and clutching her hat as if it were a lifeline thrown over the side of a sinking ship, was following along behind.

There was a waiting room in the clinic and it wasn't much different from what you'd find in the States: fluorescent lights, gleaming linoleum, a smell of bleach and floor wax to drive down the faint lingering odor of body fluids. Nurses glided through one door and out another, a trio of hard-faced women sat staring into computer screens at the front desk and a forlorn cadre of the sick, hopeless and unlucky slouched on folding chairs in an array of bloody bandages and mewling infants. There was air-conditioning, and that was a blessing. And a restroom. The first thing he did, as soon as Oscar directed them to seats in the far corner of the room, was lock himself in the men's, turn the tap on full and let the cold water (tepid, actually) run over his face. He wet his hands and worked them through his hair, which he wore long, in the fashion he'd adopted as soon as he'd got out of the service and gone off to college, no hard-liner and no fool either, because what woman in San Francisco in that day and age would look twice at a man in a crewcut? *Baby killer,* that's what they'd shouted at him when he boarded the bus at the airport, but the accusation only puzzled him. He didn't want to hear about babies,

alive or dead, or Vietnamese self-determination or the jungle that
was a kind of death in itself. He only wanted to get laid. Just that.

When he came back to the waiting room, Carolee and Oscar
were making small talk, just as if they were lounging over drinks
at the Martini Bar on the ship. He heard her say, "And your
youngest son, what's he do?" and then she glanced up with a
smile and patted the seat beside her.

"He's in computers," Oscar said. "Actually paying his own
rent, which is kind of a miracle these days, if you know what I
mean—"

"Oh, yeah, *we* know," she said, and he thought she was going
to say something about Adam, but she didn't, and that was all
right, that was a blessing, because for the first time in years, it
seemed, Adam had gone right out of Sten's head—he wasn't worrying about where he was, what he was thinking, what kind
of trouble he was going to get into next, because they were in
enough trouble themselves. "Don't we, Sten?" she said, and gave
him an odd look, as if she wasn't attached to the moment, and he
supposed she wasn't and no sense in pretending otherwise. This
was hard. As hard as anything that had ever happened to them,
and she'd had to stand there and watch it unfold.

"Maybe you want to go freshen up?" he said, sinking into the
seat. "They've got a real bathroom here, with hot and cold running water. Paper towels. The works. Knock yourself out."

"Yes," she said, rising from the chair with her black cloth bag
still looped across her chest, "I think I will," and then she was
sidestepping a child in a wheelchair and making her way across
the room.

They both watched her go. There was a crackle of Spanish
over the address system. A baby, exasperated beyond endurance,
threw back its head and began to howl. He turned to the man
beside him, to Oscar, and shook his hand. "I want to thank you
for doing this," he said.

A shrug. "Least I can do."

"What about your wife, she okay with it?" The wife, short, plain, with an expressionless face, a straw hat and an oversized turquoise necklace one of the goatees had jerked from her throat and dropped casually on the pile in the middle of the blanket, had gone back to the ship with the rest of them.

Another shrug, more elaborate this time. A smile. "Once a paramedic, always a paramedic."

"The guy's dead, isn't he?"

"Yeah, he's dead. You could see that when you let go of him. But we have to try—and I tell you, I've seen people come back to life so many times I wouldn't want to be taking odds. You do what you can and the rest is out of our hands, you know what I mean?" The loudspeaker crackled again, more Spanish. Oscar looked up, concentrating, then shook his head. "No, it's nothing, it's not for us."

"But again, thanks for this. I owe you. When we get back to the ship, the drinks are on me."

"No apologies. What you did out there was amazing, it really was. Word is"—he lowered his voice—"there's been problems lately, the kind of thing the Costa Rican government, not to mention the cruise line, doesn't want to get out. It's not just robbery. Sometimes—again, I've heard rumors—they want more than that." He shot a glance round the room, then leaned in confidentially. "They can get brutal. With the women especially. In one case I know of they raped them all, young, old, they don't care, right in front of the men. Daughters even. Kids."

"Jesus."

"So what I'm saying is you don't have to thank me, I should be thanking you."

There was movement at the door. Sten glanced up, expecting the police, but it was only another patient, a boy of ten or so, his head wrapped in gauze and the right side of his face looking as if somebody had taken a cheese grater to it. The woman with him—his mother, his aunt, maybe a big sister—looked like a saleslady from one of the high-end stores, pink dress, heels, eye shadow, but the face she wore was the face of despair.

Distracted, he watched the woman guide the boy across the floor to the admittance desk and begin making her case to the secretary there, who barely glanced up from her computer screen. The boy was unsteady on his legs, leaning into the woman for support, and Sten could see where her dress had begun to go dark under the arm and across her breast with what might have been perspiration but wasn't. He couldn't understand what she was saying, but her voice rose up suddenly to jackhammer the secretary, who kept pointing to the seats in the waiting room with an increasingly emphatic jab. The woman in pink was having none of it. Her voice raged on until there was no other sound in the room. The lights flickered. The air conditioner blew. And then, as if it had all been decided beforehand, a nurse emerged to escort her and the boy into the inner sanctum and the little sounds came creeping back, people coughing, sneezing, conversing in low voices against the pain that had summoned them there. Sten could feel his blood racing. "High drama, huh?" he said.

Oscar, who'd been watching the boy too, turned back to him. "Bicycle," he said. "Or motorbike. Bet anything." His eyes flicked to the doorway behind the desk and back again. "And a concussion on top of it."

Sten shifted in the chair, which had begun to dig into his backside. He wanted to stand and stretch, but instead he just sat there, bearing it. People crowded the room, faces everywhere. Somewhere a machine was whirring. Babies cried. Somebody's phone rang. "So what now?" he said, shifting again. "I mean, what are the police going to do—I'm not in trouble, am I?"

"You? They ought to give you a medal."

"Right, sure. But do you know anything about the laws down here?"

The thin stripe of mustache quivered and it took him a

moment to realize Oscar was working up a grin, as if all this was funny, as if now, sitting here exiled in this little chamber of horrors, the real fun was about to begin. "They ought to give you a medal," he repeated.

An hour crept by. Nothing happened. More people came dragging through the double doors and they brought more squalling babies with them, more bandages, more broken bones and abrasions, more grief, but the police never showed. Oscar, depleted of small talk, leaned back in his chair and shut his eyes. Carolee kept saying, "This is ridiculous," and Sten kept agreeing with her. Beyond the windows, the sun stood high still, though it was past five now, cocktail hour, and he couldn't help thinking about what they were missing aboard ship, the outward-spooling loop of activities that lassoed every moment, as if to sit on deck and look out to sea would crush you with boredom. He didn't need activities. He needed rest. He needed a drink to wash the bad taste out of his mouth. The Martini Bar was all ice, the bartop itself, frozen and planed smooth, and the air-conditioning was like the breath of a deep cave in the hills back home in Mendocino.

At some point, he must have closed his eyes too. He'd been thinking about the first time he and Carolee had come south of the border, a summer vacation when they were in their twenties, backpacking through Mexico, Belize and Guatemala. Carolee had stepped on a sea urchin in one of the tidal pools and the spine had broken off in her heel, which became instantly infected, and so they'd had to go to a clinic like this one, or was it a hospital? That was in Mexico, in the Yucatán. They'd waited then too, waited eternally, until finally a doctor no older than they took them into a back room strewn with medical debris, gave her a local, extracted the spine and shot her up with penicillin. Sten had had to carry her out of there. And then, two days later, he was the one who collapsed, sick with a gastrointestinal bug because he'd ordered oysters—*ostiones*—and didn't know the term the waiter threw back at him: *ceviche*. He'd expected them fried or maybe baked in an Oysters Rockefeller kind of thing, but here they were, served up cold on a plate of ice, and Carolee sitting across the table grinning at him. "They look good," she said, folding a chicken taco into her mouth. And he, whether out of some macho impulse or maybe just the stupidity of youth, sucked them out of their shells, all twelve of them, and then ordered a dozen more.

It got worse. They were snorkeling someplace—Belize, he thought it was, or maybe Isla Mujeres—and stayed out too long because it was magical, beyond compare, the reef there alive with every kind of fish you could imagine, and it wasn't just sunburn they suffered all the way down the blistered crab-red lengths of their bodies, from the backs of their necks to the calluses at their heels, but sun *poisoning*. Within hours their legs swelled up with fluid, as if they'd somehow shot over to Africa and contracted elephantiasis. They could barely walk, and she with her sore foot to begin with. Clutching at each other for support, sweltering, sick, staggering like drunks, they made their way up the street to their hotel, local rum—fifteen cents a shot at the lobby bar— their only consolation. And then, a few days later, they began to peel, and as he crouched there over the unmade bed, absently stripping the dead skin from his legs while Carolee snored beside him, he noticed the ants coming in beneath the door in a wavering dark line that snaked under the bed to climb the wall and exit through a crack below the windowpane. They seemed to be carrying something, these ants, like the leaf-cutters you saw in nature films. But they weren't carrying leaves—they were hoisting pale shriveled translucent flakes of skin, human skin.

"Give me the Nordic climes," he'd told Carolee when she sputtered awake, and told her again and again, through all these years, making a routine of it, a joke, but a joke that wasn't funny, not in the least. "Oslo," he'd say, "Helsinki, Malmö, Reykjavik, what's wrong with Reykjavik?"

And then he wasn't thinking anymore, he was dreaming. He was alone, hiking up a trail deep in the redwood forest, everything cool and dim in the shadow of the trees, his legs working and his heart beating strong and steady so that he could see it there out front of him, at arm's length, beating, beating. He kept going, up and up, till he wasn't walking anymore but gliding above the ground, sailing on stiffened wings, and that seemed perfectly natural, as if all his life this was what he'd been meant to do. He might have been a bird. He *was* a bird. But the strangest thing was there were no other birds out there with him, no creatures of any kind, no people even, nothing but the trees and the sky and the earth unscrolling beneath him in silence absolute, dream silence, a silence so profound it could be broken only by the mechanical squawk of a loudspeaker—*Doctor Hernández, venga al teléfono, por favor*—that sheared off his wings and dropped him down here in the hard wooden seat of the Red Cross Clinic, awaiting judgment.

"You were asleep," Carolee was saying. "I didn't want to wake you."

It took him a minute, so much harder at his age to come back to the world, and then he sat up and gazed blearily round the room, his eyes shifting from Oscar's face to Carolee's before dropping to the watch on his wrist: 6:15. Was that right? He blinked at Carolee. Blinked at Oscar. "Jesus," he rasped, "they going to make us wait here all day?"

Oscar—he'd been asleep too—rose from his chair, stretching. He was wearing shorts, plaid shorts, and below the hem of them his kneecaps were discolored, smudged still from where he'd knelt over the dead man in the mud. "I'll go check at the desk."

"No, don't bother." He was on his feet now too, a sudden jolt of anger searing through him as if he'd touched two ends of a hot wire together. "Come on, Carolee," he said, reaching a hand down for her, "we're out of here."

"But Sten, they haven't come yet. The police. They'll think—I don't know what they'll think."

He just shook his head, took her hand and pulled her up. "Sorry, friend," he said, nodding at Oscar, and then he was guiding Carolee back across the waiting room, out the double doors and into the scorching stink of the evening, charcoal and dogshit and the fumes of the cars, fish, dead fish, and if he brushed by the pair of policemen in their pleated blue uniforms with the *Fuerza Pública* patches on their sleeves and their faces of stone, he really didn't give a good goddamn whether they'd come to pin a medal on him or haul him off to Golgotha. He was out in the street, that was where he was, striding through traffic, calling—no, yelling, bellowing—"Taxi! Taxi!"

3.

AND THAT WAS ALL kinds of fun too, trying to commu-
nicate to the cabbie just where he wanted to go, and how did
you say "boat"? *Barco,* wasn't that it? He all but shoved Carolee
into the backseat, then slammed in himself, twisting his neck
toward the cabbie and in the process catching a glimpse of himself
in the rearview. His eyes, furious still—burning, consumed—
were sunk in a nest of concentric lines like pits on a topographic
map, the eyes of a seventy-year-old retiree pushed to the limit.
There were red blotches on his cheeks. His nose looked as if it
had been skinned. And his hair, not yet gone the absolute dead
marmoreal white of the rest of the duffers on the ship, but getting there, hung limp over his ears. But his eyebrows—his eyebrows were exclusively and undeniably white, and how had he
never noticed that? White and pinched together with the glare
of the sun that picked out the two vertical trenches at the bridge
of his nose and ran them all the way up into the riot of horizon-
tal gouges that desecrated his forehead. He was old. He looked
old. Looked like somebody he didn't even recognize. "*Barco,*" he
announced to the driver. And then, to clarify, added the definite
article: "*El barco.*"

The driver was dressed in shorts and sandals and the ubiq-
uitous flowered shirt open at the collar and he wore some sort
of medallion dangling at his throat. He didn't have an iPod, but
he sported the same wispy goatee as the bus driver and the two
thieves in the lot—in fact, and this came to him in a flash of
ascending neural fireworks, the guy could have been the bus
driver's twin brother, and if that wasn't an irritating thought he
couldn't imagine what was. All right. They were in the cab, that

was all that mattered—but the cab wasn't moving. The driver—
the cabbie—was just staring at him.

"*El barco*," he repeated. "I want to go to *el barco*."

"The boat," Carolee put in. "The cruise ship in the harbor.
The *Centennial?*"

"Oh, the boat, sure, no problem," the cabbie said, grinning,
then he put the car in gear and started up the street. A joker.
Another joker. He'd probably learned his English at Cal State.

"Ask him how much," Carolee said. No matter the exchange
rate or the deals she finagled in the shops, she was sure they were
getting ripped off, especially by cabbies. Before they'd left, she'd
gone online to browse the travel sites and make detailed lists of
dos and don'ts: photocopy your ID, leave your jewelry aboard
ship, avoid fanny packs ("one-stop shopping" in the thieves' jar-
gon), dress down, talk softly so as not to broadcast your national-
ity, stay sober, carry a disposable camera ashore, and always get
the price up front before you get into a cab.

"How much?" he said, or croaked, actually, deep from the
well of his ruined voice.

"Oh, it's not much," the driver said, accelerating, "nothing
really. Only a mile or so. I'll give you a break, don't worry." And
he mentioned a figure—in *colones*—that seemed excessive, even as
Sten tried to do the math.

"*Demasiado,*" Carolee said automatically.

The driver, and he was a cowboy too, swinging into the next
block with a screech of the tires, glanced over his shoulder and
said, "Maybe you want to go back to the clinic? Maybe you want
to wait for some other cab?" The car slowed, made a feint for the
curb as if he were going to pull over and let them out.

"*Demasiado,*" Carolee repeated.

Raising his voice to be sure he was understood, not simply by
the driver but by his wife too, Sten said, "Just drive."

✦ ✦

The first thing he did when he got back aboard and passed
through the gauntlet of rhapsodically smiling greeters, puffers,
porters, towel boys and all the rest of the lackeys who were paid
to make you feel like Caesar returning from the Gallic wars every
time you set foot on deck, was step into the shower. He should
have deferred to Carolee, should have let her have first shot at
it—and he would have under normal circumstances, but he was
too wrought up even to think at that juncture. He'd thrown
some money at the cabbie while she stood there on the pavement fooling with her hat and bag, then he took her by the arm
and marched her up the gangplank and into the elevator and on
down the hall to their cabin, impatient with everything, with her,
with the lackeys, with the card key that didn't seem to want to
release the lock—and was this the right cabin? He drew back to
glare at the number over the door: 7007. It was. And the card did
work. Finally. After he'd tried it backwards, forwards and upside
down and angrily swatted Carolee's hand away when she'd tried
to help—and why, amidst all this luxury and pampering, couldn't
they manage to code a fucking key so you could get into your
own fucking cabin you were paying through the teeth for? That
was what he was thinking, cursing under his breath, but then
the light flashed green, the door pushed open and before Carolee
could pull it shut he was already in the bathroom, stripping off his
putrid shirt and sweaty shorts to thrust himself under the shower-
head and twist both handles up full.

He must have stayed under that shower for twenty minutes
or more, he who was always so conscious of wastage at home,
who would bang impatiently on the bathroom door when Adam
was a teenager and showering six times a day, who recycled and
bought local and composted every scrap left on every plate in
the house. But not now, not today. Now he needed to wash
himself clean of the dirt of this godforsaken shithole he should
never have come to in the first place. He lifted his face to the
spray. Soaped up. Let the shower massage him, soothe him, coax

him down off the ledge he'd been perched on ever since the bus
had pulled into that mud lot. He was showering, all right? Was
that a crime? When finally he did emerge, Carolee brushed by
him without a word and locked the door behind her. An instant
later she was in the shower too, the muted hiss of the water inti-
mate and complicit.

He went straight to the phone to order a drink—a martini,
two martinis, his and hers—and something to put on his stomach,
something that didn't involve tortillas, rice, beans or fish. Pasta, he
was thinking. Pasta and a salad. And steak for her, filet mignon,
rare. He dialed room service, ordered the drinks and food and
went out in his robe to sit on the veranda and brood over the views
of the city and the bright rippling dance of the sea beneath him,
wide awake suddenly when all he'd wanted all day was a nap. He
poured himself a glass of water and took a long drink, his throat
parched, still parched, always and eternally, and when he set the
glass back down he saw that his hand was trembling.

Carolee was still in the bathroom when the knock came at
the door. Barefoot, cinching the robe around his midsection and
smoothing back his hair—still wet because nothing ever dried
in this humidity—he came in off the veranda and crossed the
cabin to the door, expecting the room-service waiter. It wasn't
the room-service waiter, but a group of four, fronted by the fun
director in her solid black heels. Beside her stood one of the ship's
officers—a man of forty, forty-five, wearing a deep tan to contrast with his whites—and behind him were two members of
the *Fuerza Pública,* as rigid as wooden soldiers in their sharply
pressed uniforms. "Sorry to disturb you, Mr. Stensen," the fun
director said, "but I wonder if I might introduce you to Senior
Second Officer Potamiamos and Officers Salas and Araya of the
local police force."

"We just wanted a word with you," the ship's officer inter-
jected, his English smooth and bland and with the faintest trace
of an accent Sten couldn't place, though he assumed it must have

been Greek. "About today's . . . incident, I suppose you'd call it. We've interviewed some of the others and we'd like to have your version of events, if you don't mind."

Sten took a step back and held open the door. He wanted to bark at them, wanted to tell them to go fuck themselves and slam the door in their faces, but all he did was shrug. "No, I don't mind," he said.

The ship's officer produced a smile, but he made no move to enter the cabin. "Fine," he said, rocking back on his heels. "Very good. Excellent. But wouldn't you be more comfortable in one of our conference rooms? Where we can sit at a table, have a bit more room? Get coffee. Would you like a coffee?"

"I'm not going to need a lawyer, am I?"

The fun director—her nametag read *Kristi Breerling* in gold letters against a glossy black background—looked as if she were about to burst into laughter over the absurdity of the proposition, but the cops never broke protocol and Potamiamos' smile froze in place. "We just want your version of events, that's all," he said. "We're cooperating fully with the local authorities, who, I'm told, are even now tracking down the other two criminals involved in this unfortunate assault on our passengers—on *you*. And your wife." A pause. He glanced across the cabin to the bathroom door. "Is she present, by the way? We'd like to have her—"

"*Version of events,*" Sten put in, cutting him off. He didn't like where this was going, didn't like it at all. He was an American citizen. He'd been attacked. On foreign soil. And the Senior Second Officer was either going to throw him to the wolves or cover the whole thing up. Or both.

"Yes, that's right," Potamiamos said. "For the record. But wouldn't you—wouldn't we all—be more comfortable in a larger space?"

"I'm comfortable here."

That was when the door to the bathroom clicked open and the cops snapped to attention. Carolee, barefoot and wrapped in one of the ship's plush deep-pile towels, stood there gaping at them a moment before she recovered herself and ducked back into the bathroom, the door pulling shut behind her with an abrupt expulsion of air.

"Well, in that case, can we come in?" Potamiamos asked, and then he paused, as if thinking better of it. "Or should we wait a few minutes to give you and your wife a chance to dress? Five or ten minutes, let's say? Would that be sufficient? We don't want to be intrusive, but, you understand, these officers do need to make their report and the ship will have to stay in port until such time as this business is concluded." The smile, which had gone up a notch when Carolee appeared, had vanished. The passenger was always right, that was the credo of the ship, of the whole cruise industry, but sometimes a passenger stepped over the line and the Senior Second Officer had to come down from the bridge or the casino or wherever he spent his time and address the situation in a way the usual ass-kissing shipboard smile simply wouldn't accommodate. The cops just stared. The fun director looked embarrassed.

It came to him suddenly that he was in control here, that they were afraid of him, afraid of the stink he could raise—*Tourists Mugged on Cruise*—afraid of lawsuits, bad press, all the retirees of the world canceling their reservations en masse and nobody collecting the precious Yankee dollars that kept the whole enterprise afloat, the true trickle-down economy, from the old folks' pensions and 401(k)s to the captain and his crew and the restaurateurs and shop owners and even the pickpockets and whores. "All right," he said, "give us ten minutes." He leveled a look on Potamiamos. "How about the Martini Bar? That work for you?"

That was the moment the room-service waiter chose to appear in the doorway, pushing a cart with the covered dishes and drinks set atop it. He was a Middle Easterner of some sort, judging from his nameplate, part of the international cast that ran the ship, from the Greek officers to the Eastern European housekeepers, one-

point-three crewmembers to every two passengers, no amenity
left unturned. When he saw the cops and Senior Second Officer there, his face fell, but Sten waved him in. "Put it there on
the table, will you?" And then, turning back to his visitors, who
couldn't have all fit in the cabin at once even if they'd wanted to,
he said, "Make that half an hour, will you?"

He wound up tasting nothing—not that it wasn't good, all the
food was terrific, first class all the way, but he was still sick in his
stomach from the ice cubes or the dirty glasses or whatever it was,
and worked up too over what was coming. He chased the pasta
around his plate, the same lobster tortellini in cream sauce he'd
practically inhaled the day before, and sat there sipping medita-
tively at his martini while Carolee dispatched her steak. She was a
good eater, always had been since the day he'd met her, no nonsense, no lingering, address your food and put it away, and how
many times had he glanced up from his plate in one restaurant
or another to see that she was already finished before he'd had a
chance to shake out his napkin? It was a sensual thing, he supposed, and that was all right because he was included in her range
of appetites too, and who would have thought it would last this
long? A lifetime. A whole lifetime.

"They're going to want to question me too, aren't they?" she
said, tucking away the last pink morsel on the tines of an inverted
fork, a faint sheen of grease on her lips. She'd changed into a pair
of jeans and a silk blouse—blue, with a scoop neck that showed
off the topaz necklace she wouldn't dare wear ashore. Matching
earrings. A touch of makeup. She'd combed out her hair, which
was darker when it was wet, but blond still and mostly natural,
though the woman at the beauty parlor back at home touched it
up every month or so.

"Yeah," he said.

"What do I tell them?"

The question irritated him. "What do you mean what do you tell them? Tell them what happened. Three shitheads attacked us and we defended ourselves."

She was chewing, the napkin suspended in one hand. A shadow flickered across the veranda, and it might have been a gull. Or no: more likely a vulture. Vultures were everywhere here, settling like collapsed umbrellas on top of every roof and telephone pole in town. "You think I'm dressed okay?"

He shrugged. He was in a pair of shorts and a Hawaiian shirt, exactly what he would have worn if he were going to the bar for a cocktail and a little recreation, as he'd done every night since the boat left San Diego. "You're fine," he said. "You're not on trial. And I'm not either. Everything's fine, believe me."

Her voice went soft. "I'm glad you were there."

"Me too." He stared down at the floor, his feelings too complicated to put into words. They'd been lucky, he knew that. And she must have known it too. "But I'm not going to be around forever," he said, lifting his eyes to hers. "You've got to learn to watch out for yourself."

"No more nature walks, is that what you're saying?"

"It's no joke, because it's not just money they're after, you know that, don't you? Anything can happen. Bad stuff, real bad stuff."

She didn't answer. She looked beyond him, out the open door to the bay and the sepia blur of the city that was like some fungus sprung up around a band of pale eroded beach and hacked green palm. He pushed his plate away. What he wanted was a cigarette, and he'd actually reached for his shirt pocket before he caught himself—he hadn't smoked in ten years now. It was times like this he missed it most. Smoking had given him something to do with his hands, the whole ritual of it, from sliding the cigarette from the pack to tamping it on the nearest hard surface, to cupping the match and drawing in the first sweet sustaining puff. The thing was, his hands had become too busy, manipulating up to two packs a day, his fingertips stained yellow with nicotine and his lungs as black as the bricks of the fireplace back at home. That was all behind him now. Now he was healthy. Now he rode a stationary bike and got out in the woods two or three days a week, keeping his hand in with part-time work for the lumber company, looking out for trespassers, squatters, marijuana growers—patrolling, if that was what you wanted to call it. The way he saw it, he was getting paid to go hiking, simple as that, best deal in the world.

Carolee set down her fork and laid her napkin across the plate, where it instantly began to color with the juices gathered there—blood, that is, and why should that bother him? A basket of bread stood beside her plate, untouched. A carafe of water. The grated Parmesan the waiter had left for him, yellowing in its stainless-steel bowl. Flies were at it now, Costa Rican flies, wafted in through the open door to the veranda. She reached for her martini glass, which bore a smear of lipstick on the rim, a transparency of red wax and the faintly striated impress of her lips, and it touched him somehow, this trace of her there, DNA, a code to outlive us all. There was a dead man in the morgue, but she was alive and he was alive too, alive together, come what may. He watched her lift the glass and finish what was left of her drink. "I needed that," she said, her voice flat and deliberate. She looked tired. "It's been a day, hasn't it?"

"It's not over yet." He wanted to add, "Some vacation, huh?," but restrained himself. Rising from the chair, he felt something click in his right hip, a tendon there, one more thing he'd managed to aggravate. He threw back his head to drain his own glass, best painkiller in the world, then patted down his pockets to be sure he had everything he was going to need, or potentially need: cellphone, wallet, passport, card key. At some point in the progression, he realized he was still holding the glass and that the glass was empty, useless, one more irritation, and without giving it even the flicker of a thought, he swiveled round and flung it high out over their private veranda and into the bright glittering sky beyond. Carolee just looked at him as if he'd gone mad till he snatched her glass up off the table and tossed it out the window too, and then he turned his back on her, rotating his wrist to consult his watch. And yes, he was angry, furious all of a sudden, as if he were back out there grabbing hold of that jerk with the gun, the dead man, the man he'd killed with his bare hands, and why couldn't the fool have picked some other group, another bus, another day?

He was squinting at his watch—half an hour, was half an hour up?—but he couldn't seem to make out the position of the hands, his eyes going on him now too, along with everything else. *Jesus. Jesus Fucking Christ.* If they offered him a drink he was going to refuse it, no matter how badly he wanted it—and he wasn't going to volunteer anything, just the facts. He smoothed down his shirt, took hold of the doorknob and shot a look over his shoulder to where Carolee still sat lingering at the table as if they had all night, as if they could have another round and order up dessert and coffee like normal people on vacation. "Come on," he said, flinging open the door on the corridor, "let's get this over with."

4.

IT MIGHT HAVE BEEN his imagination, but as they walked down the corridor to the elevator he couldn't help feeling people were making way for him, eyes meeting his and dropping to the floor, conversations suddenly hushed, men unconsciously hugging their wives closer as if he were some sort of feral beast, and what was that all about? Had the captain made an announcement? If not, he was going to have to at some point, the cruise delayed here in port for another day, at least a day, and of course everybody had cellphones, BlackBerries, iPads, all rumor consolidated into news and all news instantaneous. They knew. The whole ship knew.

Potamiamos and the two cops were waiting for them in the scoop-backed lounge chairs in a corner of the Martini Bar, the fun director off somewhere else now, her duties in the present circumstance having extended no further than applying her knuckles to the door of cabin 7007 and making the introductions. All three were sitting stiff-backed in the chairs, glasses of iced tea sweating on the table before them. They rose when he and Carolee crossed the room, even as a pair of waiters materialized from the shadows to pull out chairs for them. "And what will you have, ma'am?" one of them asked, bending over Carolee. Sten tried to warn her off with his eyes, but she was looking to the waiter. She emitted a little laugh, self-conscious all at once and maybe a little tipsy too, and said, "When in Rome . . ." And then, catching herself: "Just water, thanks."

"Sir?"

"Water. Out of a bottle. No ice."

The waiters withdrew and a moment of silence descended

on the table before the Senior Second Officer turned to the cop on his left, who for some reason was now wearing a pair of sunglasses, though they were indoors and the lighting was in no way intrusive. "Lieutenant Salas, perhaps you'd like to begin?"

"Yes, certainly," Salas said, his voice a creeping baritone, heavily accented. He shifted his gaze to Sten, or seemed to—you couldn't really tell what he was looking at, which, of course, would have been the point of the dark glasses. "Why don't you, sir, begin by giving us an account of events, what did you see, what did you do, et cetera."

Sten told him. He had nothing to hide. He'd done what anybody would have done, anybody who wasn't a natural-born victim, anyway. There was no need to go into detail about the trip itself, the state of the roads or the recklessness of the driver—not yet—so he began with the bus pulling into the lot and how everybody had descended into the sun, guidebooks, binoculars and birding lists in tow, and how he'd gone across the lot to the fat woman's *palapa*.

"And why was that?" Salas had produced a pack of Marlboros, shaking one out for himself and offering the pack to Sten, as if this were the interrogation scene in a police procedural, and that struck him as funny, so he laughed. "This is amusing?" Salas said. "The recollection? There is something amusing about the death of a man in my jurisdiction?"

"No," Sten said, waving away the pack as Carolee sat there tight-lipped beside him and Salas struck a match and touched it to the tip of his own cigarette. "No, not at all. I was thinking of something else, that's all."

The moment hung there. Potamiamos, handsome as a cutout from the cruise line brochure, tried to look stern—or worried, maybe he was worried. The thought caught Sten up and he felt the smallest tick of apprehension.

"You went to the *palapa*. And why was that?" the lieutenant repeated on a long exhalation of smoke.

"I was thirsty. It was a long ride. I dry out easily." He smiled, but it was a smile that gave no ground, lips only. Lips and teeth. "I'm old. Or didn't you notice?"

Salas nodded. "And then you went behind the stall, did you not? Into the jungle there?"

"Right. I had to piss. You know, pressure on the bladder?"

There was a moment of silence. Salas, his face unreadable, turned to the cop beside him. "*¿Qué dijo?*"

The second cop flicked his eyes at Carolee, then leaned forward, cupping one hand to his mouth. "*Para orinar,*" he said.

"Ah, I see," Salas said. "It all comes clear now—you were urinating."

The Senior Second Officer rediscovered his smile and now they were all smiling, smiles all around, *urinating,* the most human thing in the world, and what had they thought—that he was an accomplice? That he'd been hiding? That he'd worked all his life and paid his taxes and retired to come down here to this tropical paradise and mug tourists? "Yeah," he said, smiling still, but there was an edge to his voice, "I pissed on a tree back there. Any law against that?"

Apparently not. No one said a word, but the smiles slowly died all the way around. He wanted to go on, wanted to get things out in the open, wanted to throw it in their faces: *All right then, charge me, you sons of bitches, go ahead, but I'll make you regret it, all of you!* The words were on his lips when Carolee raised her water glass, ice cubes clicking, and took a quick birdlike sip. They seemed to have arrived at some sort of impasse. The room expanded, then shrank down again till it fit just exactly right. Finally, the lieutenant ducked his head to remove the dark glasses, revealing eyes that were darker still, eyes that were almost black, heavy-lidded and set too close together. "We are not here to accuse you," he said. "We are here to assist. And to clear up any difficult feelings or dissatisfactions you or your wife may have. We are gravely sorry for what has transpired and we extend our sincerest apologies."

Someone at the bar behind them let out a laugh and the lines hardened in Salas' face, lines that traced his jaw muscles and pulled tight round his mouth. He wasn't much older than his own son, Sten realized, thirty maybe, thirty tops, but his job—poking at the underbelly of things, interviewing gringos, sweeping the dirt under the carpet—bore down on him, you could see that at a glance. Sten had an impulse to reach out to him, to thank him, but he couldn't relax, not yet, not till the boat weighed anchor and they saw the last of this place.

"The man you"—a pause—"*encountered,* was a criminal, well known to us. Let me tell you, his death is no loss to the world." His lips parted and here came the smile again. "In fact, from a certain perspective, you could almost say that you've done us a favor."

The other cop nodded in assent. "One less problem. Or headache, is that how you say it? One less headache?"

"Yes," Salas agreed, "that's exactly it. Now," swinging round to face Carolee, "we will require a statement from you, señora—and my colleague here, Sergeant Araya, will assist you in that." He squared his shoulders, as if coming to attention, though he was still seated and his iced tea stood untouched before him and the cigarette burned unnoticed in his hand. "And you, sir, Mr. Stensen, I would ask you please to accompany me and the Senior Second Officer"—a nod for Potamiamos—"to another portion of this ship, a cabin we have secured for this purpose, in order for you to make identification of a man we have reason to believe was an accomplice in this business." He made a motion toward the door, sweeping an arm in invitation.

Sten remained seated. He looked to Carolee, who'd sat there wordlessly to this point. "It's okay," he said, "no worries. I'll be right back."

Potamiamos rose. He and the lieutenant exchanged a glance. The party seemed to be breaking up.

"All right," Sten said, "I'll take a look at him. But I'm not leaving this ship."

"Oh, no, no." Potamiamos very nearly clucked his tongue. "No, there's no question of that."

They walked down the corridor to the elevator, Potamiamos to his left, Salas to his right, and everybody, every reveler aboard, stared at him as if he were being led off to a detention cell somewhere, and he supposed there must have been a secure room down there in the depths of the ship to accommodate the occasional passenger or crewmember who drank too much or went floridly berserk. They had a sick bay, didn't they? And a pharmacy. And just about anything else you could imagine. They were a small city afloat and all contingencies had to be anticipated and prepared for.

He was a head taller than either of his—what would you call them?—*escorts*, but still he couldn't help feeling a sense of unease, no matter how many times he told himself he was in control, because he wasn't, he wasn't at all, and he half expected some sort of trick, a roomful of cops, handcuffs, the cloth bag jerked over his head and a quick hustle down the gangplank and into some festering hole like the one in *Midnight Express*. The tendon clicked in his knee again, once, twice, and then they were standing before the elevator and the doors were opening on a scrum of passengers in tennis togs, terrycloth robes, shorts and T-shirts, dinner jackets and cocktail dresses. The Senior Second Officer greeted them with a blooming smile and a cheery "Good evening, folks, enjoying yourselves?" while Salas held the door and shepherded Sten in amongst them. Most of the others were going up and Sten and his escorts made way for them as the elevator stopped at various decks, even as a fresh crew of tennis players, high rollers and shuffleboarders crowded in, and then they were going down, stopping at each floor, until they were belowdecks, in the crew's quarters, where passengers were not allowed.

Sten had been arrested only once in his life, for a DUI after a wedding for which he'd stood as best man. John Jarvis' wedding. J.J. They'd been in the Corps together, had seen some hairy and not-so-hairy shit, buddies over there and back here, and when they got home—the very week—J.J. had married his high school heartthrob in some wedding palace down in Carmel. Drinking preceded the ceremony, floated through it on fumes and quick nips from one flask or another, rose in a delirious clamor while the cake was cut and distributed and went on unabated long after the newlyweds had ducked away to do what they were going to do as man and wife in their room at the big hotel in the middle of town. He'd felt a bit hazy as he'd climbed into his VW Bug and started back up the coast, alone and missing Carolee, who was away in London for her semester abroad, but he had the radio—"Radar Love," cranked high, he remembered that, and "Magic Carpet Ride" too—and he had the window rolled down though he was freezing, making it all the way up 101 and Nineteenth Avenue through the city and Golden Gate Park and back onto the freeway and across the bridge, feeling clearer and soberer by the mile.

That was when the flashing lights appeared in his rearview, a cop rushing up on him so fast he thought at first the problem must have been up ahead of him somewhere, the cop after somebody else in that streaming river of taillights that made the night so cozy and inviting. He was wrong. The cruiser rode up on his tail, but he told himself that didn't mean anything, not necessarily, because maybe the cop was going to get off at the exit coming up on the right, an emergency there somewhere, an accident, a dog loose on the highway, a motorcyclist down, debris in the pass-ing lane . . . but then the cruiser swung out alongside him and it began to dawn on him that he was in trouble.

What he remembered of that night, aside from the wheezing and muttering of his fellow drunks and the reek of vomit that was so pervasive it seemed to arise from the walls themselves, was the helplessness he'd felt behind bars, locked up, incarcerated, in the can, no place to turn or even sit, except the floor—not in control, definitely not in control. He'd told the arresting officer he'd been to a wedding, the wedding of one of his service buddies—"You know," he said, "the Marine Corps? Like I served my country. Like I saw some bad shit and I know I had a couple drinks, just this once, because it was a wedding, okay?"—but it didn't do any good. He had a flashlight, the cop, and it was right there like a supernova bursting in Sten's face, in his eyes, hot and probing. Cars hissed by. It was the strangest thing, but for a moment, just that moment, he didn't seem to know where he was or where the light had come from or why it was punishing him like this. "You know you're in no condition to drive, don't you?" the cop said.

Sten just blinked at him. And then, very slowly, he began to nod his head in agreement.

But now he was in a corridor, deep in the underbelly of the ship, one man on his left, the other on his right. They walked along amiably enough, down to the end of the corridor, and then they swung into another corridor and another after that till he had no idea where he was or how to find his way back. He followed their lead, moving along blindly till Salas put a hand on his arm to guide him and they entered a room that smelled of food—of hamburgers, a mountain of hamburgers, fries, onion rings, beer—and he saw the light there, bright as the cop's flashlight, and the man it illuminated till it seemed as if he were the only three-dimensional thing in the room. Everything else was flattened as if on a screen, tables, chairs, the counter where they must have served up meals to the crew. But the man—a Tico in an oversized T-shirt sitting at one of the Formica tables, his hands cuffed behind his back and his eyes cast down—seemed to leap out at him. He wore a goatee. He was skinny, puny, barely there. He might once have held a knife in his hand.

"Is this the man that attacked you?" Salas indicated the prisoner with a jerk of his head, his voice in official mode now, ripe with accusation and contempt. "Or one of the men?"

Sten saw now that there was another policeman in the room, a guard with a holstered gun leaning against the back wall in the shadow—or relative shadow—of the lamp. He saw too that the lamp, one of those shop lights with a clamp at the base of it, was fixed to the table directly across from the prisoner and arranged so that there was no way for him to escape the glare of it, and if he went outside of himself again to think of the movies, this scene he'd witnessed a hundred times on screens big and small, it was because the movies were his only reference point for what was happening to him. It was as if he'd entered some dream, some fantasyland where there was no sun, no sky, no mud lot or bus or ship, only this. Finally—and he was on his guard now, on his guard all over again—he noticed the square of white cloth smoothed out at the far end of the table. It was a linen napkin, one of the service items on pristine display at each of the ship's restaurants and lounges, one of countless thousands that must have been washed, dried, folded and set out afresh each day. But this one was different. This one held—presented—three exhibits: a .357 Magnum revolver and two knives, switchblades with mother-of-pearl handles.

"Well?" Salas said. "What do you say?"

Sten looked to Potamiamos but Potamiamos averted his eyes, as uneasy with the proceedings as he was himself. He could feel Salas pushing his will on him, eager to get this over with, wrap it up, take the prisoner back where he belonged, to the cell in some crumbling compound with the rusting steel bars and wet concrete floor—and what else? Roaches, there'd have to be roaches. Scorpions, maybe. Who knew? Biting flies. Leeches. Toss him in the pit and leave him there. Sten wanted out too. He thought of Carolee and the other cop and how she was bearing up, and then he was focusing on the prisoner as if seeing him for the first time. The man's left eye was partially closed and a raised red welt traced the cheekbone beneath it. His scalp was close-shaved, each follicle of hair bristling like a clump of rice set down in a smooth paddy of skull-tight flesh. There was a problem with his ear, the lobe torn, dried blood coiled in the hollow there, grainy and dark, and his posture was all wrong, his body language. He looked ashamed of himself, looked guilty. Was this the man? Sten couldn't say. It could be. Certainly it could be.

"Well?"

Sten shrugged.

Salas exchanged a glance with the Senior Second Officer. "We will need a positive identification, because unfortunately"—he gestured to the weapons on the white cloth—"whatever person extracted these knives from the mud compromised any fingerprints we might have found there. Do these look like the knives the perpetrators used—in your recollection?"

Another shrug. "I don't know," he said. "But that's the gun."

"Yes, we have corroborated that."

It was then that the prisoner entered the equation, suddenly jerking to life as if he'd been hot-wired. His head snapped forward and he rucked something up—a rapid ratcheting of his throat, the pursing of his lips—and there it was on the front of Sten's shirt, dangling in a long glistening thread. "*Voy a matarle,*" he snarled, even as Salas stepped forward and cuffed the side of his face. "*¡Silencio!*" Salas roared, and then he turned to Sten and said, "Do you see? Do you see what happens when you try to treat these animals like human beings?" He drew himself up. The prisoner shrank back into the nest of his bones. The light flickered and the bloated hull of the ship seemed to rise and dip on a nonexistent tide.

"What did he say?" Sten wanted to know.

"Nothing," Salas said. He seemed abrupt, almost offended by the question. In the same moment, he removed a handkerchief from his breast pocket, and very carefully, tenderly even, he wiped the spittle from the front of Sten's shirt. "Now, I ask you again: is this the man?"

If his heart was pounding, it wasn't out of fear or excitement or remorse, but out of rage, only that. He'd never seen this man before in his life—in that instant, he was sure of it. Another Tico. Another shaved head. Another goatee. He looked first to Potamiamos, then to Salas, and finally, to the prisoner. "Yeah," he said, and he was already shifting his hips to work the long muscles of his legs and climb on up out of this hole, "that's him. That's the one."

PART II

Willits

5.

SHE DIDN'T LIKE FAST food, or not particularly—the grease they used hardened your arteries and they doused everything with corn syrup and sugar, which jacked up the calories and made you put on weight, an issue with her, she knew it—but she stopped at the place on Route 20 in Willits and got a crispy chicken sandwich, if only to put something on her stomach. It wasn't like her to oversleep, but that's what happened, and she'd had to skip breakfast and run out the door with nothing but a cup of yesterday's coffee microwaved to an angry boil—and she still wound up being half an hour late for her morning appointment. As a concession to the little voice nagging in her head, she skipped the fries and ordered a diet drink instead of regular, though she did ask for crispy instead of grilled because grilled had no more taste than warmed-over cardboard with a spatter of ketchup on it. Kutya was in the backseat, generally behaving himself, but he came to attention when she pulled into the drive-thru lane. He must have recognized the place, if not by sight, then smell, though she hadn't stopped here more than a handful of times. At any rate, he began whining and tap dancing around on the seat he'd rendered filthy despite the towel she'd spread over it, and she gave in and ordered him a burger (no bun, no condiments, no pickles), feeding it to him over her shoulder as she put the trusty blue Nissan Sentra in drive and sailed on out of the lot and down the long winding road to Fort Bragg and the coast.

There was talk on the radio, but it was mainly left-wing Communist crap—*NPR,* and how was it their signal was stronger than anybody else's?—and even that faded out once she started down the grade and hit the first few switchbacks, so she popped in a CD instead. She favored country, but the old stuff, the classic stuff, Loretta and Merle and Hank, because all the new singers with their custom-made boots and blow-dried hair were just pale imitators, anyway. And if people criticized her for being a once-divorced forty-year-old woman with no romantic prospects on the horizon who really wasn't in step with the times (*You mean not even Brad Paisley?*), so much the worse. She liked what she liked. And when she went out on a Saturday night with her best friend, Christabel Walsh, and had a few beers, she just let the music wash right over her like the vapid stares of all the losers lined up at the bar who were too small-minded and self-absorbed to ask a woman to dance.

No matter. She dwelled within herself. She was content and self-sufficient. She had her own business, she had Kutya, a rented two-bedroom clapboard house that looked down on the crotch of the Noyo Valley and half the horses in the world available to her anytime she wanted to ride. If another relationship came along, fine. If not, too bad for him—or them, whoever they might be—because she wasn't desperate, not in the least, not even close, and there was no way in the world she was going to pretend to like Brad Paisley or whoever because to her it was all just more of the same singsong bastardized crap, and she'd told Christabel that and she'd tell anybody else who might want to stick their nose in too.

So there she was, driving in her own personal property with her dog by her side and a living to earn, winding down Route 20 so she could get to the Coast Highway and head forty-four-point-five miles south to the little flyspeck town of Calpurnia, where there were three horses—and, if the veterinarian showed up on time, at least one sable antelope with three-foot horns—that needed her ministrations. It was the middle of the summer. The sky was clear, the sun fixed like a compass point ahead of her. When she looped around a turn and saw the coast off in the distance, it was clear there too, the fog burned back and exiled in a linty gray band out at sea. Was she wearing her seatbelt? No, she wasn't, and she was never going to wear it either. Seatbelt laws were just another contrivance of the U.S. Illegitimate Government of America the Corporate that had given up the gold standard back in 1933 and pledged its citizens as collateral so it could borrow and keep on borrowing. But she wasn't a citizen of the U.S.I.G.A., she was a sovereign citizen, a U.S. national, born and raised, and she didn't now and never would again acknowledge anybody's illegitimate authority over her. So no, she wasn't wearing her seatbelt. And she didn't have legal plates, or the sort of plates the republic of California deemed legal, that is (the sticker that had come with the ones on the car was long since expired because she wasn't about to play *that* game), and if she was traveling on the public roads in her own personal property, it was her business and nobody else's.

When the cop pulled her over, he claimed it was because she wasn't wearing a seatbelt, but of course he would have had to have raptor's eyes to see that from three hundred feet away where he was fooling nobody behind a roadside clump of madrone except maybe the drifting black vultures overhead. She'd watched him swing out behind her, pulling a U-turn and settling in on her tail with his gumball machine spinning and his siren whoop-whoop-whooping. She might have gone half a mile or more before she finally pulled over—in a spot at the mouth of a dirt drive that seemed sufficiently safe, the whole road to this point bristling with jagged pines and dried-up weeds that snatched at the side of the car every time she drifted toward the shoulder. Looking back on it, she supposed she could have stopped sooner, and she supposed too that that might have had something to do with this particular cop's agitation, but you did what you did and you couldn't have regrets, not in this life that just marched you on toward the grave day by day.

He was lean, young, fresh-faced. He had to tap at the window three times before she rolled it down. Kutya lurched forward to give him a low warning growl and then he was barking and she didn't do a thing about it. Let him bark, that was what she felt. It was his right.

"Do you know why I stopped you, ma'am?" the cop said.

Of course she did: he was the oppressor and she was the oppressed. She said nothing.

"License and registration," the cop said, raising his voice to be heard over the clamor of the dog. "And proof of insurance."

What she told him in response, in a voice as steady as she could hold it, even as Kutya settled into a ragged gasping continuous low-throated bark and people slowed to gape at her as if she were some circus attraction, was that she was not engaged in a contract with the republic of California. "I'm a sovereign citizen," she said, speaking as clearly as she could, given the noise of the dog and the clank and hiss of the traffic as all the white-haired Baby Boomer tourists applied their brakes and then stepped back on the gas once they'd got a good look. "You have no authority over me."

The cop just stared at her. After a moment he flipped up his sunglasses so she could see the fine red fissures of irritation fracturing his frog-belly eyes. "Maybe you didn't hear me," he said, "but I asked for your license and registration."

She said nothing. Just fixed her gaze straight ahead to where the road ran on into the sunshine past a field of stiff yellow grass and a shadowy fringe of trees, the road that ran true to her destination, to the place where she had business when she had no business here at all.

"Ma'am?"

She turned her head back to him, locked her eyes on his, and her heart was going, all right, because she could tell where this was leading and it scared her and made the anger come up in her too, and why couldn't they just leave well enough alone? "I told you," she said, "I have no contract with you."

"Does that mean you refuse?"

"Let me repeat," she said. "I—have—no—contract—with—you."

He shifted his boots in the gravel along the roadside, a dull grating intolerable sound that got Kutya back up into the high register. The cop put his hands on his hips, as if to show her where the gun was and the nightstick and handcuffs too. He said, "I'm going to have to ask you to get out of the car."

"No," she said. "I won't."

"Suit yourself." He straightened up then and stalked back to his car, where she could see him in her rearview as he leaned in, pulled out the cord of the radio mike and started moving his lips.

Ten long minutes crept by. Each one of them, each second, dripped acid through her veins, and she thought of just putting the car in gear and driving off, but resisted because that would only make things worse. Kutya—he was a puli, a white puli—settled into the discolored basket of his dreadlocks and fell off to sleep, thinking the threat had passed. Foolishly. But then he was a dog, and dogs had other concerns.

Finally another cruiser appeared, lights flashing, siren scream-ing, swooping on up the road behind her like a black steel shroud and nosing in at an angle so close to her front bumper she thought it was going to hit her. In the next instant she was staring across the passenger's seat of this new car and into the face—the hard demanding unforgiving put-upon face—of a female officer, who picked something up off the seat, squared herself and swung out of the car. Next thing she knew, both cops were there, one on either side of her, and Kutya was back on his feet, back at it again, barking in a renewed frenzy that just made everything that much harder.

"Good afternoon," the female cop said, her eyes roaming over the interior as if she was thinking of making an offer on the car. "I understand that you refuse to comply with Officer Switzer's request for identification, is that right?"

She said nothing.

The female officer—she was tall, thin, no shape to her at all, and she wore no makeup, not a trace, not even lipstick—asked her to get out of the car. Or no, commanded her.

She said nothing.

"Just to be sure you understand me," the male cop cut in now—he was stationed by the passenger's-side window, leaning in so he could watch her, and if that didn't make her feel paranoid she couldn't imagine what would because this was like being squeezed between two pincers and it was wrong, intolerable, a violation of every natural right there was—"I have to inform you that state law requires you to show a valid driver's license, registration and proof of insurance at the reasonable request of a peace officer."

She threw it right back at him. "*Reasonable?* You call this reasonable? You have no authority here—you're nothing more to me than a man dressed up in a Halloween costume."

"If you refuse," he said, the muscles tightening around his mouth, "we will have no recourse but to remove you forcibly from your vehicle—"

"Which will be impounded," the female added, as if they'd switched speakers on a stereo, his voice assaulting her on the right, hers on the left. "And your dog will be taken to the shelter." She paused. A top-heavy camper swished delicately past them, ten miles under the limit. A pickup going the opposite way swung with elaborate courtesy off onto the shoulder to give it room and then continued on in a slow-motion crawl. "And you yourself, if you don't comply this minute, will be arrested, I promise you that—and I personally will escort you to the county jail."

It was hopeless, she could see that. The day was ruined. The week, the whole month. This was the mega-state in all its glory. She'd stated her status in plain English and they still didn't seem to understand. Well, they could go to hell, all of them. She started screaming then, calling them every name in the book, shouting "TDC! TDC! Threat, Duress and Coercion!" over and over again, even as the female forced open the door and took hold of her by her left arm and Kutya, good dog, faithful dog, went right at her.

✦ ✦

They took her to the county jail in Ukiah, retracing her route back up Route 20, though now she was in restraints and in the backseat of a police cruiser, separated by a heavy wire grid and Plexiglas shield from the female cop, whose right hand, resting at one o'clock on the wheel, sported two bright shining flesh-colored bandaids where the dog's teeth had broken the skin, though it wasn't much more than a scratch. Her own car was back alongside the road, awaiting the tow truck, and Kutya—poor Kutya—after having been poked, prodded and muzzled by two numbnuts from Animal Control, had been forced into a boxy white van, which must have been somewhere behind her now, on its way up this same road to the animal shelter, also in Ukiah. She'd missed her appointment, of course—and for what, for nothing, for a seatbelt?—and she'd had no way of letting the Burnsides know she wasn't coming, that she'd been unavoidably and illegally detained and wasn't just blowing off her responsibility, and who could blame them if they went online and found another farrier to shoe their horses and trim the hooves of their sable antelope? She had a reputation to maintain, a business to run, and she was doing no harm to anybody, doing nothing more than using the public byways as was her inalienable right, and now look at the mess she was in.

Still, as the cruiser looped through the turns and climbed back up out of the Noyo Valley, she began to rethink her position, until degree by degree she felt the indignation cooling in her. This was going to cost her. Fines, towing and Christ knew what else. They'd make her renew that sticker, and there'd be paperwork, a layout of cash she really didn't have and every sort of hassle the authorities (*authorities,* what a joke) could devise. By the time they arrived at the police station and they'd photographed and fingerprinted her, given her her one phone call—to Christabel, who else?—and escorted her to an empty cell and locked her in, she was contrite. Or no: *chastened* was a better word. And enlightened. Enlightened too. These people didn't recognize her status, didn't know a damned thing about the Uniform Commercial Code or her rights under it, and they didn't care either. They had all the power, all the muscle, and she was nothing, reduced to this, to groveling and ass-kissing and giving lip service to the System, as if she was grateful they'd assaulted her and taken away her rights and her property. All right. If that was how they wanted it, fine. She sat in that cell and kept her mouth firmly shut and fed her hate and resentment till Christabel showed up an hour later with the bail money and she was out.

"I told you," Christabel said, once they'd slammed into her pickup in the lot out back of the station. "You may have your theories or beliefs or whatever, but these people? They don't care. They're on another planet—this planet, planet earth." She gave her a look, all eye shadow and glistening black mascara. "And you—you're in outer space. I mean it, Sara. I really do."

Christabel was two years older than she was, also divorced, also childless. She'd kept her figure and had men sniffing after her seven days a week, but she was done with men, or that's what she said, anyway—at least till the next one came along. She was Sara's best friend and here she was proving it all over again, taking time out from her work as a teacher's aide at the elementary school to be there for her, but she was wrong on this, dead wrong.

"It's not theory," she said. "It's law. Natural law."

"There you go—I mean, don't you ever learn?" They were heading out of the parking lot now, the police lot, and the idiot dinger started in because she wasn't wearing her seatbelt. "And buckle your belt, will you?"

Contrite? Who was contrite? Not her. "No," she said. "No way."

That was when Christabel hit the brake so hard she nearly went through the window. "I swear I'm not going another inch until you buckle up—and not just because of what happened here and not for safety's sake either, but because I can't stand that fucking noise one more second!"

"You don't have to shout," she said. "I mean, there's nothing wrong with my hearing." Still she didn't touch the belt. It was as if her hands were paralyzed.

The noise kept up, *ding-ding-ding,* a beat, then *ding-ding-ding* and *ding-ding-ding.*

"Sara, I'm warning you, I mean it, I do—"

She let her gaze roll on out over the scene. She was calm now, utterly calm. Traffic flicked by on the street. *Ding-ding-ding. Ding-ding-ding.* A girl who honestly couldn't have been more than sixteen went by pushing one of those double baby strollers as if there was nothing wrong with that, as if that was the way people were supposed to live. She looked over her shoulder and saw that there was a car in the lot behind them, a face trapped in the blaze of the windshield, some other soul trying to get out of this purgatory and back to real life, but nobody was going anywhere unless something changed right here and now. Christabel was glaring at her, actually glaring.

In the next moment, and she hardly knew what she was doing, she flipped the handle and pushed the door open wide, and then she was out on the sidewalk, her feet moving and the door gaping behind her, hurrying down the street as fast as her boots would take her, thinking, *The bank, the bank before it closes.* And Christabel? Christabel was just an afterthought because she wasn't going to sit there arguing. She had to get to the bank because she knew she was going to have to suck everything out of her savings and put it into a cashier's check if she was going to get the car out of hock. That was the first priority, the car, because without it she was stuck. Once she had it back, the minute they handed her the keys, she'd head straight to the animal shelter, because when she thought about how scared and hurt and confused that dog must have been, it just made her heart seize. He'd never been separated from her since she'd got him as a pup, never, not for a single day, and what had he done? Just defend her, that was all. And now he was locked up in a concrete pen with a bunch of strays and pit bulls and god knew what else. She didn't care what anybody said, and they could go ahead and crucify her, but that was as wrong as wrong got.

6.

BUT THEN THEY WOULDN'T let her car go until she went down to the DMV and had it properly registered (their words, not hers), yet in order to do that she had to show title to the car, which was at home in the lower drawer of her filing cabinet, which in turn meant calling Christabel and eating crow (*I'm sorry, I was upset, I don't know what came over me*) so she could get a ride back up to Willits and then down again to the DMV, which was closed when she got there, of course, as was the animal shelter, and that was hard, the hardest thing about this whole sorry affair. She could see through the glass of the door into the deserted lobby and hear the dogs barking in back, could hear Kutya, and there was nothing she could do about it. She must have banged on that door for ten minutes but nobody came, and the noise she made, the noise of her frustration and anger, meted out with the underside of her coiled fist, just made the dogs bark all the louder.

Behind her, in the lot, Christabel sat in the truck with the engine running. "They're closed!" she shouted, hanging half out the window. "Can't you see that? They're closed!"

She almost broke down then, so frustrated her eyes clouded over till she could barely see, but she didn't break down and she didn't give up either. Instead she worked her way around back, looking for a way in, a gate with a padlock somebody had forgotten to secure, a chainlink fence she could scale, and all the while the dogs barked and howled and whimpered from deep inside. She circled the place twice—there was a rear door, locked, and from the feel of it, bolted too—then made her way back across the lot to Christabel.

"Well?" Christabel demanded. "Did I tell you? They're closed.

Shut down." She held up her phone. "Hours, ten to five, Tuesday through Saturday."

"You don't have a crowbar, do you, anything like a crowbar? A jack handle?"

"Are you crazy? They probably have cameras—everybody does. You're probably on film right now. You can't just—"

"The bastards," she said, spitting the words out, so saturated with grief and hate it was coming out her pores. "Jesus. I was just going to work. Isn't that what they want in this rip-off society, people working? So they can stick their hands in your pockets?"

The pickup rumbled in a soft smooth way that was like its own kind of melody. A steady float of exhaust ghosted across the lot. Christabel pulled down her sunglasses to squint against the light that flattened her features and picked out the vertical trenches between her eyes. "You're not talking about the IRS again, are you?"

She didn't answer. Just stared at the building and listened to the barking of the dogs as it wound down now to a confused gabble and then stopped altogether.

"Because I've heard it all already. And you don't pay taxes, anyway, do you? Or fines either." She paused. The exhaust tumbled on a breeze that came up out of nowhere, rich with chemical intoxicants. "Get in the car," she said. "I'm tired."

"So am I."

"Well, get in."

This was why people firebombed buildings. And how she'd like to bomb the police station and the DMV and this shithole too . . . but then Kutya was in there and she couldn't hurt him, couldn't even think of it. Most people—and Christabel was one of them—didn't understand that government by the corporation was no government at all. Didn't understand that it was the Four-teenth Amendment that converted sovereign citizens into federal citizens by making them agree to a contract to accept federal benefits—and taxes and all the illegal and confounding maze of laws that come with them. Taxes on your taxes. Do this, do that. You don't like it, go to jail. But that amendment was unconstitutional and if you subscribed to it you were just a slave of the system and had no rights at all except what they doled out to you with one hand while helping themselves to your paycheck with the other. How had it ever come to this? How could people be so blind, so stupid?

It all came down on her in that moment in a funk of hopelessness, because what was the use? She'd fight them, she'd continue to fight them and do everything in her power to live free and beholden to no man or woman, fight till there was nothing left of her but bleached white bones spread out in the dirt, but not tonight, not now. There was nothing she could do. She was beaten. She ducked her head so that her hair fell in her eyes till the wind lifted it again, then climbed into the pickup and slammed the door.

"Where to?" Christabel asked, softening her look.

Christabel was a good friend, a true friend, the best she'd ever had, the one person who was there for her, wading through the shitstorm no matter what came down. And she was right, of course—they couldn't sit here all night. Sara just shrugged.

"How about a drink? After all you've been through don't you deserve it?" A little laugh. "Not to mention me."

The truck rumbled. A plastic bag chased the breeze across the blacktop. She fixed one last look on the ugly buff building with its cheap knee-high vertical windows anybody could step right through and let out a sigh. "I don't care," she heard herself say.

They wound up going to a brew pub on State and she tried a pint of something called Mendo Blonde, but it tasted of hops and metal and just gave her gas, so they went over to Casa Carlos and had margaritas and chicken tacos and she ate too much and had at least two too many drinks. She didn't even know she was eating, she was so upset. The food just seemed to disappear, tacos, beans, rice, basket after basket of the chips she dipped mechanically in the little cruets of salsa that began to clutter the table till there was no room to rest your elbow or even a forearm. And the margaritas too—as soon as she set down her empty glass there was a new one there to replace it. By the time they made it back home to Willits (twenty minutes on a darkened highway that seemed like hours), she was too exhausted to do anything more than collapse in bed after Christabel dropped her off. She didn't even bother to turn on a light or pour herself a glass of water, just undressed in the dark, flinging her clothes in the direction of the chair in the corner, the house woeful and empty without Kutya there so that every creeping sound of the night was magnified, and if she was the kind who cried herself to sleep, she would have done it. She woke at intervals throughout the night, feeling as if she was being strangled in her sleep, a heavy shroud of sorrow and regret pulled up over her like a comforter made of dross.

She was up at dawn, her every mortal fiber aching, and her first thought was for Kutya. Christabel had agreed to drop her at the DMV before she went in to work, but that was two long hours away, and so she made herself a pot of coffee and some wheat toast and went out on the front porch to watch the sun ease its way down into the valley and illuminate the tops of the pines and firs and redwoods that had been the support of generations of loggers since the first settlers made their way up from the coast. She kept checking her watch, the minutes dragging as if they had anchors attached to them, and then the newspaper arrived to reiterate its falsehoods and outright lies, but she was too worked up to concentrate on it and she found herself pacing round the yard, back and forth, as if she were in the cell still—under lock and key, restrained, constrained, helpless—until Christabel's pickup turned off the main road and came up the drive.

The people at the DMV barely glanced at her, lost in their wilderness of forms and regulations and computer printouts. She was the first one in the door when they opened. There was the usual crap, the flag, the linoleum, the chairs and desks and eye charts, all paid for by the wage slaves of the U.S. of A., one little sinkhole of bureaucracy amongst a million of them. The man behind the front desk could have been anybody, and if he realized he was a minion and servant of the corporate state, he gave no indication and she wasn't about to inform him either. All she wanted was the signed, sealed and approved scrap of DMV paper to tape to the inside of her windshield. Which she got in due course. Money changed hands, naturally, but she wasn't going to worry about that now because now she needed her car back so she could drive to the animal shelter and retrieve her dog before he whined himself to death—and what must *he* have been thinking? That she'd abandoned him? Given up on him? Told them to lock him away with all those strays they euthanized as if they had no more animate soul than a bug?

She got a surprise at the impound yard, which she'd walked to, ten long blocks, but it was a pleasant surprise, if you can call having your property stolen from you and paying to get it back pleasant in any way, shape or form. But there was Mary Ellis, one of her longtime clients, standing behind the bulletproof glass in the office, and she was sympathetic to the point of rallying to the cause—oh, she knew the arresting officer, all right, Joanie Jerpbak, and she was a queen bitch, daughter of a retired CHP officer who was the original son of a bitch—but more money, a lot more money, changed hands despite the sympathy, and then it was on to Animal Control.

Barking was what she heard when she pulled into the lot, barking that seemed to rise to a frenzy as she stepped out of the car, and what were they doing to them in there, goading them with cattle prods? She remembered her husband—ex-husband— telling her a story about how they trained the police dogs down in Sacramento. He was in college then and the apartment he was renting was on the second story of a building that looked down on the backyard of the K-9 academy, where they kept and trained the dogs. One afternoon he heard the dogs going crazy and looked out to see a figure dressed like the Michelin Man with a pair of Belgian shepherds tearing at him. He had a stick in his hand—he was the aggressor, the bad guy—and he didn't shout, "Bad dog!" No, what he was shouting was "Good dog!" over and over again. That was how they trained them. That was the kind of people they were.

Her throat was dry and her heart was pounding when she stepped through the door, the barking from the pens in back rising in volume and yet another functionary standing there gazing at her from behind another desk. They murdered dogs here, that was what she was thinking, *euthanized* them, and from the sound of it, provoked them just for the pleasure of it. She didn't say hello or state her business, but just gave the functionary—a woman in her twenties dressed in khaki shirt and shorts—a shocked look. "What are you doing to them back there?" she demanded.

The woman—girl—smiled. "They're all excited," she said, and the smile widened. "It's feeding time."

Feeding time. Did she feel foolish? Maybe. A little. She shifted her gaze to the bulletin board on the side wall, which was plastered with head-shots of dogs and cats up for adoption, and then to the cats themselves, ten of them or so, each in a separate cage tricked out with a mini hammock, as if they were on vacation with all the time in the world at their disposal, as if they were happy to be here, when the truth was they were only waiting for their appointment with the furnace in back. There was an antiseptic smell about the place, a scent of formalin and Simple Green, and something else she couldn't quite place, something caustic. The counter before her offered brochures on pet care, vaccinations and neutering and a hallway led to another door, the one that gave onto the inner sanctum. "I came for my dog," she said, bringing her focus back to the girl. "I would've been here last night, but you were closed."

"Name?"

"Kutya."

"Kutya what?"

"Just Kutya, that's all. I mean, does a dog have to have a last name?"

The girl let out a laugh. "Sorry," she said. "Your name, I mean."

"Sara Hovarty Jennings. That's H-o-v-a-r-t-y, Jennings. They took my dog away from me yesterday afternoon, the cops, when they impounded my car. And they brought him here."

Still smiling—they'd broken the routine, shared a joke—the girl focused on the screen of her computer and tapped away at the keyboard. Sara stood there at the counter studying the girl's face while the dogs barked distantly and a pale finger of sun poked in through one of the windows she'd briefly considered smashing the night before. She watched the smile fade and then die. "I'm sorry," the girl said, looking up at her now, "but we can't release the dog at this time."

"What do you mean? I'm the owner. Do you need proof, is that it?"

The girl looked embarrassed, the way people do when they're about to drop a bomb on you. "No," she said softly, and Sara could see that it wasn't her fault, that she was sympathetic, some-body's daughter just doing her job. "It's that—well, the report says here that the dog bit someone, is that right? And that you don't have a certificate of rabies vaccination?"

Sara went numb. She just shook her head. The dogs barked and barked, but it was joyous barking—they were barking for their kibble and the cold comfort of their cages.

"She'll have to be quarantined for thirty days—"

"He."

"He will, I mean. It's right here, see?" She swung the moni-tor round so that Sara could see the regimented blocks of words suspended there, as if they meant anything, as if the official who'd typed out the order had any authority over the dog she'd raised from a puppy so tiny he couldn't even climb the two steps to the back porch.

"My dog doesn't have rabies," she said.

But the girl was ahead of her here, the girl, who despite her youth, sympathy and good humor, had been in this very position before, a girl in uniform *just doing her job.* "I'm sorry," she said. "We can't take that chance. It's the rules."

7.

TWO LONG DREARY PLAYED-OUT days dragged by, every ticking minute a new kind of torture. She couldn't eat. Couldn't sleep. The TV was just noise and every book and magazine she picked up might as well have been written in code for all the sense it made. She paced back and forth across the kitchen floor till she practically wore a groove in it and shunned the ringing phone, though caller ID told her it was Christabel or one of her clients or—endlessly—her mother calling from her condo in San Diego to magnify her complaints and whisper the details of her confidential crises in a voice so thin and reduced you might have thought it was coming from beyond the grave. Either that or the phone was tapped. Who knew? Maybe it was.

She'd tried to reason with the girl at Animal Control but all she got was "Sorry" and "Those are the regulations" and "There's nothing I can do," and then she tried to educate her so she could comprehend what a free-born citizen was and how her arbitrary rules didn't apply, but that wasn't working, not a chance, and finally she'd lost it, actually snatching something up off the counter—a ledger of some sort—and slamming it to the floor with a sharp reverberant boom that startled them both. The girl pulled her cellphone out then and informed her she was going to have to leave or she'd call the police. "And I mean it too," the girl said, her mouth bunched in a pout, and she *was* a child—a willful, stupid child. And how could you argue with a child?

On the morning of the fourth day, which was a Saturday and the last day the shelter would be open till the following week, she knew she had to do something—she could feel Kutya's spirit crying out to her just as intensely as if he were right there in the room with her—but she couldn't imagine what it might be. It was seven o'clock. She made herself some coffee and a packet of oatmeal. Suddenly the phone rang—her landline—and this time she picked it up.

A familiar voice came at her, but at first she couldn't quite place it. "Sara?"

"Yeah?"

"Cindy Burnside."

"Oh, yeah. Hi."

"We were expecting you on Tuesday, or did you forget?"

"No, I'm sorry, I didn't forget—I ran into some trouble and I should have called you, I know, but, well, it was the police. They impounded my car." Her voice went thick. She was on the verge of tears. "And Kutya. They've got Kutya down at Animal Control."

"What? What are you saying?"

"He bit the cop that pulled me over. Nipped her, really. Barely broke the skin if you want to know."

There was a silence.

"But it's okay now," she said, "I got the car back. I can come this morning, if you still want me—"

And so there she was again, driving in her own personal property down the brake-eating road to the coast, listening to Hank Williams feeling sorry for himself, her seatbelt unfastened and the windows open wide. She tried not to think, weaving in and out of the dense bastions of shadow the big trees threw up across the road, but she kept coming back to Kutya and the girl at Animal Control and the vertical windows and the locked back door as if it were a chess problem that only needed sufficient brain power to solve. There was practically no one on the road, which was fine with her because there was nothing worse than following some overcompensating idiot's brake lights around every real or imagined turn, but by the time she was halfway to Fort Bragg the fog had climbed up the hill to meet her, locking everything in its gloom. She rolled up the windows, and then it got progressively darker and wetter till she had to flick on her lights and the wipers too.

She saw no cops, hidden or otherwise, and she made it to Calpurnia in good time, considering the fog. When she pulled into the long dirt drive at the Gentian Burnside Preserve it wasn't ten yet and that was a good thing because she still had unfinished business in Ukiah. As she rolled up to the barn, Cindy emerged from the house dressed in jeans and a sweater, her hair loose around her shoulders. It was cold. Everything was beaded with moisture, the fog even thicker here. "You poor thing," Cindy said, coming across the yard to her. "Did you get your dog back yet?"

She could only shake her head, the question so fraught and painful she had to bite her lip to keep from venting right then and there. She tried to keep her personal life separate from her business and didn't like to make excuses—it wasn't professional—or lay any of her political views on her clients unless they were receptive, and the Burnsides definitely weren't receptive, or not the way she read them anyway.

"Cup of tea?" Cindy offered. "And I've got a loaf of three-grain bread I baked yesterday if you want a bite of something—"

Cindy was in her fifties, an heiress to some corporate fortune—Sara never could remember which—who bankrolled her husband's obsession with preserving African ungulates that were on their way to extinction in the wild. She didn't put on any airs. If you didn't know, you'd never guess she was worth a hundred million or two or three or whatever it was. She seemed content to live out here on their hundred and twenty acres, riding her horses and helping her husband manage the herd of sable, roan and kudu antelope and the Hartmann's and Grevy's zebras roaming around the place as if they'd stepped out of a nature film. She didn't have a dog because of the animals—there were breeding females amongst them, that was the whole point, and they saw any canine as a threat, no different from jackals or the piebald wild dogs that tore their calves to pieces out on the savanna—and when Sara was there she was always careful to keep Kutya in the car. But then Kutya wasn't in the car. He was in a cage. In Ukiah.

"No, that's nice of you, Cindy, but I've got a day ahead of me—lots of complications—so I better get right to it. The vet coming?"

"He was out on Tuesday so we went ahead without you. It was Corinna? She was favoring her left hind leg and so he darted her and did a thorough exam—there was some inflammation there and he didn't know exactly what was causing it, so he's got her on prednisone. And since she was down, he did the hoof trimming himself." They both looked off to where the corral narrowed and the fences started and you could see some of the animals in the distance. "So it's just the horses today," Cindy said, turning back to her. "No big deal. Nothing to worry about. These things happen, right?"

"Yeah," Sara said. "Yeah. But why do they have to happen to me?"

She worked quickly, trimming the horses' hooves, cutting out the excess hoof walls and dead sole and then reshoeing them, letting her mind go free. All three horses—two mares and a gelding—knew her, so there was no problem there, just the routine she'd gone through a thousand times. The work settled her, the simple movements, the tools in her hands, the living breathing presence of the animals. She was in the car and heading back up the driveway by noon, feeling the sense of accomplishment she always felt on a job well done (and a payment received), but as soon as she got out on the main road it all came rushing back at her. The quarantine period was for thirty days. Thirty days. There was no way she was going to accept that.

She might have been pressing a bit, going faster than she should have considering the fog—at one point she came up on the pale ghost of a Winnebago moving so slowly it might as well have been parked, and she had to swing blindly out into the opposite lane to avoid hitting it, something she'd never do normally. There was no one coming, thank god, but she told herself she had to get a grip even as her speed crept back up again. The radio gave her classic rock, tunes she'd heard ad nauseam, but she was bored with her CDs and just let it play. She was tapping idly at the wheel, drumming along with the beat, jittery still from her morning coffee and the prospect of what lay ahead of her, when the sun broke through not half a mile after she'd turned back onto Route 20, and if it wasn't exactly an omen, at least it was nice. Off went the wipers, down came the windows. The breeze was cool and fresh and it carried the deep dry scent of the conifers that climbed up the grade as far as you could see in both directions. She'd just swung into the first of the wide sweeping turns after the long straightaway up from town when she saw the figure there on the side of the road—a man, a young man, backpedaling along the shoulder with his thumb out.

She wasn't naïve and she didn't have the highest opinion of human nature—or intelligence—but she made a point of stopping for hitchhikers, on these roads, anyway, whereas she would never even consider it down in the Bay Area where you had all sorts of nutballs and weirdos and stone-cold killers running around. Anybody hitching here was a local, most likely, and everybody couldn't afford a car, she understood that. There was still something of the hippie spirit up here, long hair, bandanas, brothers and sisters all, and half the population of the county growing marijuana as a going proposition. She pulled over and here he was, hustling up the shoulder to her.

He didn't have long hair. Didn't have any hair at all. He was wearing some sort of fatigues or camouflage—it wasn't deer season yet, was it?—and he was shouldering a backpack with a canteen looped over it. She saw a perfectly proportioned skull shaved to the bone, pale arching eyebrows that were barely there and a pair of naked eyes squinting against the sun. He was tall, six-one or -two, and he had to duck way down to toss his pack in on the backseat and then fold up his legs to squeeze into the seat beside her.

"Hi," she said, smiling reflexively, and it came to her that she knew him somehow, maybe from one of her clients or the bar scene or maybe she'd picked him up before. He looked young, but he was old enough to drink, mid-twenties, maybe—and who was he?

He gave her a blue-eyed stare, his eyes drifting away from her face as if he were stoned or just wakened from a dream.

"Where to?" she said, putting the car in gear and throwing a quick glance over her shoulder before rumbling back onto the roadway in a storm of dust.

He didn't answer, as if he hadn't heard her, and he wasn't looking at her now but sitting there rigidly as if he were at the dentist's, staring straight ahead.

She tried again. "You going far?"

"Ukiah," he said without turning his head, his voice soft and subdued, fluttering up from somewhere deep inside him.

The trees flashed by. She leaned into the next turn. "You're in luck," she said.

She wound up doing most of the talking, general subjects mainly—the tourists, the weather, how dry the forest was this time of year and how the fog down on the coast seemed thicker than usual—and when she got specific with regard to the absolute worthlessness of the song that was on the radio he didn't offer an opinion one way or the other. Whether he was an Elton John aficionado or wanted to poison his well or was utterly indifferent, she couldn't say, but she'd thrown it out because she certainly wasn't shy about her opinions and laying them out there was the best way to open people up. It didn't open him up. He just stared out the window, his shoulders stiff as a coat hanger. In fact, the only thing that seemed to get a rise out of him was when she told him about Kutya, how they'd impounded her car and taken him away from her. He gave her a sidelong look then, his head and neck still locked in position, straight forward, and murmured, "Yeah, they took my car too."

"Really? Why? What happened?"

He just shrugged. "You know how it is," he said after a moment.

"Yeah," she said, stealing a look at him, "tell me about it."

The day glanced off the windshield. She gave the car some gas to get up the grade and there was nobody ahead of her, which was nice, but there was a whole phalanx of motor homes twisting down the hill in the opposite direction, big groaning fortresses of metal that seemed ready to fly out of control on every turn, and what kind of person would drive something like that? Somebody clueless. Somebody who was a slave to the corporation and the oil companies and didn't even know it. She goosed the accelerator and the engine faltered till she goosed it again and another gear kicked in. A lone car flashed by, heading down, then there was a log truck, empty, rattling and clanking till you couldn't even hear the radio, and then, emerging suddenly from its shadow, a cop car, the windows opaque with sun. That was when her passenger came to life, whipping round in the seat as the cruiser blew past, shouting "Fuckers!" out the window and stabbing both middle fingers in the air. He was right there, leaning into her, and she could smell the sharp ammoniac taint of his breath. "Fuckers!" he shouted. "Fuckers!"

It was over in a heartbeat, the cop car gone and vanished round the bend behind them along with the motor homes and the log truck, but she couldn't seem to catch her breath. All she needed was another confrontation with the police. What was he thinking? Who was this guy? Was he on drugs, was that it? "Jesus," she exploded, "don't do that, are you crazy?"

She gave him a hard stare, but he was looking right through her now, his jaw set so that the muscles stood out in a ridge that ran up into the hard unyielding shell of his skull. He never even blinked, just turned his head, rigid and erect and unmoving all over again. She repeated herself—"Are you crazy?"—but he didn't answer. She was on the verge of pulling over and telling him to get out because this was too much, she just couldn't risk it, not now, not today, when it came to her: she knew him, of course she did. "I know you," she said.

She shot a glance at him, then her eyes went back to the road. "From Fort Bragg High? I used to sub there." Another glance. "You're Sten Stensen's son, aren't you—Aaron? Or no, Adam— Adam, right?"

He didn't turn. Barely moved his lips. "My name's Colter."

Colter. He wasn't fooling her. Sten had been principal until he retired, and this was his son, Adam, the one who'd caused so much trouble for everybody concerned. She'd had him in class a couple of times—he'd had hair then, long hair, puffed out and braided into dreadlocks, an inveterate doper who wore Burning Spear T-shirts and affected a Rasta accent. Adam. Adam Stensen.

"Colter," she said musingly, lingering over the *r*. "Is that a nickname? Or an online moniker or what?"

He wouldn't answer and they were silent for a while. There was just the buzz and thump of the radio, the whoosh of the breeze and the sibilance of the tires catching and releasing the road. She wanted to instruct him, wanted to tell him she felt the same way he did about the corporate police in their jackboots and shiny patrol cars and let him know about the Uniform Commercial Code and the Sovereign Citizens' Movement and the straw man and all the rest, but she kept her peace—at least for now—because a plan was already forming in her head. By the time they hit Willits and turned south on 101 for Ukiah, it was as firm as it was going to get. "You know," she said, and they were the first words she'd uttered in the past fifteen minutes, "when we get to Ukiah? I mean, before I drop you off at, where was it, the sporting goods place?"

He didn't turn his head, but he was listening, she could see that.

"It won't take five minutes," she said, watching him now, even as her eyes darted back and forth to the road ahead of her. "One quick stop, that's all."

8.

He was going to cooperate—he liked the idea, she could see that—but he insisted she had her priorities backwards. "You take me over to Big 5," he said, "and *then* we go to the animal place." It was the longest speech he'd given since he got in the car. "Because I don't want to get hung up here, you understand?" He was looking at her now, actually looking at her, as if he'd come out of a trance.

"They close at five," she said, "and I'm not going to leave my dog in there one more day, no way, José—"

"Look," he said, pointing to the clock on the dashboard. It showed one-forty-five. "There's a ton of time."

"But my dog's in there, don't you get it? Every minute he's locked up is like driving nails into my flesh. No, I'm sorry, but Kutya's first—"

He shook his head. "You want my help, it's Big 5 first. You don't, you can let me off anywhere. Here. You can stop here."

They were on the outskirts of Ukiah now, traffic thickening, the sun glaze brushed over everything like a coat of varnish. Big 5 was on East Perkins, more or less in the middle of town, and Animal Control was on the far side, heading south. She was recalculating—she needed help if she was going to get Kutya back, and nobody else, least of all Christabel, would be willing to go through with it because she was afraid, they were all afraid, everybody she knew—when he reached into the back for his canteen, unscrewed the cap, took a long swallow and offered it to her.

She tried to brush it away. "No thanks," she said. "I'm not thirsty."

"You know what you need?" he said, pressing it on her. "You need to relax. Go ahead, take a hit."

What she was trying to do was stay focused and humor him at the same time, because those were the cards she'd been dealt, so she took the canteen and lifted it to her lips. She'd expected water or maybe a sports drink, but that wasn't what she got—it was alcohol, booze, a quick sharp burn of it in her throat. "Jesus," she said, and the surprise of it made her laugh, "what is that—jet fuel?"

"One fifty-one."

"What? Rum, you mean?"

And now he was smiling for the first time. "Gets you where you're going. But here, turn here, that's East Perkins—"

They went into the store together, as if they were on a date or something, and if that felt a little strange, she didn't mind. She needed to keep an eye on him. If she was attracted to him on some level she told herself it was only because he was malleable—or potentially so—and she was willing to ride with that. No harm, no foul. Once they were done here they'd see to her problem and once that was over she could foresee offering him a lift back as far as Willits, and if he wanted to come in and see where she lived, maybe drink some wine and sit out on the porch, that was okay too. Omelets. She could make omelets. She had eggs and cheese, red pepper, tomatoes. And she could always whip up a salad. That was what she was thinking as the automatic door swung open for them and they stepped into the artificially illuminated cavern of a place that smelled of pigskin, gun oil and saddle soap. And plastic, plastic in all its thousands of guises.

"Wait here," he whispered as they came through the door, and he had his head down, as if he was afraid of being seen or called out. Then he was gone, slipping down the aisle toward the fishing and hunting section where the fiberglass rods poked up like antennas and the rifles glinted in their display cases. There was hardly anybody else in the store, aside from the checkout guy—young, short, dark hair, his earlobes distended by a pair of shining black plugs—and two teenage girls trying on running shoes. The thought came to her that he was going to rob the place—or at least shoplift—but she put it out of her head. He was Sten Stensen's son. And yes, he was trouble. But he wasn't going to do anything crazy—and if he did she'd cut him loose in an eyeblink, just slip out the door as if she'd never seen him before. She wandered over to a display of biking gloves and matched her hand size to the hard plastic package that read *Women's Medium.*

It didn't take him ten minutes. She'd moved on from the gloves to a display of detachable water bottles, reflectors and helmets *for all your biking needs,* though she didn't own a bike, and when she looked up he was at the cash register, pretending he didn't know the guy with the earplugs. He set two handbaskets on the counter, the one filled with expensive freeze-dried meals, the other with what looked to be an outdoor cook kit and a hunting knife in a fancy strap-on sheath that probably ran ninety or a hundred dollars. Not one word passed between him and the checkout guy. He paid with a crumpled twenty and the guy rang something up, popped the cash register, and gave him back a ten and a five. Adam ducked his head, shot him a grin—"You have a nice day," he said—and then the guy wished him a nice day too and Adam was out the door, his back to her, striding briskly for the car. She gave it a minute, taking up one of the water bottles and then replacing it on the display stand before making her way to the door, trying not to look at the guy with the earplugs, but she wavered just as the door pulled back for her and saw that he was studying her, with interest.

Adam was already in the car when she got there, stuffing the silver-foil packets of food into his backpack. She slid in beside him and shut the door. "Got a good deal, huh?" she offered, turning the key in the ignition and ignoring her seatbelt, which she could do with impunity because she'd long since disabled the dinger or nanny buzzer or whatever you wanted to call it.

"Let's just say I have a connection." He gave her a smirk, tearing at the packaging that housed the cook kit (more hard plastic) and casually dropping it out the window. By the time they were rolling out of the lot, he'd slipped the shining aluminum kit into the pack, along with the knife, which he didn't even glance at, and he was lifting the canteen to his lips again and again offering it to her.

"No," she said, "not now. Not till we get Kutya." She smiled. "Then we can celebrate."

"Party," he said, and his voice had gone mechanical, as if he were thinking about something else altogether, as if he weren't even there. "Party on."

Was he drunk, was that it?

"I'm a party animal," he said in the same detached voice. "A real, a *super,* party animal."

"Yeah," she said, swinging out onto the highway, "yeah, me too. But you're going to be all right for this, aren't you? What we discussed?"

Nothing.

"Listen, Adam—"

"Colter."

"Colter. I need five minutes, that's all. And then, if you want, we can go back to my place—in Willits, at the top of the canyon?—and party all we want. I've got wine. I can make us omelets. You like omelets?"

No response. He was rigid again, staring through the windshield as if it was the transparent lid of a coffin.

"Okay," she said, "okay, fine. Five minutes. That's all I ask."

She got lucky, because when they came through the door at Animal Control, it wasn't the girl behind the counter but a middle-aged man with dyed hair and a severe comb-over, and he was busy explaining adoption procedures to a couple his own age who

sported identical his-and-hers paunches. Adam was grinning, for
what reason she couldn't fathom, except that he was drunk, he
must have been drunk, but he'd roused himself when they pulled
into the lot and now he edged right in, saying, "Sir? Sir, could I
ask you a question?"

The couple turned to stare at him. The man behind the counter, who'd been in the midst of enumerating the virtues of a dog
named Dolly, lifted his head to give him an annoyed look. "Just
a minute," he said.

"But"—and here Adam, soft-voiced to the point where you
could barely hear him, calibrated his tone till it was a kind of rising whine—"I have a question, just a simple question."

The man just blinked at him.

And her? She was making like she didn't know him, as if
they'd come in separately, two strangers interested in dogs. And
cats. She went over to the brochures and made a show of selecting
one of each, a pet lover who only wanted to be informed about
the rules and regulations, about safety and health and the special
needs of kittens and puppies.

"About spaying?" Adam said. "You do spaying here, don't you?"

"Yes," the man behind the counter said, "yes, of course. But
if you could just wait a second until I'm done with these people,
who *were* here before you—"

The woman gave Adam an indignant look, then turned back
to the conversation. "Dolly's housetrained, right?"

"Oh, yeah," the man lied, because how would he know?
"They all are."

And then Adam, inserting himself between husband and wife
at the counter so that each had to take a step back, let his voice go a
notch higher. "How old do they have to be before you spay them?"

The Animal Control man blinked again, but he was there
to inform people and the response was all but automatic. "Six
months or so."

"You use a scalpel, right? Betadine, make it nice and clean. Do you do it yourself—I mean, personally?"

That was when she drifted down along the far side of the counter and away from the little group gathered there behind her, her neck bent as if studying the brochures in her hand, and nobody even glanced at her as she ducked into the hallway, turned the handle of the door and slipped inside. She found herself in a corridor with an office of some sort on her right and an open door at the far end. She moved cautiously, a step at a time. If there was somebody back there she'd play dumb—she was looking to adopt, that was all, and was this the way to the cages? But what if it was the girl from the other day? She could be back here, she *would* be, dispensing kibble, filling water bowls, hosing down the floors. What then—another stare-down? Or something more, something harder, something worse? There was one thing she knew: she wasn't leaving here without her dog. A sharp smell of urine hit her. She could hear the animals moving and rustling beyond the door, a clack of nails on concrete, a furtive yip, whining. She steeled herself and went on.

As soon as she came through the door and started down the row of cages, the dogs—there must have been forty or more—sprang up off the concrete floor, scrabbling at the wire mesh and crying out for release, but where was Kutya, where was he? They were barking now, every last one of them, raising a clamor that was sure to bring the attendants running—the girl, wherever she was, and the man from the front desk and who knew who else? "Kutya!" she called, "where are you? Come on, boy! Kutya!"

He was in the last cage down, looking cowed, as if he'd done something wrong, as if it was his fault he'd been locked away in here, and she felt sick with the thought of what he'd been put through. It was a crime, that was what it was, and she was beyond caring now—just let them try to stop her. In the next moment she had the cage door open and she was clicking the leash to his collar and bulling her way out the rear door, the one that gave onto the fenced-in courtyard and the parking lot beyond.

The dog seemed to sense her urgency and he didn't hang back to fawn on her or lick her hand or jump up. He had his head down, his paws moving in a brisk businesslike trot, following the leash and the quick clatter of her boots around the corner of the building, across the pavement and up into the backseat of the Sentra, which was parked just out of sight of the front windows. She fell into her seat, slammed the door, her heart pounding. "Stay," she growled at the dog. "Stay. Get down!" And then the engine fired up and she put the car in gear, telling herself to be calm, that everything was all right, just fine, no one had seen a thing, but her hand trembled on the wheel as she swerved across the lot and pulled up parallel to the front door.

He was in there still—she could see him through the near window, his scalp shining in the light. What was wrong with him? Why wasn't he coming? She couldn't help herself and she knew she shouldn't do it, but she tapped at the horn, twice, two sharp little bleats, and still he stood there at the desk, apparently jawing on with the Animal Control officer when he hadn't said twenty words to her all the way up the hill. She leaned forward. Kutya began to whine. And now she hit the horn again, more insistently this time, and saw him glance up, a confused look on his face. They were all four of them staring now and she didn't want to do it, didn't want to hit the horn again, but she did, grinding her palm into it.

And now there was movement, a shuffling of position as if he were swapping shirts with the couple at the counter—or dancing with them—and he was still talking, his jaw still going. What was wrong with him? She beeped again. She saw him detach himself from the little group and then he went out of her line of vision until he appeared again at the glass door, which snatched at the light as he pushed it open and came down the walk to her. But— and this was strange too, strange and maddening—he just stood there staring at the car as if he'd never seen it before. She rolled down the window. "Get in!" she said.

He just stared, gone off again.

She barked out his name—"Adam!"—even as Kutya came tumbling over the backseat and into the front where he was plainly visible and the shapes inside the building seemed to coalesce, three faces wedded in one and staring out the window at her. "Goddamn you, get in!

"Adam!" she warned, and she was half a beat from just leaving him there, dumping his pack out into the lot and turning her back on him, when his face changed and he came round the front of the car to pull open the passenger's-side door, scoot the dog off the seat and slide in. She was already in gear, already tugging at the wheel and hitting the gas, when he turned to her, full-face, and said, "I told you, my name's *Colter.*"

PART III

Northspur

9.

HE COULDN'T STOP LAUGHING, giggling like he was in junior high and Mr. Wilder was throwing his voice to be Huckleberry Finn one minute and Nigger Jim the next, because this was the way it was supposed to be, sticking it to them at the Big 5 and at the animal place too, one-upping them, one-upping the world, and she was giggling too so that every time he found himself winding down she'd start him up all over again, best thing ever, huge, just laughing and laughing, and what he was thinking was that she was all right, cool, or close to it, even though she was too old and didn't have any qualms about displaying her uptight side for all to see, leaning on the car horn and barking at him in the parking lot to the point where he'd almost told her to go fuck herself and forget about the ride because he could just stick out his thumb and not have to listen to her shit or absorb it either. But he was racing now, the little wheel inside his brain spinning at top speed, everything on the highway shooting by as if they'd gone into hyperspace though there was no one chasing them and when he snatched a look at the speedometer he saw she was doing fifty-five, exactly fifty-five, as if the engine had a governor on it. Or a robot arm. He tried to picture that and all he could see was a bolted-together metal head where her head had been just a second ago and a mechanical arm reaching down under the steering wheel and through the instrument panel and into the superhot engine until she began to say something through the giggles and her real head popped back on her shoulders with all its lines and grooves and stingy retreating bones and the eyes that kept snapping at him like rubber bands. He needed a hit of 151. Or maybe he didn't. Cars exploded all around them. He lifted the canteen to his lips and drank.

What she was saying was, "So you think you might want to come back to the house? To celebrate?" Another rush of giggles. Her hair was in her face. A silver bracelet sparked on her wrist, Morse code, a signal, a definite signal, *long, short, long, long, short.* He passed her the canteen and watched her press it to her lips. The dog—the dog had dreadlocks and that rocked him—poked its head between the seats and breathed a gas fog of stinking breath between them. "You up for it?"

The wheel began to slow. He came back to things the way they were or had to be and saw her all over again. She was old and he didn't like her squirrel-colored hair and he hated the way she'd said I know you and called him Adam, but she had big tits and her boots were made out of snakeskin and they had pointed toes with silver strips worked in, shit-kicking boots, and she was a shit-kicker and so was he. "You don't know me," he said.

She grinned at him, big lips, soft lips. The cars had stopped exploding and the highway ran true now so that he knew it and knew where he was and the dog breathed its stinking breath and she said, "Maybe, maybe not."

"I could rape you," he said.

"Go ahead and try."

There was no independence in the world, just dependence, and the animals were dying and the sky was like a sore and everything had a price tag on it. It wasn't like that when the mountain men came out of the east and went up into the Plains and the Rocky Mountains when the country stopped at the Mississippi and the hostiles ruled all the territory beyond. That was when John Colter went up amongst the Blackfeet on the Missouri River and did his deeds. This much he knew from the history books—and the internet too but the internet had about one fiftieth of the information the books gave you—and when he could concentrate, when the wheel slowed and everything came back into focus, he could sit in one place for hours and read the same passages over and over, *Give Your Heart to the Hawks* and *The Mountain Men* and *John Colter: His Years in the Rockies,* with its picture of Colter on skis in the snow and facing down a whole village of braves and their mad snarling dogs. His favorite place, the place where he kept his Army Survival Guide and his books on trapping and fishing and living off the land, was his grandmother's house when she was alive and the rain was coming at the windows like the ocean turned upside down and the Noyo swelled up and gouged at the banks and took the big logs and boulders down with it so you could hear them grinding like teeth. Everything was safe then, the room warm with the woodstove, something cooking in the kitchen, the bed made for him in the spare room so he didn't have to go home and see his father there in the chair in the living room with the what-did-you-do-for-me-lately look scored into his face like a mask out of some sci-fi flick the aliens wore to make them look like upright lizards. The mountain men lived free and they never had to say *Yessir, Cap'n, to no man.* Beaver, that was what they were after, beaver hides—plews—to make the felt for the high hats everybody wore across the sea in London and in New York and Boston too, and the beaver were theirs for the taking and there was nobody in that day and age tougher and savvier and more independent than Colter.

"You want a glass of wine?" she was saying to him. "Two-Buck Chuck, but if you blow on it and let it sit a minute it's not half bad."

Somehow he was in her house, though he couldn't remember how he'd got there, the chain of events, that is, the movement of the car, the opening and slamming of the doors, boots on the porch, key in the latch, none of it. Her house was white, everything painted white, though there were dark smudges of human dirt on the cabinets and doors and the frame of the doorway without a door that led from the living room, where he was, to the kitchen, where she was, throwing her voice like a ventriloquist with a dummy in her lap and who was the dummy here, who was the receiver, what was the message?

"I drink it," she said, and let out a laugh. "If it's good enough for me I guess it's good enough for anybody except maybe the president and his wife and the CEOs of the major corporations, so what do you say? Join me?"

He watched her. She had big tits. They were right there, underneath a T-shirt screaming with the letters TDC in a glossy lipsticky red that was the color of the blood John Colter spilled when he had to, when they wouldn't leave him alone, the white men and redskins alike. Her big tits swayed like water balloons as she came into the room now with the bottle in one hand and a glass in the other and he watched the way the neck of the bottle kissed the rim of the glass and the vacant space inside it filled red, but a darker red, wine-red, and then he had the glass in his hand and he was draining it in a gulp.

"Whoa," she said out of her soft lips, "I guess you are a party animal, *Colter*. But I'm making us omelets, so just hold on," and here she was filling his glass again. "You want music? I can put some music on. What do you like?"

All right. He was sufficiently slowed down now to appreciate what was going on here. This was called interaction, words spilled and words sucked up, the phase of things you needed to get through if you were going to get laid and he was going to get laid—everybody talked about getting laid, Cody and everybody else he'd ever known—and he'd been laid before so he knew all about it, twice, on two separate nights, and here she was, whatever her name was, padding back into the kitchen on her feet that were bare now to go through with the ritual of food preparation when all he was seeing was Dara Spinelli from high school with her eyes like lasers she never closed the whole time. She had big tits too. She sat atop him in the backseat of his car before they took it away from him and rubbed herself into him and shucked off her shirt and there they were, her tits, and he took hold of them and put his mouth to them and then he got laid. "You got any Slayer?" he heard himself say.

"Slayer? What are they, rock?"

He shrugged. She didn't even know *Slayer*? It came to him that she lived in a different world, but then everybody lived in a different world, boxed off, dead to life, the seas turned to acid and the Chinese taking over because they were the new hostiles and if you had ten million Colters you couldn't beat them back. "Pantera," he said. "You got any Pantera?"

She let out a laugh and he didn't like that laugh, or not particularly, and she held out her hands, palms-up, as if he'd stumped her. "Why don't I just put something on and you relax—you've had a hard day shopping and dog-liberating, right?" And here came the giggle again. "Chill," she said, "just chill. I won't be a minute."

The dog was on the rug in front of the couch, inches from his boots. Dreadlocks. Dreadlock dog. That was cool. He thought of Bob Marley and Jimmy Cliff, thought of his camp in the woods that nobody knew about, thought of ganja and opium and the poppy plants he was growing from seed in two hundred and twenty-seven black plastic pots so the gophers couldn't get at them. He smelled onions. Garlic. Heard the sizzle of the pan and realized there was music playing, old-timey music, corny as corny can be, and felt his boner straining at his zipper the way it did when he was looking at porn when his grandma was out in the garden or at the supermarket or when she was dead, dead the way she was now, dead six months and he in that house still and still talking to her, at least when the wheel was spinning. When it wasn't, when he was clear, he was out in the woods, tending his plants and building his bunker because it was all coming down, all the shit of the world and the pollution and the death of everything and he was going to be prepared for it, a mountain man himself and no two ways about it.

✦ ✦

They ate right there in the living room with its white walls that
were so bright they were like gunshots bursting in his ears till
she turned the overhead light off and the yellow-glass lamp in
the corner took over. She poured more wine and settled in beside
him on the couch, her legs jackknifed under her and the soles of
her bare feet showing dirt on the balls of her big toes and on her
heels, the skin yellowed there and the other toes clenched like
miniature fists clutching at the rim of a cliff that wasn't a cliff but
only a flat broad short-of-white couch pillow that connected with
the couch pillow he was sitting on so that every time she bent
forward to the coffee table which was really just a wooden chest
with brass handles on either end he could feel the buoyancy of
her as if they were both out in the ocean and treading water. And
those black slashing things circling around them, those fins cutting the surface? They weren't sharks, they were dolphins, grinning dolphins, happy dolphins, tail-walking dolphins showing off
their tricks to such a degree that he felt nothing but gratitude
for them and if she was touching him now, touching his jeans,
his thighs, his crotch, that was all according to plan. He stopped
treading water and her face was right there, closing in on his, and
she kissed him, her lips soft as the inside of things and tasting of
garlic and butter and what was that herb, that herb his mother put
on everything till it tasted like soap? Cilantro. He hated cilantro.
But not now, not on her lips, not while she was unzipping him
and loosening his belt and putting her tongue in his mouth.

In the morning she wanted him to stay, fussing around in the
kitchen with a coffeemaker and a hot griddle and talking at such
a clip she barely drew breath, telling him about the seminars she'd
taken in Redemption Theory and how they'd really opened her
eyes. "Do you know that everybody born in this country has a
straw man behind them worth six hundred and thirty thousand
dollars, which is what allows the government, or what passes for

government, to take out loans on the backs of us all?" she asked, or no, demanded of him as if he were arguing with her when he wasn't, when he was clear and just sitting there at the kitchen table with a mug in one hand and a fork in the other. "Unless you call their bluff. Unless you stand up to them and write checks against your straw man and start to draw that money down and keep them off your back permanently—"

In the night, in her bedroom that was as black dark as alien space—darker, because out there at least there were stars—he'd held tight to her and her big tits and soft lips and done it twice without seeing anything or being seen and that was anonymous and it calmed him till he blacked out and slept and woke up clear and with the wheel quiet inside him. Now he was eating and she wanted him to stay, and the dog was crunching kibble over a blue plastic bowl set in the corner, the sun shining and something that wasn't much more than static playing on the radio on the counter by the sink, and he cut her off in the middle of her straw man speech to say, "I have to go. You know why?"

She was pushing things around on the stove. She shifted her head to look at him over one shoulder. "Why?"

"Because they're going to be coming for you."

"Who?"

"Who do you think?"

"How do they know it was me? Nobody saw us. For all they know I could sue them for letting somebody steal my dog out of the pound—"

He had to laugh, but it was a noiseless laugh and his lips never moved. "Sherlock Holmes," he said.

She gave him a puzzled look.

"You don't have to be Sherlock Holmes. It's your dog. Who else would steal it?"

Her hair was a mess where he'd run his fingers through it in the dark and the pillow had flattened it on one side and for an instant it seemed to catch fire in the sun coming in through the window, every wild wisp of it burning like a halo of jumping flames. He could see the smallest things, the fine leather creases at the corners of her eyes, a single translucent hair stabbing out beneath her left ear, and finer still, till he could see the microscopic mites living and fucking and shitting in her eyebrows, in everybody's eyebrows, every minute of every day. "Yeah," she said, "I thought of that, but there's nobody to take him for me, to hold him, I mean, till the thirty days are up—he doesn't have rabies, I swear it . . ."

He said nothing. Just sat there watching her mites wave their segmented legs even as he felt his own mites stirring in the valleys between his eyes, and then the mites were gone and he was clear again. Mornings. In the mornings he was clear, or mostly so, and he knew what was happening to him and knew that dope and alcohol made it worse—or better, definitely better—and that all his plans, the plans he talked up in his own head and out loud too, with his own lips and tongue and mouth, were going to come to nothing, that the poppies would die and the hostiles would come for him and he'd lead them on a merry chase, but that in the end everything in this life was just shit and more shit.

"Could you take him? Hide him, I mean—just for a few days?"

"I can't have a dog."

"You've got your own place, didn't you tell me? Near Northspur? On the river there? That's only like fifteen miles or something and there's nobody around out there, right? Like even if Kutya barks, nobody's going to hear. Or complain. Or even know." She was looking at him as if she could see right through him, two naked eyes hooked up to her brain and taking in information like the feed on a video camera. "I could drive you there now and you could just—he's no trouble. Really."

"My grandma wouldn't like it."

"Talk to her, will you? Or we both could. I'm sure if she understood the circumstances—it's just temporary, that's all—she'd want to help out."

He couldn't picture that. Couldn't picture the dreadlock dog in the house that was his private universe behind the eight-foot cement-block wall he'd built around it to keep them out, all of them, because the fact he kept trying to bury was that his father was selling the place to some alien and had already told him he had so many days from that day whatever day that was *to clean up your crap and get out and I'm not going to tell you twice,* which was why he'd set up the camp in the woods in the first place.

"No," he said, "no," and he was shaking his head. "She wouldn't like it."

IO.

JOHN COLTER WAS TWENTY-NINE, four years older than
he was now, when he signed on with Lewis and Clark for the
expedition to explore the Louisiana Purchase and open up the
west. He'd been raised on the frontier in Kentucky, a wild place
back then, more comfortable sleeping rough than in his own bed
in the cabin he shared with his parents and his brothers and sisters
and one uncle and his uncle's wife, and if the other farmers' sons
were content to walk behind a plow, he wasn't. He was a free
agent from the earliest age, earning his keep by way of hunting,
fishing and trapping, and in no need of a trail to carry him out or
bring him home again either. As a child, he took to disappearing
for days at a time, and then, as he got older and ran through his
teens, for weeks, and no matter how far he roamed or in what territory, he was never lost, born with an uncanny ability to orient
himself no matter where he was. He was like an animal in that
regard, like a fox—or better yet, a wolf, an outlier with his nose
to the wind.

Lewis and Clark took him on as scout and hunter, and while
he left St. Louis with the expedition and stayed with it for more
than two years, exploring the course of the Missouri River and
going overland to the Columbia and ultimately the Pacific Ocean,
he never made it back to civilization with the rest of them. It happened that on the return trip, while they were retracing their
route through the Dakota country, a pair of trappers, heading
west, stopped to camp with the expedition and tried to persuade
Colter to come with them—he knew the country and they didn't.
He'd be their guide and their partner, three-way split. Plews were
fetching ten dollars a head back in St. Louis, so it would be like

stealing candy from a baby, easiest thing in the world, trap beaver and get rich—not that Colter cared about money much more than as a means to keep him in powder and balls, but the idea of staying in the country appealed to him. He went to Captain Clark for permission to muster out and he gave it to him, though there wasn't a man in that company who didn't think he was out of his mind, more than two years on the trail and civilization within reach—women, drink, clean sheets, news of the world and the celebrity that would come down to them all—and yet all that meant nothing to him. That was for other men, weaker men. He wanted to go out into the wilderness and take what was his and if anybody stood in his way, Cheyenne, Crow or Blackfoot, he'd take them too.

What became of the trappers, nobody knows, but at some point—a month in, two—Colter had got fed up with them, and who could blame him? Even with Lewis and Clark he was mostly on his own, out ahead of the expedition, breaking trail, hunting meat, camping solitary against the fastness of the night. The trappers—Joseph Dixon and Forrest Hancock—bickered, gave out with opinions, expected him to do things their way, two votes to one, as if setting traps and roasting beaver tail over a cottonwood fire was a democratic process. By spring of the following year—this would have been 1807—he was heading back down the Missouri in a canoe, his plews gone and stolen after a party of Blackfeet had surprised him. He had nothing to his name but his knife and rifle and a leather pouch with his powder, balls, flint and steel inside, and he had no destination either, though he had a vague notion of going back down to St. Louis just to see what would turn up.

He never made it. He ran into another expedition at the mouth of the Platte River—a conglomerate of fur traders under Manuel Lisa who were ambitious to set up a trading post–slash–fort—and he agreed to go on ahead, to go back, that is, and scout for them. His job this time was to contact the Crows in their scattered villages and spread the news about the trading post and how they could exchange furs for steel knives, mirrors, blankets, beads and baubles, which he did. In the process he became the first white man to discover what would become Yellowstone Park and managed to get himself shot in the right leg while fighting with the Crows against a party of Blackfeet. The Crows weren't especially sympathetic or grateful either. They moved on and left him to his fate. But what kind of fate was that? Dying out there with a suppurating wound while the buzzards settled in for the feast? No, no way. Totally unacceptable. He wasn't ready to leave this planet because he was too tough for that, too determined and resilient—and yes, independent—so he favored his good leg and walked three hundred miles back to the fort on the Platte.

This was what he knew, what the history books revealed, and if he closed his eyes while she sat beside him in the driver's seat humming one of her lame country songs and the dog hung his head over the seat and breathed its meat-reeking breath in his face as the car yawed down Route 20 on the way to his place, he could picture how it must have been, Colter fighting down the pain till it went from something that filled him like an air pump inflating his skin to a hot white pinpoint of light that cooled with every step he took. Three hundred miles. Who could walk three hundred miles today, even on two good legs? Not to mention that Colter had no PowerBars or beef jerky or anything else, not even an apple, which people today took totally for granted as if apples were like air, and he had to forage all the way, subsisting on roots, frogs, snakes, the things he shot and feasted on only to leave what he couldn't carry to rot when he moved on. That was legendary, that was a feat, but it was nothing compared to what came next—Colter's Run, when he was naked and barefoot and a whole army of Blackfeet braves was chasing him down, all of them pissed-off and screaming and taking aim at his naked shoulders with their spears held high. He ran, and they chased him. And if he was faster than they were, even on their own ground and with their feet protected by moccasins, it was because he was John Colter and they weren't.

He knew something was wrong the minute they turned into the dirt road and heard the distant discontinuous clanging as if the world were made of steel and coming apart at the seams. The windows were down. He'd been staring into the side mirror, staring into his own jolting eye and seeing the door panels fixed there like blistered skin and the dog slavering out the back and smearing the fender with a shiny outwardly radiating web of spit and mucus that immediately turned brown with flung-up dust when they went from pavement to dirt, and he wouldn't look up. He wasn't ready yet. He was listening to the tires, a clean spinning whine of perfect harmony on the blacktop that gave way to an angry thump and pop as they rocked over the wash-board corrugations worked into the road to his grandmother's house—to *his* house—because it was better than listening to her, to Sara, who kept trying to radicalize him against the government when he was already a thousand times more radical than she was. Nobody governed him. They were all just criminals anyway, every politician bought and sold by the special interests and the cops nothing more than their private army—he knew that and she didn't have to tell him. But she did. On and on till her voice seemed to be coming from someplace other than her mouth and lips and larynx, as if it was riding radio waves on its own special channel.

But that clanging. Somehow he knew what it was and who was making it, though he'd never heard that exact sound before and couldn't have said how he knew unless it was some sixth sense like the sense that told Colter when there were hostiles about. She was saying, "They might come to my house but I'll just play dumb and say, 'I thought you had him' and then get angry and say, 'What are you telling me—that he got away? Or what, you didn't . . .'"—she turned to him, grinning, pretending to be someplace else talking to somebody else and not him at all—"'send him out for adoption?' And then I'll pause and let my face go dark. 'Or no, don't tell me you *put him down*? Because if you did—'"

The house was there under the trees and the river was down below it. Ever since the cops had taken his car away he'd had to hitch into town for groceries, though his mother would come pick him up, was happy to come pick him up—and she'd done it a couple of times—but that wasn't independent, and after a while when she pulled up to the house that used to have a phone before he uprooted it and tossed it in the river where it could go deep and talk to the minnows and steelhead in every human language, he would duck out the back door, slip over the wall and into the woods, and then he went to the locksmith and changed the locks so she couldn't get in.

Sara said, "Is this it?," and he nodded and she put on her blinker to turn into the gravel drive even as he saw the bishop pines screaming with sunlight and the three brown plastic over-flowing trash cans no one ever seemed to come and pick up and the big object, the real thing, the thing that slammed at him like a missile shot out of nowhere—his father's car, parked in the shadow of the wall like it belonged there.

"Shit," he said. "*Shit.*"

The car lurched to a stop. She put it in park, cut the engine and turned to him. "What's wrong?"

He just pointed at the car in front of them, a new Toyota hybrid his father had bought as a retirement present to himself, a statement on four wheels that might as well have had a loud-speaker attached to it trumpeting its miles per gallon and crying out against the spoliation of the earth and the four hundred parts per million of CO_2 in the air. That was a good thing, he wouldn't argue with that—it made sense to cut down on gas-guzzling, of course it did—but if you really wanted to get serious you'd just send the car back to Japan and use your own two legs to get around. His father didn't need a car. Nobody needed a car. That was what feet were for. Tell it to Colter: he didn't even have a horse.

The clanging faltered, intermittent now, and then it died altogether so that the little noises—of insects, the river, birds in the trees—came back to establish themselves in a soundloop that was as steady as the beating of his heart. Out of the car went the dreadlock dog the minute Sara cracked her door and then they were out in the yard and the dog was lifting his leg against something that hadn't been there before, rubble, a pile of rubble that looked like busted-up cinder block. And then the clanging started up again and he thought of his father and how his father had got in his face when he saw the wall for the first time, shouting "Where's your brain? You build an eight-foot wall without a doorway, what are you thinking? Or are you thinking, are you thinking at all?"

His father had shouted for a good fifteen minutes and then gone home and come back with a stepladder and he'd watched him—an old man with a scorched-earth face—climb up to perch crotchwise on the lip of the wall and hoist the stepladder up behind him so he could ease it down the inside, and then his father was there, in the compound, and he was shouting all over again.

"It's to keep people out," he'd said in his own defense. "I can climb it. And I don't need any ladder either."

But now, now there was a doorway-sized hole in the wall and a pile of busted-up cinder block in the yard and even before the dreadlock dog had got done with his yellow arc of piss here came another fractured block, flung through the doorway to clack against the pile and send the dog off yipping as if he'd been hit, which he hadn't. Sara snapped a look at him like he was the one who'd thrown the thing and called comfort to the dog while those little brown birds with the forked white tail feathers shot like bullets across the yard and the sun flared and flared

again. That was the moment his father appeared in the jagged
new doorway, dressed in his hiking boots and jeans, his T-shirt
sweated through and a pair of stained work gloves on his hands.
His father's face took up a wondering look and then discarded it.
"Adam," his father said, and his tone was neutral because he was
surprised to see Sara there beside him, as if she'd crawled out of
some secret passage deep under the earth like a gopher or a mole,
a thing that went around on all fours, and *Let's do it doggie-style,*
she'd said the second time, *do you like it doggie-style?*

"Hi, Sten," she said, and he watched his father's eyes fall into
their twin sinkholes for just an instant as he tried to place her and
then his father said "Hi" back and added her name, to prove he
knew her. And more: his father was calculating, the two of them
in the same picture, her with her big tits and the dreadlock dog
that was sniffing at his leg now, putting two and two together,
fucking in his mind, fucking, fucking.

"Nice to see you again," Sara said, and his father dredged up
a smile for her. "How's retirement treating you? You did retire,
right—isn't that what I heard?"

His father put both his palms on his forehead and swept his
hair back, gray hair going to white, the kind of thing a Blackfoot
brave would have prized on a dripping scalp, then unfastened the
rubber band pinching his ponytail, patted the loose hairs in place
and refastened it, all in three seconds flat. This was his characteristic gesture. Or one of them, anyway. Hair. He had hair. "That's
right," his father said. "Just got back from a cruise, in fact. Down
south. Maybe you read about it? Or saw it on TV?"

She was wearing her jeans and shit-kicking boots, nothing to
see there, so far as fucking was concerned, but her big tits were
sticking out of a little turquoise blouse the size of a rag and you
could see her navel too. And her belly. Her belly that was like a
wave at sea and just as soft once it washed over you. "Oh, yeah,"
she said, "yeah. Of course." She raised her right hand to smack
her head in a *duh!* kind of way. "That must have been terrifying."

His father shrugged.

"I heard it was three of them. Mexicans, right? In Mexico?"

"Costa Rica."

"Costa Rica? Jesus, I thought that was supposed to be safe—"

"Yeah, well, nothing's safe," his father said, and why did he look at *him* as if he'd had anything to do with it? He wasn't there. He didn't kill anybody. "It could happen anywhere. We were just lucky, that was all."

"Three of them," she repeated, "and they were armed and you had nothing but your bare hands? I'd say that's more than luck."

Another shrug, his father the hero, the killer. "You let two of them get away," he heard himself say. He could feel his father's stare boring into him, but he wasn't going to look up and acknowledge it—he was watching the way Sara's reptile boots shifted in the dirt, the two little silver gleams there at the toes of them, *shit-kickers.* "So did the guy's eyes pop out or what? Like a frog when you step on it?"

"Adam," his father said, and he heard the tone of it and knew it, the tone that cut him down to size, diminished him, made him nothing more than a boy, a child, an infant, as if what he said was always stupid and irrelevant and nobody wanted to hear it.

"What," he said, throwing it back at him. "You killed him, didn't you? You ought to know."

"Adam. Come on, now. That's not the point, you know that. Sometimes—"

And here she cut in, as if she was on his father's side now, as if she and his father were some sort of tag team and everything he'd done with her, from one-upping the Animal Control idiots to drinking Two-Buck Chuck to fucking in the dark didn't count for a thing. "It was self-defense."

He'd been clear, or a little clear anyway, but he wasn't clear anymore, a sudden buzz of noise in his ears and then the dread-lock dog started barking and the trees took it up, all the Sitka spruce and Doug firs and bishop pines and new-growth redwoods running up into the hills and barking in chorus. He needed a hit of something, pot, hash, opium, acid, and where was the canteen, what had he done with the canteen?

"Adam, it's all right," his father said in his hollowed-out reptile's rasp of a voice, the voice that was meant to be comforting and copacetic but was really nothing more than a hiss, and his father took a step toward him, the gloves swelling his hands till they were King Kong hands, black and rubbery and made to crush things. "We're okay here, there's no rush, and we're going to find you a new place to live, believe me, we will—"

"My name's not Adam," he heard himself say, and there was somebody else speaking for him now, Colter, Colter speaking, "because Adam was the original man and I'm not the original anything."

Sara was right there, right there between them, leading with her midriff—that was the term, her midriff, her bare midriff—and she said, "Adam's been helping me. He's great. He's been a great help. What we need is a place to keep the dog—Kutya?—for a couple of days. Because my landlord? She's being a bitch about having a pet. And I was wondering if, well, Adam said he'd help me out—if it's okay with his grandma, that is. And you, you of course."

So his father was taking this in and the trees were barking and his father knew it was all a lie and his son had been fucking her, though he didn't want to admit it to himself, and the three of them were standing there *outside the wall* just jawing away as if they were in one of the plays they'd put on in the auditorium in high school.

"Well, good, good," his father was saying. "I'm glad he could help, and as far as his grandmother's concerned, well, she passed on six months ago now, so that won't be a problem. Right, Adam?" A look for him now, drilled full of holes and every hole a question mark punctured with little barbs. "Happy to accommodate you—I mean, if it's okay with Adam it's okay with me."

Everything was so nice, everything so perfect, his father on

his best behavior because of her, going out of his way to be reasonable and understanding, just like he always was in his office
at school with his big arms laid on the desk in the short-sleeved
button-down shirt he wore without fail, winter and summer. As
reasonable as the guidance counselor and the parade of shrinks
marching through his life as long as he could remember. And
what was it the last one said, Dr. Rob Robertson, Robert's son,
just call me Rob, the head-thumping diagnosis that was supposed
to end it all and stop the wheel and make everybody happy? *A
problem of adjustment to adulthood.* Yeah, sure. In spades. And then
he *was* an adult, eighteen and out of school, and that was the end
of the shrinks. He had acid instead, he had alcohol, pot. And here
he was, adjusting to adulthood, right here, right now.

"Big hero," he heard himself say in the most sarcastic voice
he could dredge up, and he was looking at the ground, at the
dreadlock dog, at the pile of busted-up cinder block. "John Colter
would have killed them all—*I* would have killed them all."

They just looked at each other, the two of them, as if he'd
been speaking Chinese.

The urge he had, right then, was to take them by surprise,
dash through the new doorway, circle round back of the house
and go right up over the wall and out into the woods, just to get a
little *peace* for a minute, and was that too much to ask? And he was
going to, he was going to do that, just as soon as he wrapped up
this conversation or dialogue or trialogue or whatever it was, and
so he squared himself up so he was his father's height—*Straighten
up, straighten your shoulders and stand up straight, be a man,* that was
what his father was always telling him, had been telling him, harping on it as long as he could remember, from elementary school
to junior high to senior year and the half semester at Humboldt,
which was about all he could stand—and he was fed up with it and
he did something he never did, looked him dead in the eye and
said, "And one more thing, in case you're wondering—I fucked
her. Isn't that right, Sara? Isn't that right? Didn't I fuck you?"

II.

HE DIDN'T WAIT AROUND to see the look on his father's face because that was then and this was now and now he was already up and over the back wall and across the Noyo because the rains had stopped for the season and there were places you could wade, no problem, his boots wet and squishing and his pants soaked to his knees, moving fast, army double time, up beyond the cabin where the dog-faced man lived with his fat grub of a wife and ugly squalling kids who didn't deserve to live, not on this planet, anyway, and a good mile and a half beyond that to where he'd made his own clearing on timber company property with the chainsaw he'd lifted from one of the cabins down around Alpine and then trimmed the branches off the logs and stacked up the logs to make his bunker. What he needed was sunshine. Sunshine was essential to plant growth. Any fool knew that. And you didn't get sunshine in a pine forest unless you took down the trees as quietly as you could considering the noise of the chainsaw that beat at your ears and went right inside of you whether you used ear protection or not, but there were ways around that. For one thing, who was there to hear, anyway, aside from the dog-faced man whose name was Chip Moody and who'd hated him on sight and the feeling was mutual? Or the old white-hairs like his father the timber company paid to hike around the woods and make sure the Mexican gangs weren't out there carving up marijuana plantations and poisoning everything that moved? For another thing, he was smart enough to do most of his cutting in the middle of the day when people were at work or when the Skunk Train was taking a load of tourists up and down the tracks to Northspur and back and all the hard metallic noises of the world ran confused.

He wasn't thinking because his father had set him off, his father always set him off and his mother did too, but not as instantly and not as thoroughly, and when he emerged in the clearing he realized he'd forgotten to bring his pack with the new knife and the cook-kit and the freeze-dried entrées that were better when they took on a little smoke from the fire than anything you'd cook yourself. And his canteen. His canteen was still half-full of 151 and he had his baggie of buds and his blunt and matches in the side flap of the pack, which was in the backseat of her car and he wanted all that now. His stomach rumbled. He could see the pack there on the dirty seat with its filthy rumpled towel and the white clumps of dog hair scattered around like weeds growing out of it, but the dirty seat was in the back of the blue car that was parked behind his father's car and he had to fight down a cresting wave of paranoia and regret that slammed at him so hard he had to sit down on a stump in the middle of the field just to swim through it and catch his breath because what if she'd forgotten the pack was there and gone back up the hill to her house and left nothing behind but the dreadlock dog? Or worse, what if she'd stolen it, stolen everything? And worse, worse, worse, what if she'd broken a window in the house and crawled in and got at his stuff there, what if she took his rifle, his porn, the six hundred dollars he kept against emergencies in the Safeway sweet pickle relish jar behind the couch?

It was a hateful thought and it made him miserable right through to the bone, and he sat there on the stump looking across the field of stumps that was as long as a football field but narrower, much narrower, so as not to attract attention from the air, where the sheriff's department was always doing flyovers looking for growing operations, sat there staring at where his bunker was disguised on the hill with the brush he'd cut and the camo cover over it and at the marshaled lines of black pots glinting under the sun, but getting no satisfaction from any of it. He was hungry because he hadn't eaten anything since breakfast at her house and the lack of food, the loss of it, gnawed hard at him, because here he was out in the woods without his stuff like some weakling, like some tenderfoot who'd run away without giving it the least smallest little niggardly thought. "Niggardly," he said to himself, said it aloud, and then he was chanting it as he pushed himself up and started back across the field, niggardlies dropping like spit, ten of them, a hundred, *niggardly, niggardly, niggardly.*

He saw smoke rising from the woodstove chimney at Chip Moody's dog-faced house and the car pulled up there under the sun, so he circled around through the trees without showing himself because why should it be Chip Moody's dog-faced business what he did or where he went? The woods were quiet, no birds, no bugs, nothing moving. Light fingered through the bare trunks of the trees. The dirt smell was strong, humus, pine needles, rot. He heard somebody beeping a car horn off in the distance and thought of his house again, of Sara and her car and his father and the clanging mallet, and hurried down the hill to the river where he just glided across the water like those lizards in the nature shows that go so fast they never break the surface. Then he was there, back at the house, and he wasn't calm, wasn't calm at all.

The first thing he saw was the dog, its fur in violent motion, and it was barking at him, once, twice, till the trees took it up and then suddenly stopped because the dog came up to him and stuck out its wet snout so he could take it in one palm and feel the electricity go out of it, tail wagging now, the dreadlock dog here to stay whether he had anything to say about it or not. Then he saw her car and then he saw the vacant space where his father's car had been and everything sucked back down from hyperspace and slowed to a crawl, all the visuals good and fine and everything as it was except for the door-shaped hole in the wall and the frame his father had cemented in there and the flat metal door propped up in the shade, ready to hang. Hang a door. He said that to himself, then said it again. All right. There would be a door into the compound. But it was metal and metal was better than wood and he'd have a key to it and he'd lock it and keep everybody out for as long as that was going to happen.

His next surprise, beyond the dog and the fact of her car being there while his father's wasn't, was the smell of food, a loud red shout of a smell he'd known since he was little—spaghetti sauce, that was what it was, floating atop the scent of the garlic powder in the clear plastic container you had to thump against the counter before you could get anything out of it. He stepped through the gap in the wall and saw that the door to the house stood open behind the dark mesh of the screen door, and that stopped him a moment. How had that happened, unless she *had* broken a window or his father somehow managed to get a key or change the locks back or somebody forgot to lock up when he went hitching up to Ukiah yesterday afternoon? No matter. He stepped into his own house as if he were a stranger and there she was, her back to him, rattling around in the kitchen like somebody's mother. Or wife. There was music on the radio—that came to him next— and everything that was familiar about the place, which he kept neat, shipshape, he did, looked different now because she was in the middle of it like some force field that bent and distorted things, and if he thought of his grandmother, it was only the briefest stabbing spike of a thought because she turned then and saw him and smiled.

"Hey," she said, "where've you been?"

There was sun, late sun now, evening sun, spilling through the kitchen window, and it took hold of her and held her there. He didn't answer. Couldn't answer. Nobody knew about the camp in the woods and nobody was ever going to know.

A pot hissed on the burner behind her. There came the tap-tap-tap of the dog's nails on the hardwood floor and the dog brushed by him like a shrub on legs and entered the picture, right there, beside her.

"Your father went home," she said. "He had to pick the lock to let me in—and I hope that's all right." She stopped to swipe a strand of loose hair back behind her ear with the pinky finger of her left hand, her characteristic gesture. Or one of them. She had hair too. Squirrel-colored hair. "I just thought we might have something to eat because, you know, with Kutya here and I don't have to work tomorrow, I just thought I might as well, you know, stay." She was grinning. She had something in her hand—a stirring spoon, his grandmother's stirring spoon with the rust flecks in the shiny metal and the hard yellow plastic handle. "What do you say about that?"

What did he say? He said nothing, not yet. This was a concept and it was going to take a minute for it to seep in because he hadn't thought it would go like this, not when he was out at the camp and knew that he'd left his pack behind in the backseat of her car, where it still was, the 151 and all, but right now, in this moment with her there and the dreadlock dog and the light spilling through the windows till his grandmother's stirring spoon glowed like a wand, a magic wand, he felt so close to calm it was like a spell had come over him. And yet, and yet—there was something there still to keep the wheel spinning, and it was his father, the thought of his father, who'd gone home now, for now, but would be back anytime he pleased and with a new doorway to walk through too.

"You talk to my father?"

"Yeah. I knew him, you know, from school."

"You talk about me?"

She shrugged. "A little."

"What did he tell you?"

The dog pulled his front end low to the floor and stretched, the banner of his tail waving as she bent to him to scratch his back, right there in his sweet spot, but what she was doing, whether she knew he knew it or not, was stalling so she could think of what to say next. She straightened up. He was ten feet from her, in the living room still, watching the light. "He said you were going through a rough patch."

A rough patch. That hit him like a slap in the face and he had to laugh, but it wasn't like the laughter in the car after they'd stolen the dog back, but more of a noise that caught in his throat as if he'd swallowed something and couldn't get it out. "Rough patch," he repeated and laughed again. "Did he tell you about the playground? About my car? About the Chinese? Did he tell you I don't have a job?"

"No," she said, and she crossed the floor to him and squeezed his arm at the bicep, leaning in to touch her soft lips to the side of his face. "All he said was you'd hit a rough patch, but I don't care about that. I like you, you know that?"

He didn't answer.

"And since I'm here anyway I looked in the refrigerator— which is impressive the way you keep it, neat, neater than mine, by far—and found the hamburger there and the chicken sausage, and since you had all these spices and cans of stewed tomatoes and whatnot, I just figured I'm hungry and I'll bet you are too. Okay? So let's have some wine and maybe sit out back for a while and let the sauce cook down. You're going to like the way I make spaghetti. Everybody says it's the best."

She was holding on to his arm still and the light was flowing over the dog where it lay in the rug of its fur on the kitchen floor and the smell of the simmering sauce was tugging at his glands, the salivary glands that looked like trussed-up sacks of tapioca pudding in the illustration in his biology text from school, and another phrase came to him that had nothing niggardly in it at all: *Go with the flow.* He said it aloud, "Go with the flow," and she gave his muscle another squeeze.

PART IV

Mendocino

12.

THE WHOLE IDEA OF a vacation, of a travel vacation, was to clear out the cobwebs, put your troubles behind you and come home refreshed. Well, it hadn't quite worked out that way, had it? As he reminded Carolee every chance he got. His stress level was so high the first week home he had to go to the doctor to check on his blood-pressure medication and see about a refill on his Xanax, which he never took anymore, not since he'd shut the door behind him at the high school for the last and final time. It wasn't enough that they'd been attacked or that the ship had been delayed in Puerto Limón for a full twenty-four hours while the Costa Rican bureaucrats conferred with the cruise line bureaucrats and the State Department flunkies so that when the boat did finally get to Miami they'd missed their flight to San Francisco or that the flight they did manage to get on was delayed for three hours because of fog on the other end—no, it was the press, the press was the real and continuing plague because they kept the whole thing going when all he wanted was to turn the page and forget about it. They didn't care what he wanted. They never even asked. They just came after him.

Within an hour of his walking out of that room in the bowels of the ship, even before he and Carolee had got through the first bottle of Perrier-Jouët sent compliments of the captain and delivered by Kristi Breerling herself, his cell began ringing. Exhausted—wiped—and half-drunk too, he wasn't thinking and just put the phone to his ear and rasped, "Hello?"

A voice came back at him, an unfamiliar voice, distant but clear. A man's voice. "Mr. Stensen? Sten Stensen?"

"Yeah?"

The voice gave a name and an affiliation and without pausing to draw breath began hammering him with questions, each
more inane and intrusive than the last—"What was it like out
there? How many of them were there? How do you feel, you
feel any different? You *are* a senior citizen, right—seventy years
old, is that right? A war veteran? Did the alleged attacker say
anything to you? He had a gun? Or was it a knife?" He tried
to answer the man's questions as patiently as he could, though
Carolee was hissing at him to hang up and all he could think of
was the cruise line's slogan—*Experience World-Class Indulgence*—
and wonder how in Christ's name this reporter had managed to
get his cell number, but finally, after a question about his service
record—*In Vietnam, was it?*—he broke the connection even as the
call-waiting light flared and he shut the thing off and stuffed it
deep in his pocket.

"Who was that?" Carolee demanded.

"I don't know. Some reporter."

It was dark out over the water. They'd pulled the sliding door
of their private veranda shut to thwart the mosquitoes and whatever
else was out there—vampire bats, he supposed. The champagne in
his glass had gone warm. He took a sip and made a face—it tasted
like club soda with a dash of bitters and no more potent.

Carolee was giving him her severe look, her mouth drawn
down and her eyebrows pinched together, a crease there in the
shape of a V she'd been working on for sixty-four years now. "You
don't have to talk to those people," she said.

The glass went heavy in his hand. He could barely hold his
head up. "Yeah," he said, "and you don't have to swat flies either."

Of course, part of the problem that first week was that he couldn't
seem to say no. He was a celebrity, an instant celebrity, the story
plumbing some deep atavistic recess of the American psyche, and
forgive him, because he knew it was wrong in every way, but

after the third or fourth interview he began to feel he was only getting his due: *Ex-Marine, 70, Kills Tour Thug*; *Quick Thinking Saves the Day*; *Costa Rica Tour Hero*. If he stopped to think about it he would have been ashamed of himself—he was being manipulated, and worse, glorified not for any virtue, but for a single act of violence that haunted him every time he shut his eyes—but he didn't stop to think. He'd never been interviewed on the radio before—or on TV either—and that shot up the stress level, of course it did, but he went through with every request until the requests began to trickle off in the wake of newer and riper stories, the mass shooting of the week, the daily bombing, the women imprisoned as sex slaves and all the rest of it.

There were calls from Hollywood too, producers making promises, naming sums, gabbling over the line like auctioneers—and that was what this was, an auction, make no mistake about it—but none of them ever followed through and he never received a letter from a single one of them let alone a contract or, god forbid, a check. But he didn't want a check, didn't want to be inflated any more than he already had been—who in his right mind would ever want to see a movie made out of his life, anyway? *The camera pans down the street to focus on a frame house in need of paint in the sleepy lumber town of Fort Bragg, California, and there he is, ten years old and emerging from the front door to do something dramatic like walk to school, and here's his mother calling to him like June Lockhart in* Lassie, *then we shift to the high school years, the junker car, the prom, Vietnam, college and Carolee, the birth of their son, student teaching, the rise up the rocky slope to the great and shining plateau of school principal, and all of it circling round the cruise ship and the blighted dirty jungle and one climactic moment to justify it all, this American life.* Who would they get to play him—Sean Connery? Tommy Lee Jones? Travolta? Absurdity on top of absurdity.

As it turned out, he did agree to one TV appearance, gratis, with a station out of San Francisco, which sent one of their newswomen and two support people to the house and filmed him sitting in the rocker on the front porch with the blue pennant of the ocean flapping in the distance. When it aired that night on the six o'clock news, he saw himself loom up on the screen like something out of one of the Japanese horror flicks he'd loved as a boy—*Rodan,* maybe, or *Godzilla*—his eyes blunted, his face scaled and gray and his big fists clenched on the arms of the chair as if he was afraid of falling out of it. *Were you scared?* the TV woman asked him and he said he was too angry to be scared, his voice like the leaky hiss of an air hose. *It all happened so quickly,* she prompted. *Yeah,* he rasped, looking into the camera with his face absolutely frozen, *something like that. And you just reacted? Yeah,* he said, *I just reacted.*

By the second week, things had died down to the point of extinction as far as the press was concerned, but he couldn't go anywhere without somebody giving him a thumbs-up or calling out to him, people he didn't even know. It was as if he belonged to them now, the whole community, as if he'd graduated from being a retiree and homeowner to another level altogether. And that might have given him some satisfaction—it did—but somehow all he could see was Adam's face, twisted in a sneer. *Big hero.* Yeah. Sure. That about summed it up. What was he going to do, run for mayor?

And yet still, at odd moments and always while Carolee was out or occupied elsewhere, he couldn't resist googling his name to see what would come up. Most of the articles repeated the same information (and misinformation, one adding ten years to his age and another spelling his name variously as Sternson and Stevenson), but every once in a while he would find something new, a detail revealed, a tidbit that put everything in a fresh light as if the incident were reconstructing itself for him like a jigsaw puzzle. He was at it one fog-obliterated afternoon, surfing away, the world reduced to the dimensions of the screen in front of him, when he came across an article he'd somehow managed to overlook (or maybe it had just been posted, who knew?—the internet worked in mysterious ways). This was a fuller account of the AP story that had appeared just about everywhere, and as he scanned it, his eyes jumped to the one detail the other reports had left out as if it had no significance at all: the name of the dead man. To this point, he'd been anonymous—the thug, the mugger, the thief—and now he had a name: *Warner Ayala*. And more: here was his biography, compacted in two lines of print. He was twenty-four years old. A resident of Jamaica Town. He'd built up a long rap sheet of minor crimes from the age of twelve on and he was a suspect in a string of attacks on tourists and local residents alike. Or had been. Warner Ayala. And here was his movie, here was his life.

"Warner," he repeated to himself, saying it aloud like an incantation, "Warner," and all at once he was thinking of the parents, the siblings, cousins, grandparents, a father like himself who was mourning his dead son even now. It was as if someone had crept up and struck him a blow from behind, all of it rushing back in that instant, the sun, the mud lot, the fierce unrelenting intimacy of his body entangled with this other one, and he felt so filled with self-loathing and despair it was all he could do to lift his finger to the off button and make the whole thing disappear.

It was three-thirty in the afternoon. The fog sat in the windows. It was very quiet. The blank screen gave him back a ghost image of himself, of his ravaged face and unfocused eyes, the presence still there, still awake and alert and corrosive, even as he pushed himself up from the desk and the world came back to him in all its color and immediacy. Paneled walls. The den. The framed photo of Adam, eleven years old and holding a stringer of half-grown trout aloft with a smile uncomplicated by anything beyond the joy of the moment. Another picture there, of him and Caroleee, squinting into the camera against a fierce tropical sun and no older than Adam was now. And another, of his mother, dead twenty years and more, a ghost herself. Next thing he knew he was in the kitchen, washing down a Xanax with a cold beer, and then he went into the living room and started a fire, as much for the cheer as the warmth of it. He felt hopeless. Felt like shit. The pill wasn't working or the beer or the fire either.

For a long while he just sat there, moving only to stir the coals, the clock on the mantel ticking louder and louder and the fire hissing and the four walls closing him in until some sort of curtain seemed to lift inside him, dark to light, and gradually he began to come out of it. Here he was, still ambulatory, with his mind intact, or mostly so, sitting before a fire in the shingled ocean-view cottage they'd traded up to get—and get at a steal, jumping on it when the recession hit and the values plunged. Even better: he'd finally managed to escape Fort Bragg, winding up here in the religiously quaint little tourist village of Mendocino, population 1,008, where you could get fresh-baked bread every morning and afternoon and the world's best coffee anytime you wanted. Enough, already—he wasn't one to feel sorry for himself. What was done was done. Move forward. Shake some pleasure out of life. He got to his feet, groggy from the beer and the pill, but inspired suddenly: he was going to call Carolee and tell her to come home, right away, because he was taking her out to dinner—at the Bistro, the place she liked best.

Her phone rang but she didn't answer and it went to voicemail. "Call me!" he shouted into the receiver and then rang the number again. She was down in Calpurnia, helping out at the animal preserve there where she liked to volunteer two days a week, but it was getting late—past five now—and they would have fed the animals already, wouldn't they? Or shoveled up the shit or whatever they did? Maybe she was in the car, maybe that was it. He was trying to picture that, his wife, driving, the fog strangling the headlights, her gray serious eyes fixed on the road, which was slick and wet and deserted, when she picked up.

"Hi, Sten," her voice breathed in his ear, "what's up?"

"Where are you?"

"I'm just getting in the car."

"Good. Great. Because I'm taking you out to dinner at that place you like."

"The Bistro?"

"Yeah."

"What's the occasion?"

"We're going to celebrate."

He heard the muffled thump of the car door slamming shut, then the revolving whine of the engine starting up. "Celebrate what?"

"I don't know," he said. "I just feel like celebrating. Life, I guess."

There was silence on the other end.

"You there?"

The faint distant crunch of gravel, tires in motion, then her voice coming back to him: "Sounds fine to me."

"Okay," he said, "okay." Everything was precious suddenly, his life, her life, the lives of the animals and of everybody else out there on the slick wet roads. He felt so overwhelmed he could barely get the words out. "You be careful out there, huh?"

The restaurant was in Fort Bragg, eight miles up the road from Mendocino. It occupied the second floor of a brick building the size of a department store that had once housed the operations of Union Lumber and it was floor-to-ceiling windows all around so that if you got a window table you could sit there and eat and feel as if you were floating over the whole town and the ocean too. Though it was the middle of August and the tourists were out in force, they got a window table without having to wait at the bar because the hostess was a former student at Fort Bragg High and recognized him, though he didn't recognize her. "Who was that?" Carolee asked, once they were seated.

"Beats me," he said, looking up at her, feeling good, if a bit shaky still. "At this point, they all look the same to me."

There were menus, drinks, a basket of hot bread. He went through the bread without even realizing what he was doing, hungry suddenly, though he hadn't got a lick of exercise all day.

"You *are* hungry," she said. "Don't tell me you didn't eat any lunch?"

He ducked his head, grinned. "No, I had something."

"What?"

"I don't know—a sandwich. Or cereal, a bowl of cereal." The fact was, he couldn't really remember. He had a sudden vision of himself laid out flat in a nursing home, gasping for breath, all his vitals dwindled down to nothing. Old man. He was an old man. "But tell me, how was it down there," he said, to cover himself, "—they get any new zebras in? Or what, giraffes? Or are they fresh out over there in Africa?"

"Same old," she said. "But really, I don't know why you have to make fun of them. If it wasn't for the Burnsides and a handful of people like them, people who care, those zebras and antelope would be gone from the face of the earth."

"Then why don't they send them back? Because that's where they belong, isn't it? I mean, zebras in Mendocino County—give me a break. What does he think, he's Noah or something?"

She was having a martini, three olives on the side. That was her trick: olives on the side so you get more gin, a matter of displacement—or lack of it, that is. She took a long slow sip, watching him. "That's the idea," she said. "Eventually. When things are, I don't know, more stable over there."

"Right," he said, and he felt his spirits crank back up and it had nothing to do with the Xanax, or did it? "Because they'd just eat them now, right? Probably the minute they got off the boat." The mountain zebra was almost gone in its native range, he knew that much, and the Grevy's too. The kudu weren't doing all that much better.

"*Stable,*" she repeated bitterly, sweeping her hair back. "It's a joke over there. Places like Sudan or Somalia, even Kenya. Everything's guns. Tribes. Guerrillas." She paused to back up and give it an exaggerated Spanish pronunciation: "*Gare-ee-yas,* I mean. Not gorillas—gorillas we could use more of. A whole lot more. But that's the mentality over there—shoot everything that moves."

"Over here too," he said.

She was silent a moment. Then she said, "What are you thinking of having?"

"Me? Fish. What about you?"

That was when he glanced out the window to the street below and saw Adam climbing out of an unfamiliar car that had just pulled up to the curb—a Japanese thing, pale blue, that suddenly became familiar, because here was that woman, what was her name, emerging from the driver's side to join him on the sidewalk. From this angle—he was right above them—he saw only the crowns of their heads and the flat plateaus of their shoulders, Adam's head shaved to the bone and glowing in the light trapped beneath the fog. The woman—her name came to him then, Sara—wore her hair parted down the middle, a crisp white line there as if her skull had been divided in two. They seemed to confer a moment and then started across the street to the pizza place and the bar there, Adam in the camo outfit he seemed to wear perennially now and Sara in jeans, boots and a low-cut top that displayed the deep crease between her breasts, bird's-eye view.

"Isn't that Adam?" Carolee said.

"Yeah, he just got out of the car there."

"Who's that with him?"

"Sara. The woman I told you about—from the other day?"

A silence. The restaurant buzzed around them. They watched the two of them cross the street, mount the curb and disappear into the pizza place—the pub that sold pizza, that is—Adam hunching in ahead of her, no thought of standing aside or holding the door, but that was only typical, that was only to be expected, that was Adam.

"She's old for him, isn't she? She's got to be forty."

"That's his business."

"I mean, what's she even doing with him?" She was leaning to her left, at the very edge of the table, squinting to peer out the window, though there was nothing to see but the closed door and above it the neon sign doing battle with the fog. "She's a piece of work herself, is what I hear."

He just shrugged, took a sip of his martini. He'd given up worrying about Adam a long time ago—or at least he'd tried to. Adam had problems. He'd always had problems. There'd been shrinks, a whole succession of them, but once he turned eighteen they had no control over that, and even after the last time he'd been arrested and evaluated by a state-appointed psychiatrist they still couldn't get access to the records. Privacy laws. He was an adult. Living in his own world. And while that world had its intersections with theirs and they did what they could—helped him with money, gave him a place to live where he could have some privacy and do his thing, whatever that might be, putting up walls, obsessing over the Chinese, calling himself Colter—he kept pushing them away till there was no point in it anymore.

"Cindy Burnside says she's got some pretty strange theories; I mean, really out there—as in right wing? As in conspiracies? Anti-everything? You know she got arrested for refusing to show a cop her license and registration?"

"She's fine," he said. "He's fine too."

"Fine? Where's he going to live when we close on my mother's house? With her?"

He didn't have a chance to answer because the waiter suddenly appeared with two fresh drinks, two more martinis, which would put them both over their self-imposed limit, if they were going to drink wine with dinner, that is—and they were. But there was the tray, there the perspiring glasses, there the waiter, smiling. "We didn't order those," Sten said.

The waiter—fiftyish, in white shirt and tie, his hair slicked tight to his skull—gestured to the couple sitting two tables over. They smiled, waved. Did he know them? "Compliments of the gentleman and lady," the waiter said.

"I don't want another martini," Sten said. "I'm not even half-finished with this one—"

"They want to buy you a round," the waiter said.

He wanted to say *For what? Why? I don't even know them,* but they were already raising their glasses to him and here was the man giving him the thumbs-up and then the peace sign—or maybe it was the *V*-for-victory sign—and he said, "Yeah, sure, okay," and in the next moment he was raising his glass in return.

"That was nice," Carolee said.

"Real nice," he said, and he couldn't keep the sarcasm out of his voice.

She must not have caught it because the next thing she said was, "The sturgeon sounds good," and then, in non sequitur, "I thought Adam wasn't supposed to go in there? Piero's, I mean."

"That was a long time ago," he said.

"They don't eighty-six you for life?"

He stared into the fresh martini—and he wasn't going to rush even if it was getting warm before his eyes because he wouldn't have strangers dictating his life to him—before he looked up and said, "If every time somebody got a little rowdy they eighty-sixed you for life all the bars in the world would be out of business."

"A *little* rowdy?" And here was that look again, the one that bunched her eyebrows. "I'd say he was more than a little rowdy—and what did that wind up costing us?"

He felt the irritation come up in him, despite the Xanax, despite the gin and the whiff of vermouth riding atop it. "I don't know," he said. "Can't we talk about something else?"

13.

THE NEXT MORNING, EARLY, he found himself back in Fort Bragg, at the grocery there—the cheap one, the one the tourists didn't know about—pushing a cart and working his way through the itemized list Carolee had pressed on him as he went out the door. The place was over-lit, antiseptic, as artificial as the flight deck of a spaceship, and at this hour there were more shelf-stockers than shoppers. That was all right. He liked the early hours, when things were less complicated. He'd been up early all his life and though everybody said the best thing about retirement was sleeping in, he just couldn't feature it. If he found himself in bed later than six he felt like a degenerate, and he supposed he could thank his mother for that. And his father. The work ethic—once you had it, once it had been implanted in you, how could you shake it? Why would you want to? Relax, he kept telling himself. Keep busy. Relax. Keep busy. The last thing he wanted was to wind up sitting in a recliner all day staring at the TV like some zombie or pulling on a sun visor to chase a golf ball around the fairways with a bunch of loudmouthed jocks. Or bridge. He hated bridge, hated games of any kind. But how *did* you relax? That was the problem he was trying to resolve—and certainly world-class indulgence wasn't the answer.

He seemed to have a package of meat in his hand, T-bone steak, slick and wet and red, and when he set it in the cart, there was a fine glaze of blood on his hand, and no place to wipe it off. Some stores provided paper towels to ease the unpleasantness of this little reminder of precisely where that steak or chop or chicken breast originated, but not this one. He stood there a moment, rubbing the pink glaze over his fingertips before surreptitiously wiping it off on the soft plastic wrapper of one of the packages of hamburger buns stacked on the display case behind him.

When he turned back to the cart, reaching down to reassemble the things there and check them against Carolee's list—1% milk in the plastic jug, pickles, cookies, more meat, pasta, beans, rice—he felt the twinge in his lower back again, the muscle there balky still. It seemed to bother him more in the mornings, stiffening up overnight despite the form-fitting neoprene pad Carolee had stretched over the mattress, but then he hadn't slept on that pad or in that bed—their bed—the previous night. He'd wound up on the narrow single bed in the guest room because Carolee was in one of her moods. And it wasn't all her—he'd been in a mood too, absolutely. And why? Because after they'd finished their celebratory dinner, she'd insisted they go across the street and into the pizza place where Adam was, where Adam had been for the better part of an hour. "For an after-dinner drink," she said, taking hold of his arm as they came down the stairs at the restaurant.

"They don't have after-dinner drinks there. Only beer and wine, remember?"

"An after-dinner wine then."

They were passing by the bar on the lower level—the door swung open on muted lighting and inflamed faces—and he said, "Why not have one here? A real drink, a cognac or that Benedictine you like. I'm wined out, if you want to know the truth." They were in the hallway now, moving toward the front door. "Or actually, I've had enough. More than enough. Let's just go home, huh?"

She was chopping along in her short swift strides, tugging at his arm as if leading him on a leash. "I want to go to Piero's," she said.

And he stopped, right there, right at the door, to tug back at her. "Let it go," he told her. "Drop it. He's a big boy now. He's an adult. You can't just go around spying on him—"

"I'm not spying on him. I just want a drink at Piero's, all right? Is that a crime?"

"No," he said, "but stalking is."

She'd jerked angrily away from him. "I can't believe you," she said, pushing through the door and out onto the street while he followed in her wake, the folds of her dress in violent motion, her perfume an assault on the damp night air, perfume he didn't like, had never liked, perfume she wore just to make his eyes water. He made a note to himself to find the little bottle amidst the clutter in the bathroom and dump it in the trash when she wasn't looking, but then of course she'd just go and buy another bottle and he'd dump that and she'd buy another one, a losing proposition all the way round. He hadn't gone two steps before she swung round on him, combative, her legs braced, hands on hips. "He's my son. *Our* son." She took in a deep moist breath and blew it out again. "I just want to get a look at her."

The fog softened the lights of the buildings up and down the street. There was no traffic. No noise, no sound of any kind. Even the ocean, no more than five hundred yards away, was silent, as if the waves had been sucked back down the beach before they had a chance to break. "Right," he said into the stillness, "like we just happened to be passing by and got a sudden craving for pizza, at what—nine-fifteen at night? When we're normally sitting in front of the TV and thinking about bed? He's not stupid, you know."

Her face was contorted, angry, the lines at the corners of her eyes etched in the faint tricolored glow of the neon across the street. "I'm going in there," she said. "Whether you're coming or not."

What he did then was take hold of her arm—or no, he snatched it with a sudden jolt of violence that seemed to explode inside him. "You're going nowhere," he rasped, his voice locked tight in his throat.

She tried to pull away but he held on to her, his hand clamped just above her elbow, feeling the bone there, the humerus, and how weightless and weak and fragile it was. She was angry enough to curse him, except that she never cursed—in her quaint moral universe, women didn't use offensive language, only men did. "Let me go," she demanded, "you're hurting me."

He didn't know what had come over him but it was all too much—Adam, Warner Ayala, the martinis sent over by two total strangers as if they could buy his approval, as if he'd asked for it or wanted it in any way, shape or form—and he just tightened his grip till all he could hear was the furious chuffing intake of her breath and the kick and scrape of her heels on the pavement. This was a dance, a kind of dance, more jig than polka, and it might have gone on till one or the other of them gave in, but then a car came up the street, headlights sifting through the fog to pin them there as if they were onstage, and he let her go. At which point she lurched back a step and then, without so much as a glance, stalked across the street and into the bar, leaving him with no choice but to follow.

It was a tiny place, claustrophobic, smelling of hops and cold sweat. There was an L-shaped bar that seated ten maybe, kitchen beyond it, a narrow hallway, a cramped array of tables. People were packed in shoulder-to-shoulder, chattering away in a percussive animal hum. In the old days there would have been a dense haze of cigarette smoke and a whiff of marijuana too, but if you wanted to smoke now it had to be outside, on the street. Behind the bar was a chalkboard featuring the brews on tap, with brief descriptions, the most pertinent of which seemed to be alcohol content. One of the ales, Sten noticed, was listed at 11.9% alcohol by volume, which must have had a real kick to it, but then that was the point, wasn't it?

Carolee was standing at the bar behind a cluster of people, mostly young, who were hunched over their elbows and their pints of stout, pilsner and ale. Nobody was drinking wine. And Carolee, her shoulders tense with agitation and her hair tucked haphazardly up under the collar of her coat, made no move to flag down the bartender. Her hands were clasped before her as if she were patiently awaiting her turn, when in fact her eyes were fixed on a table in the back, the last one down the narrow hallway which gave onto the restrooms and the rear exit. She was trying to be discreet, trying to look like a thirsty, gracefully aging woman who was only waiting for her pint of 11.9% ABV ale, but she wasn't doing much of a job of it—she just looked awkward, that was all. No matter. Adam's back was to them. He was leaning into the table, apparently staring down into his beer, while Sara, her face animated, did the talking. And gesturing. She was really going at it, her face running through all its permutations, her hands dancing and fluttering as if she were directing traffic on top of it, and what was the subject? The problems horses had with their hooves? The DMV? Dogs? Or was she just talking, was she one of those people—women, for the most part—who just talk to round out the sonic spectrum? Which would have cast Adam in the role of listener, but then Adam never seemed to pay much attention to anyone, off in a trance half the time, as if it wasn't words that had meaning but the sound itself, voices sawing away like instruments in an ever-expanding orchestra. Sten eased his way through the crowd and tapped Carolee on the shoulder. "Okay, you've seen her," he hissed, "now let's get out of here before she spots us—or Adam does."

Carolee wouldn't look at him. She made a pretense of studying the chalkboard. "I want a beer," she said.

"A beer? I haven't seen you touch a beer in ten years."

"All right, a wine. A pinot noir. Get me a glass of pinot noir."

There was music playing over the sound system, a thin drift of high harmonies rising above an insistent guitar, the volume turned just low enough so that you couldn't actually hear it except at odd intervals, though you knew it was there. He shuffled his feet. Put his hands in his pockets. He felt bad. Felt conflicted. Carolee was going to get her wine, that was as certain as the law of diminishing returns, and he was thinking he could maybe maneuver her back toward the door, as far from Adam as possible, and hope for the best. But then what was he thinking? What was wrong here? Why couldn't they just stop by their own son's table and say hello as if they'd drifted in at random? (*Yeah, they'd been to a movie and had a craving for pizza and what a surprise to see you here, but we won't keep you, no, no, just go ahead and we'll see you later, okay?*) Because Adam wouldn't believe them, that was why. Or maybe he would. You could never tell with him.

If all this was about making a decision, it was taken out of his hands, because Sara looked up then, her eyes languidly scanning the room, till they settled on his and then Carolee's. He watched her face change. First she looked puzzled, as if she couldn't quite place them, but then she smiled and waved and ducked her head to say something to Adam, who seemed to stiffen in his seat. His head was down still, the muscles at the back of his neck bunched, but he didn't move or respond. He might have been frozen in place, might have been a statue. There was a lull. The music emerged. Somebody shouted out something inane, the way people tend to do in bars. And then, very slowly, Adam turned in profile to glance over his shoulder. The look he gave them—his parents, his own parents—shaded from incomprehension to hate, to a look of such ferocious contempt you would have thought they'd come to tear the flesh from his bones. In the next moment he was up and out of the seat and hurtling down the hallway, past the kitchen, past the restrooms and right on out the back door. And Sara, the horse lady who was fifteen years older than he was and no paragon herself, gave them a fleeting apologetic smile before she snatched up her purse and hurried out after him.

But now it was morning and Sten was in the supermarket, arching his back to take the crick out of it, Carolee's list clenched in one hand and the steak seeping blood at the bottom of the cart, getting on with his life. Eggs. Hadn't she mentioned something about eggs? He scanned the list, her handwriting a neat rounded script that flowed like music on the page, handwriting that was as familiar as his own, but he saw no eggs listed there. What the hell, he was thinking, reaching for the carton anyway, thinking better safe than sorry, when he became aware that someone was standing right there beside him, too close for casual contact, someone who started off as a pair of running shoes and shorts climbing out of the floor and turned out to be Carey Bachman, who used to teach social studies at the school till his wife's cosmetics business took off and made earning a paycheck extraneous. He was in his mid-forties, with a narrow slice of a face dominated by his milky protuberant eyes ("Fish-Eyes," the students had called him behind his back) and he was dressed in a T-shirt though it was fifty-eight degrees outside and colder in here, what with the refrigerated air of the meat and dairy displays, and he should have been smiling, but wasn't.

"Carey," Sten heard himself say.

Still no smile. Sotto voce: "Hi, Sten." A glance over his shoulder, conspiratorial. "Listen," he said, "you see what's going on here?"

See what? What was he talking about?

Carey led with his chin, eyes up, then down again, and Sten looked across the aisle to see three—no, four—Mexicans pushing a pair of overloaded carts. They were dressed in work clothes—boots, jeans, long-sleeved shirts—and each wore a brand-new Oakland A's cap pushed back on his head with the bill jutting out at an odd angle, as if it were a fashion trend. Other than the caps, which they might have got at a ballgame at the Coliseum the night before, there was nothing to distinguish them. Three were young—teenage or early twenties—the other middle-aged. They could have been anybody. "Yeah," he said, "I see them. What's the deal?"

Carey gave him a look of disbelief. "What's the deal? 'Take Back Our Forests,' that's the deal. Remember, you came to the first meeting? Before you went off on vacation—on that cruise?"

It came back to him now, though so much had happened in the interval he'd completely forgotten about it, and even if he hadn't he still couldn't fathom what Carey was talking about. It was seven-fifteen in the morning. He'd had too much to drink the night before. The overhead light cut into his eyes. "Yeah," he said. "So?"

"This is just what we were talking about. This. Right here. Right now." Carey was having trouble containing himself, but he dropped his voice as the Mexicans wheeled past and turned into the next aisle over.

Sten saw that their carts were loaded with staples, four-pound bags of Calrose rice, dried pinto beans, cellophane-wrapped boxes of instant noodles and what looked to be half the ground meat in the store, but still he just stared at Carey, the moment unwinding in slow reveal. Take Back Our Forests had been Carey's idea—his and Gordon Welch's, who managed the local B. of A. branch— and it wasn't a vigilante group, not at all, a designation they'd bent over backwards to deplore. No, it was a citizens' group—an association of concerned citizens, property owners, businessmen, locals all—that had risen up spontaneously in response to what was going on in the forest. The drug cartels—La Familia, the Zetas, Sinaloa—had come north, had come here, to grow marijuana on state and federal land, bypassing the need to smuggle product across the border, and in their wake they'd brought violence to the Noyo Valley, to Big River and the Mendocino National Forest. And worse: they poisoned everything, putting out baits for rabbit, skunk, deer and bear, even poisoning the streams. The calculus was simple: a dead rabbit wouldn't be girding the base of the plants to get at the moisture there and a dead deer wasn't going to browse the nascent buds—or a dead bear either or a marmot or a squirrel or anything else that ate, moved and breathed—and the best way to ensure that was just to poison the drinking supply. Hikers had been shot at. Fishermen. Hunters. People were afraid to go into the woods.

"I was out for my morning run," Carey said, and then he broke off to crane his neck and peer down the aisle. "Mules," he said. "These are the mules. You see what they're buying?"

Sten shrugged. "Maybe it's a church group. Maybe they're going on a picnic."

"Bullshit."

They stood there a moment, blinking in the light. Sten wanted a cup of coffee, an English muffin, maybe a soft-boiled egg—and a nap, definitely a nap. He watched a heavyset woman who looked vaguely familiar—another early-morning shopper—stump by with a handbasket bristling with celery, seven or eight bunches of it, and wondered what that was all about—cream of celery soup? Carey put a hand on his wrist. "Listen, we've got to follow them, you know that, don't you? To find out where the camp is—"

"Why not just call the sheriff?"

"Don't be naïve. There's no law against buying groceries. And even if they're illegal, which you damn well know they are, the cops are prohibited from checking their status—they can't even ask because it might abridge their precious rights, to which everybody is entitled the minute they set foot in this country, whether they're drug dealers or not. The cops are useless, you ought to know that." He was going to say more, all ready to go off on a rant, but he suddenly stopped himself, motioning with his eyes, and here came two of them with their cart that was heaped now with peppers of every description—jalapeños, serranos, green, red, yellow, orange—and a pyramid of tortillas in the family-sized packages, twenty, thirty or more. When they'd turned down the next aisle, heading for the checkout stand, Carey let go of his wrist and lowered his voice to an urgent whisper. "You got to help me out here."

Sten was noncommittal, but he was aroused: more dark little men, more criminals. And here, right here in the U.S. He was no racist—he'd seen the demographic shift in the school population over the years, the Swedes, Norwegians, Italians and Poles who'd worked the lumber mills when they were a going concern giving way ever so gradually to the Hispanics who cleaned their houses, repaired their cars, stocked the shelves in the supermarket and made up the beds for the tourists, and it had meant nothing to him, immigrants in a nation built on them—but when they destroyed the land, drove people out of their own parks and forests, it was another thing altogether. He'd seen their abandoned camps deep in the woods, the mounds of trash, the carcasses of the animals, oil and pesticides leaching into the ground, the abandoned propane tanks and crude listing shacks. It was a matter of ecology as much as anything else. Save the forests. Save the trout. The salmon. The deer.

"We're going to have to use your car. Because I told you, I jogged here"—Carey picked at the front of his T-shirt in testament—"and mine's all the way back at home."

"Follow them? Isn't that a little extreme?"

"We stay back, way back. Just till we see what road they turn off on."

"Then we call the sheriff?"

"Yeah, then we call the sheriff."

I4.

THEY WERE DRIVING A new Ford XLT pickup, white, with Nevada plates and dust-streaked sides, which only seemed to confirm Carey in his suspicions, as if every Mexican had to be driving a beater prickling with rakes, shovels and blowers, as if it were a condition of their lives on this planet, as if the stereotype was the only type. "Stolen," he said. "Bet anything."

Sten just nodded. But it was odd, he had to admit it. He wanted to think they were traveling mariachis, the construction crew for some millionaire building a getaway in the hills, a church group, real and bona fide, but as he sat behind the wheel of the Prius in the parking lot, Carey at his side, and watched them load the groceries into the bed of the truck, he knew he was fooling himself. He'd tried to appear casual at the checkout stand as the girl there, a Latina with heavy purple eye shadow who might or might not have been a student at the high school, scanned his items. Hovering over the counter in his jeans and sweatshirt, he went quietly about the business of bagging his forty-two dollars and thirty-five cents' worth of groceries, nothing amiss, the most ordinary thing in the world, but out of the corner of his eye he was watching the Mexicans in the next checkout lane while Carey kept a lookout at the door. They had a third cart he hadn't noticed before, this one filled with plastic jugs of water, half a dozen twenty-four-packs of Tecate and a couple bottles of E&J brandy, real rotgut, not at all the sort of thing you'd take on a church picnic.

The men huddled there in their askew caps and they didn't say a word, not to their own checkout girl or to each other either. They looked at nothing, at the wall, at the floor. When the customer ahead of them—the woman with the celery—had concluded her transaction, they came to life, juggling things from the carts to set them neatly on the rolling black conveyor belt. Sten took his time so he could study them, the three young guys doing all the work while the older one stood there watching the display on the computer screen as if totting up every item in his head. The bill, which the older man paid—in cash—came to over seven hundred dollars.

There was a row of cars separating Sten's Prius from their pickup, and if they noticed him and Carey sitting there, they gave no indication. They were focused on what they were doing, and they were quick and efficient, the groceries transferred from the carts in minutes, and then the older man got behind the wheel while two of the younger ones slipped in beside him and the third sprang up into the bed in a single bound, nimble as a gymnast. Sten waited until the Mexicans had backed out of their spot, conscious of Carey, who'd gone quiet with the tension of the moment, and then put the car in drive and slowly followed them out of the lot. The street they were on—Franklin—paralleled the Coast Highway, which was the town's main thoroughfare and lively with traffic this time of year, what with all the tourists either coming or going, even in the morning, especially in the morning, because tourists liked to get right up, gulp down their coffee, eggs over easy, three strips of bacon and hash browns and hit the road to invade the next charmingly decrepit coastal town before everybody else got there. He was surprised when the pickup turned left—no signal, just a lurch—and headed down the block to turn right on the Coast Highway, where they'd be more visible to any patrol car that might happen by. But then—and he had to remind himself lest he get carried away—they really hadn't done anything, had they? Aside from pumping seven-hundred-odd dollars into the local economy, and what was wrong with that?

"Watch it," Carey said, "watch it!" and he saw that he'd come up too close on them, almost rear-ended them in fact, swerving now, at the last moment, as the pickup—no signal—swung into a gas station and he rolled on by, the blood pounding in his temples and his hands locked on the wheel, trying his best to look innocuous. And old. Old and befuddled. No problem there.

Carey's voice came at him again, insistent: "Pull over. Here. Behind that van."

He flicked on the signal, did as he was told. The gas station was a block behind them. Glancing in the rearview, he saw the white truck ease up to the pump there and one of the men—the one in back—jump out to flip open the gas tank and insert the nozzle before hurrying inside to pay, in cash, because what drug dealer, what grower, would use a credit card?

"Jesus, Sten, what are you thinking? You almost hit them."

And now he began to feel the faintest tick of irritation. He hadn't had his breakfast, his groceries weren't getting any fresher, he was tired and fed up and here he was chasing phantoms while Carey Bachman barked orders at him. "But I didn't," he said, and gave him a steady look. "Did I?"

They waited there at the side of the road till the pickup was in motion again, its blunt hood and massive grill nosing up to the street as a clutch of motor homes lumbered by, and then, without warning, the pickup was cutting across both lanes and heading back in the direction they'd come from and Carey, his voice rising, jerked up so violently in his seat the whole car rocked on its springs. "Cut a U-ey, quick, quick!" he shouted. "They're turning left. Hit it, come on!"

The Prius was built for gas mileage, not the Indianapolis 500, but it had enough acceleration to get you through a tight spot if your reflexes served you and Sten's did. He was able to pull out front of the first creeping motor home and slash a U-turn with a minimal squeal of the tires and a single admonitory blast of the startled driver's horn, and he kept his foot on the accelerator until he was fifty feet from the tail of the pickup, which continued half a block south before making an abrupt left back up the street they'd just followed it down. All right. He slowed, hung back, watched the pickup continue straight on up the road, the sun just beginning to poke through in the distance to illuminate the world in a soft wash of color, and did his best to keep up without being too obvious about it.

Carey had gone rigid but for the bounce of one agitated knee. "They're heading straight up into the hills," he cried, his voice thin with excitement. "Didn't I tell you? Huh?"

Sten wanted to say, *What does that prove?*, but he was feeling it now too, more certain by the minute that Carey was right, that they were onto something. A load of groceries like that? There wasn't much up here, once you got out of town—a couple of ranches, deep woods, the Georgia Pacific property he or Carey or one of the others hiked twice a week to make sure nothing like this was going on, to report it, which was what they were going to do now, just as soon as they saw where the illegal operation was. He didn't say anything, just focused on the white gleam of the pickup ahead of him, which wasn't doing much more than forty-five or so. He eased up on the accelerator. Held tight to the wheel. A car appeared around the next corner, coming the opposite way, followed by a battered pickup, its bed stacked high with baled hay—horses out here, a smattering of cattle, chickens, turkeys (and weed too, that went without saying, but that was different because what people did on their own private property for their own consumption—citizens, American citizens—was nobody's business but theirs). The Prius shook ever so slightly with the motion of their passing, and then the road was clear but for the white pickup with the shadowy figures inside and the man in back propped up against the cab and looking straight at them, his gold-and-green hat flashing in the light like a homing beacon.

Weed. The great lure of the North Coast, the Gold Coast, Pot Alley. They grew grapes in the Anderson Valley, but they grew pot in the hills. It had been going on as long as he could remember.

"They're signaling," Carey said, and his voice seemed to come out of nowhere, startling him. He saw that the pickup had its right blinker on and that it was slowing now to pull over on the shoulder in a tornado of dust and it took him by surprise. His first instinct was to hit the brakes, not knowing what else to do. "No, no, no, don't stop," Carey hissed, "whatever you do, don't stop," and here they were, right on top of them, giving him little choice but to continue on past, staring straight ahead as if the pickup on the shoulder was no more significant than the trees, the rocks and the litter along the roadside. He was going slowly, too slowly, and he could feel their eyes on him, arrogant eyes, angry, suspicious. "Goose it," Carey said, and he was staring straight ahead too.

They drove on up the road, Sten snatching a look in the rear-view while Carey slouched low in the seat so he could study the side mirror. The white pickup just sat there, the dust dissipating, and then they were around the next turn and it was gone. "What now?" Sten asked, and he wasn't really asking, just thinking aloud.

Carey was agitated, hyper, frazzled with the adrenaline running through him, the way it was in battle, when your glands pumped chemicals into your bloodstream and action was the only off-valve to bring you back down again. "Just keep on," he said, his eyes swollen in their sockets. "Or no, pull over. Pull over and wait till they go past again."

Sten flicked on the blinker, looking for a spot up ahead, and there it was, a patch of bleached-out dirt on the edge of a dropoff, and in the next moment he was swinging onto the shoulder, generating his own tornado of dust. Unfortunately, he was barely off the road, the turnout so narrow the driver's-side wheels were still on the blacktop, and he had a fleeting vision of a logging truck roaring round the turn to peel off the left side of the car—and how would he explain that to Carolee? Not to mention the insurance company?

The engine shut itself off, dutifully. There was no traffic. He lifted his eyes to look into the mirror. "What if they don't come by? What if they already went past their turnoff just to fox us and they're doubling back?"

Carey turned a stricken face to him and jerked his head round to stare out the back window, where the road lay silent and the sun swelled to brighten the surface till it might have been freshly oiled. "Just wait," Carey said.

"Wait for what? They're gone, I tell you." Another glance in the rearview. The bushes gilded in light. The soaring trees. Everything as still and innocent as the beginning of time. "I'm for turning around."

And then suddenly the pickup was there, rounding the bend, looming huge in the rearview. It gave him a jolt. He could feel his heart going. He snatched a quick breath and kept his hands firmly on the wheel, as if it were in danger of breaking loose and disintegrating before his eyes. The truck was moving at a good clip, but it slowed abruptly as it came up even with them and both he and Carey turned their heads to stare into the faces of the four men, no pretense now, the truck twice the size of the Prius, big tires, big cab, and it came to a halt right there beside them. It was a staring contest, that was what it was, and he was thinking they would be armed and why wouldn't they be because this was no church group and these were no ranch hands, thinking *What have I got myself into?*

The man behind the wheel, the older one, had a face that sucked up the light, his eyes red-rimmed and sleepy, but the look he gave Sten was unmistakable. Sten had seen it all his life, on the football field, in the service, from the punks at the high school who thought they were men when they didn't have the faintest notion of what a man was, the look that said, *Don't fuck with me.* Five seconds, that was all there was to it. Nobody said a word, though the windows were down and the one in the passenger's seat was close enough to spit on, and then the tires jumped and the pickup shot up the road to vanish round the next turn.

"Call the sheriff," Sten said, and in that instant he had the car in gear and he was lurching out onto the roadway, pedal to the floor, something gone awry in him now, the switch thrown, and he could no more have turned around and gone back home than cut off his own hand. This was America, this was his turf, where he'd been born and raised, not some shithole in the jungle somewhere. "Son of a bitch," he said.

And Carey? Carey was clutching at the passenger's strap with one hand and trying to work his phone with the other. "Slow down!" he shouted. "It's not worth it. Jesus, Sten, you're going to kill us."

The trees careened past, tight turns here, the coast far below them now, dips and rises, timberland, better than fifty inches of rain up here on the slopes each winter and thirty-nine below, rain that swelled the streams and percolated into the soil and pushed the biggest trees in the world—living fossils—up into the sky. The tires shrieked. Air beat in the window to slap at his face. "I can't get any reception," Carey said, as if it mattered, and then the white flash of the truck's tailgate shone through the treetrunks up ahead and he eased off on the gas, in control now, because they might have had the advantage on the open highway, but here the smaller vehicle was more than a match for them.

He settled in behind them, giving them space—fifty feet, as if the Prius was equipped with an invisible tape measure, as if it was one of those super cars out of a James Bond movie. The one in back, his face a sharp blade of light beneath the upthrust bill of his cap, stared right through them as if it was all nothing to him, as if he wasn't a criminal, as if he wasn't going to go out there and open up cans of tuna and sardines laced with carbofuran to poison the bears and raccoons and fishers and anything else that dared get in his way. Well, all right. He was past caring about niceties now. He was going to follow them till the wheels fell off—or they ran out of gas. Yes. Right. And that was another advantage of the Prius.

Carey said nothing. He kept fiddling with his phone, though it was futile, any fool could see that. There was no reception here—they were in the middle of nowhere, what did he expect? Ten minutes drifted by, fifteen. Sten focused on the shifting white tailgate so fiercely it began to blur, swelling and receding, a ghostly thing, almost illusory, a thing that floated out ahead of him, snaking through the turns, vanishing in the dips and emerging again, no rhythm, no logic, just movement. He kept hoping for some traffic, for another car, for anyone to signal to or flag down, but there were no other cars on the road, not this far up, not today. The road narrowed, became a channel through a sea of redwood and fir, and still the pickup rolled on and still Sten sat fifty feet behind it.

And then, abruptly, the Mexicans pulled off on the shoulder and Sten hit the brakes, put on his blinker—pointlessly, but it was an old habit—and followed suit. There was a logging road off to the left and a hundred feet on and he wondered if that was their destination, if they had their camp somewhere in there and didn't want to give it away. They were stuck, that was what he was thinking. Couldn't go forward, couldn't retreat. Check and mate.

After a while, the driver of the pickup shut down the engine. The sun climbed higher by degrees. Shadows shortened. A jay called from the woods. "What are they doing?" Carey asked. "Why are they stopping here?"

"See that road up ahead?" He indicated it with a thrust of his chin.

"You think that's where they're headed?"

Sten shrugged. His stomach rumbled. "They're in a spot now. They hadn't counted on us being here, that's for shit sure."

Another fifteen minutes ticked by on the dashboard clock. And then finally, inevitably, the driver's door of the pickup flashed open and the older Mexican stepped out and started back down the road toward them, his steps slow and measured, the cap still at the same jaunty angle. His face was flat, boneless, almost as if it had been scooped hollow, and his nose was flat too so that Sten wondered if he'd once been a boxer. Or a rodeo clown.

The man came up to the window and leaned down to look in at him. "You need help?" he asked, his accent slow and stopped-up so that "help" came out as "hell."

"No," Sten said, shaking his head for emphasis. "No, we're fine."

The man seemed to consider this a moment, his look unwavering, a hint of menace seeping like a tincture into his squinting brown eyes.

"How about you?" Sten said. "You need help?"

Sighing, the man drew himself up and said, "No, we doan need no hell," and then he looked off in the distance as if to find the words there for whatever was to come next.

Carbofuran. It was one of the deadliest pesticides known to man. A couple drops of it would kill you. And what happened to the bears? They died clawing at themselves, their guts on fire.

"You sure?" Sten said.

Another sigh. The man bent to look in the window again, his eyes hardening. It was then that he let the flap of his shirt fall open so that Sten could see the polished wooden handle of the revolver tucked in his waistband, but that was a mistake and it was going to cost him because he didn't know who he was dealing with here.

Sten shoved open the door so suddenly the man had to step back, and then he was out on the naked strip of pavement, unfurling himself to his full height so that now he was the one looking down. "You know what this is?" he demanded and he could feel it coming up in him all over again and there was no stopping it, though the man shot a look to his compatriots, who flung open the doors of the pickup even as the acrobat in back sprang out and began coming down the road toward them and Carey hissed, *Sten, come on, it's not worth it, let's go.* "This is America, you son of a bitch. The United States of America. You get that?"

The man rocked back on his heels, his eyes locked on Sten's, and for a moment Sten thought he was going to spit at him the way the prisoner had in Costa Rica, but that didn't happen and a good thing too because he was a beat away from losing it. Here was guilt. Here was the shit of the world come home to roost right here in the redwoods. The man scuffed his boots on the pavement, then swung round without a word and started back for the truck, his arms outstretched to usher the other three along with him. Sten watched them climb back in. The doors slammed. Sun glinted off chrome. And the truck sat there—and so did Sten— till the minutes became hours and Carey, in over his head, talked himself hoarse on the theme of giving it up, of getting out of there before somebody got hurt, because they weren't vigilantes, were they?

Finally, and by now it was past noon, the pickup's engine roared to life and the driver cut the wheels hard even as the man in back—the acrobat—leapt down and started up the road on foot. He was lithe, tall, rabbity, and by the time the driver had turned the truck around and started back down the hill, he was jogging up the road, the bill of his cap pulled down tight now, fashion sacrificed to exigency. "Where's *he* going?" Carey wondered aloud.

Sten didn't answer. He just put the car in gear, swung a U-turn and followed the pickup back down the road, all the way down, past the supermarket and back out onto the Coast Highway, where it turned north and kept on going. At speed. And here was where the big engine had the advantage, though Sten tried gamely to keep up. By Cleone, they'd lost them, but Carey got the 911 dispatcher on the phone as soon as they were in range. "What do I tell them?" he asked, his face blanched and the armpits of his T-shirt soaked through with nervous sweat.

Sten went silently through the list of crimes—Being Mexican; Driving a New Ford XLT; Buying Too Many Groceries; Acting Suspicious—but he was already signaling, already looking up the road for the next left so he could turn round and head home. It was one-twenty in the afternoon. The meat was rotted, the milk gone sour. And the eggs. Nothing worse than the smell of rotten eggs. He turned to Carey, Carey with his bouncing knee and too much white in his eyes, Carey in his jogging togs, Carey the vigilante. "Just tell them they were brandishing a weapon," he said. "That ought to do it."

PART V

The Noyo

15.

"DOESN'T HE SCARE YOU?"

She was in the kitchen of the house on the banks of the
Noyo, a weak sun sifting through the trees, and Christabel, who
didn't even know him and who was probably jealous—definitely
jealous—had called to see how she was getting along in exile.

"No," she said, "not at all." And that was the truth. Adam
could be as strange as strange got, no doubt about that, but what
Christabel didn't understand was that underneath there was an
essential sweetness to him, a boyishness, an innocence you didn't
find in the types that took up space in the bars and stomped up
and down the aisles of the hardware store with the oh-so-pleased-
with-themselves smirks on their faces, which, sadly, seemed to be
the only types available to women like her and Christabel. Plus,
he was young. And handsome. A whole lot handsomer than her
ex, Roger, who'd let himself go till he wasn't much more than a
belly with pants on it—or anybody she'd dated since. And built.
She told Christabel that, as if she needed any justification, because
who she dated was nobody's business but hers, not even her best
friend's.

"He's like a rock. I don't know what he does—I don't see him
lifting weights or anything—but he's hard all over."

"Don't get dirty on me now."

She laughed. "I'm not. Really, I'm not. Just stating the facts."

There was a long exhalation on the other end of the line,
Christabel blowing out the smoke of her cigarette, and she could
picture it, the way she threw her head back and pursed her lips
as if she were channeling the smoke through an imaginary portal
in the sky and sending it right on up to heaven, to God Himself,

who, after all, was the one who invented nicotine. "You're just a cougar, that's all."

She didn't deny it. In fact, it brought a smile to her lips. "Who me?" she said, and they both laughed. Then she said, "I thought you gave up smoking?"

"I did."

"So what's that puffing I hear?"

"Just having a little taste to see what I'm missing. Isn't that what you're doing—with Adam? Because don't tell me you're serious—"

It had been a week since she'd moved in and if he hadn't been around much, that was all right. He was mysterious, always out in the woods, and when he wasn't he was lying supine on the couch in a clutter of books and notepads or just staring into the gray void of the TV, which looked as if it hadn't worked in years. If he had anything to say at all it was about Colter—Colter this and Colter that, the same story, over and over. And the cops, the cops really lit him up. Ditto the Chinese. Colter, the cops and the Chinese, those were his themes. When he was talking, that is, which wasn't much. He disappeared early each morning, before she was up, but he was always there for dinner and always glad to see the food dished out on the plate, whether it was meat loaf or mac and cheese or bean burritos. Glad for the sex too. She'd never known anybody like him—it was as if he'd been locked up in a cage his whole life. He wanted it. He needed it. He was hungry for it. And so was she. She'd been abstinent so long she'd forgotten what it was like to have your blood quicken just thinking about some-body, to feast on the smell of him, to find yourself getting wet even before he had his clothes off, even before he touched you.

"You want to meet him? See for yourself?" A pause. "He's sweet. He really is."

Christabel said something back, but it was garbled, hampered by the connection, the signal weak out here in the woods, and there was no landline—Adam had ripped it out. And why? He claimed the phone had been listening to him, spying on him, and if she doubted that—CIA, FBI, his mother, the Chinese—she couldn't fault his paranoia. Or was it even paranoia—or just wariness, just being hip to reality? They were listening in on everybody and tracking their e-mails too, and that was a fact.

"You're breaking up," she said. "It's me. Wait a minute"—and she stepped out the back door—"is this better?"

"I said, after what you've been telling me, he sounds pretty strange. Even if he is a stud."

"What's strange? Everybody's strange. You're strange. I'm strange."

"You can say that again."

"No, seriously, you want to come for dinner?"

"When?"

"I don't know, tonight?" It was a Saturday, the day they usually got together for dinner someplace and then the whole hopeless charade of bar-hopping, singles night out, as if there'd be any male in any of those places who would be of interest to either of them, every last one too old, too young, too stupid or too married.

"Come early. We'll have cocktails. Four-thirty? Four, even?"

A silence, as if Christabel were weighing all the stacked-up options of her glittering social life, and then she said, "I don't even know how to get there, like what road, it's not even marked, right? And that's another thing—it's just crazy what you're doing. You can't hide out forever—"

"A week isn't forever."

"What then—you going to stay the full thirty days till the dog's out of quarantine? You think that's going to satisfy them? You can't just—why don't you at least take him to the vet and have the vet give him a shot or some kind of certificate or something?"

It was as if somebody had laid a cold hand on her back—or no, an ice pack. All her fear and hate gusted through her like an

Arctic wind and froze her right there in place, her boots stuck fast in the dirt, her frame as rigid as the cinder-block wall and the trees that stood motionless all around her. Christabel was right: she couldn't stay here forever, plus Sten was closing on the place and there'd be a new owner soon. And where did that leave her? She couldn't go back to her own house because they'd be looking for her there, at least till the quarantine was up, and Christabel's apartment was the size of your average cell at the House of Detention and she wouldn't have her anyway because she couldn't risk harboring a fugitive. And that was just how she'd put it, Christabel, the coward, the wuss: *harboring a fugitive.* Bow down and kiss their asses, why don't you? *I could lose my job,* she'd said.

The fact was, Sara had already taken the dog to the vet and already mailed the proof of rabies/parvo vaccination to the court, knowing it most likely wouldn't fly since Kutya had bitten the cop *before* he was vaccinated. But it was better than nothing. At least she was trying, though they had no right in any of this except the right of might, the right of their fraudulent and blatantly uncon-stitutional laws and their storm troopers in the shiny taxpayer-bought cars. And the judges and the courts and the DMV and all the rest of the parasitic bureaucracy they'd imposed on the Amer-ican public. It was a house of cards just waiting for somebody to blow it all away. The leeches. The bloodsuckers.

"I already did," she said. "But I'm not going to stand around and wait for some dickhead in a patrol car to pull into the drive-way with a warrant, I'm not that stupid. And I'll tell you another thing: I blew off the court appearance too."

"Great. That's just fucking brilliant. What do you want to do, go to jail?"

No, she didn't want to go to jail, but there was no way she was going to bow down to them because that would just make her a slave like everybody else. In three weeks she'd go back to the vet and have him certify that the dog didn't have rabies, not then or ever, and if they still wanted to come after her for a bogus misdemeanor charge of obstructing police operations (!!!), well she'd take that risk. And bet anything—bet anybody—they'd forget all about it. Really, even in their puffed-up sick little world they must have had better things to do than harass somebody over a dog and a seatbelt. Like catch a couple serial killers or rapists maybe, wouldn't that be a start?

"Whatever," she said. The sun was warm on her shoulders, already defrosting her. Birds sang in the trees. It was a beautiful day, a glorious day, and here came Kutya around the corner of the house to rub up against her leg and sit at her feet in a cascade of hair. Chicken cordon bleu, that was what she was thinking, the classiest thing she knew how to make, because this was an occasion, or it was going to be, and she wasn't cowed or bowed or stranded like some refugee floating on a raft, and Christabel was going to see that and appreciate it and they were going to party on down as if she didn't have a care in the world. "Christabel? You there?"

Another long exhalation, *pfffhhhh*. "Uh-huh."

"Listen," she said, "let me tell you how to get here . . ."

Then she was in the kitchen, cleaning up after breakfast. She'd made eggs over easy and Canadian bacon with fried tomatoes on sourdough toast, enough for two (cooking for two already a habit, after all these years of cooking for one, one only), even though Adam wasn't there to share the meal. She'd wakened at first light to the gentle release of the bedsprings and there he was, naked and slipping into his camouflage pants, in too much of a hurry to bother with underwear. Or too manly. Or juvenile or whatever. He didn't look at her, didn't even glance in her direction. Thirty seconds was all it took to lace up his boots, throw on a shirt and disappear into the bathroom, where she heard the buzz of his electric razor. She'd watched him shaving two mornings ago just for the thrill of it—her man, hard as rock, shaving his chin, his cheeks, circling the taut slash of his mouth, then running the razor up over his skull and down the back of his neck, thirty seconds more, and he never once looked at himself in the mirror. And why was that? Mirrors spooked him, or so he'd told her over their third glass of wine at dinner that night. "Why?" she'd asked. He'd just turned away and in that soft breath of a voice said, "I don't like what I see in there."

This morning she'd got out of bed while he was in the bathroom, throwing on a terrycloth robe his grandmother had left behind, and followed him into the living room. "You going out in the woods?" she asked, though she already knew the answer—and knew too not to pry. He had something out there, a bunker, a fortress—it could have been a treehouse, for all he let on—and it occupied him all day every day. Or maybe he was hiking. Maybe that was it. Whatever it was, it sure kept him in shape.

He didn't answer. Didn't even bother to nod. It was morning and in the morning he didn't have much to say. They were close at night, in the dark, very close, but what they were doing together didn't need words. When he'd been drinking, which was a pretty regular thing—daily, that is, and she joined him because why not?—he'd open up to her as much as he was capable of. He wasn't a talker. That was all right with her. She could talk for two.

"You want me to make you a sandwich?"

Still nothing. He just slipped on his backpack, took up his rifle and slung it over one shoulder. She noticed he was wearing the knife he'd got at Big 5, the sheath looped over his belt at hip level. And he had his canteen, of course, dangling from the pack, and whether it contained 151 or water she couldn't say. His boots shone—he polished them every night, the sound of the rag snapping back and forth the last thing she heard before he came to bed. Everything about him seemed to gleam in the light, from the boots right on up to the barrel of the rifle. For her part, she didn't know one rifle from another—guns didn't interest her—but this one was some sort of military thing with a clip on it. "What's with the gun?" she asked. "You going hunting?" And then she tried to make a joke of it: "Bring me back a couple of squirrels. I make a mean squirrel stew."

He'd glanced up at her then, as if seeing her for the first time. His eyes were clear, a bright transparent blue that went so deep she could have been looking into the ocean and seeing no bottom to it at all. "For protection," he said.

"From what?" And she couldn't help herself: "Cougars?"

If he heard her, if he recognized she was making a joke, he never let on. "People," he said, "motherfuckers, creeps, assholes. Cougars eat deer, people eat everything."

"And they're not going to eat you?"

He gave her a smile then—his version of a smile, anyway, the corners of his mouth lifting ever so subtly in acknowledgment—and started out the door, ducking his left shoulder automatically so as not to strike the lintel with the muzzle of his rifle. She wanted to call out to ask him if she should expect him for dinner, but checked herself—she wasn't his mother. She wasn't a nag either. And what he did, for as long as he was going to do it, didn't matter to her. This was temporary. It was a week. Maybe it would go three weeks more. Or maybe . . . but she didn't want to think beyond that.

She went to the door and watched him stride to the cement-block wall and go up and over it as if it were nothing. Like Jackie Chan. Or the new James Bond, whatever his name was. And what was that martial arts thing called, where you just run right up a wall? *Parkour.* Adam was a master of that. Of course, he could have just strolled through the doorway his father had made, but he refused to—he wouldn't acknowledge it, didn't even seem to see it. If it was up to him he'd seal it up again, she knew that, but then it would be pretty inconvenient for her when she wanted to haul in a load of groceries or take the dog out for a walk, and what was she going to do, use the stepladder? Plus, how could you sell a house with no way in? And Sten intended to sell it, no matter how his son felt about it, and he'd taken her aside and told her as much. The house was in escrow and he didn't want anything screwing up the deal—the buyer was a friend of his and Carolee's who was taking the place as is, grandmother's furniture and all, and he'd agreed to let Adam stay on till the end of the month. Her guess was that they needed the money to pay down the mortgage on the new place in Mendocino, which had ocean views, and ocean views were anything but cheap.

Crossing the yard herself now, Kutya trotting along behind to pause and pee and sniff at her ankles, she came through the doorway just in time to see Adam heading down the slope to the river. The sun glinted off his shaved head and sparked at the muzzle of the rifle, and then he was in the shadow of the trees and she lost him a moment before he reappeared on a bend in the path, moving fast, double time, always double time, as if somebody—or something—was after him.

She'd just got done with the dishes when her phone rang. Without thinking, she hit "talk" and put it to her ear. "Sara here," she said, figuring it was one of her clients—or maybe somebody new. She was in the Yellow Pages, both in the phonebook and online, and she could never have too much work. The money was good and she worked hard for it, which was why she was never going to give another nickel to the feds, or what—the Franchise Tax Board, and what a joke that was.

"Sara?" The voice was a man's, deep, a froggy baritone.

"Yes?"

"Sara Hovarty Jennings?"

It was right about then that she began to regret having answered, because what client—or potential client—would ask for her by her full name? "Yeah," she said, and all the brass had gone out of her voice. "Who's this?"

"This is Sergeant Brawley of the Mendocino County Sheriff's Department." A pause to let that sink in. "And I'm calling to urge you to come in voluntarily to the Ukiah station and surrender your dog"—the rattle of a keyboard—"Kutya. Is that right? Kutya, isn't it?"

Stupidly, she said, "Yes."

"Let me apprise you that there is a warrant out for your arrest—for failure to appear—and that we have video evidence showing that you entered Animal Control with an accomplice at 2:35 p.m. on Saturday, August 10, and illegally removed your dog from quarantine. What do you have to say to that?"

"I'm quarantining him myself," she said, feeling up against it now, more angry than scared.

Another pause. More rattling. "And where might that be?"

"I mailed a certificate of rabies vaccination to the court— what more do you want from me, blood?"

The voice, which had been deep, calm and blandly officious to this point, rose in pitch—and color, color too, as if any of this mattered to him, as if it was anything more than some idiotic imposture: "We want, or no, we *require* you to surrender your person and your animal immediately on penalty of—"

That was all she heard, because in the next moment she had the phone down on the kitchen floor and was grinding it underfoot—they could track you, track you anywhere, the phone like a homing device, like your own little flag of surrender. For a moment she was too angry to think, and if she just kept grinding the phone under her heel and if the plastic frame of it was gouging the linoleum floor Adam's grandmother had kept up through all her failing years, well, she would worry about that later. At the moment, she couldn't seem to catch her breath, she was so upset. She kept telling herself to calm down even as the dog, with his dog's radar, sensed that something was amiss and began to whine, his nails tapping out an elaborate distress signal on the slick linoleum.

As soon as she'd had a chance to catch her breath she began

to rethink things. Already she regretted smashing the phone. Yes, the number had been compromised, no doubt about that—obviously the police had hacked the phone records to get her cell number, but without a phone how would her clients reach her? How would she schedule appointments? How would she live? Even now people could be calling her—or the home phone, where they'd just get a message. Which she couldn't receive and couldn't answer. And if she didn't call back, they'd just go to somebody else, and there went her business. She looked down at her hands and saw they were shaking.

She needed to go to the market for groceries—and to stop in at Radio Shack for a new phone, one of those cheap disposable things that came with a prepaid card. But she was in no condition to drive, not now. So she did the only thing she could think to do: clean. Cleaning always calmed her, the Zen of it, the mindlessness, take up a sponge and some Ajax and go deep. For the next two hours she did nothing but sweep, scrub and polish, rechanneling her energy into something productive. She wasn't going to let them get to her, she was determined about that. Christabel was coming over for a nice dinner and they were going to celebrate, the United States Illegitimate Government of America be damned. She took out the trash and carried the recycling to the car. Retrieved the mop and cleaned and waxed the linoleum in the kitchen, though she'd just done it the day before, then soaked a sponge in bleach and ran it over the grout around the sink by way of eradicating the ugly black tendrils of mold there, working an old toothbrush over the problem spots till they disappeared. Next, she proceeded to the living room, where she took up the oriental rug and carried it outside to air it, flinging it high to drape over the wall, then went back in to sweep and wax the oak floor before turning to the bedrooms.

The house had two: the late grandmother's, which was fussy and cluttered with keepsakes and bric-a-brac, the walls hung with corny pictures of anthropomorphized chicks and puppies and kittens, and Adam's, which was where they'd been sleeping. His room was Spartan, nothing but the essentials, though she did find his bong, a couple of rolled-up Bob Marley and the Wailers posters and a handful of tie-dyed T-shirts tucked away in the back of his closet, along with a cardboard box of old video games and action movies. Typical stuff. Boys' stuff. It made her smile. And that smile broke the spell. They couldn't trace her—she could have answered that phone anywhere, could have been on a job, cruising along in her car, roaming the aisles of the food store, how would they know? Sergeant What's-His-Face probably had a list of sixty people to call—and harass—and it was nothing to her. They'd never find her. The tools. The corporate tools of the U.S.I.G.A. who couldn't begin to comprehend anything other than what their bosses dictated to them, and wasn't that the way the Fascists took hold and the Communists too? Through ignorance and propaganda? Just keep the people in the dark and whatever you do don't let them read the Constitution.

She swept the bedroom, taking her time, then she vacuumed for good measure and made up the bed with fresh sheets, and then—once she felt calm again, as calm and unruffled as if she were at the tiller of a sloop cutting across a spanking sun-drenched bay—she put the dog in the car and drove on into Fort Bragg, to the cheap market there, the one the tourists didn't know about, to pick up the boneless chicken breast and the ham and Gruyère and seasoned bread crumbs for the cordon bleu, as well as asparagus, new potatoes and two bottles of wine for her and Christabel and a six-pack of Old Stock Ale, 11.9% ABV, for Adam, after which she stopped in at Radio Shack to get herself a new phone.

She had everything ready by four, the table set, the cordon bleu and potatoes ready to slip into the oven, the asparagus rinsed, drizzled in oil and laid out on a separate pan and the first bottle of wine (a mid-range California red, on special, but a step up from Two-Buck Chuck and certainly drinkable, especially after it sat out for a while) opened and decanted to give it some air. Adam wasn't back yet, but he generally turned up around cocktail hour, looking to get a buzz on. She'd got into the habit of putting out potato chips or crackers and cheese or mixed nuts or something, he was that hungry, as if he hadn't eaten all day—and maybe he hadn't, unless he was eating the freeze-dried meals he'd got such a deal on at the Big 5. She fed Kutya so he wouldn't be begging at the table and she'd just sat down with the three-by-five card she kept in her wallet to put some of her clients' numbers into the new phone when she heard the sound of a car coming up the road. Expecting Christabel, she rose with a smile, tucked the phone away in the front pocket of her jeans and went out the door, across the yard and through the gap in the wall, Kutya at her heels.

But this wasn't Christabel's pickup rolling to a stop out front, but a Prius, a silver Prius, and for a moment she drew a blank. Then she recognized Sten's face there behind the windshield and understood. He'd come to hang the metal door that had been sitting there all week, that was what she was thinking, but then she saw that his wife was with him—Carolee, whom she'd never met, or not formally—and began wondering if she'd have enough for two more people, and beyond that how all this was going to go down with Adam. And Christabel. Because Christabel was expecting a party, just the three of them, that was the whole point. But the doors flung open, slammed, and there they were, Kutya circling round them and barking as if they were intruders, which, in a way, they were. "No, Kutya," she called. "No bark. Get down now."

Carolee wore a puzzled expression—or inquisitive, maybe that was a better word—and she didn't even seem to notice the dog, just fastened her eyes on Sara's and tried to simulate a smile to cover herself. It was a motherly smile because she was a mother, in her sixties—Adam's mother—though she looked younger, what with her blond hair, worn long and parted so it fell across her face. She was wearing dressy sandals, white shorts and a pink blouse with plenty of room in it. Compared with her husband she was almost a dwarf, three or four inches shorter than Sara herself, and here she came, still ignoring the dog, right on up to her to extend her hand, squint into her face and say, "You must be Sara."

Well, yes, she *was* Sara, and she didn't like the scrutiny she was getting here, wondering in that moment just exactly what Sten had told her, not to mention Cindy Burnside and whoever else. She held it all in, taking the limp hand in hers before exchanging a quick look with Sten to gauge his reaction before saying, "Nice to meet you." And then, in extenuation—of what, she wasn't sure: moving in with their son, occupying a house that was in escrow, having a barky unkempt Rasta dog, being alive and drawing breath—she added, "I was just cooking."

Carolee dropped her hand and let her smile fade and come back again, as if it were battery-operated. "Nice to meet you too," she said, and now she looked to Sten, "—finally." The dog was sniffing at her bare legs, her toenails newly done, in a shade of red just this side of orange, and she turned back round to ask, "Is Adam here?"

"No, he's out," Sara said, and she should have left it there, but didn't. "In the woods?" She shrugged, let her eyes fly up, her smile complicit. "You know Adam."

Carolee wouldn't give an inch. She just stood there staring into her eyes, cold as anything. "Yes, I know Adam," she said, and the way she said it was like a sword that plunged right in and worked its way out the other side. "He *is* my son, after all."

Check, she was thinking, and she was staring right back and just as hard. *You're the mother and I'm nothing, just some random fuck, isn't that it?* She almost said something else she would have regretted—this woman was a friend of Cindy Burnside, after all, and she could spread her poison far and wide and no doubting it— but instead dropped her eyes. "Listen, I've got plenty—I mean, I was expecting a friend, and Adam, of course—and if you want to stay for dinner that would be great, I mean, we'd be honored . . ."

"Sounds good," Sten said, "but we really just stopped by for a couple minutes. I was thinking I'd hang that door and Carolee wanted to go through some of her mother's things—"

Without another word, without even bothering to glance at her or even pretend she'd picked up on the invitation, Carolee just brushed right by her, passed through the gap in the wall and went on across the yard and into the house to leave her standing there with Sten, who looked—what was it?—pained. The sun glinted in his hair. He was wearing Ray-Bans, so she couldn't see his eyes, but the rest of his face seemed to shrink away, the Amazing Shrinking Man, now you see him, now you don't. This was hard for him. It was hard for her too.

"Really," she said, "I'm making chicken cordon bleu—it'd be no trouble."

"No," he said, letting one hand rise and fall, "we can't stay. I brought a couple of boxes—" And here he stepped over to the car, flipped open the rear hatch and raised them in evidence, eight or ten new cardboard boxes, folded flat. "Most of the junk's going into the dumpster, but there are things she's sentimental about, though Christ knows where we're going to put it all." He let out a laugh. "You're supposed to be scaling down at my age."

"Yeah," she said, nodding, as if she could know. "But how about a drink? You'll have a drink at least?" She smiled. "I've got wine open. And I make a killer margarita."

For the next half hour she tried to stay out of the way as Carolee stomped in and out of the house clutching boxes stuffed with odds and ends and Sten tinkered with the door to get it flush, looking in odd moments like Adam, but she didn't want to go there. Like father, like son. Though she couldn't feature Adam hanging a door or changing a washer or anything like that. He was more the outdoors type, and here it came to her with the force of revelation: more the *horticultural* type, more the grower, the pot farmer, and why else would he be so secretive out there in the woods all day every day? She tried to picture it, the spiky-leafed plants, a whole field of them nodding in a gentle breeze and Adam hauling water up from some creek, working his muscles under the blaze of the sun. It was time he let her in on the secret. Time he trusted her. And showed it.

Then the door was hung and Sten had a margarita in his hand, which Carolee, looking daggers, had refused, and she had no choice but to put the potatoes in to bake though she wished they would just leave before Christabel showed. Or Adam. Adam could waltz in any minute now—it was close to five and his internal clock would be ticking—and who knew what kind of reaction he was going to have? As like as not, he'd just jump right back over the wall and disappear. Like at the pizza place. They were having a nice discussion, even if Adam was a bit rocked on that ale and the hits of rum he kept sneaking from the canteen, and she was explaining Redemption Theory to him, how Roger Elvick had uncovered the whole fraud the government was perpetuating by issuing birth certificates so they could use every baby born as collateral for the loans the Federal Reserve gave the government after they went off the gold standard and how they'd put him away in some mental hospital and given him electroshock just for telling the truth to people, when she looked up and saw Sten standing there in the crowd by the bar with the blond woman she'd assumed was Carolee, and that was the end of that.

Adam had let out a low hiss of a curse, then turned his head to look and cursed again. Before she could think he was up and out the door and she had no choice but to follow him. Thing was, she couldn't find him. He wasn't in the car. And she sat there and waited for half an hour or more, till after Sten and his wife had left and gone up the block and around the corner to where they must have parked their own car, and then she drove around for another hour, going up and down the back streets that went ghostly in the fog. She saw cats. A coyote. A couple of drunks stumbling home. But no Adam. Finally, she'd given up and gone back to the house—which had to be fifteen miles from town, but what else could she do? When she woke in the morning, he was there beside her, curled up in the fetal position.

Now, trying to make small talk with Sten while dodging his wife and sipping her own margarita—she'd made a pitcher, frozen limeade, triple sec, tequila and the juice of a couple limes for the extra kick—she heard the crunch of tires on the gravel out front, which would have been Christabel. Finally. She was almost an hour late, typical of her, but why couldn't she have been a little later, just this once?

They were on the porch, sitting at the redwood picnic table and talking about the glories of nature. Sten swirled the dregs of his drink around the bottom of the glass and showed every indication of wanting to get out of there but Carolee was still rattling things around in the house. You could smell the potatoes now, which meant it was time to put the cordon bleu on. "How you like staying out here in the woods?" he was asking in a general way, trying to be kind. "You are staying here now, aren't you?"

"Yeah, I guess so," she said, appending a little laugh, as if to say it was as much a surprise to her as to him. "Just temporarily. For a few days, I mean. Till I sort things out with my landlady."

"Peaceful, isn't it? Seen any deer? Coyotes?"

She was distracted, picturing Carolee trotting out to her car with an armload of things and encountering Christabel before she could introduce her, but she wasn't going to let it show. "One coyote," she said, looking past Sten to the new metal door, which had been propped open with a rock. "He comes by like every night, or so far, anyway, at eight-thirty or so, right on schedule," she said, but then she broke off and gave him her richest smile. "That'll be my friend, Christabel?" And then, maybe because she wanted his approval or at least a little acknowledgment of common ground—two educators, *three*—she added, "She's a teacher's aide."

16.

CHRISTABEL WAS WEARING HER black jeans, heels and a red spandex top that displayed her figure to good advantage, the sort of outfit she wore when they were going bar-hopping, which was a little puzzling because they weren't going bar-hopping tonight, as Sara had made abundantly clear, or at least thought she had. They were going to have a homey night, drinking and laughing and eating a nice meal, and they were going to sit out here on the porch and feed the mosquitoes because Adam would definitely be more comfortable out of doors with a new person to deal with—if he stuck around, that is, and there was no guarantee of that. And while he likely wouldn't be too thrilled to see Christabel there, whether on the porch or in the house or anywhere else, he was going to have to get used to it because she wasn't about to give up her whole life however far this thing went. Plus—and she'd be the first to admit it—she wanted to show him off. If Christabel was jealous over the phone, just wait till she got a look at him.

Unfortunately, Christabel was out of sorts. She appeared there in the propped-open doorway with an exasperated look on her face, her lips pursed and her eyes beaming out all kinds of lethal rays that could have dissolved flesh and stone alike, because she'd been lost on a succession of dirt roads for the better part of the last hour and only found the place after stopping some old lady out walking her dog and having her draw a map on the back of a greasy McDonald's bag. Sara didn't know that, or not yet, but she shot her a frantic wave, in stride, hustling across the yard to intercept her and warn her about Sten and Carolee. Not that it was a huge deal or that she was apprenticing for the role of daughter-in-law or anything like that because Adam *was* strange and a week of hot sex didn't make a relationship (though it was a damn good start and no denying it), but that the whole thing was awkward, her moving in and their happening to show up now of all times. Because this wasn't really her house. And she didn't really belong here.

Before she could warn her off, Christabel was saying, "Shit, Sara, I've been lost for an hour and my phone kept flashing that fucking infuriating no service light—"

"Hi," she said, trying to smile and signal with her eyes at the same time, before turning to where Sten stood on the porch. "Sten, this is my friend I was telling you about?" Kutya surged round Christabel's ankles, yapping out his joy as she made her introductions: "Christabel, Sten; Sten, Christabel."

Then they were all on the porch and Sten was taking Christabel's hand in his own and looking down the front of her blouse the way all men did when they liked what they saw, whether they were sixteen or sixty (or seventy in this case). "Nice to meet you," Sten said, grinning like a gargoyle. He held her hand a beat too long, his eyes going from her face to her tits and back again. "I'm Adam's father."

And Christabel gave it over just like that. The frown was gone and here came the megawatt smile, the attraction mutual and all the social niceties spread out on the board. "Nice to meet you too. And I'm looking forward to meeting your son." A pause. Was she actually licking the corner of her mouth? "Sara's told me so much about him." A laugh. "All about him, in fact."

Chitchat followed—she'd heard he was retired and he'd heard she was a teacher's aide, and she was, at Brookside Elementary, up in Willits, Special Ed, must be a tough job, oh, yeah, it was, but rewarding, you know?—and then the screen door pushed open and Carolee was standing in the midst of them, her arms encircling the last of the boxes. Sara saw the neck of a ceramic lamp with a staved-in shade poking out of the top, along with what looked to be a sheaf of children's drawings on paper gone yellow

with age and a blue cloche hat with a pheasant's tail feather knifing out of it.

Carolee was sweating, though it wasn't hot out at all—in the
low seventies, if that. She'd tucked her hair behind her ears to get
it out of the way and the skin at her temples glistened. She gave
everybody present a sour look. "Don't tell me," she said, homing
in on Christabel, "—not another one?"

"Here," Sten said, "let me take that," at the same instant Sara
heard herself say, "You need any help?"

Carolee didn't need any help. She was the mother and this was
her mother's house. She didn't need any more introductions and
she absolutely didn't need to be wasting energy on social ameni-
ties or even being civil. Half a beat, then the box was in Sten's
arms and the two of them were heading down the steps and out
the gate. Sten called "See you later" over his shoulder, and then
they heard the slamming of the rear hatch and the two car doors,
followed by the sucking whoosh of the car starting up and the
stony protest of the gravel as the tires rolled on over it.

"Well, *that* was nice," Christabel said. They were both still
standing there on the porch, Sara with a half-empty margarita
in one hand and a bottle of wine in the other, Christabel in her
black heels that were already floured with dust, looking to the
empty space in the cement-block wall as the aroma of the baking
potatoes wafted out through the screen.

"Yeah," Sara agreed, hardening her voice despite the fact that
for some unnameable and untouchable reason, she felt like crying.
"But really, what do I care?"

"It's just a fling, right?"

"Yeah," she said. "That's all it is."

The cordon bleu was done and set atop a trivet on the counter
in the kitchen and she and Christabel were sitting at the table
on the porch drinking the last of the margaritas preparatory to

getting into the wine, when they heard a noise from inside the house, a thump, then the wheeze of a door on its hinges. "That'll be Adam," Sara said, feeling relieved, though she wouldn't let it show on her face. He was late and she'd begun to worry that tonight of all nights would be the one he wouldn't show. She'd told him she was thinking of having a friend over for dinner one night—a girlfriend, her best friend, somebody he was really going to like—and though he hadn't reacted she couldn't help getting the idea he wasn't all that excited about the prospect.

Christabel turned to look over her shoulder. "What is he, a ghost? I thought this"—pointing across the yard to the metal door, which still stood open—"was the only way in? Or what, has he been hiding under the bed or something?"

She felt a tick of irritation. "Don't be like that."

"Like what?"

"You know: catty. Superior. And don't you go talking down to him either." There was another thump from inside and Kutya, who'd been lying at her feet, raised his head, moderately interested, before letting it drop again. "If you want to know, he just goes right up and over the wall—like Jackie Chan in that movie? It's part of his training. Keeps him fit." And then she turned her head too and called out, "Adam? Adam, you in there?"

No response. All the sounds of the world came crowding in, the birds, the insects, the soft rush and gurgle of the river that wasn't much more than a stream this time of year, though it kept on dutifully flowing through all its bends and pools and on down to the harbor below.

"Training for what?" Christabel raised her eyebrows.

"I don't know, just training. He likes to keep fit." And then she called his name again: "Adam, we're out here." A pause, listening: still nothing. "I thought we'd eat out on the porch tonight—"

She was just about to get up and go in to see what he was up to—he was going to do this for her, be presentable, be *cool*, if she had any power over him at all, and she did, because he liked what she was giving him and he needed it too, just to get whole, to be whole and not some spooky recluse staring off into space and saying the first thing that came into his head. His grandmother used to cook for him and before that his mother. Now she was cooking for him—and no, she wasn't old enough to be his mother, but then his mother never went to bed with him either. And here she had to laugh: *At least I hope not.*

"What's so funny?" Christabel was leaning into the table, setting her glass down over its wet imprint in the wood, then lifting it and setting it down again as if it were the most delicate operation in the world. She was looking up at her, a collusive smile on her face. She'd already heard about the sex—Sara had told her everything, in detail, because she couldn't help herself—and now she was expecting more.

"Oh, I don't know," she said, "just thinking of something, that's all." Then she was pushing herself up. "Let me go get him. I mean, dinner's ready and I don't want the meat drying out—plus, I think it's time we poured some of that wine, don't you?"

Christabel gave her a sloppy wide-lipped grin. "Hear, hear!"

She was feeling it herself, two and a half margaritas on an empty stomach, as she pushed through the screen door and into the living room, with its pine paneling gone dark from half a century of smoke, the old ladies' lamps and wood-framed pictures and the couch that was older than she was. "Adam?" she called. Another thump, a shuffling of feet, and there he was, framed in the kitchen doorway, a beer in one hand, a half-gnawed portion of cordon bleu in the other. There was a crescent-shaped smear of dirt or grease or something on his forehead just over his left eye, and the boots he was always so careful with were crusted in mud, which had in turn left the kitchen floor a mess. "Jesus," she said, "what happened to you—you fall in a swamp or what?"

She didn't expect him to answer and he didn't. He just stood there chewing, alternately lifting the chicken and the beer to his mouth.

"Christabel's here, I was telling you about? We've been drinking margaritas and I think we're a little wrecked." She let out a
giggle, the whole room composing itself around the silhouette of
him there in the doorway, pixel by pixel, as if she were watching
TV, which is how she knew just how wrecked she was and knew
too that she'd have to put something on her stomach tout suite.
"But dinner's ready and we're going to eat out on the porch, so
why don't you . . ." She trailed off. "I mean, just clean up and
come join us, okay?"

He didn't move, but that was typical and he didn't say anything either, which was also typical. "My father," he said after a
moment.

"Sara?" Christabel's voice. "You in there? Need any help?"

"In a minute," she called over her shoulder and turned back to
Adam. "What about him?"

"He was here."

"They both were, your mother too, and I'll tell you, she
treated me like dirt. And Christabel too."

"If he touched anything, I'll kill him," he said, and now he
was coming toward her and the light caught him so that she could
see he was mud all over, pants and shirt and his hands too where
they dangled from the soiled sleeves.

She put her hands on her hips. "He just hung the door, is all,"
she said. "Your mother took a couple boxes of things from your
grandma's room—"

His face changed suddenly, hardened up as if it had been set
in concrete. "Shit," he spat. "Shit on her. And shit on you too."

"Me? What have I got to do with it?"

"You let her."

"I didn't let anybody do anything. This is their house, not
mine, remember?" She felt a little woozy suddenly and she wanted
to go over and give him a kiss, mud or no, but instead she just
cocked her head back and said, "If you want to get any tonight
you better behave yourself. So go in and get washed up—and take

your boots off first, you're tracking the place all up—and then you come out and meet Christabel and make nice." She lifted her wrist to squint at her watch, the hands of which she could just barely make out because her reading glasses were on the kitchen table next to the recipe book. "Dinner is served—or will be—in five minutes flat. Hear me?"

When he did show up at the table—with another beer, which must have been his second or third, and the canteen too—the mud was gone and his fingernails were clean, but he wasn't wearing any clothes at all, only the towel cinched round his waist. Which he made a show of dropping when he pulled out the chair and sat down. Christabel, nonchalant, or at least pretending to be, said hello, but Adam ignored her. It wasn't much past six but they were in the shadows here, the sun having sunk away into the canopy of the trees, and while it wasn't cold yet it was getting there. You could see that Adam's chest and arms were stippled with gooseflesh and his nipples were hard, though he wasn't shivering. Let him play his games, Sara was thinking, but after she'd filled his wine glass and topped off Christabel's and her own, she couldn't take it any longer and finally had to ask, "Aren't you cold?"

"Toughens you," he said, though he wouldn't look into her eyes.

"I was just going to get up and put on a jacket—what about you, Christa? You cold?"

But then Adam was talking, a miracle, as if a stone had cracked open and become fluent. "Colter wasn't cold. Colter was butt-ass naked when they chased him—and that river he jumped into? That river was like ice."

Christabel was just staring, running her eyes all over him, and she had that little smirk on her face. "Uh-uh," she said, "I'm not cold," and then, to Adam: "So you're a nudist, huh? Sara never told me or I wouldn't have bothered with all these clothes myself. Here," she said, and she actually reached down, arched her back and worked the spandex top up and over her shoulders, pausing there a moment before pulling it over her head and balling it up on the table in front of her. She was wearing a black lace brassiere underneath and she was all gooseflesh too.

"Oh, come on, grow up, the two of you." Sara was sitting there clinging to her wine glass, not upset, not yet, but maybe something less than amused. A whole lot less.

"You said you wanted to show me off," Adam said in an even voice, and then he was rising from the chair so you could see all of him, cock, balls, pubic hair, everything. "Isn't that right, Sara?"

All she could think to say was "Not at the table" and she was going to add that his mother must not have taught him any manners at all, making a joke of it, but checked herself—she didn't want to provoke him because you never could tell what he was going to do next.

It wouldn't have mattered because in the next moment Adam was gone—present, but gone, veering off into one of his reveries or spells or whatever you wanted to call it—his gaze focused on a point over Christabel's head, on nothing, and his voice took on a weird metallic timbre as if there were a microphone stuck in his throat: "Party on down," he said, echoing her, mocking her. "How about a threesome? You ladies up for a threesome?"

That seized her up, all right. She was no prude, but this was just him pushing her buttons to see how far he could go. He was still posed there, staring off into space, but now he was getting hard by degrees, click, click, click, and she couldn't have that, not in front of Christabel, so she did the first thing that came to mind— she took up one of the grandmother's antique-gold linen napkins and snapped it at him, right there, right where it hurt most, and what did Christabel do? She just burst out with a laugh.

Okay. Fine. But Adam got the message, both hands shooting to his groin, and then he sat down, wrapped the towel back around him, and without another word put his head down and began to eat. Christabel watched him a minute—fork to mouth, his jaws grinding—then let out a hoot and said, "What fun!", shook out her top and pulled it back over her head, though it didn't do her sprayed-up hair any good. And herself? She laughed too, couldn't help it, and in the next moment, as the sky pulled down and the bats shot out of the trees to explode overhead, they were all three of them laughing to beat the band, and when they were done with dinner they went on into the house and built a fire and sat around it, watching the flames leap up the chimney and holding tight to their wine glasses until at some point, Adam, still wrapped in the towel, got up and slipped out the door and into the night.

17.

IT WAS THE MIDDLE of the second week when she began to wake up to reality, at least that portion of it that had to do with money and earning a living. She'd had two jobs the week before, one all the way up in Redwood Valley, which would have been no problem if she'd been at home because that was practically in the neighborhood, and the other down in Navarro, at the winery there, where she saw to the owners' horses on a regular basis, but that meant burning up gas and since she didn't want to use her credit card—they could trace it—she had to use cash and her cash was running low. Most of her income, the lion's share (or horse's share, actually), came from her trade and the connections she'd made over the years, but she relied on subbing to supplement it and school was still out for the summer. And even if it wasn't, how could they call her if she wasn't home?

To complicate things, she didn't have her calendar—or most of her clients' numbers either, aside from the few she'd kept on the card double-folded in her wallet—and she was sure she must be missing appointments. For the past three mornings now she'd awakened with a jolt from dreams of fucking up, of being late, lost, unable to get where she was going in the hazy geography of dreamland that was clogged with wrong turns and the butts of horses galloping steadily away from her. That made her nervous. Irritable. She'd even snapped at Adam over breakfast when he started going on about Colter. "*Colter,*" she'd spat, slapping the flat of her hand down on the counter, "fucking Colter! I've only heard it like ten thousand times."

He was sitting at the table, forking up French toast, and he shot her a look that should have warned her off, three parts hurt and one part pure slingshot rage.

"Can't you ever talk about anything else? Like what you're doing out there in the woods all day long? Huh? Like what you're *growing*?"

What happened to the plate he was eating from, his grand-mother's china plate with the rose-cluster design on it? Up against the wall, syrup and all, and then down on the floor, in pieces. And Adam? He looked hate at her, then bulled right by her, and if she lost her balance and slammed against the kitchen cabinet it was nothing to him because he was snatching up his pack and jerking the rifle over his shoulder and then he was over the wall and gone without a word.

So she was sitting there in the kitchen in the aftermath of all this, brooding over things, Kutya licking the scraps off the floor and the sun trapped in the morning fog, which had managed to reach this far up just to depress her further, when it came to her that what she needed was to get into her house, whether they were watching it or not. She needed her calendar, where she'd always been careful to write out her appointments under the date, along with phone numbers, and in the case of word-of-mouth referrals, addresses. And she could use some clothes, having packed hastily to say the least. She was bored with what she was wearing—boots, jeans and the same two tops, in rotation—and figured Adam must be too. She hardly ever wore a dress, but she had half a closetful, including a cute yellow sundress with a scoop neck that still fit her in all the right places. Maybe Adam would like to see her in that, just for a change, to spice things up. And here she went off into an erotic daydream, him sitting there on the couch with the towel wrapped around him, already hard, and her coming across the room to climb atop him and lift the skirt up so he could see she wasn't wearing anything underneath . . .

It didn't take her long to convince herself that they wouldn't be watching her house. She was too small-time. She hadn't killed anybody, had she? And she told them she was quarantining the dog, though it was just plain stupid because anybody could see he didn't have rabies and what was a little scratch on some scrawny lady trooper's hand? A quick raid on her own house, that was what she was thinking. But not in daylight—it might be totally paranoid to think they were watching the place twenty-four/seven, but it was very much in the realm of possibility that they'd send a patrol car by once in a while just to see if there was a vehicle in the driveway. No, she'd go at night. Tonight. Late. Adam would love the idea because here was another chance to stick it to them, and all at once she was replaying the scene at the animal shelter, how her blood had raced, beating like a drum circle, and how the two of them had laughed in the car as they rolled down the highway free and clear, laughed till they were gasping for air and she put a hand on his thigh and asked him if he wanted to party and he did. Oh yes, he did. With gusto. And the party was still going on.

When he came in around six he was wired on something, he wouldn't say what, still pissed over what had happened that morning. "You're out of line," he told her, glaring at her, standing there poised over the sink in the kitchen that was sunlit and warm and peaking with the aroma of the homemade lasagna she'd sweated over half the afternoon. "Way out of line. Because for your information I'm not growing nothing."

"Anything," she said automatically.

Still the glare. "Nothing," he said carefully. "I'm not growing nothing."

It wasn't really in her to be repentant—that just wasn't her, sorry—but she tried her best to placate him, keeping her mouth firmly shut and handing him a margarita when he came up for air after dipping his head to the faucet and letting the water run over his face and scalp, saying everything she had to say with gestures, as if she were a deaf-mute. There was no mud on him, not a trace, though his boots were thick with trail dust, and he took the margarita without comment and went out to sit on the porch with it. She gave it a minute, then brought the pitcher out to him and her own glass too and they sat there in silence, pouring till the pitcher was empty. He wouldn't look at her the whole time and she took the hint and made as if she were wrapped up in her own thoughts, the two of them sitting there in silence, getting a buzz on, but she couldn't help sneaking glances at him—and not just to gauge his mood but because she loved watching him, the way he moved, the delicacy of his smallest gestures, how he circled the rim of the glass with his thumb and forefinger and brought it to his lips, his eyes narrowing in on something she couldn't see, beautiful eyes set off with a girl's lashes, eyes like flowers, like flowers in a field.

Then she served him the lasagna and poured him a beer—and poured herself one too, though the carbs went straight to fat on her—and when he started in on Colter and the Chinese she listened to as much of it as she could take before cutting him off. "Adam," she said. "Listen, I'm sorry about this morning but the thing is I need some things up at my place—I mean, this is great here and all, but I feel like I'm camping out, you know what I'm saying?"

He shrugged as if it was nothing to him.

"My address book, for one thing. I need to get hold of everybody and make sure I'm not screwing up my appointments—and clothes, I need to pick up some clothes. Like a dress. Would you like that—me in a dress?"

Maybe he would, maybe he wouldn't. But he wasn't going to show her anything.

She dropped her voice till it was a purr in her throat: "What do you say to going up there tonight? Just you and me. Late, like maybe midnight or one maybe, when nobody'll be around?" Her own lasagna was getting cold. She tapped the fork on the edge of the plate, *tap-tap, anybody home?* "A raid," she said. "Let's call it a raid."

She was watching him closely, like that first day in the car, and she could see she was having an effect. He'd gone still, the beer clutched in one hand, fork in the other. After a moment, he set down his beer and swiveled his neck to bring his eyes to hers, and he wasn't staring through her now—now he was seeing her.

"Well," she said, "what do you say?"

"Cool," he said. "I'll bring the rifle."

"What? What are you talking about?" His eyes were on her still and he was holding on to that half-formed grin of his that seemed to stick in the corner of his mouth as if his lips just couldn't lift it all the way up. "No," she said, "no way. That's just crazy."

She hated guns and she put her foot down, or tried to, because this really was overkill, not to mention a recipe for disaster, but five hours later there they were following the track of her headlights up the hill on a moonless night, his gun propped between them—not in the trunk, not laid out flat on the floor in the backseat—and a pair of night-vision goggles dangling from his neck. He'd drawn two slashes of oil or greasepaint or whatever it was under his eyes like the players you'd see on *Monday Night Football* if you were unlucky enough to be bar-hopping in the middle of it and he was so amped up he kept talking about the plan, what the plan was and how they were going to execute it—his word: *execute*.

"Look," she told him, leaning into one of the wicked switch-backs that seemed to chase the car all over the road (and she wasn't drunk, not even close—just a little buzzed), "it's all in good fun, but that thing isn't loaded, is it? It's not going to go off and blow a hole in the roof or anything—?"

He didn't answer. She'd already extracted a promise from him that he wasn't going to do anything more than just sit there in the car—which she was going to park down the street from the house, out of sight—and wait for her. Ten minutes, that was all she was going to need and he could just sit tight, okay? Was he cool with that?

They hadn't seen a single car since they'd turned onto the

highway and that had helped with her blood pressure, which must have been spiking despite the alcohol in her system because she was regretting ever having mentioned this whole fiasco to him— she should have just waited till he was asleep and snuck on up the road by herself and he'd never have been the wiser. But she'd wanted some moral support (that was a laugh: it was more like amoral support where he was concerned) and things had sort of ratcheted out of control. He was a boy, playing war games. She could understand that. But this was no toy rifle and if he saw a cop, any cop, anywhere, who could tell what he might do? And what would that make her—accessory to murder? It was bad enough that the next time a cop stopped her she'd be going straight to the county jail, and while she wasn't ready to accept that or genuflect to the system either, she was still smart enough to stay out of its way as much as possible. You couldn't fight them. Look what had happened to Jerry Kane. She'd tried to tell him about that, how the pigs had shot dead one of the gurus of the movement, the foremost, the very man whose seminars she'd attended and who'd opened her eyes and revolutionized her life, gunned him down in a Walmart parking lot in Arkansas and his sixteen-year-old son along with him, but it just seemed to go in one ear and out the other.

"I said, that thing isn't loaded, right? Because if it is, I'm just going to turn around right here and now. You hear me?"

His voice, soft as fur, came at her out of the darkness: "Jesus, you sound like my mother. But you're not my mother, right?"

And that got her, that reminded her of what was real, what counted, what she was doing here on this dark road. With him. "No, baby," she said, softening, and she reached out her hand to him. "I'm not your mother, I'm your lover. And when we get home, watch out."

So that was that. Whether the gun was loaded or not or whether she was going to enter into a contract with the sheriff's department under threat, duress and coercion and go to jail for the better part of her natural life or wind up shot herself or just assert her right to travel in her own personal property to her own house and reclaim the personal property she kept there was anybody's guess. But it was late and Willits wasn't exactly Times Square and they'd be turning off well before they got into town proper and there really wasn't anything that could go wrong. She was just being a slave and a coward even to think it. The cops were asleep. And so was everybody else.

18.

WHEN THEY WERE COMING up on her turnoff she couldn't decide whether to use her signal or not, but then she figured not, because if anybody was watching why broadcast her intentions? "This is it up here," he said suddenly, fully alert and ready for anything, and she was impressed that he could pick out the road in the dark even though he'd only been to the house once. He was smart—and he'd been born with an internal compass too, no ravine or trail or gulley or back road too remote for him, the kind of person who would always land on his feet no matter where you tossed him. And if there was one thing he wasn't, it was a coward. Or a slave. He might have been in outer space half the time, but if ever there was anybody born who would take them on, no holds barred, he was the one. And maybe that was suicidal, maybe it was mental—it was, it definitely was—but as she turned into the dark lane between the two vestigial fenceposts that picked the thread of it out of the night for her, she was glad he was there. If anything happened, which it wouldn't, she'd at least go out in a blaze of glory.

The front end let out a little shriek and then the tires were hissing along the blacktop and she flicked off the headlights, just in case. "Blaze of glory," she said aloud, tailing it with a nervous cackle, and she was as crazy as he was, *Jesus.*

She pulled just off the road a hundred yards from her house, then thought better of it and swung a U-turn so the car was facing the other way in case they needed to make a quick exit. With no moon, her house was in darkness, nothing showing there but what the stars gave up. Ditto the L-shaped ranch house of her closest neighbors, the Rackstraws, an older couple with grown children out of the house and a dog so ancient and decrepit it had forgotten how to bark. "Okay," she said, her fingers wrapped around the door handle, "you know the drill. I'm just going in the house, my own house, that's all, for like ten minutes. And you're just going to sit here, right? Don't even get out of the car. Okay?"

She watched him a moment, the profile of him, too dark to see his features—all she could tell was that he was staring straight ahead, out the windshield and down the road the way they'd come. And that he was wound up, strung tight as wire. "Okay?" she repeated and leaned in to peck a kiss to his cheek before she slipped out of the car and started up the road.

As soon as the door eased shut and she was out there in the night, her tension began to fade. This was her home, her turf, the place where she'd lived for the past eight and a half years since she'd given up on Roger, the place where she walked Kutya and exercised her clients' horses in the fields and sat out on the deck in the evenings to watch the sun slip down over the distant gray band of the ocean. What was she afraid of? It was her right to be here—it was anybody's right. This was a free country. Or so they claimed.

Everything was quiet but for the soft percussion of her heels on the pavement and the intermittent grinding of a solitary cricket in the dark dried-up field to her left. Her night vision came back to her incrementally as her eyes adjusted, though she could have found her way blindfolded. Her strides lengthened. She breathed in the night air, fragrant with a lingering sweetness the afternoon sun had pulled out of the weeds and wildflowers, and she felt freer than she had in a long time—at least since that idiot cop had come after her and turned her whole life inside out.

Before she knew it she was heading up the gravel drive, the pea stone—pale in contrast with the darker void of the yard—looking almost as if it were illuminated. It crunched underfoot though, so she stepped off into the dirt: no reason to make noise if she didn't have to. She fished the keys from her purse, a faint tinkle of metal, and she was actually heading for the front door before catching herself. She stopped, listened, telling herself she was just being crazy, then slipped round back anyway. Another tinkle as the key turned in the lock and she was in.

For a long moment she stood just inside the kitchen door, in the darkness, debating whether to turn the lights on. She could smell the garbage from all the way across the room, whatever was in there when she'd left gone rancid and probably attracting ants too—they were a problem in this place, always had been, black rivers of them flowing in under the door and darkening the counters, the walls, even the ceiling sometimes. No matter. She'd deal with all that later. Now she just needed to get her address book and her calendar and some clean clothes—and that dress, or maybe a couple of dresses, like the yellow and white polka dot, which was real summery and looked great with her strappy sandals—and then lock up and forget about the place for a while. Let the ants have it.

Ultimately, she did turn the lights on, first in the kitchen, then in the hall where her desk was, and finally in her bedroom. She didn't bother folding things, just stuffed a couple blouses, some underwear, another pair of jeans and her dresses and sandals into a kitchen-tall garbage bag and rolled up the calendar and tucked it in her purse. She was getting ready to leave, giving things a final look-over, trying to think what she was forgetting—she had her address book, her checkbook, her moisturizer and nail polish remover, the special shampoo she used for dandruff, stamps, envelopes, a beach towel and her bathing suit, just in case he wanted to go swimming some afternoon—when the first rattling burst of gunfire split the night in two and she just about jumped out of her skin.

Talk about panic, talk about going from the launching pad straight up into orbit in the space of a single heartbeat, well here it was. She didn't have time to think, just run. Later she would find that she'd bruised herself above her left knee, but she couldn't for the life of her recall how or when, just that it must have happened in those first few panicky seconds when she was racing through the house to shut off the lights and slam through the back door and out into the blinding dark, where the sharp crackling rattle of gunfire split the night open all over again. But what was it? Where was it? She stumbled across the yard, clutching her purse and the garbage bag to her chest, the night unfolding in layers till she could see again, her breath coming hard and her feet pounding across the gravel—there was the pale outline of the drive, there the dark erasure of the road and the still darker hump of her car planted rigid and unmoving at the side of it and she was running even as the light flashed on in the Rackstraws' front window and the dog that hadn't made a sound in the last five years started howling as if it had been set on fire.

And where was Adam, where *was* he, no shape or shadow of him in the passenger's seat as she jerked open the driver's door and flung her things in, calling "Adam! Adam!" in a hot fierce whisper that sounded in her own ears like a scream. Her fingers trembled as she rifled through the purse for her keys and then she had them in the ignition and the engine jumped to life and the headlights flew out like heat-seeking missiles and there he was, Adam, right there in front of the car, the rifle tucked under one arm and the twin pinpoints of his eyes throwing the light back at her.

"Jesus!" she shouted, her head out the window now. "What are you doing? Get in the car, get in!" Something changed behind her, something qualitatively different now—another light, the Rackstraws' porch light, floodlight, whatever it was—and somebody's voice, a man's voice, Jack Rackstraw's, thundering, "What's going on down there?"

"Adam," she said, "Adam," and it was like a plea, a prayer, an invocation to get them out of there, and she couldn't leave him, she couldn't, but her heart was going into overdrive and she actually had her hand on the gearshift to shove the thing into reverse and back away from him when the door pulled open and he slid into the seat and slammed the door shut again and she hit the accelerator with a foot that really didn't know what it was doing beyond finding that place where the tires would grab and the car would hurtle off into the tunnel the high beams carved out of the night.

"Kill the lights," he said, and it was the first thing either of them had said since he'd got in the car. They were out on Route 20 now, heading back down the hill, and there was nobody behind them as far as she could see, but then that didn't mean anything, did it? They had helicopters, whole fleets of cruisers, guns and more guns. She was going too fast, she knew it. The tires screeched. She jerked at the wheel. She was in a state, close to breaking down and screaming her head off, susceptible, fully susceptible—but this didn't make any sense to her. Shut off the lights? Now? On the highway? In the dark?

He repeated himself, his voice honed and hard: "I said, kill the lights."

She swung wildly through a turn and then looped back the other way, through the next one, her palms sweating and her eyes jumping at the road ahead. "I can't," she said, "we'll go off the road. I can hardly see as it is—"

"Here," he said, and he was thrusting something at her—what was it? Heavy plastic, slick glass: the night-vision goggles.

"I can't—what are you doing?"

"Slow down," he said. "Watch the road."

And then they both froze, the sound of the siren riding up on them out of nowhere. A whoop, a scream. It jabbed right into her, shoved itself up under her flesh like a hypodermic scoured with acid. This was it, she knew it, she was done, doomed, everything she'd built in her life gone out the window—she wasn't going to have to worry about being a slave to the system anymore because she was going to be a prisoner of it. In a jail cell. With what—a tray of mush and insta-food shoved through a slit in the door three times a day? She wanted to pull over, wait for the inevitable, but she didn't. She just kept on driving, kept on going down, one turn, then the next, but where was the siren coming from—behind them or out in front?

There was a whoop, another whoop, then it faded, then whooped again. "Are they—?" she asked, but never got to finish the question because here came the sheriff's dead-black cruiser hurtling up the hill in the opposite lane, lights flashing, one suspended moment as the thing rocked past them, Adam motioning with the gun and she furious and spitting "No, no!" at him, and then it was gone and vanished round the next bend.

"The pigs," he snarled. "The fucking pigs."

She didn't feel as if she was driving anymore but sailing, and not across some calm picture-postcard bay, but into a dark maelstrom dragging her down to some darker place still. She stabbed at the brakes, hard, and the force of it threw them both forward—seatbelts, who needed seatbelts?—and he hit the windshield with a sudden heavy wet resonance she could feel like a blow to her own body, the car careening toward the trees, everything held in the balance before it caught on the hard compacted dirt of the shoulder and straightened itself out, and still she was driving and still they were going downhill.

When she could talk, when the words came back to her, stingy, squeezed, caught in her throat, she asked him if he'd hurt himself, was he okay, was he bleeding?

He didn't answer. But she could feel him there at her side, glowering, outraged, all his jets on high. A minute passed. Two. The trunks of the trees flipped past like cards in a fanned deck.

"Here," he said suddenly. "Stop here. Turn."

She saw a dirt road rushing up on the right, a wide mouth of nothing cut between a ragged avenue of trees, and for once she did as she was told.

✦ ✦

Later, after they'd rocked and swayed for what seemed like hours over a series of pits and craters and washboard corrugations, a campground appeared under the canopy of the trees, her head-lights catching the glint of metal, cars there, half a dozen of them, parked in darkness, and he told her to pull over and shut down the engine. "Here?" she said. "Yeah, here." She switched off the ignition and killed the lights and everything vanished. The dark-ness was absolute—they might as well have plunged down a mine shaft somewhere, no trace here even of the stars. And if there were campers out there, they weren't sitting around campfires roasting marshmallows, not at this hour. They must have had tents, but in the instant before the lights went out she hadn't seen any. *Aren't you afraid of him?* Christabel had asked.

Well, here was the test of it. And the answer? Yes and no. Yes, she was afraid he was going to do something crazy, like shoot off his goddamned gun, which he'd already proved fully capa-ble of doing, but no, she wasn't afraid to be there with him in the blackest depths of the blackest night she'd ever dreamed or imagined. He was right there beside her, breathing steadily. She could smell him, the sweat of him, the neat's-foot oil he used on his boots, a faint chemical drift of the rum on his breath. He'd brought her here because that cruiser was going to turn around, he was sure of it, because their car was the only one on the only roadway through these hills, one way in, one way out, and now they were safe because no cop would ever think of looking for them here—no cop even knew it existed, she'd bet anything. She breathed out, breathed in. Closed her eyes and opened them again and it made no difference. All right. So they'd had an adventure and here they were, together, in the dark.

All the adrenaline had gone out of her or been reabsorbed or whatever was supposed to happen to it and she felt a deep peace steal over her. "What now?" she asked, though she already knew.

His voice came at her out of the void. "We sleep."

"Just sleep?"

He didn't answer but she could picture him wearing his little smirk, which was answer enough for her.

"You want to get comfortable?" she asked. "Like in the back-seat?"

There was the sound of liquid sloshing around its container, liquid in motion. "You up for a hit of rum?"

"No, I don't think so." She was hot for him, hotter than ever, excitement running through her like a burn, but she had to ask him one more thing before she pulled her blouse up over her head and dropped her bra and let him nuzzle there like the child he was. "Adam?"

"Colter. Call me Colter."

"What were you shooting at? There was nobody there. You weren't even supposed to get out of the car."

He was silent a long while. Finally, he said, "You accusing me?"

"No. I'm just, I just want to know what you were shooting at—"

"Hostiles," he said, his voice as disembodied as if she were talking to him on the phone, long-distance, the words dropped down and filtered out of the buzz of the universe and nobody listening in but her and her alone. "I told you," he said, "they're everywhere."

PART VI

The Jefferson

19.

THEY WERE UP ON the forks of the Missouri, where the Jefferson, Madison and Gallatin rivers come together in what's now Montana, trapping beaver and stacking up plew after plew because this was virgin territory, under control of the Blackfeet, and the Blackfeet had their own ways of dealing with trespassers, none of them pretty. Depending on their mood, they might cut off your fingers, one by one, then your toes, your ears, your lips. Or jam splinters of pine up under your flesh and set them afire or strip the skin from your limbs and hold the bleeding ropes of it up in front of your eyes so you could focus on what they were doing to you. And through it all you had to laugh in their faces to show how impervious you were to pain in the thin hope they'd put a swifter end to it. Cry out, whimper, whine, plead, and they'd take their time with you. And get creative too.

Colter had a single companion with him this time, a black-bearded trapper named John Potts who talked too much and ate too much but was tough enough and had his own traps, which cost ten dollars each—as much as you'd get for a hide—and were like stacked-up gold out there in the wilderness where there was no way to manufacture or repair them. They were heavy cumbersome things of iron and they had to be set out and held in place in the swift cold water by means of a stake driven into the bottom. The trappers would save the castor glands of beaver they'd killed and work them into a redolent paste that reproduced the scent the animals marked their territory with. They used this to cap a second, thinner stick that stuck up out of the water just high enough so that the beaver would have to step on the pan of the trap to boost himself up and get a sniff of it. Once the jaws closed on him, he'd dive and eventually drown.

Nobody knows how many traps Colter had but Adam liked to think of him as having ten, ten at least—more than Potts, anyway, because Potts was his inferior in everything, whether it was paddling upriver against the current all day or jerking meat or catching beaver to make the money to get him back out into the wilderness to catch more. What time of year was it? Fall. Fall, when the beaver pelts begin to thicken out again with winter coming on. Colter's leg had healed by this point, though the scar was still puckered and red and he must have been thinking he'd just as soon have grown a new leg as be confined back at Fort Lisa with all those people around him and nothing to look at but bark-peeled logs and a big dull muddy river that had been all beavered out. He didn't like people. Or not much, anyway. Not as much as being out there under the spreading sky and depending on no one but himself and why he'd taken Potts along no one could figure. Maybe Potts bribed him. Maybe that was it.

But there was a morning, first light, when they were checking the traps they'd set out the previous morning on a fair-sized creek that fed into the Jefferson—dusk and dawn, that was all they could risk, lie low through the day and don't even think about starting a cookfire, making do with jerky and hardtack and whatever came to hand that didn't need a flame under it—when Colter's sixth sense kicked in. They were in their canoes, sticking close to the alder and willow that overhung the banks, silently going about their work. Fog steamed like breath out of the water and hung there, though it would soon burn off and leave them exposed. Colter was for packing it in, but Potts, greedy Potts, wanted to keep on till all the traps had been checked and re-baited. This was the part that always got to him, how Colter, who knew better, had hooked up with this clown and then gone against his own better judgment. But there it was. And still—*still*—even after they heard the clatter of hooves on the shore above them, Potts insisted that it was just a herd of buffalo coming down for a morning drink. Insisted, and spoke out loud too, though, of course, it was in a whisper. He must have said something like *Don't be a pussy* or whatever the equivalent was back in the day.

That was when the Blackfeet appeared, a horde of them, painted, mounted on their ponies. There must have been two or three hundred of them or more. It wasn't a war party, Colter could see that at a glance—there were women and children with them, crowding in now to peer over the bank at the two interlopers in the canoes. Maybe they'd only be robbed, that was what he was thinking—hopeful, always hopeful—and he made a peace sign and called out a greeting in their own language. He had maybe a dozen phrases in the Blackfoot language and could understand more than he could speak. Crow was the language he knew best. He could speak that fluently, but then the Crows, along with the Flatheads, were the enemies of the Blackfeet, which brought up a further complication—what if one of them recognized him as the sole white man who'd fought on the side of the Crows six months earlier? As for Potts, Potts didn't speak anything. He just sat there in the canoe, looking as if he was going to shit himself.

One of the braves waved them into shore and they had no choice but to comply. Both canoes hit the sandbank at the same time and Colter sprang out to stand up straight and face them down to show he had no fear, but Potts wouldn't get out. *They're going to kill us,* he said in a choked voice, *but they're going to torture us first,* and he tried to back the canoe away but one of the braves took hold of the paddle and then, when Potts went for his rifle, the brave grabbed that. At this point, Colter, who was stronger than any two of them combined, waded in, snatched the rifle away and handed it back to Potts. (Why, Adam always wondered, when they should have just waited them out? What was he thinking? Or maybe he wasn't thinking, maybe he was just reacting.) That, unfortunately, started a chain of events no one could stop. Potts pushed back in his canoe and it shot out to midstream, at

which point one of the Indians let fly with an arrow—*shush*—
and there it was, embedded in Potts' left hip, blooming there, the
feathers trembling like rose petals in a breeze. And what did Potts
do next? Snatched up his rifle and shot the closest Indian to him,
which was the one who'd tried to take it away from him, now
hip-deep in the water and looking hate at him. An instant and
it was done. And in the next instant every brave there was using
Potts for target practice.

So Potts was dead, dead in a matter of seconds, and Colter
was standing there on the shore amidst all the hostiles howling
like scorched demons and the women sending up their weird ululations of grief over the dead brave and half a dozen Indians in
the creek now and wading to the canoe to drag it back to shore.
Where they went at Potts' corpse like a butchers' convention, the
women especially, hacking at him till he was unrecognizable, just
meat, slick and wet and red. And Colter? Still there, still standing,
still staring out unflinchingly, in another place altogether, ignoring them.

What was that like, seeing your companion gutted and dis-
membered out of the corner of your eye and not thirty feet away?
How could anybody have just stood there instead of panicking
and trying to make a run for it? Colter did. Five minutes, that
was all it took for them to finish hacking at Potts till there was no
more left of him than a skinned rabbit, and then they turned to
Colter. Everybody was jabbering at once, crowding in to threaten
him with hatchets, spears, the points of arrows and knives, their
faces contorted and their mouths flung open so that every word,
every shriek was delivered in a thunderstorm of spit. And they
stank. They really stank. Stank worse than corpses come back
to life. As if it mattered. As if anything mattered to Colter other
than somehow saving his own skin. In the next moment he was
stripped naked, his clothes sliced off him by the squaws' knives,
and here was what was left of Potts' organs flung at him to spatter his chest with blood. One woman—the widow who'd been a

married woman ten minutes before—was brandishing something in his face, flailing him with it, and what was it? White, flaccid, a twist of pubic hair and the sorrowful deracinated sack of what had been Potts' testicles and the other thing attached to it, limp and bright with blood, and it could have been a turkey neck, stripped of skin and feathers, but it wasn't.

So *what* was he shooting at? Was she serious? Movement, that was what. Who knew who was out there, whether it was the officers of the law or the Chinese smuggled up from Mexico on the panga boats they abandoned on the beaches till there were more pangas than seals and bundles of kelp combined or just some dog-walking shithead who was already dialing 911? And if he strapped on the night-vision goggles and whoever it was was gone in the space of those twenty seconds, what did that prove? That they were elusive. That they were smart. That they were watching him harder than he was watching them and that they were watching her too. He'd seen movement and so he fired, just to keep them off, just to let them know what his Chinese Norinco SKS Sporter semi-automatic assault rifle could do in the hands of somebody who really knew how to use it no matter what his father said or tried to say when his Aunt Marion gave it to him for his twenty-third birthday because her husband was dead and you didn't have any use for a rifle when you were dead unless maybe you were a zombie and his Uncle Dave might have been a zombie in real life but definitely wasn't going to be coming out of his grave anytime soon.

Whatever. But then she was barking at him and he thought she was going to run him down with the car she was in such a panic, which wasn't cool-headed at all and he was ashamed for her and wanted to say something about that, about tactics and coolness under fire, but the words wouldn't come. He was flying, the sound and feel of that rifle pumping him full of helium gas like a balloon lifting off into the sky, and for the first few minutes he just sat there seeing the headlights streaming out into the night and knowing how wrong that was. *Kill the lights,* he told her, knowing they'd be coming, and it was no different from the deeds they'd done in high school, slowing down to hang out the window and obliterate somebody's mailbox with a baseball bat or egging the gym teacher's house because he was a Nazi, and always with the lights off so you could slip in under the radar. *I can't,* she said, and he was about to reach over and flip the switch himself when the siren started in and he knew just what to do and where to go because the pigs were flat-out stupid and so what if there was only one road going down? *Here,* he said. *Stop here. Turn.*

And then they were in the dark and the lights *were* off and he guided her the first part of the way with the goggles, at least until they'd put a couple of curves between them and the main road so there was no chance of any U-turning pig seeing their running lights or anything else and then he let her switch the headlights back on and everything was cool. She calmed down finally and when she calmed down she started chattering away about anything that came into her head as they went bumping over washboard ripples and slamming through potholes, everything a uniform drifting dirt-brown and the leaves more gray than green and the tree trunks like pillars supporting a whole other road above them, a black road and starless. He wasn't listening. The wheel was spinning but spinning slower now and she was there beside him, Sara, a human being, a word mill, a talking dictionary, big tits jouncing with the up and down of the car springs, her voice coming too fast at first but gradually slowing as she got used to the fact that they'd one-upped them yet again and there was no chance of being caught by anybody, not now or later.

Some time passed, or must have passed, but he didn't notice. She was still talking. "So what did you think of Christabel?" was one thing she said but he didn't answer so she said it again and this time he was right there with her.

"Is she Chinese?"

"*Chinese?* Christabel? What are you talking about? Christabel Walsh? That's Irish. And her mother was a McCoy."

"She looks Chinese."

"Christabel? Come on, Adam, what planet are you on? She's no more Chinese than I am. Or you, for that matter." Her big tits bounced. The trees caught the light. "What is this obsession with the Chinese, anyway?"

He didn't want to tell her about the incident in San Francisco, whenever that was, years ago, he guessed, and he didn't want to tell her that the Orientals were conduits to the other worlds and the Chinese star proved it. It was too complicated. And he didn't really feel like getting into all that now, so he unscrewed the cap on his canteen and had a hit of 151 and just repeated what he'd already told her because she was trying to understand and he had to give her credit for that. "They're the new hostiles," he said. "I told you."

More ruts, more bouncing. The car spoke its own language, low and steady, a kind of robot growl that never gave up and he could look right through the dashboard and into the engine and see the pistons there, the valves and connecting rods, pumping and pumping like sex, robot sex, car sex, steel on steel. "What do you mean," she said, "like economically?"

"Are you crazy? Who's talking about *economics*? Economics is shit." He stopped there, looking for the words that right then started marching across his line of vision, left to right, as if he was reading from a script and that was nothing new because everything in this world was scripted like some lame reality show and everything had been said before a billion trillion times, *How are you today, Fine, How are you, Fine, Have a nice day, You too.* His head hurt where he'd banged it on the windshield, but there was no blood. She drove. The car growled. "Let me ask you something"—she was pissing him off she was so stupid and he wanted her to know it—"because sometimes I wonder about the college you went to and if you were paying attention at all."

"So ask."

"Where did the Indians come from?"

It took her a minute. "Asia? The land bridge, you mean?"

"What we ought to do?" he said. "If I was president?"

"What?" A little bleat, and that was funny, because her voice got jerked on a string by the next pothole.

"Nuke 'em. Nuke 'em before they nuke us," and he was picturing it now, everything melted, everything ash. "Or hack all our computers and send us back to the Stone Age. No money, no food, no electricity, no nothing."

"That wouldn't be so bad, would it? It'd give the animals and the environment a chance to come back. We'd need more Colters then, wouldn't we? People that could live off the land?" Her face was turned toward him, light on one side, dark on the other, quarter moon. She was right. Back to the Stone Age. More Colters. Live off the land. And get ready for the hostiles, because they were coming and they would just take what they wanted and nobody to stop them.

She was quiet a moment. The car thumped. The night squeezed in. She didn't know it yet but they were going to have to stay out here all night long, at the campground, where they'd blend in with the others. It would be cramped in the car and she might not like it but that was how it was. There was a blanket in back. He had a couple PowerBars and she always carried a bottle of water in the car. They'd sit there in the dark. They'd get high. And not just on rum and marijuana, but what he had in his shirt pocket, a surprise, first fruit of his poppies, the sap he'd worked into little dried-out balls you could smoke just like that in a pipe you made out of foil and could use once and toss away and nobody the wiser. Then they'd have sex. She'd open up to him—she always opened up to him, hot and greasy and with that smell of her like some animal with its scent glands on display, like a beaver, and it came to him then that that was why it was called beaver. *Beaver shot,* he said in his head. And then he said it aloud: "Beaver shot."

"What?"

He didn't say it again, only thought it: *Beaver shot.* And money shot, that was when you pulled it out and squirted their beaver or their tits or belly. Spermatized them.

"I said, if the whole corrupt society broke down, that wouldn't be so bad, would it?"

"No," he said softly, "no, it wouldn't."

Days flipped by, he wasn't sure how many. She was there in the house, cooking, cleaning, picking lint out of the Rasta dog's fur and spreading for him every night, and he was out working his plants, slitting the seed pods with a razor and letting the milky stuff drip out till he scraped it off and rolled it into a ball. When he had enough of it, when he was satisfied with the product, he was going to sell it—Cody, Cody was going to help him out on that end because he really couldn't feature tramping up and down the street looking for heads and freaks and tourists who might or might not be interested—and he was going to take the money and put it in a jar and hide that jar in a secret place so he could be independent of everybody and everything *forever.* He'd build another bunker, deeper, farther, and he wasn't ever going to come back.

Problem was, he had a wicked case of poison oak. It was in between his fingers, blisters so big there it hurt to make a fist. And he'd somehow managed to get it on his cock, pissing, most likely, but then you had to piss and to get it out you had to touch yourself and that's where the poison oak got in. He'd heard that if you ate some of the leaves you'd be immune and he'd tried that when he was twelve or thirteen and all that had happened was he had blisters on his lips and in his mouth and halfway down his throat so he couldn't even eat for a week, so that, to put it mildly, was bullshit. Anyway, he needed calamine lotion and she'd gone to the store and gotten it for him and now, right now, with the sun straight up overhead, he was skirting the dog-face's property and heading back to the house to dose himself with it, especially down there where every step chafed him and the itch was a thing you couldn't scratch because that would only make it worse but he was scratching it anyway and it was bringing tears to his eyes.

Down one slope, across the river that was less a river every day, up the other slope and through the trees to the house, the wall there, and then up and over the wall and into the yard. Two whispers: his feet touching down. The dirt. Yellow weeds. Sun. A hole the Rasta dog had dug, no bigger than a birdbath. One tree, puny, leaves drooping. And what was this? A bicycle up against the wall, cinnamon red, with dirty white tape wrapped around the handlebars, and that was strange because Colter didn't have a bicycle, bicycles hadn't even been invented yet, and where had that come from? He'd already shrugged out of the backpack and propped the rifle against the wall, but now he straightened up, alert suddenly, his sixth sense kicking in. That was when he heard the voices. That was when he made himself small and slipped round the corner of the house to peer in the window and see his mother there and now his father too, shapes shifting in the sun raking through the glass to cut their heads off and replace them with haloes like in the church with Jesus and Mary but his father wasn't Jesus and his mother was no saint either.

Slip away, a voice was telling him, whispering to him, *slip away over the wall and go deep before they know you're here,* and he realized he could see through the house because the curtains were gone, see all the way across the rugless bare boards, out through the windows on the other side and beyond that to the door his father had cut in the wall. Which stood open. Propped open. And why, if every time his father showed he was going to prop the door open, had he bothered to put that door there in the first place? For security? To keep everybody out? Or in? But there was something there, a vehicle, the broad white flank of it suddenly blasting up at warp speed to spread itself atop the wall, black let-

tering there, or the tops of letters, letters wearing hats, and for
the tiniest hemidemisemiquaver of a second it was a puzzle but
a puzzle anybody could have solved: *U-Haul.* That's what it said.
They had a U-Haul here. And what did that mean? That meant
they were taking things. That meant the alien was moving in,
into *his* house, into his grandma's house, and he could see it now,
the alien in the cemetery with his shovel and digging, digging,
digging till he had her dead body dripping beetles and grubs and
he threw it over his shoulder and came right back and laid her out
on the bed to be his bride like in *The Evil Dead* or one of those
movies, he couldn't remember because they were all the same.

He wanted something. It wasn't 151, it wasn't pot or opium
or acid or a two-foot-long submarine sandwich heaped with pro-
sciutto, provolone and pickled Tuscan peppers. No. It wasn't any
of that. It was Sara. Sara was what he wanted. And he rose now,
confused, because where was she, and that was when the Rasta
dog must have seen his shadow because the Rasta dog was barking and they saw him there in the yard and his father was waving
him in, waving like the braves on the shore before they peppered
Potts. *Peppered Potts*—he was saying it, saying it aloud—and here
they were, his father, his mother and Sara, all of them out the back
door and into the yard and the Rasta dog too, barking and incit-
ing the trees till the trees were barking along with him.

"Adam," and it was like a chorus, "you're here."

There was no denying it though he wished he didn't have
poison oak and wished he'd just stayed out there in the woods so
he wouldn't have to crawl through this big dripping heaped-up
pile of bullshit and worse bullshit yet to come, so he didn't deny
it. "Yeah," he said, and he tried to put a smile on his face but it
wouldn't come. He stared down at the ground.

And now his father: "Art Tolleson's moving in tomorrow. So
that's it. All she wrote. If you want anything, personal things, you
better take it now."

And his mother: "We fixed up a room for you? At the new

house? It's just temporary, I know, and we'll help you find something, I don't know, more suitable—"

His father: "When the time comes."

Sara said nothing. She was just standing there. He was staring
at the ground—or no, at her shit-kickers. "What about Sara?"
he heard himself say. "What are you going to do, bury her too?"

His father: "What in Christ's name are you talking about?
Stop with this crap. Enough. I've had it up to here." A glare. "You
can turn it on and off just like that, can't you? Isn't that right?"
Nothing. Nobody. The sun, the dirt, the weeds, the shit-kickers.
"Well, turn it off. Or take your meds or whatever it is you need
because the fact is—the reality—the house is no longer ours."

His mother: "Sten. Don't be like that." Softer now: "Adam,
come on, it's all right. She can, she can maybe, for a few days, I
mean, at our house—"

And Sara, finally: "He can come with me. Stay at my place.
For as long as he wants." And then, shifting her face or at least
the voice coming out of it as if her head was a loudspeaker but he
couldn't say, not really, because he wasn't going to look up because
if he looked up he'd be part of their reality and he didn't want
any part of being a part of that: "It's okay, the thirty days are up,
no problem. We'll just help your parents clean up a bit and then
tonight"—a pause for his father's benefit, and she was the saint now
and where was her halo?—"we'll go up the hill. Sound good?"

It didn't sound good. Nothing sounded good. He wanted his
parents out of there—hit "enter" and just beam them up, haloes
and all—and he wanted it to be night so he could go in and
fuck Sara in the dark. "Personal things," he said, spitting out the
words. "Peppered Potts. Dog-face Moody. And Art Tolleson, I
don't know if you noticed"—raising his eyes now as if they were
the high beams on the car—"is an alien."

His father took two strides forward, his father the giant with
his hands like catcher's mitts, and he was livid. "That's rum on
your breath. You're drunk. And Jesus knows what else."

THE HARDER THEY COME

He just shrugged, but it was afternoon and afternoons were never good and here went the wheel, spinning, spinning.

"Now you get your ass in there and pack up your crap"—stinking breath, hostile breath—"and you can come to our house tonight, both of you, or you can go to her house, I don't really care—"

"Yeah," he was saying in that other voice, the one that was like vinegar up your nose, "and you can go fuck yourself too. Big hero. Why don't you just kill me too—wouldn't that be easier? Isn't that what you want? Isn't it?"

Then his father shoved him, hard, didn't hit him but shoved him, and he was a rock because he hardly felt it and didn't even take a step back but when his own arms jerked out and he was doing the shoving they were like two pistons pulled right up out of the engine block and his father reeled, his father stepped back, but then his father came at him again and it was ugly, *he* was ugly, as ugly as Potts, and maybe his mother got into it too, trying to separate them, her voice gone up into the high register till it was like an air-raid siren, and that really was all she wrote, finally and absolutely, because his father was in the dirt now and his mother too and he was gone, rifle, backpack, knife in its sheath, up over the wall and into the high weeds and gone, pure gone.

20.

LATE, BLACK DARK, THE frogs doing their thing along the creek and the crickets in the high grass, no other sound but the whisper of his boots. He circled the place twice to make sure there was nobody around and it wasn't till the second recon that he noticed her car there because he wasn't expecting it and the shadows were like loam and the loam was piled up till it was buried, absolutely. What did he feel about that? He felt a quickening, not the wheel now, though it was humming along, all right, but in his blood, in his cock. Her car. Her car was there though it should have been gone by now and her with it. He was in cover, crouching, and if he itched, he was going to take care of that because he was going to go into that house whether his father liked it or not—or Art Tolleson the alien or whoever—and he was going to get the calamine lotion he'd come for earlier and, more importantly, he was going to go down behind the couch Art Tolleson was inheriting as part and parcel of the deal and extract the sweet pickle relish jar with the six hundred dollars in it and then they'd see just how independent he was. He lifted the night-vision goggles to his face and took a good long look at the car and there she was, her head lolling back and no doubt the Rasta dog there too on the floor someplace or the seat beside her and what was she thinking, what was she doing? It made his skin prickle to think of the answer, made his cock hard: she was waiting for him.

The Rasta dog let out with a whole boiling cauldron of yips, snarls, barks and high-throated yowls the minute he touched his hand to the car door and here was her face, dumb with sleep and pale as the underside of her feet, fixed in the gap where the scrolling-down window slipped into the doorframe. She called him by name, his old name, the one he'd rejected, but he didn't care, not now, and he didn't bother to correct her. Then she asked if he'd had anything to eat, but he didn't answer. He said, "I want to get in the house. He didn't change the locks again, did he?"

"I don't know," she said, her voice sticky, like taffy. "I don't think so."

"Because I'll smash every fucking window in the place . . ."

Stickier still: "What do you need, baby?"

"Calamine."

"I've got it here with me in the car. Come on, get in. We'll go up to my place—just for tonight. Or longer. However long you want. It's okay. It is."

He held out his hand. "Give it to me."

It took her about six weeks, fumbling around with her purse and her suitcase and all the bags of groceries and crap, the dog whining and stinking and breathing out his meat-eating breath and her turning on the dome light, which was so wrong and so untactical and so just plain idiotic he couldn't have even begun to explain it to her, but there it was, the plastic bottle cool and round in the palm of his hand and their skin touching like two flames as she handed it over.

She tried again. "Come on," she said, "let's go. I'm tired."

He ignored her. Yes, his cock was hard, but so was Colter's through a thousand black nights and freezing dawns, and it was something you just had to deal with. Discipline, that was what it was called. What soldier, what mountain man, worried about sex? You got it when you could and if you didn't have it you just learned to do without. It wasn't like food. Or plews. Or balls and powder for your rifle. Of course he could have gone through the front gate, which was unlocked—he tried it—but that would be giving in to his father and his father's scheme, so he went over the wall, and when he got to the front door he tried his key and his key worked but that didn't mean anything because it was just more of the same. No, what he was going to do was what he'd envisioned all the way back: he was going to break in, break things, let people—let his father—know just how he felt.

There were rocks in the yard that fit his fist as if they'd been shaped and eroded and pressed deep in the earth over all the eons just for this purpose, just for smashing windows, and no one to hear or care. Except Sara. She was there shouting at him after the picture window in front gave up the ghost—the *ghost,* and that was funny, this one's for you, Grandma—and then she actually tried to stop him, to grab at his arm as he went for the next window and the next one after that, methodical now, with all the time and purpose in the world.

Sometimes it was a good thing to put the brakes on the wheel and slow everything down and the 151 and the opium did that but then you were vulnerable because you weren't alert and ready for action and when you shouldered your rifle and went up the trail to your bunker you felt like you were wading through water, as if the air wasn't air anymore but something thicker, denser, something dragging you down like the too-thick atmosphere and too-heavy gravity of the aliens' planet. The Chinese planet. The planet where they lived and bred and sent out their scouts to come after you. So he stopped the opium—Colter didn't need it and neither did he—and traded off a couple marble-sized balls of it to Cody at the pizza place in exchange for six hits of acid and a chintzy little baggie of what Cody said was coke but was really meth. No matter. Stay awake, *get* awake, and march, march all day long till your legs didn't know they were attached to your body.

Weeks went by. Or he thought it was weeks. Maybe it was days, maybe it was months, but the important thing was he was in training and he could go like Colter when Colter walked those three hundred miles and he knew every trail in all these woods and forests and he didn't even need trails because there was nobody in that whole poisoned corrupt police state of Mendo who knew the country better than him and never had been, not since the mountain men themselves. He was doing it, he was finally doing it, living free, and no, he'd said no to Sara that night, the night of the broken glass, because he didn't want to be dependent, didn't want to go soft on her baked lasagna and her big soft lips and big soft tits and all the rest of it. *No,* he'd said, *no, get off me!* And she did. She got off him. She gave up. He smashed glass and a whole lot more and she got back in her car with the Rasta dog and the taillights cut a stencil out of the night, red stencil, red stencil receding, *Have a nice day, You too.*

But now, today, whatever day today was, he had a problem— and it wasn't poison oak because that was dried up now and it wasn't the shits, though come to think of it he did have the shits and that was from drinking out of whatever stream whether it was in the state forest or running through the lumber company property like silver music playing all on its own or maybe the Noyo, never the same river twice, everything in flux, including his fucked-up bowels—and that problem was backup. He'd begun to realize—or no, the realization slammed into him like the hundred arrows that transfixed Potts—that he was vulnerable on his own turf where anybody could see his plants and maybe the bunker too if they looked hard enough and hadn't he spotted a helicopter going over just the day before? And all those jets, high up, like silver needles threading the sky, every one of them equipped with super-secret spy cameras? Too much, way too much, and he'd really let his guard down this time, hadn't he?

A new bunker, that was what he needed, a backup plan, a place to retreat to if it came to it, anybody could see that and you didn't have to be a tactical genius to appreciate the value of it. So he had a shovel and a bow saw he'd taken from the Boy Scout camp on the Noyo which was abandoned now for the season because the Boy Scouts were all back in school and he was heading overland—no sense in showing himself on the roads—to a place he knew of six miles north, very secure, high ground surrounding the pool a spring made when it pushed out of the mountain. Pure water, that was what he was thinking. A spring. None of this bacteria and giardia and human waste the aliens fed into all these other streams. He went through the trees, down a ravine, up the other side, double time, and the air was cool and the bugs asleep, and when he got there he unwrapped a handful of Hershey's Kisses for the sugar rush and then used the little soft foil wrappers to make himself a blunt and smoke out while he contemplated the arrangements.

The Boy Scouts, that was what he was thinking about. They were another kind of pathetic, crybabies and dudes and the sons of dudes, and they hadn't really needed the sleeping bag he spread out by the side of the spring so he could lie back and watch the tops of the trees stir and settle and stir again before he got down to digging. And cutting. Maybe he closed his eyes. Maybe he drifted off. It didn't really matter because he was dreaming when he was asleep and dreaming when he was awake and if the two dreams intertwined that was the way it was meant to be. What it was that woke him out of the one dream and sent him rushing into the other was a noise, the dull airtight thump of a car door slamming shut, but how could that be? How could there be a car out here? *Unless*—and the qualifier shot out claws to grab him down deep in his gut where he was already cramping—unless he hadn't done a proper recon because he wasn't a soldier at all or a mountain man either but just another unhard unprepared unfit version of the fat kids with their bags of Doritos he used to play *World of Warcraft* and *Grand Theft Auto* with before he pulled the plug on all that. Mountain men didn't need video games. Mountain men didn't need to waste hostiles by proxy. Who wanted to be connected? Who needed Doritos? Who needed fat kids? And nerds. Half of them were probably in China, Chinese nerds. No, he was *disconnected* and proud of it and had been since he was what, fourteen, fifteen?

But what about that noise? What about that slamming door? How could you have a secure backup position within earshot of a logging road? Cursing himself, knowing he'd fucked up, he came fully alert in that instant. Silently, he took up the rifle and rose to his knees, listening, trying to determine what direction the threat was coming from. The rifle had a pistol grip, which he'd wrapped in black electrical tape for the feel of it, the tactile sensation of knowing it was in his hand, wedded to it like skin, so he could feel his finger on the trigger with no interference and squeeze off rounds at will, thirty rounds to a clip and two more clips in the backpack and another 208 rounds of dull-silver Wolf 7.62mm bullets in there too. He could hold off an army. He would. Just bring them on.

Everything was silent. Some kind of peeping started up—a bird, or no, one of those chickaree squirrels, the kind that don't know a thing beyond eating and shitting and fucking but cling to the high branches and bitch all day long, anyway—and that peeping was an unfortunate thing because it covered the sound of footsteps coming up the slope along the streambed. That and the noise of the stream itself. And that was crazy. How could you develop a defensive position and anticipate the enemy with all this racket? An electric bolt shot through him. He wanted to shout out to the squirrel to shut the fuck up. He wanted to blow him away, eradicate him with one blast, and then what? Then stomp his rodent head till it was just mush . . .

The voice came out of nowhere. "Hey, you," the voice said, the voice demanded, "what do you think you're doing in there?"

He was startled, he admitted it, and he hated himself for that, taken by surprise because he hadn't done a proper recon and even after he'd been alerted to the presence of hostiles he had to go off dreaming about squirrels. He was still on his knees. He could feel his fatigues getting wet because there was moss here beside the sleeping bag and moss was like a sponge and now he felt the pressure on his bowels too until he was like Potts about to shit himself in that canoe. The source of the voice, where was it? It seemed to be everywhere. And he was a fool, a fool. He slipped off the safety, hating himself.

"There's no camping here," the voice went on, and here was the source, a hostile with fish eyes and a flat fish head and shorts and hiking boots, coming toward him through the draw where the stream started down out of the spring and carved its own way, silver music, "and no trespassing either. This is Georgia Pacific property. Can't you read?"

His defenses were down and so he said that, said, "My defenses are down."

The hostile was fifty feet from him, red-faced, barking, everybody barking twenty-four/seven and he was tired of that, give it a break, give my ears a fucking break, and the hostile was saying, "You pack up your crap and get out of here," and that was when he pulled the trigger, twice, *pop-pop,* and it wasn't like *I didn't even know my finger was on the trigger* because he did know and he took aim the way he had a thousand times in target practice and the two shots went home and dropped that hostile like he was a suit of clothes with nobody in it.

Long time. Long, long time. He just sat there, right where he was, and smoked another blunt, the chickaree still at it, the spring pumping out water like it was never going to quit. A few mosquitoes came to visit and after a while there were meat bees and a couple bluebottle flies dancing over the dead man who might have needed to be buried and might not have. Colter never buried anybody, not hostiles, anyway, and Fish-Eyes was definitely a hostile, even if he did look like that teacher from school. What he did do though, finally, was push himself up to go and stand over the corpse the way Colter would have done and he briefly entertained the notion of collecting a scalp here, his first scalp, but rejected that. The man was on his back. He'd been shot through the gut and then, in recoiling from that shot, he must have turned slightly so that the second shot went through his right arm and on into the side of his ribcage. A hole there, but not as big as the one in his gut. His shirt—a T-shirt with some stupid logo of some stupid organization on it—was very wet and very red with the color of the cinnamon bicycle that was propped up against the wall back at the house that used to be his. The eyes weren't looking at anything. And the mouth—the mouth definitely wasn't giving any commands or issuing any threats, not anymore. But the whole thing didn't look right to him and he was seeing a bright shearing radiance of colors and things breaking down into their constituent parts and then reassembling again, only not in the same way, not the same way at all, and what he was feeling was pain, sharp and demanding, pain in his own gut, and he didn't think twice about it, just pulled down his pants and squatted there and took a rank and violent shit.

He needed something, that was what he was thinking, Imodium or maybe if it was giardia, some kind of prescription. He couldn't just go around sick in his stomach and shitting all the time, could he? No. That wasn't going to work. He'd have to go into town, to the drugstore there. But if he needed a prescription, where was he going to get that? For the moment though the problem was the shit he could smell in his own nostrils and so he hiked his pants halfway and crabwalked over to sit in the spring and clean himself off, then he dried himself with leaves— not poison oak, just leaves—pulled his pants back up, collected his things and went off into the woods, heading upslope. He knew a place up there, remembered it, could picture it even now, where there was another spring. Maybe, he was thinking, just maybe, if he gave it a real good recon, it would turn out to be a primo spot, exactly what he was looking for.

And then let them come. Just let them.

PART VII

Fort Bragg

21.

STEN WAS AT THE gas station, pumping gas and working the squeegee over the broad glass plane of the Prius' back window, seven-thirty in the morning, sun shining, on his way down to the harbor with a spinning rod to fling a lure across the mouth of the channel there and see if anything cruising in from the sea would like to take it in its scaly jaws. All the years he'd been working he told himself he loved fishing the way he had as a boy, nailing steelhead and salmon in the Noyo, Big River, the Ten Mile and out on the ocean too, told himself that as soon as he had time he was going to fish till he dropped. But he didn't. Or hadn't. In fact, this was the first time he'd touched the rod in longer than he could remember, and he wasn't fooling himself—he knew he'd put his gear in the car and come out here this morning just to do something, just to get out of the house and shake the rust off. If he caught anything, so much the better—that would be a bonus—but the real deal was to kill a couple of hours before he went back home to see if the bushes he'd trimmed yesterday had grown back or the caulk he'd replaced in the kitchen a week ago needed replacing again.

He was thinking of another gas station, one that was long gone now, where he'd worked the summer before his senior year in high school. Three young Italians—or maybe one of them wasn't Italian—had pooled their resources to open the place. They were in their early thirties, he guessed, but back then they seemed old to him, and they were enthusiasts, full of jokes and high spirits, their own bosses now and sure to rake in a fortune. One of them, the one who might not have been Italian—Gene, his name was Gene— did bodywork and the other two, Tony and Rico, were mechanics.

What they needed him for was to pump gas, check tires and oil and coolant, and to dole out Green Stamps against their eventual redemption. Different times then. He'd worked seven a.m. to seven p.m. and every day at noon Rico would go to the sandwich shop and bring back subs for all of them—and beer, a can of which they would let him have instead of soda though he was underage. They made him feel good. Made him feel like a man.

Where were they now? he wondered. Dead, he supposed. Dead and buried and rotted away to nothing, the casket collapsed on itself, their bones bare and gray and losing heft by the day. People asked him what his philosophy was, as if by being principal—having been principal—he was schooled in the thoughts of the great thinkers, and what's more, was a great thinker himself. Well, he had no philosophy. He just lived and drew breath like any other creature, more acted upon than acting. There were Jesus, Santa Claus and God when he was little, but they'd gone the way of slingshots and training wheels, the apprehension of death—the first intimation of it—canceling out everything else. What was his philosophy? Kill or be killed, eat or be eaten. Or no, that was too harsh. Just be, that was all. What was coming was coming and there was no sense or comfort in worrying about it. Other people went to church, other people played golf, served on committees, ran charities. He went on a luxury cruise. He went fishing. And if Carolee should die before him, he faced a world of woe so deep and catastrophic he didn't think he'd be able to see himself through. Definitely not. No way in the world. He kept a gun in the house, a Glock 9mm he'd always prayed Adam would never find when he was a squirrelly kid and into everything, and that gun would have its use sometime down the line. Retirement plan? Sure, the good and giving Glock Firearms Company would see to that.

So he was morbid, so he was bored, so he was pumping his own gas and letting his mind tick through the past and present like one of the mutating tapes of the home movies he'd made when Adam was a kid before he saw the utter futility of it because who was ever going to watch them and how could you hope to stop time? There was a breeze. It lifted the hair around his ears and laid it back down on his shoulders, the lightest part of himself, but heavy all the same. Then a GMC Yukon, fire-engine red, slid up on the other side of the pump, and Art Tolleson's face was there, suspended behind the sheen of the window like an old towel hung up to dry.

Art didn't say hello and he didn't smile. He looked like somebody carrying an armful of raw eggs as he eased out of the car and climbed up onto the island separating the pumps. "Did you hear?" he asked.

"Hear what?"

"They shot Carey Bachman."

"Who?"

"Who do you think—the Mexicans."

Art stood there blinking at him, the tentative expression gone now, subsumed in something harder. He looked pained, looked angry, as if he'd been shot himself, Art Tolleson, friend, neighbor, former colleague, a lifelong bachelor in his early fifties who taught English at the high school, and whether his sexual orientation had been a matter of conjecture in the faculty lounge or not never factored into the school board's perception of him because he drew students like a magnet, male and female alike, and never a complaint or even the hint of one. He had a high nasal English teacher's voice and a slack body, but as if in compensation—and to still rumors—he dressed as if he'd been born and raised in a logging camp, workboots, jeans, plaid shirts, and made a point of attending the full range of sporting events at the school. He hunted in the fall. Fished in the spring. And he'd done Sten a huge favor by taking the house off his hands, though the day he took possession was a disaster, every window in the place smashed out, glass everywhere, the coffee table staved in and the toilet in the guest room—Adam's room—shattered in porcelain fragments that lay scattered across the floor like unearthed bones, the water three inches deep and flowing out under the door. Sten had cleaned up the place himself, paid for everything, and he and Carolee had put Art up in the guest room at their place till the glazier got done because it was the least they could do. As for Adam, he hadn't laid eyes on him since—or heard from him—and that was a month ago. "He needs help," was what he said to Carolee, but what he was thinking, exhausted now, fed up, terminal, was *Goodbye and good riddance; there's no paternal or even human sympathy left because the well has run dry. It's dried-up and blown away.*

"What are you talking about? What Mexicans?"

Art should have been wearing glasses but he wasn't—contacts, had he gotten contacts? Or what, laser surgery? Art gave him a strained look, ever so slightly myopic. "They found him last night, up on the north logging road—you know, the one where there were all those downed trees last spring?"

He didn't have anything to say to this. He was picturing the Mexican with the pistol tucked in his waistband, the Don't-Fuck-With-Me clown with the scooped-out face. That picture went gray and broadened out till it was like a shovel whacking him in the back of the head. His blood pressure rocketed. Here it was, right in your face. The only surprise was that it hadn't come sooner.

Art, myopic Art, was studying him out of his dull brown eyes, expecting some sort of response, but Sten was thinking about Carey, trying to picture *him,* and drawing a blank. All he could see was the Mexican, duplicated over and over again.

"They shot him twice is what I hear and left him there to die. That was night before last so there's no telling how long he suffered. And then"—he hesitated, his eyes jumping in their sockets—"the animals got to him. After he was dead, I mean. Or I think. I hope."

There was nothing to say but he had to say something so he said, "All right," and what that meant—*I've heard enough* or *I feel your outrage* or *The tank's full*—he couldn't have said himself.

Art said, "We've got to do something."

"Yeah," Sten said, or heard himself say because he wasn't all there yet, "definitely. Definitely we have to do something."

"You have a gun?" Art's tone was nasal but elevated with emotion, and he might have been reading out a line from David Mamet or Arthur Miller to his drama class. *You have a gun?*

Sten didn't answer him, or not directly, because he didn't want to go down that road because that road led to people getting shot in the woods, led to poor Carey with his hot head and thumping knee getting it not once but twice until he was dead, dead, dead. Take Back Our Forests. Fine. Sure. But not that way. "They ought to call out the National Guard," he said. "Sweep the whole fucking forest."

"That's an idea. Really. That's what they ought to do." A pause, a look, direct, eyeball to eyeball. "But Carey's dead. And they're still out there. Right now. Laughing, probably laughing about it."

Sten got his receipt out of the metal slot, tucked it in his wallet, swung open the door and settled into the seat. "We'll talk," he said before slamming the door, starting up the engine and edging out onto the highway. A quick glance for Art in the rearview, and there he was, looking small and lost, the big red truck looming over him. Somebody waved from a passing car, somebody who looked familiar, though he couldn't place him, and he actually started toward the harbor, driving along like anybody else on the way to a morning's fishing on a day of precious sunshine under a sky lit bright and without a cloud to cast a shadow, before he put on his blinker, swung round and headed back home. The fish would be relieved, at least there was that.

Carolee was in her nightgown still, sitting at the kitchen table with a cup of coffee and the crossword puzzle out of the *Chronicle,* and she barely glanced up when he came in. "Back so soon?" she murmured. She was wearing her glasses and staring intently at the page before her, trying to break the code, and this was her way of staving off the boredom and filling the hours when she wasn't enjoying world-class indulgence aboard a cruise ship in the sunny crystalline waters of the Caribbean. Her hair shone in the light through the picture window, outside of which, in the intermediate view, birds flapped and clustered at the feeder, while in the longer view the sea sparked distantly under the sun. She was barefoot. The flesh bunched at her chin as she compressed the muscles there in concentration. "What's a seven-letter word for earthworm?"

The answer—*annelid*—sprang into his head, cribbed from a mimeographed sheet of multiple-choice questions in Bio 101 a thousand years ago, but he didn't give it to her, didn't say anything in fact. He just stood there, shaken more than he cared to admit—and now he *was* seeing Carey's face, the excitable face, the anxious one, the face he'd worn on the day they'd chased the Mexicans halfway across the county. He tried to picture him dead, but he drew a blank. Hard to picture anyone dead because there was a spirit there, a soul, the animating principle, whether you believed in God the Father and all the ministering angels or not, and that spirit was more specific even than the body that contained it. Carey was dead. There'd be a funeral. The community would come unglued. Vengeance is mine, saith the Lord. Maybe so. But not this time.

"Sten?" Looking up now, the glasses at half-mast on the flange of her nose. "Did you hear me?"

What he said was, "They got Carey."

She gave him a numb look, her pale wondering eyes riding up above the frames.

"Carey Bachman. The Mexicans. They shot him."

"What are you saying?"

"I'm saying he's dead, what do you think? He's dead. Carey's dead."

She wasn't indifferent, or not exactly—he could see the alarm germinating in her eyes and unfolding its petals across her face, color there, blossoming—but she didn't jump up from the table and tear out her hair or set up a wail of grief or even, and he couldn't help noticing this smallest detail, let go of the pencil gripped neatly between her thumb and first two fingers. The requisite questions dropped from her lips—*How? When? Where? How had he found out? Had they caught the killers? Was there no place safe anymore?*—and yet there was no shock in her tone, no outrage, no engagement. And why was that? He knew why. Adam. Adam was why.

She'd spent the previous afternoon at the Burnsides', helping Cindy and Gentian with the animals and the tours they gave daily. But it wasn't only Cindy and Gentian: Sara had been there. She came down on a regular basis, every six weeks or so, to shoe Cindy's horses and file their teeth, and there she was, in her boots, jeans and a no-nonsense T-shirt, her hair tied back in a ponytail and her hands roughened by the work. Carolee had said hi, uneasy, maybe a little embarrassed because of the scene out front of the house the last time they'd seen each other, Adam attacking his own father and his own father down there on the ground, but she was aching for news of Adam and here was her chance to get it.

Cindy, always the gracious hostess, had set out a platter of tuna- and egg-salad sandwiches for them, late lunch, with a scoop of homemade potato salad and carrot sticks and a drink of her own concoction, two parts cranberry, one part each of sparkling water and diet 7Up. Nice. A nice lunch. Cindy was always going out of her way like that. They were sitting there, she and Cindy, talking about the antelope and Cindy's hope for a mating pair of giraffes one of the zoos was offering them, when Sara came out of the bathroom where she'd been cleaning up. She looked good. She'd combed out her hair and put on some makeup and if she was forty she didn't look it. More like thirty.

There was some business talk—the horses, the antelope, the fact that the vet was doing the hooves on the zebras, sable and

kudu now and Cindy hoped Sara didn't mind but it was just easier that way since he had to be there to dart the animals in any
case—and then Cindy excused herself to go to the kitchen and
put on the water for tea and Carolee and Sara had a moment to
themselves. "How are you?" Carolee asked. "Everything okay?"

The other woman tugged at her fingers for a minute as if to
loosen the joints—she worked hard and had the calluses to prove
it—then gave a smile so fleeting it was dead on arrival. "I'm not
getting laid, if that's what you mean." She picked up her glass,
rattled the ice cubes, drained what was left in the bottom. "So
things could be better, yeah. A whole lot better."

Carolee was puzzled. And maybe a bit offended too—she'd
never been a fan of that kind of talk—but she forged on because
she had no choice and if this woman with the flaring eyes and
low habits and mad theories was going to wind up with Adam
she needed to be understanding, needed to give her the benefit of
the doubt, needed, above all else, to pump her for information.
"But what about Adam? How's he doing? Is he helping out, is he
okay?"

"Adam? I haven't seen Adam since that night, that time, I
mean—at the house?"

This information came down on Carolee like a rockslide, just
buried her, the way she told it. They'd both assumed he was with
her, and the news came down hard on him too—if he thought
he'd washed his hands of his son he was fooling himself. Adam
was there, always there, as persistent as a drumbeat in the back of
your mind, the rhythm you can't shake, the tune you can't stop
humming—he was his father, still and forever, and he'd tried to
be as good a father as he could through all these years no matter
how hard he rubbed up against Adam's will and his delusions and
his pranks, if you could call them that. He was Adam's father. He
loved him. And here he'd been entertaining his own delusion of
Adam living in a kind of half-cracked (which meant half-sane)
parity with this woman, Sara, who at least dwelled on Mother

Earth and had a job and could cook for him and feed him and be his mother and lover rolled in one. *I fucked her. Isn't that right, Sara? Didn't I fuck you?* It was like throwing coins in a wishing well. He'd made his silent wish, the wish he couldn't say aloud because then it wouldn't come true. And what was it? That Adam was somebody else's problem now.

Carolee had been stunned silent, sitting there with her mouth open. "You mean," she said, "he isn't with you?"

Sara, piggy Sara, Sara with her flaccid cheeks and fat thighs, too-old Sara, slutty Sara—no suitable lover for *her* son, not even close—had shaken her head emphatically and her eyes had moistened. "And I want to apologize—for that night, I mean. I stayed there till like ten or eleven, waiting for him? And when he came back I tried to stop him smashing things up, but he wouldn't listen." A catch in her voice, and in that moment, just for an instant, Carolee softened again. "And he wouldn't come. Believe me, I tried"—and here was Cindy with the teapot nestled in its cozy—"I tried so hard I had bruises up and down my arm for a week after. But he wouldn't listen. And he wouldn't come."

Now, in the kitchen, with the birds at the feeder and the newspaper folded down flat on the table, Sten felt nothing but anger. Carey was dead, the gangs had taken over, there'd be beheadings next, corpses hanging from the bridges like in Tijuana, the forests lost and all hope of peace and tranquility flown out the window, and all she did was tack up a checklist of questions, as if she cared, and then went back to her crossword. "Annelid," he said, snapping out the syllables as if each one had a flail attached to it. "Seven letters for earthworm."

"Oh, Sten," she said, shaking her head side to side. "I know, I know. I'm just worried, that's all. Where is he, that's what I want to know—"

"He's at the funeral home. Or the morgue."

"Maybe we should call Cody's parents—maybe he's with Cody."

"I'm talking about *Carey*. Carey Bachman. He's at the morgue. Can't you get that through your head?"

It was a pointless conversation and it ended, as if at the bell between rounds in a prizefight, with the ringing of the telephone, which happened to coincide with the feverish buzz of the cell in his pocket. He was the ex-principal, the ex-Marine. He was the hero. The one they gave the thumbs-up to and bought unwanted drinks for. And now they were calling to see what they should do, everybody, the whole town buzzing and stirred-up and scared, and they would keep on calling through the rest of the morning and on into the afternoon.

22.

THE MEETING—THERE HAD to be a meeting—was scheduled for seven the next night in the high school auditorium, Gordon Welch presiding. Over two hundred people showed up. The initial meeting, the one that got Take Back Our Forests off the ground, had been held in Gordon's den (his man cave, as he liked to call it, with a kind of rote obnoxiousness he seemed not even dimly aware of), and there were exactly eight people in attendance, all male but for Susan Burton, who owned the coffee shop on Main Street and who supported any and all causes that had to do with salvation, whether of stray cats, Romanian orphans or the land we trod, the water we drank and the air we breathed. As Sten remembered it, they talked a whole lot of nothing for two solid hours, Carey giving speeches and Gordon taking over when he ran out of breath, the stuffed heads of big-game animals from three continents staring incongruously down on them from their vantages on the paneled walls. Sten wasn't exactly sure what a kudu was, but he had a feeling that the one with the twisted black horns must have been a kudu—or was that a sable?—and couldn't help wondering how the Burnsides would feel about its presence there amongst them. But the Burnsides weren't there. And neither was Carolee.

What was resolved? The color of the T-shirts they were going to give out at the coffee shop by way of drumming up support and the configuration of the Take Back Our Forests logo that would grace the breast pocket and the back too (a clever melding of the letters *T, B, O* and *F* to represent a tree-spiked hillside Carey had devised with the aid of Photoshop). And a vague promise of future meetings, a letter-writing campaign and the involvement of law enforcement. There was no urgency. They were operating on rumors. On the sightings of Mexicans at the supermarket and the hardware store. On statistics. The only real evidence was the dead zones the growers had left behind, to which Sten was an eyewitness and said as much.

But this was different. Now Carey was dead, shot down and murdered, and people were out for blood. If it felt strange walking down the corridor and stepping into the auditorium, Carolee on his arm, Sten tried not to show it. He'd been back a few times since he retired, easing the transition for the new man, John Reilly, clearing out his things, saying his goodbyes after a lifetime, but here he was in the very auditorium where he'd called so many meetings and assemblies himself, where he'd been in charge and was in charge no longer. That was all right with him. He was fine with that. He was here to bear witness and lend his stature to the moment and the cause and whatever was to come. They were not vigilantes, that was the thing to remember, and that was what he was going to emphasize when it was his turn to speak because he knew where violence took you, knew better than most, and if he thought of Carey he thought of that day in the car and the rage that had come over him. Whether the man with the gun had been guilty or not, he'd been ready to take him on, ready to snap, a heartbeat away—it was the Mexican who had the sense, who was cool enough to suss out the situation and back down. For the moment. But then he was out there still, wasn't he?

John Reilly brought the meeting to order and said a few words about Carey, about how much he was loved and how much he would be missed—clichés, but necessary clichés, the very same ones that had been on his own lips through all the afternoons and early evenings he'd had to preside over public chest-barings like this, the accumulated grief, juniors and seniors struck down in auto accidents, a girl with a sweet teardrop face who played the violin dead of leukemia, colleagues gone in an eyeblink. This was for the students, who were sober-faced and attentive for a change, the first three rows congested with them, shining with them, their heads glossy with reflected light. Their parents and the rest of the townspeople filled the rows behind them, their faces anything but sober. They looked angry, vengeful, looked like vigilantes. He saw that Carey's widow, Sandra, wasn't there, her grief too raw and unconstrained to make a public show of it, and that was a small mercy. This wasn't a memorial. That would come at the funeral home later in the week, as soon as forensics did what they had to do and released the body. Carolee would send a card and they'd be there, both of them. He'd be expected to say words and he would, the same words John Reilly was saying now.

Next was Gordon. He wore a suit and tie, his dyed hair left gray at the temples by way of lending him gravitas—he was a banker after all, and Sten didn't grudge him the artificial touches, though he was something of an attitudinizing ass and tended to think a little too much of himself. What he talked about, and he was shrewd enough to keep it brief this time, was the ecology. The resources the north country had been blessed with—timber, water, fish and game—and how they belonged equally to all citizens, rich and poor. They were our legacy and they had to be preserved, for the generation sitting here tonight and the generations to come. Right before he sat down, he delivered the kicker: "And we're not going to let anybody take them away from us— not the criminals or their gangs or anybody else." The applause was thunderous.

Sten was up next and he was to be followed by the real draw of the night, Rob Rankin, the county sheriff, who was going to have to do a whole lot of explaining and lay down a soft smooth wrinkleless carpet of reassurances. And then take questions. Which, judging from the mood of the crowd, could be an occasion for some real bloodletting. At any rate, Sten took the podium to a groundswell of applause and after eulogizing Carey in a way he hoped went beyond the usual—Carey truly cared, not just about the environment but about democracy and the legacy we were leaving our children, and he'd actually gone out and done something about it, patrolling the woods to make us all safer—and then reminded everybody present that nothing had been established yet aside from the fact that whoever had committed this crime was armed and dangerous and not to be trifled with. The sheriff was doing his best to identify the perpetrators and bring them to justice. In the meanwhile, it was imperative—he'd actually dredged up and dusted off the word, his officialese come back to him like a second language—that everybody just stay calm.

He'd paused at that point and gazed out on the crowd. "We are not vigilantes," he said, "and we are not going to fly off the handle and take matters into our own hands because that'll do nobody any good, least of all Carey Bachman. Respect him. Respect his memory." Another pause. Nobody believed him, he could see that. *Senior Citizen Kills Tour Thug.* All right. He'd done his best. He wasn't principal, he wasn't mayor, he wasn't the sheriff. What he was was an American citizen, a *senior* citizen, and he felt immeasurably tired all of a sudden. The auditorium seemed to swell and recede. His back ached. He felt a headache coming on. The thing was, everything just seemed so hopeless, so utterly, blackly, irremediably hopeless.

"And now," he said, his voice echoing in that acoustic desert till it came back to him as the last desperate gasp of a man withering under the sun that wasn't the sun at all but the 1,500-watt theatrical spotlight installed by Rainier Holcomb, the deaf electrician, now dead, under Sten's own mandate, "I'll hand the mike over to Sheriff Rankin." He nodded at the radiant bald head and glittering badge of the loose-limbed man in uniform sitting amongst the twelfth graders in the front row. "Who'll say a few words and then take your questions." Then, gathering himself up, he went on back to find his seat beside Carolee.

The rest turned into a kind of drowsy meditation, the auditorium overheated, the sheriff droning on in a sleepwalker's voice, the questioners by turns timid and outraged but performing their roles just exactly as expected, *Should we keep our doors locked? Is it safe to be out at night? Why don't you arrest them at the supermarket, tell me that? You want perpetrators, I'll show you perpetrators!* Twice he felt the sharp reminder of Carolee's index finger probing his ribs and realized he'd drifted off, an embarrassment at any time but doubly so now, here in the high school auditorium with Carey dead and people looking to him to provide guidance and support. Problem was, he didn't want to provide guidance and support. He just wanted to go home. To bed.

Finally, as things were winding down—the sheriff had been asked the same question for the sixth or seventh time and gave the same tired answer, to wit, "We'll know more when the facts are in," and somebody said, "So you don't advise going out in the woods right now, for any purpose?" and the sheriff said, "No, not really, not until we clear this thing up"—Sten felt himself come awake in a way he'd never been awake before, as if he was an animal seized in the jaws of a bigger animal and shaken helplessly. *The woods. Out in the woods.* He'd actually placed a call to Cody Waters' parents—yesterday, with Carolee fretting and all the shit raining down around them—and got Cody's cellphone number and gone outside where she wouldn't hear and punched it in. A voice answered—"*Digame*"—and he thought he had the wrong number but persisted anyway. "Cody?" he'd said. "Is that you?"

"Who's this?"

"Sten. Adam's father?"

A silence. Then, "Yeah?"

"Was that Spanish you were talking?

"I guess."

Another silence.

"Listen, I was calling because I wanted to ask if you've seen Adam lately. You know he moved out of the house by the river, right?"

"Yeah, I guess."

"We just, well we haven't heard from him and we were won-dering if maybe he was up there with you—"

"No, no, he's not here. I haven't seen him in like a month maybe."

There was static on the line, a faint sizzling in the background. "Did he say what his plans were? Where he's living?"

He could picture the boy on the other end of the line, the sharp slash of his nose, the sloped shoulders and Don't-Even-Ask look, the dreadlocks he and Adam used to wear before they gave up reggae for rap and then death metal and shaved their heads, before they went military and developed attitudes and started pushing the buttons of the police and everybody else too. When they were kids. Just kids.

A sigh. The sizzle of static. "I don't know," Cody said finally. "In the woods, I guess."

23.

THERE ARE THE NAMELESS fears and there are the named ones too. When he was a child his nightmares weren't of ghouls or monsters or people chasing him with knives and axes and decapitated heads, but amorphous things, neither human nor animal, the fear that sat in your stomach, inside you, and you couldn't define it or shake it either. That was what this was like. He didn't say a word to Carolee, but the morning after the meeting he was up early, earlier than usual—first light—and he didn't bother with breakfast because if he started fussing around in the kitchen she'd wake up and ask him where he was going and he'd just have to lie to her. His daypack—water in a bota bag, granola bars, binoculars, Swiss Army knife, matches stuffed in a plastic pill container to keep them dry, foil space blanket and GPS beacon for emergencies—was hanging on the coat tree where he always put it when he came in from one of his surveillance hikes. He pulled on a baseball cap—Oakland A's, how about that?—patted down his pockets to make sure he had his wallet, keys and cellphone, and then headed out the door.

He drove up the north road, slowly, rolling over pinecones, fist-sized rocks, sticks and twigs and scraps of vegetation that had been pulverized by the tires of the emergency vehicles, looking for the spot where it had happened. Art had told him it was by the spring up there, no more than a thousand yards off the road, just follow the creek on up and you can't miss it. Well, he couldn't have missed it anyway because the tracks of the ambulance and the sheriff's four-wheel drive came together there, crosshatching the road where they'd had to make their three-point turns to return with the body and whatever evidence they'd discovered. Which thus far was being kept secret. He'd tried to get Rob Rankin to tell him but Rob just shook his head. "Can't disclose that. Sorry, Sten. Ongoing investigation."

There would have been shell casings. And the bullets themselves, the ones they dug out of Carey's dead flesh. That would have been something, at least. But what he wondered—and here he was, following a wide beaten path uphill through the bracken at the feet of the trees, the morning still, nothing moving and nothing sounding off, not even birds—was just what caliber those casings and bullets had turned out to be. Were they from a handgun? A revolver? An old wood-grip .38 or .45 some scoop-faced son of a bitch kept tucked in his waistband like a Hollywood cliché? *Badges? We don't need no stinking badges.* Or something else. Something else altogether.

The only sound was the trickle of the stream, no wind in the trees and that eerie absence of birdcall, as if the place had been poisoned, as if the Zetas were just over the next rise with their human mules and their booby traps and their carbofuran. He never had found out what happened that day when they'd lost sight of the white truck and Carey phoned 911—there was nothing in the paper and he could only assume the Mexicans had gone off on a side road somewhere and waited an hour or two before doubling back. It was nothing to the cops. They had a whole lot on their hands and if every 911 call about people brandishing weapons didn't have a scripted ending, so much the worse. But it was quiet. Too quiet. Quieter than any forest he could remember. He pricked up his senses. The air was damp with a funk of rot, of moss and mold and things breaking down, and underneath it the smell of water bubbling up out of some dark place. He forced himself to move slowly, step by step, studying the shadows where they deepened in clots of vegetation, listening hard, as if the perpetrators would be anywhere within ten miles of here—what did he think, they were going to kill somebody and then come back and lick the blood off the rocks? After a moment he went down on one knee to peer into the stream and see if he could detect any life there, nymphs, water boatmen, minnows as dull and gray and natural in these waters as the brick-red platys were in theirs. The water was pellucid. He saw nothing, not even a water strider.

He continued on up, the trees standing silent, the bushes increasingly beaten down and the ground raked over as he came closer to the dun scallop of rock where the spring emerged from the side of the mountain. There was a tree down just in front of the pool the spring made, cover for anyone lying in ambush, but then why would there be an ambush in this place? There was no plantation here, that was obvious. The trees were dense, closed in, the sunshine minimal. It was a water source, of course—they needed water, and they were known to divert whole streams as well as run drip lines hundreds of yards out into their makeshift clearings where they'd sacrificed the trees for the greater good of profit and criminality. What if—and he was speculating now—Carey had come upon a couple of them checking out the location or even laying out plastic tubing to take the water down to the road, to a catchment there or a tank in the back of a brand-new white Ford XLT pickup with all-terrain tires?

But no, that didn't make any sense. They wouldn't have shot him—that would only bring attention to themselves, bring the heat. They might have cursed, might have made a crude gesture or two and spat out a garble of Spanish and English—Spanglish—to proclaim their innocence, *We are hikers, señor, only hikers,* and then gone on their way. To avoid the confrontation the way they had the day he and Carey had followed them to a standstill. They didn't want to kill anybody, not unless someone got too close to the growing operation, either by design or accident, and even then the better part of them—the mules—would just melt away into the undergrowth when the DEA or the sheriff's department pulled a raid. Who wanted to be a hero? Who wanted the attention?

No, that wasn't the answer, that wasn't the answer at all. He was standing there on the very rock, the smooth clean water-burnished slab of granite where they'd found the body—the chalk marks there still—and if he was studying the grain of the rock for bloodstains it wasn't out of idle curiosity or morbidity or even a desire to mourn a friend. There was a mystery here, a puzzle he had to solve for himself before Rob Rankin and his forensics team did, and it was tied up with that fear, the nameless fear that was mutating now into a named fear, named and punishing and inadmissible.

Suddenly, and he didn't quite know why, he was calling out his son's name. "Adam?" he shouted, obliterating the silence. "Adam, are you out there?"

PART VIII

Ukiah

24.

SO ADAM WAS GONE. Adam was crazy and Adam was gone. That hurt. It did. Hurt her more than she would ever admit, not even to Christabel, and Christabel was there for her, sitting over her strawberry margarita with a long face saying, "You want to talk about it?" They were at Casa Carlos in Ukiah, Friday night, a month after Adam knocked her down, trashed the house and kept on trashing it till she thought he was going to hammer his way right on through the walls. She was crying that night. She'd tried to stop him, tried to bring him back up the hill where they could settle in and be like they were before, but he wouldn't listen to her and he wouldn't stop either. She screamed his name, screamed it over and over, the shock and confusion wadded in her throat till she thought she was going to choke on it, and then she cursed him, stood out in the dark yard and cursed him to the tone-deaf clank and clatter of things breaking, shattering, falling to pieces. Crying still, she'd put Kutya in the car, started up the engine and swung round in the driveway. "You son of a bitch!" she shouted out the window. "You shit! I hope you die and rot in hell!" Then she put the car in gear and drove on up the hill, listening to Hank Williams, only Hank, and crying in harsh hot jags that took the breath right out of her body.

She didn't tell Christabel any of that—that was personal. Personal even from her. What she did tell her was that they'd had a fight—Adam was upset because they had to move out and he started taking it out on her—and that it was over, or probably over, ninety-nine and a half percent sure if you wanted to figure the odds. And what did Christabel say? "I don't see what you saw in him, anyway." She'd paused to blow out smoke. "Except his bod. But he was trouble with a capital *T* and don't you try to deny it."

Now, in one of the dark booths along the back wall where the black velvet tapestry of Selena hung beside one of a snorting bull in a shadowy arena clotted with even shadowier faces, with the candle guttering in its rippled glass urn and the corny Mexican music tweedle-deeing through the speakers in a sad travesty of normalcy and joy, she felt like crying all over again. That, and getting drunk. They were already on their second pitcher, the remains of her beef enchilada and Christabel's macho burrito congealing in grease on the plates before them—she really did have to start eating healthier and she made a promise to herself in that moment, albeit a drunken promise, to start tomorrow—and things had begun to blur a bit.

"I mean, beyond the sex," Christabel said, her fluffed-up hair and the candlelight giving her a weird Halloweeny look, "what did he ever do for you? Did he contribute? Pay for anything?"

"I don't want to talk about it," she said. But she did. And in the next breath she said, "He could be so funny."

"Right. Like that night he sat down to dinner buck naked—"

And then they were both laughing and she picked up the pitcher and topped off their glasses, the frothy pink confection like something a child would lap up, cotton candy made liquid, but it packed a punch, no doubt about that. Plus, she was driving because Christabel's pickup was in the shop with some mysterious ailment that was probably nothing but would cost five hundred, minimum, of that she could be sure. The way mechanics took advantage of women, especially single women, was another kind of disgrace, as if things weren't bad enough already . . .

The bill came. They divided it up and left a two-dollar tip on a thirty-six dollar charge because when you really thought about it the service was lousy and the food worse and the decor right out of a Tijuana whorehouse, and so what if the waiter gave them a dirty look when they were going out the door, he could go fuck himself, they could all go fuck themselves. Right. And then they were on the street, the air cool on her bare arms, September nearly gone already and October coming on, time dragging you through the year as if it had hooks on it, one holiday after another, Memorial Day, Flag Day, Fourth of July, Labor Day, and then the big ones, Halloween, Thanksgiving, Christmas, New Year's, and all of it in service of what? Shopping. Spend, spend, spend. Make the corporations that much richer and the people that much poorer. Really, the only way to get off that wheel was to drop out and she'd told Christabel that till she was blue in the face, explained it over and over, patiently, in detail, and still she didn't get it. Or wouldn't.

Jerry Kane got it. And Jerry Kane died for it. He just got fed up to the point where quoting the UCC code and declaring his status to whatever Fascist disguised as a policeman just didn't cut it anymore and so he took up arms because they gave him no choice. The final straw, or the next-to-final straw, was when they arrested him in Carrizo, New Mexico, at what he called on his radio show a "Nazi checkpoint, show me your papers, Heil Hitler," a checkpoint set up for the sole purpose of harassing citizens, both natural-born and slave-state, and, of course, extracting money from them, moola, hard cash, as if they were anything more than just roadside bandits out of the old time, the lawless time when you protected yourself and your own and lived free. It wasn't any different from what happened to her. They stopped him for no reason except that they had the guns and demanded his papers and when he refused to enter into a contract with them they hauled him off to jail under threat, duress and coercion and what he did was file a counterclaim alleging kidnapping and extortion against the arresting officers and the justice of the so-called peace of the so-called court. And then, two months later, he was on his way back from one of his seminars in Vegas to his home in Florida, and it happened all over again, and who could blame him if he just turned around and defended himself from fraud, malice and yes, *kidnapping*. Yet again.

He'd had enough. And when the two cops came up to the white van that was his own personal property on one of the highways and byways guaranteed for free and unencumbered access under the Uniform Commercial Code, he started shooting. West Memphis, Arkansas, Crittenden County. Two oppressors shot dead. But that wasn't enough because the cops tracked Jerry Kane and his son to that Walmart parking lot and two more cops went down in a shitstorm of bullets and Jerry Kane and his sixteen-year-old son gave up their lives for it. For what? For seatbelts? For *papers*?

"Uh, Sara—Sara, earth to Sara?"

It was cold. She was rubbing her arms on the street that was all but deserted and the neon sign out front of Casa Carlos was like icing on a frozen cake and Christabel was standing there beside her trying to be funny. "Yeah," she said. "Okay, okay."

Then they were walking to her car, the sound of their heels like gunshots echoing out into the night and the traffic lights going red and green and red again and nobody there to know or care and Christabel was saying, "You going to be all right to drive?" and she was saying, "Don't worry about me, I'm fine."

So she drove back to Willits on the road she could have driven blind and dropped Christabel off, a few pairs of headlights coming at her, nothing really. She was minding her own business and thinking ahead to Kutya and how he would have been missing her and holding his pee because he was the best-trained dog in the world and totally considerate of her, and if things seemed a bit blurrier than usual, that was all right, that was because it was dark and getting darker and she was sticking to back roads only now, taking a circuitous route home in the event there were any clowns in cop uniforms out there on the main road looking to harass, detain and rob people traveling in their own personal property to their own personal residence. Route 20, that was what she wanted

to avoid, and she did, cutting a big rectangle or maybe a trape-
zoid around it, twice having to back up and pull U-turns because
she somehow wound up on dead-end streets. But Route 20 was
where she had to go at some point if she was going to get home,
and finally, after having circumvented—or rectangavented—the
intersection at South Main, she found herself out on the darkened
highway at something like eleven o'clock at night. Minding. Her.
Own. Business.

And then it all started over again, as if she were caught in a
time warp. One whoop, then the lights flashing in the rearview.
The shoulder of the road, the narrow view out the windshield.
The sounds: bugs in the grass, the overzealous roar of the cruiser's
engine straining even in neutral, the declamatory tattoo of the
officer's boots first on the pavement and then on the tired dirt
strip of the shoulder. The lady cop, the very one, bloodless, thin
as a post, no lipstick, and something like joy in her eyes. The
flashlight. The commands, *License and registration, Proof of insurance, Step out of the car,* and the same answers, or answer: "I have
no contract with you."

But they had the guns. They had the handcuffs. And they had
their way with her.

25.

THIS TIME SHE HAD to spend the night—in the drunk tank—with two other women, both in their twenties and both as dumb as boards and so polluted they couldn't have stood up straight let alone driven an automobile, while she—she herself—was hardly drunk at all, and no, she wasn't going to get out of the car and no, she wasn't going to breathe into the Breathalyzer or stand on one leg or touch her fingertips to her nose or anything else. And why? Because SHE DID NOT HAVE A CONTRACT WITH THE REPUBLIC OF CALIFORNIA. And never would have. They could hang her, she didn't care. But Kutya, poor Kutya, he was the one that had to suffer, just like the last time. He wasn't in the Animal Control, but he was locked in the house and his bladder must have been bursting and what a trial of his conscience and all his training to have to go into the kitchen and take a sad guilty dribbling pee on the linoleum there. Where it would puddle. And stink. And dry up in a stain that would eat through the wax and take some real elbow grease to get out.

The judge was unsympathetic, a dried-up old bitch who looked as if her hair had been glued on. The bail money was doubled this time because of her failure to appear on the previous charge, and since Christabel didn't have the money she'd had to go to a bail bondsman at an interest rate that would have put countries like Greece and Spain right under. Then there was the same charade at the impound yard, more bucks out the window, and she had to dig into her super-secret savings fund, the money she'd got when she and Roger split up and he bought out her interest in the house, money she'd told herself she'd never touch because it was going to be a down payment someday on a house all her own—once she'd saved up enough on top of that to meet the piratical amount they wanted because the banks hadn't got done raping America yet.

She paid off Mary Ellis at the impound yard, Mary too embarrassed to even mention the fact that this was the second time around and too much of a slave of the system to do anything more than just take the cashier's check with a face carved out of lead and stamp her receipt. As far as the bail bond was concerned, she couldn't leave Christabel hanging with that, so she took out the full amount to give her, five thousand dollars, because she had no intention of showing up for her court date. They'd got Jerry Kane, but they weren't going to get her, never again.

What she was thinking was that the Republic of California was a place in which she no longer wanted to reside. It was the ultimate nanny state, everything you did short of drawing breath regulated through the roof, a list of no's half a mile long posted on every street corner and the entrance to every park in the state. You couldn't smoke on the street. Couldn't park overnight, couldn't pay your toll in cash on the Golden Gate Bridge, couldn't buy something on the internet without the sales tax Nazis coming after you. You couldn't even start a fire in your own woodstove or natural stone fireplace on a cold and damp and nasty winter's day down in Visalia, where she'd lived with Roger through her unenlightened years, lest you run afoul of the air-quality control board, and don't think you can sneak around the regulations because you've got a whole squadron of snitches and tattletales living right next door and across the street to report you out of sour grapes because they're too whipped and beaten down to start up their own pathetic little fires.

No, what she was thinking was Nevada. Maybe Stateline. Anything goes in Nevada and if she found a place in Stateline she'd be within striking distance of all those rich yuppies in Lake Tahoe, who all had horses that needed regular shoeing and TLC like horses anywhere. Or maybe Kingman, in Arizona. She'd been there once, just passing through but also to visit the funky little trailer court on old Route 66 there as a kind of pilgrimage, because that was where Timothy McVeigh had lived before he met Terry Nichols. Now *there* was a soldier, there was somebody who wasn't going to take it anymore. Though maybe that was a bit extreme. She wasn't violent herself and didn't really believe in it and whenever his name came up she had to admit that maybe he had gone too far—she couldn't see taking lives, though you could hardly call them *innocent*. Live and let live, right? Unless they keep on kidnapping you, keep on regulating you, keep on sticking their hands deeper and deeper into your pockets until you've got no pockets left.

Anyway, she entered into a contract with the court (TDC), picked up her car and drove home, where the poor dog ran and hid under the bed because of what he'd had no choice but to do on the kitchen floor, and that just made her all the more crazy. The subsidiary effects. They never thought of that. Never thought of what innocent creatures—truly innocent—they were torturing with their seatbelt laws and their drunk-but-not-drunk-enough nighttime patrols when anybody who wasn't already asleep wouldn't have given two shits if the streets were flowing with Cuervo Gold. But enough. She must have spent half an hour just standing there in her own kitchen, looking down on that piss stain on the floor, before finally she got down on her hands and knees and wiped it up, and then, because she wasn't herself—she was trembling, actually trembling, she was so upset—she got out the mop, the bucket and the plastic bottle of Mop & Glo and redid the whole kitchen, just to take her mind off things.

She was just finishing up when her cell rang. It was Christabel.

"Just checking in," Christabel said. "You all right?"

"I'm not hungover, if that's what you mean. I wasn't even buzzed last night. Not when they pulled me over. I mean, we did eat, didn't we?"

"I feel so bad."

"Bad? Why should you feel bad? The one that ought to feel bad is me. And the System. The System ought to feel bad, so bad it just rots from the inside out."

"What I mean is, I should have been driving. I should never have let you, I mean, with what happened with the police last time around—"

She could hear Christabel breathing on the other end of the line, a series of deep, wet, patient breaths that were like a sedative. She could feel herself calming down. Christabel. Her best friend. Where would she be without her? "Don't worry about me," she said.

"Well, I am worried."

"They can't touch me."

"What are you talking about, Sara—they've locked you up twice in the last, what, two months now?"

"What I'm talking about is I'm not going to be around, I'm out of here—I've had it, Christa, I really have—"

"Please don't tell me you're going to be like this again. If you skip out on this—"

"Don't worry, I've got the money, I'm not going to burn you."

"If you skip out they're going to put you in jail, don't you realize that? Don't you get it? And not just for an hour or overnight either."

She began to realize that on top of everything else the conversation was making her extremely unhappy, this conversation, even if it was with her best friend, even if Christabel only wanted to make her feel better, but she wasn't making her feel better and maybe that was why she couldn't help snapping at her. "So what are you now, a legal expert?"

"Oh, come off it, Sara—it's just common sense."

"Sure, and what do you know? You're just a slave like all the rest of them. If you'd just read your Fourteenth Amendment, just *read* it—"

"*Sara*—"

And then she was quoting, from memory, because she was rankled and riled and she had to do something, " 'No state shall make or enforce any law which shall abridge the privileges or immunities of citizens of the United States; nor shall any State deprive any person of life, liberty, or property, without due process of law; nor deny to any person within its jurisdiction the equal protection of the laws.' You want me to go on?"

Nothing.

"Because I will. Because that right there is the essence of it, when the states gave up their rights and made all freemen on the land into federal citizens and then along comes the Social Security Act, surprise, to establish accounts in debit on every one of us, not to mention Roosevelt taking us off the gold standard—"

"Sara! Sara, listen, will you?" And here was Christa shouting at her, actually shouting at her because she didn't want to hear the truth and never had. "Sara, I haven't got time for this. I'm sorry. I got to go."

"Yeah," she said, and if her voice was bitter right down to the dregs, so what? "I got to go too."

26.

SHE WAS AT THE stove two days later, making a pot of low-cal chicken vegetable soup (tenders sautéed in safflower oil with garlic and onions, chicken stock, zucchini, tomatoes and snow peas from her garden), late afternoon, a glass of zinfandel on the counter beside her, everything as still as still can be. Kutya was asleep on the floor, in the cool place by the sink. A faint breeze, just the breath of one, came in through the screen windows. Quartering the tomatoes and dicing the zucchini, occasionally taking a sip of wine and gazing idly out the window to where the hummingbirds were buzzing each other off the feeder, she felt herself easing into a kind of waking dream, and wasn't this the way life was supposed to be? No worries. Just living in the moment. Normally she would have been listening to the radio, but she'd spun through the dial twice and there was nothing but crap on—classical, with the stick-up-the-ass announcers who sounded as if they'd had all their blood drained out of them the minute they turned the microphone on; Mexican talk; Mexican music; Mexican car ads; classic rock with the same playlist they'd been rehashing for the last half century and, if you didn't like that, the alt rock that was such crap even the musicians' mothers couldn't take it—and so she was listening to the house breathing around her, to the jay outside the window and the neat controlled tap and release of the blade on the cutting board.

She hadn't heard from Christabel since the night before last, since their fight, if you could call it that, but what best friends didn't fight once in a while? You weren't really close with somebody unless you could let it all hang out—that was what intimacy was all about, going deep, getting under each other's skin, taking the good with the bad. That was what she was thinking, elevating the edge of the cutting board now to guide the zucchini and tomatoes into the pot and wondering if she had any mushrooms left in the refrigerator because mushrooms would give the soup a little more density and add a nice subtle flavor—the creminis, the chewy ones—when the strangest feeling came over her, almost as if a ghost had materialized in the room behind her, and that was even stranger, because she didn't believe in ghosts. She believed in graves, six feet down, and the spirit trapped in the body. That rotted.

Still, she couldn't help turning her head to look over her shoulder as the steam from the pot rose around her and the garlic sent up its aroma to sweeten the room, but there was nothing there. The strangest thing—she'd have to tell Christabel about it. To the refrigerator—yes, there were the creminis—and then to the sink to rinse them and again to the cutting board. Then the feeling came back, stronger now, and she turned around again and there he was, Adam, standing in the doorway, arms akimbo, trying to smile. "Adam," she said, naming him, just that, but she was soaring inside.

He was in his fatigues, the knife strapped at his side, his boots scuffed, his face and scalp tanned as deeply as any lifeguard's. Behind him, in the hallway that led to the living room, she could see the dark mound of his discarded pack and the thin shadow of the rifle leaning up against the wall. The dog, too lazy and spoiled to do his job properly, lifted his head suddenly, gave a soft woof and trotted over to him. Adam hadn't moved or said a word, but now he reached behind him, ignoring Kutya, who was wagging his tail in recognition and sniffing at his pantleg, and produced a plastic Ziploc bag that seemed to contain a dark smear of something that might have been chocolate but wasn't. "I got the shits," he announced.

She was going to ask if he was hungry, if he wanted a glass of wine, if he'd been out there camping in the woods all this time (the answer to that was obvious, just from a glance at him), but instead she said, "You need Pepto-Bismol? I've got those little pink tabs, I think, and maybe a bottle too." She looked at him dubiously. His pants were stained. He'd lost weight. She could smell him from all the way across the room.

He didn't answer, just repeated himself: "I got the shits."

"Or maybe something stronger? Imodium? I think I might have some in the medicine cabinet . . ." And she started for the bathroom but he just reached out and grabbed hold of her in his arms that were like steel cables and pressed her to him, hard, so hard it was as if he never wanted to let go, and then he was kissing her, the plastic bag flapping behind her so that she could feel the inflexible zippered edge of it digging into her where her pants pulled away from her blouse, and she held on to him just as tightly and kissed him back with everything she had.

Later, after she'd put his clothes in the wash—and whatever else he had in his backpack, another set of fatigues, crusted socks, undershorts that looked as if they'd been used to swab out a latrine—and left him alone in the shower with a bar of soap and a bottle of shampoo, she went to the pantry to dig out the egg noodles and sprinkle them over the pot where it was simmering on the stove so he could get something more substantial than diet veggie soup in him. As for the shampoo, he'd looked at it as if he didn't know what it was—somehow, even out there in the woods, even while suffering diarrhea (giardia, that was what he insisted it was), he'd managed to keep his head shaved, and his face too. She'd even teased him about it as he stepped out of his clothes and handed them to her, saying, "I thought mountain men were allowed to grow beards," but he didn't respond because there was a whole lot else going on inside his head right then with his body full of parasites and the thinness of him and just the simple basic need of a good hot shower, but he did give her his partway grin and he was hard, hard right there before her, and he let her reach out a hand to his cock and give it a friendly tug before he shut the door and stepped into the shower.

Once he'd had his shower, he strolled into the kitchen and sat down at the table as if he'd been doing it every day of his life, grinning his strained grin and saying he was hungry enough to eat a hog or maybe a dog and they both looked at Kutya and burst out laughing. He was wearing her terrycloth robe and nothing else and it rode halfway up his arms and bunched in the shoulders. It was blue and it brought out the blue of his eyes, which was a nice contrast (she'd almost said pretty, or thought it) with his suntanned skin. The first thing he did, right off, was drink two beers, hardly pausing for breath, and then he had a glass of water and washed down a palmful of Imodium tabs. "Cool," he said. "Niiiice," drawing it out till the final *c* was like air hissing out of a balloon. He gave her a long penetrating look, his lips glistening with the water, half of which he'd spilled down the front of the robe. From the look he was giving her she'd expected him to say something suggestive, but he didn't. "You got anything hard?" is what he said then. Or asked.

She was at the stove, stirring the soup, which was just about ready, and she set down the spoon, crossed the room to him and took hold of his arm, just above the rolled-up sleeve, and said, "Yeah, I've got you."

But he stared right through her as if he hadn't processed that at all, and she supposed he hadn't, because he was Adam, no different from how he was a month ago, right there with you one minute and gone off the next. What he said was, "'Cause I'm all out of one fifty-one."

So she poured him a glass of bourbon and he threw that down like a cowboy in one of the flickering westerns the old movie channel showed every other night. "More?" she asked, but the bottle was back on the counter behind her and she thought maybe he'd had enough, especially considering the purpose she had in mind once they'd finished supper and retired to the bedroom.

He held out the glass.

"Sure you don't want to eat first? Put something on your stomach?"

Well, he didn't. Or not yet, anyway. There was the glass framed in his hand, the nails dirty still despite the shower, half-moons of dirt worked in under them and up under the cuticles too, and she wondered if he'd sit still for a manicure at some point. She swung away to retrieve the bottle and poured for him, the neck kissing the glass, and when she tried to tip it back he just held her hand till the glass was full. "If you're going to party," she murmured, leaning into him so he could feel the weight of her against him, feel her heat and how much she wanted him and how glad she was that he was back, communication of the flesh and communion too, "then I'm going to pour myself another glass of wine."

He'd always had a good appetite, burning up calories by the thousands out there in the woods keeping himself like a rock, but he outdid himself this time. He ate as if he was half-starved, and considering the problem he was having, she supposed he was, most of whatever he'd been eating probably going right through him. She made him a sandwich—smoked turkey and cheddar on brown bread, with mustard, mayo, fresh-sliced tomato and let-tuce from the garden—and that was gone by the time he started on his second bowl of soup so she made him another one. If she didn't eat a whole lot herself that night it was because she was watching him, this miracle of dynamic energy and concentrated movement that had blown back into her life, and because she was being careful about her weight and had to pick around the egg noodles. She did have three glasses of wine, though, and that made her feel as if she were floating free right along with him.

What did they talk about? Nothing much (thanks, Christa, for asking)—the woods, which for all she could get out of him, seemed to be full of trees; her latest victimization by the System; Stateline, Nevada, and Tahoe, did he like Tahoe? And giardia, of course. Giardia and shit. There was a cherry pie she'd bought in a moment of weakness yesterday and she set that out in front of him, and he seemed interested, but then the stomach pains got to

him and he disappeared into the bathroom. After a moment she
pushed the pie away from her so as to resist temptation but then
slid it back and had just the tiniest sliver, licking the sweet con-
gealed cherry filling off her fingers before getting up to put on a
CD and start cleaning up.

He was in there forever, doing what she couldn't imagine,
though it came to her that he was maybe just slumped over the
toilet, in real pain, and she was remembering that time in Mexico
with Roger when she'd got the *turista* and felt as though somebody was alternately running a screwdriver through her and
pumping her gut full of swamp gas. When he did emerge, finally,
he was naked and dripping with water from the shower, his second shower, and he had the Ziploc bag in one hand. Which he
held up in front of his face and shook once or twice to make sure
she was focused on it. "You got to take me to the doctor," he said
in his soft, soft voice, and he wouldn't look at her, as if he was
embarrassed by his own weakness.

"The doctor? I don't know any doctor. And they wouldn't be
open now, anyway."

"The emergency room. They have to like take anybody, right?"

Of course there was the whole rigamarole of insurance and who's
your primary-care doctor and fill out this form and this one too,
but the surprise was that Adam actually had insurance through
his father and they had his name and information in the computer
from a previous visit or visits he'd made, one time apparently after
he'd gotten bloodied in a scuffle at Piero's and another after he'd
driven his car through the fence at the playground, something
he didn't want to talk about but kept mentioning all the time, as
if he'd padlocked it away and couldn't remember the combination. The waiting room was packed to the walls with people who
didn't have health care, illegals, white trash, working stiffs who
couldn't afford rent let alone seeing a doctor because their two-

year-old was vomiting blood. It stank worse than any stable she'd ever been in and she had to thank her lucky stars she'd never been sick or she didn't know what she would do. If things were the way they should be, the way they once were, with freemen on the land associating with each other on a by-need basis, then she could have just bartered with some doctor who kept horses and eliminated the middleman, the tax squeezer and the accountant and the whole shitty bureaucracy that had brought her here tonight. With Adam. Because he had giardia and they really didn't have any other alternative.

They sat there for three and a half hours, him running to the bathroom every ten minutes and her paging through the magazines that were two years out of date and so encrusted with filth she'd be lucky if she didn't get tetanus or something just from touching them, until, finally, they called his name and he went into the back room with the nurse and she watched the clock and got angrier by the minute. Or not angry, exactly. It was more like disappointment. She didn't want to be here with the screaming babies and the old men with the bloody bandages wrapped around their bleached-out skulls and the illegals so sick with whatever it was they were like walking bags of infection. No, she wanted to be home. In her own house. With Kutya. And Adam.

Forty-five minutes more—they had to run his stool sample under the microscope to confirm the diagnosis he'd already made, and yes, it was giardia, very common in these parts, and that was the danger of drinking unchlorinated water, even from the purest-looking mountain stream—and then he was walking right by her in the waiting room as if he didn't recognize her, locked in one of his trances, and she scurried across the room to catch up with him and take him by the arm and lead him out the door and into the parking lot. And that was where things got interesting.

Because there, right in front of them, pulled up neatly to the curb and with its gumball machine idly spinning, was a police cruiser, just sitting there, the engine running and the gasoline the wage slaves had paid for—she'd paid for—cycling through it and spewing out the tailpipe as carbon monoxide to pollute the atmosphere even more than they'd already polluted it. There was no one in the cruiser. No one in sight. And what she was thinking, despite Adam and her hurry to get home, was that a chance had presented itself to her out of nowhere, a chance to get back at them, if not to get even, because she'd never get even. Adam walked right by it, the prescription they'd given him clutched in one hand, the bag of shit in the other, and why he didn't just dump it she didn't know.

"Adam," she called. "Adam!"

He stopped, turned, gave her that maddening look as if he'd never seen her before in his life.

"Why don't you get rid of that bag—there, in the trash receptacle." She'd come up even with him now, the pavement like a dark lake spreading open before them. "Come on," she said, "snap out of it," and he let the bag drop from his fingers, where it would lie undisturbed till the gardeners came in the morning with their rakes and blowers.

"Yeah," he said vaguely. "Okay, yeah."

"Listen," and she pulled in close to him, lowering her voice, "there's something we got to do. It'll take like sixty seconds, that's all. Can you drive?"

He shrugged, an elaborate gesture under the yellow glaze of the streetlamps along the walk. Then he grinned, or tried to. "What you got in mind?"

What she had in mind was very simple, nothing as complex or radical maybe as what a Jerry Kane would have come up with, but a plan nonetheless: she was going to fuck up that cruiser, whether it was the one the lady cop had used to cage her up in or not, and she was going to do it by putting something in the gas tank and destroying the engine so that when the cop came out of the hospital he—or *she*—would be going nowhere. But what? Dirt? Sand? Or no, and now the solution came to her fully formed:

sugar water. It just happened that in the backseat of the car was a present she'd got at the hardware store for Christabel, a kiss-and-make-up present. A hummingbird feeder. Christabel had been commenting on the hummingbirds last time she was over, the two of them sitting out on the porch and watching them hover and feed and shear off again, as greedy as vultures, and when she saw the feeder on sale at the hardware store she bought it and then went home and made up the sugar water, one cup sugar to four cups water, and left the thing in the back of the car so she wouldn't forget it when they got together again.

All right. She didn't know the mechanics of it, but she'd heard this was a good way to really fuck up an engine or maybe even blow it up if that was possible, and why not? They'd screwed her over enough, that was for shit sure. She and Adam had reached her car now and she steadied herself a minute before unlocking the door and handing him the keys. Giving the parking lot a quick scan to be sure no one was watching, she pulled open the back door and reached in back to unscrew the cylinder from the feeder. "Listen," she said, straightening up and looking him in the eye to be sure he was with her, "just start up the car and wait here—just wait, and no craziness now—till I get done with that cop car over there, and then I stroll away and you pull up and we drive out of here, easy as you please."

He got into the car, inserted the key, turned over the engine.

"Then," she said, "we go back home." She paused, leaning in the window to reach out and touch him on the shoulder—she was always touching him, she loved to touch him, to put her imprint on him, her skin to his.

"Cool," he said.

And then she was striding briskly back up the walk, pressing the glass cylinder close to her body on the side away from the hospital with its lights and windows and the patients in their beds there who might or might not be looking out on the parking lot. Anyone seeing her would assume she was going to her car or heading back into the emergency room because she'd just gone out for a breath of air—or a smoke, a verboten smoke—and here was the cruiser, still running, the light atop it still revolving, and she was right there, her fingers working at the metal flap of the gas tank, thinking it must be locked, they'd have to keep it locked or everybody'd be doing this all day long, the shits, the pathetic wasteful cruel inhuman shits, only to find that it was true—it was locked and it wouldn't give. A quick look around: nothing, nobody. The gumball machine chopped up the light. Her heart was pounding. In the next moment she slipped around to the driver's side—gliding, flowing as if she were made of silk—cracked the door and reached in to run her hand over the dash, and where was it, where was the release? On the floor. Yes, on the floor. Then she had it and it gave and she was back around the car again—thirty seconds, that was all it took. And every gurgling ounce of the sugar water, every drop, went home, right into the greedy gullet of that cage on wheels, that tool of the oppressors that was a tool no more.

Let them suck on that. See how they liked it.

Adam was all right behind the wheel—no Dale Earnhardt, but fine just the same. He kept the car between the lines and he didn't go over the speed limit though he couldn't seem to stop laughing. "Just wait," he kept saying, snorting with laughter, "just wait till they, what, go to nail somebody, and the engine seizes up on them. That was great. That was genius."

It was. It was great. She'd gotten her little bit back and she'd got Adam back too. They went home and went to bed and he couldn't get enough of her, hard and hot and sweating in the dark, her man, her beautiful man. He'd missed her. And he didn't have to tell her, not in words, because she could feel it, oh, blessed lord, yes, feel it all night long.

But then—and she wasn't surprised or at least that's what she told herself—she woke to daylight poking through the blinds and the bed was empty and the house too. She didn't have to go out into the hallway and look to see if his pack was there or run barefoot out the back door to watch for him in the field across the way. He was gone and she knew it, vanished like smoke, human smoke, as if he wasn't made of flesh at all. But he was, oh yes—flesh and bone and hard unyielding muscle—and she knew that better than anybody. He should have stayed—she'd wanted him to and would have told him as much if she'd had the chance—but he had his own agenda, doing whatever it was he did out there in the woods.

It wasn't ideal, far from it. She'd rather have him there, rather be making coffee for two instead of one—and eggs and toast and whatever else he wanted. The house felt empty without him, though he'd been in it no more than what, twelve, thirteen hours? It saddened her. Standing at the counter in the kitchen that still vibrated with the aura of him, she poured herself a cup of coffee and gazed out the window to where a hummingbird no bigger than her thumb was sucking sugar water from the feeder through the miniature syringe of its bill, a creature innocent of cops, internal combustion engines, wages, taxes, slavery. A free bird, a free bird on the land. She blew on her coffee to cool it and told herself to be patient—one way or the other he'd get tired of it out there and then he'd be back, she was sure of it.

Just give him time.

PART IX

The Plantation

27.

COLTER DIDN'T HAVE THE shits. They probably didn't even have giardia back then, let alone the little yellow 400 mg metronidazole tablets they gave you to cure it. What they did have was hostiles, thousands of them, maybe hundreds of thousands, though the white race had done their best to bring those numbers down, what with smallpox and gonorrhea and rum, whiskey, vodka and gin. But here they were, the Blackfeet, terminally furious and flinging Potts' bloody genitalia at him, and the only issue was not if but how they were going to put him to death. Braves kept lurching up to him, right in his face, tomahawks drawn, then jerking back again, as if to rattle him, but he kept calm because he saw that some of the higher-ranking ones, the chiefs, had withdrawn a ways to sit around in a circle and think things through. Why be hasty? They had all day, all night, and if he lasted that long, the day after that. He felt his heart sink, though he wouldn't let his face show it. After a while the ululations dropped off and the young braves, the hotheads, held back in deference to their elders, but you could see they were aching for the moment they'd be set free—and gloating too over the prospect of what mold of sport the elders were devising for them.

Naked, with Potts' blood drying on his chest and shoulders, Colter stood rigid, trying to focus his mind. He could make out something of what the elders were saying—some were for the death of a thousand slits, others for making a target out of him so they could improve their aim the way they had with Potts, maybe even take wagers as to which of them could drill him the closest without killing him outright. He had enough of their language to get a sense of all this, but not enough to plead his case—if he was doing anything at that moment it was trying to form the Black-foot words in his head, when only the language of their enemies, the Crows, or Kee-kat-sa, as they called themselves, would rise up out of the depths of his brain, which was, understandably, under a whole lot of stress at the moment.

Finally, one of the chiefs—tall, bleak-faced, with reddened mucousy eyes and skin jerked by the wind and sun—pushed himself up and ambled over to stand face-to-face with him, practically nose-to-nose. Colter could smell him, the tobacco he sucked through his pipe, the sweat of his horse, the dried buffalo meat and pounded meal he'd had for breakfast. They stood like that for a long moment, Colter naked and vulnerable and wanting only to sprout wings and fly on out of there, the hardest thing to keep your back straight and not give in to the impulse to protect your gut—a reflex, really—and guard against a sneak blow that would double you up and leave you gasping in the dirt. "Are you a fast runner?" the chief asked, but Colter didn't understand him, so after a long moment, the chief repeated himself and he got the gist of it. This was hope. A particle of it, anyway. He'd heard of similar situations, in which a tribe would let their captive run for his life so they could have the sport of the chase, like fox and hounds, except that the ground was festooned with prickly pear and the fox had no moccasins to protect his feet and even if he did there was nowhere to escape to or even hide in all that flat deserted plain.

And what did Colter say, in his accent that must have been a kind of insult in itself? "Not really."

The chief bored into him with his rheumy eyes, wondering if he could believe him—or should—or if it even mattered. Even if Colter was the fastest man alive, how could he hope to outrun a hundred or more hopped-up spear-flinging braves, each of them vying to be the one to avenge the death of their tribesman, their friend, their relative, their father or son or brother? After a minute or two of this—enough to make Colter feel the extra weight of paranoia, wondering if the chief had been there for the fight with the Crows and was just now beginning to place him—the chief turned his back on him and returned to the circle of elders. Things got quiet. Children stared at him out of wide unblinking eyes. A dog came up to sniff him and raise its hackles before slinking away. The elders were talking in low voices now, as if they'd reached consensus, and he strained to hear what they were saying but couldn't catch a word of it.

Another eternity went by, every minute of it precious, however fraught, because he was alive still and thinking and breathing and pumping blood on planet earth. He just stood there, staring straight ahead, as if he didn't care one way or the other what they did with him. It was cool still, the temperature just above freezing despite the sun that had come up over the horizon now, but he didn't feel it—if anything, he felt overheated, as if he were wrapped in furs and lying in front of a bonfire. Maybe he had an itch on the back of his neck or under his arm—people had itches all the time—but he didn't dare scratch it or even move a fraction of an inch. Finally, the first chief, joined now by a younger, angrier-looking one, strolled across the beaten dirt to him, taking his sweet time. He was nodding, nodding assent, and when he was right there in front of Colter again, nose-to-nose, he said, "You go out there on the plain and then"—he gestured to the young braves, who'd begun to remove their leggings and line up for the chase—"we see how fast you run."

So Colter, taking his sweet time too, ambled out across the plain, expecting at any moment to hear the shout go up behind him but forcing himself to walk so as to get as much distance between himself and his pursuers as he could before he broke into a run and set them off. Most people wouldn't have had the presence of mind Colter had—they would have taken off sprinting and the Indians would have been on them quicker than flies on shit—but it served him well. He must have gotten a hundred yards out before the shout went up, but it wasn't so much a shout as a mad blood-crazed shriek of three hundred voices, the women ululating all over again and the braves howling like beasts. Colter didn't let it distract him and he didn't look back. He knew right where he was—it was six miles straight across the plain to the forks of the Missouri, the big river, and if he could somehow reach that and maybe get in the water ahead of them and flail his way downstream he had a chance, the smallest, tiniest, infinitesimal chance, of surviving.

Colter ran. He kept his head down, watching his feet, trying to avoid the spines of the cholla and prickly pear and whatever else was out there. His legs felt strong, though he'd spent the better part of the past month sitting in a canoe, and he never slowed his pace, sprinting the first mile as if this wasn't about endurance but speed, only that. The braves—and what had they been doing all their lives except letting their ponies do the running for them?—began to drop out, one by one. Those closest to him flung their spears at the pale retreating wedge of his back but they weren't near enough to be accurate and he could hear the spears clatter on the stones behind him. Encouraged, he kept running, and if anything, increased his speed.

Then there was the second mile, the third, and he was halfway there by his calculation and still alive and in one piece, though his feet were bloody and pierced with cholla spines and his lungs were on fire. But at least he still had lungs and that was better than the alternative, better than Potts, whose own innards were just food for dogs at this point. After a while, and he was running now for the sake of it, for nothing else but that, just running as if he'd never done anything else in his life, he risked a glance over his shoulder and saw to his amazement that there were only three braves anywhere near him. So what did he do? He poured it on, running faster than anybody before or since, and by the time he reached what he guessed was the fifth mile and could see the distant declivity where the river cut its banks, there was only one brave behind him, the fittest one in the whole camp, young, streamlined, his spear stabbing out before him as he pumped his arms with each stride.

No matter. Colter was outrunning him. Or could have or would have but for the fact that he felt something hot and viscid running down the front of him, his own blood, some essential thing ruptured inside of him from the sheer pounding stress and high anxiety he was putting his body through. He was bleeding out both nostrils, that was what it was, his chest and even his thighs smeared with blood as if he'd been plunged in a vat in one of the slaughterhouses back in St. Louis, and he knew that things had come to a head, to the point of crisis, flip a coin, live or die. So what he did, even as the brave gained on him and was about to take aim and hurl his spear at any second, was stop in his tracks and whirl around to face him. It was a good move. Because the brave, fittest and fleetest of the whole tribe, had been focused all this time on the shifting target of Colter's soap white shoulders and now suddenly here was Colter's face and chest bright with blood and Colter running no more. "Spare me," he called out, but the brave had no such intention. He cocked the spear over his right shoulder, leaning into his throw in midstride, but unfortunately for him he caught his foot at that moment and pitched face-forward into the dirt, the spear slamming down in front of him to quiver in the ground.

Colter was on him in that instant, jerking the shaft out of the earth and bringing the business end of the spear down on the writhing Indian with such force that it went right through his ribcage and pinned him to the turf like an insect. That was a moment. And Colter felt it not so much in his brain or his heart, but in his legs. He was bloody. His feet were raw. One of his pursuers lay dead on the ground, but here came the rest of them letting out a collective howl of rage and disbelief when they saw their fallen comrade, and there went Colter, running, running.

28.

IT WAS A LONG hike from her place, down through the wooded canyon that was like her two spread legs with the river the wet part in the middle of it, but it was nothing to him and he could have walked it five times a day if he wanted to, but he didn't want to. He'd got his prescription and that was going to stop the shits—it already had—and he'd got the sex he really didn't need but wanted, anyway, another weakness. Poison oak. The shits. Sex. If he stopped to think about it, it scared him. A voice—and it wasn't in his head, but out there in front of him somewhere, hidden in the leaves—started ragging on him. *Boy Scout,* it called him. *Girl Scout. Brownie. Weakling. Dude. Fag. Wannabe.* After the first hour he stopped listening because that voice was the voice of defeat and if you had discipline you could take your weakness and transform it into strength, the same as you could take a fat kid with a bag of Doritos and make him lift weights and run a treadmill instead of playing video games and firm him up in a month. Basic training. Run the hills, climb the ropes, get hard and stay hard. His father had been a Marine and he'd been hard once but now he was old. And soft. Still—and this came to him at odd moments, like now—he *had* gone over there and waxed gooks and then as an old man went down to waste some Costa Rican alien with his bare hands and you had to give him credit for that. Even if he was clueless. Even if he didn't have even the faintest hint of the threat the hostiles posed, but then why would he, living in his clean and perfect upscale ocean-view house in Yuppiesville, California?

The day was cool and he hardly sweated at all, plus his clothes were clean, courtesy of Sara's washer and dryer, and if he regretted not having stayed on at least for one day more, at least till he could have gotten to the grocery store and maybe Big 5, he had to dismiss it. He was on a mission, never forget that. Maybe that alien had interrupted him, had showed him how weak and mindless and just plain stupid his first attempt at establishing a backup position was, and maybe that was for the best because he hadn't been prepared, had he, but now he was or he was going to be. He'd already cached some things at the second camp, which was an hour's hike from the one he'd had to abandon, the one he'd had to say *mission aborted* to, and on a different watercourse entirely, high ground, absolutely, and no road within miles. He was on his way there now, hurrying, hurrying, and there were planes overhead, always planes, glinting, and it was just a matter of time before it was drones, which were just another kind of robot, and his wind was good and his legs were strong even if his pack was overloaded and pulling ever so slightly to the right and he really didn't feel like stopping to shift things around. What he had in there were the items he'd acquired from Sara that she wouldn't be needing, anyway, like what was left of the bottle of bourbon and some cans of beef stew (extra weight, but totally tasty, especially over a campfire, and easy too because all you needed was a can opener and you could set the can down in the coals and then eat right out of it when it was ready), plus a hatchet and an adjustable wrench he'd found in some alien's cabin on the way up and then stashed for the return trip.

But wait: was he lost? He seemed to wake up suddenly, the sun a jolt to his system the way coffee was, but she hadn't made coffee and he hadn't wanted it because she was asleep in bed and snoring with her mouth thrown open when he slipped out the door, and he realized he was disoriented, to the south of where he wanted to be, and how he came to realize it—and come awake— was because here was somebody's cabin hidden in the trees and a dirt road curling up in front of it like a cat taking a nap. All right, he was thinking, why not? And he circled the place three times, doing his recon, until he determined with ninety-nine percent accuracy that there was nobody home. Up on the porch now, locked door, casement windows, drawn curtains. Hello, anybody there?

A tap of the stone he dug out of the dirt and the near window had a fist-sized hole in it that allowed him to put his hand in, rotate the latch and pull the windows open so that anybody could have just stepped right over the sill and into the place that was only two rooms, woodstove, rag rug on the floor, a rusty dusty musty smell, and what was this? A .22 rifle hanging from two hooks over the stove and wouldn't that make a nice close-up kind of weapon if somebody sawed off the barrel and filed it clean?

He lost himself there for a while and that wasn't cool, that wasn't military, and he would have been the first to admit it. But so what. He liked the feel of the place, liked the old armchair with the dog hair on it and the stuffed deer head sticking out of the knotty-pine wall across from it—and he liked the liquor too, a handle of vodka, two-thirds full, papa bear, mama bear, baby bear. He found a hacksaw in the toolshed and a vise and file there too. Food in the refrigerator, ham and cheese, yellow mustard, soft white sourdough bread that toasted up just perfect. And what was that tapping on the roof? It was rain, that was what it was, first rain of the season, and if it swelled the streams he wasn't worried. All that hurry, and for what? In fact, he just took a time-out and built a fire in the woodstove and sat there through the back end of the morning and into the afternoon, drinking somebody else's vodka and modifying somebody else's .22 rifle, and didn't think anything at all.

What woke him was his sixth sense. He heard the rain, heavy now, sizzling like the deep fryer at McDonald's, and something else, an automotive noise, but the wheel inside him was barely turning at all and the vodka seemed to just press down on him till he felt like a deep-sea diver in one of those old-fashioned deep-sea suits with the riveted helmet and the long trailing air hose that seemed to rise up into infinity. It wasn't weakness and it wasn't the vodka, or not exactly, and it wasn't the warmth of the wood-stove or the fact that he could have lived in this cabin himself, all by himself, and built a wall around it too . . . it was just that he was feeling cool, equal to anything, and he was just waiting to see who or what was coming through that door because he had a sawed-off .22 in his hand that was just like a pistol, that he could use as a pistol in any tight place, and a box of shells for it too that was just lying there in the drawer of the coffee table next to a deck of cards that had been thumbed through so many times the lamination was practically worn right off each and every one of them. And he'd looked. He had. And saw that the deck was missing the ace of diamonds—not the ace of spades, the ace of diamonds—and what that meant or didn't mean he couldn't say. He wasn't superstitious. Or maybe he was.

Footsteps on the porch. Key in the lock. And there she was, an old lady with white hair and a what's-up face who could have been his grandmother if his grandmother wasn't dead already and buried and probably being dug up at that very minute by Art Tolleson, whoever he was or turned out to be when you peeled his mask off. It took her a minute, hanging there in the doorway as if she couldn't decide whether to stay or go, the rain hanging like a gray sheet behind her and smelling of release and new life for the plants, the animals, the gullies and creeks and rivers. "Who are *you*?" she asked and before he could answer asked what he was doing there. Or what he thought he was doing there.

The door stood open. The old lady had three plastic bags of groceries dangling from her purple-veined hands. Her hair was wet on top and two long strands of it, one on either side of her puzzled face, were plastered wet to the skin there. "Who am I?" he said. "I'm Colter. What was the second question again?"

The rain sizzled behind her. It was really coming down, a real worm-washer. She didn't seem to have heard him. She just stood there, the bags dangling. "What are you doing in my house?" That was what she wanted to know, and if there was an edge to her voice now, that was because she'd begun to take in the scene, the open window, the vodka, the fire, the metal shavings on the floor and the vise he'd clamped to the edge of the coffee table to steady the blade. And the guns: his rifle, propped up against the armchair with the dog hair on it, and the modified .22 he held in his hand. Which used to be a rifle. And used to be hers.

She deserved an answer and he felt so lazy and peaceful and calm he decided to give her one—and to be as pleasant about it as he could too. "Enjoying your hospitality," was what he said, even as another sound entered the mix, the rattle of a dog's toenails on the boards of the porch, and here came the dog himself, a miniature poodle sort of thing, old and arthritic and with the dark stains of his drooling eye fluids darkening the white fluff of fur on either side of his snout. He didn't even bother to bark. Just stood there next to the old lady, dripping.

"You get out of here," the old lady said then, and it wasn't the dog she was talking to.

He held up a hand. Everything was okay, couldn't she see that? There were no aliens here. And she wasn't Chinese, not even close. So what he did was push himself up from the chair and go over to the window and pull it shut. "Sorry about the glass," he said, and then, forgive him, he couldn't help himself, he was laughing. "But you forgot to leave me a key."

She did have a telephone, but he didn't care about that. It was the same ugly sort of thing his grandmother'd had, no cellphone, cellphones didn't work out here, but just a big black box of a thing that was so heavy you could have beaten an elephant to death with it. He didn't want to alarm her so he didn't jerk the wires out of the socket but just bent down and gently removed them, then straightened up and dodged past her with the phone and its trailing wires in one hand and the .22 in the other, and tossed the whole business out into the rain. (The phone, that is. Not the .22. The .22 he was going to need.) Then he pushed the door shut behind her—she still hadn't moved, though the dog was really tapping up a storm now on the bare boards of the floor, all worked up about something.

"Listen," he said, and the look on her face was breaking his heart because it was exactly the look his grandmother used to give him when she was pissed at him, "I really want to thank you for your hospitality. And I'm going to have to go soon. I've got, well, a lot"—and he waved one arm to show just how much he did have to do—"but with this rain and all, I think we might as well get comfortable, at least for a while. Don't you?"

The time he drove the car through the fence at the playground he'd gone outside of himself for a moment there and knew what he'd done the minute the kids started scattering like rabbits across the dead grass and the scooped-out sandpit under the monkey bars, which were what stopped the car finally. The monkey bars were made of hollowed-out steel and they were cemented in place like a big metal beehive, and that was what set him off in the first place. To this day he couldn't go past it without picturing the thing as some alien Chinese spacecraft just touched down and disgorging all these shrieking little half-sized hostiles who turned out to be kids, just kids. It was hard to explain, and he'd tried to explain it, tried hard, first to the pigs on the scene, then to the court-appointed lawyer and then to the judge and the shrink they assigned him. "Hey," he said, "give me a break, it was an accident. And yeah, okay, I was on 'shrooms, all right? Is that a crime?" But it was. And he shouldn't have said that or admitted it or whatever and he knew he'd fucked up the minute it was out of his mouth.

They sent him away for evaluation but he didn't have a record and he was mostly clear while he was in the *facility* as they liked to call it *euphemistically* and they gave him meds, more meds, and released him to the custody of his parents and he went back to school and got bored and hung out with Cody and got high and higher and finally moved in with his grandmother and turned eighteen and began to get serious about the outdoors because he saw his destiny then as the first true mountain man of modern times. He read all the books. He worshipped Hugh Glass, who in some ways was as tough as Colter, a former pirate turned mountain man who had a run-in with a grizzly that left him mauled and broken and all but dead so that his so-called friends abandoned him and he had to crawl a hundred fifty miles and live on roots and lizards till he got his strength back and hunted them down and put the fear of God in them. He was going to call himself Glass at first, just Glass, but then Colter came into his life, and the name was so much cooler, and so was the man too.

The rest was history. And maybe someday they'd be writing him up in books. The scene at Piero's was the one they'd have to embroider a bit because the fact was he'd seen some things there he didn't like and got into it with some of the resident aliens and if truth be told got the living shit beat out of him to the tune of two fractured ribs, a chipped tooth and a seriously disarranged nose. He knew better now. Now he had his Norinco and his .22 and his Jungle King fourteen-inch hunting knife with the serrated edge on top, which was enough to discourage twenty hostiles. As for the thing at the Chinese consulate in S.F., that wasn't even worth mentioning.

What brought it all up though was the old lady who looked more and more like his dead grandma as the afternoon fell off into evening and the rain kept up and he tipped back the bottle and just talked his heart out to her because that was what the peacefulness of her cabin and her presence too brought out in him. She was pissed, no doubt about that, and when he told her to just sit down and stop fussing she did it, but she didn't like it. He was talking and she kept interrupting him, kept complaining, kept *bitching,* till he had to tell her, twice, to shut the fuck up. At some hour—it was still gray out and that was good because he had to find his way back—he thanked her one more time, gathered up his things and went on out to the door to flip the hood on her car and rip out the distributor cap before hunching his shoulders under the straps of his pack and humping into the woods, already wet through to the skin.

He woke shivering in his sleeping bag, which had somehow got wet too, despite the fact that he'd spread a camo tarp over the bunker and dug a runoff trench with the stainless-steel folding shovel he'd borrowed from the Boy Scouts. Permanently. The thing was, though, he was clear and knew right where he was, which was Camp 2, the one high above everybody and everything. He opened his eyes on the tarp, bellied now with accumulated water so that it looked like the bottom end of a brontosaur—or a dragon, Smaug the Impenetrable, scalier than shit—and heard the soft spatter of the dying rain in the trees, along with the crash and roar of the swollen creek coming out of the spring, and right away felt sick in his stomach. It wasn't the shits. Or maybe it was, but only partially. He was hungover, that was what it was, drunk-sick, because he'd taken the old lady's handle of vodka with him and never got around to building a fire for the beef stew or anything else and had just lain there under the tarp, listening to the rain and smelling the deep ferment of the woods while sucking on the bottle like some half-witted mewling little baby that didn't know any better till his mind went blank and he passed out to wake up now, here, with the rain spattering and the spring roaring. Feeling like crap. Or no, warmed-over crap, crap that wasn't even fresh but just heated up in a pan and served to all the shit-eaters of the world in some alien soup kitchen.

First thing he did was climb up over the lip of the bunker, which was three feet high, just exactly right for cover and defense both, and get down on all fours to puke, and then he dug out one

of the little yellow giardia pills and washed it down with spring
water because no one was going to tell him *this* spring was con-
taminated because if it was then the whole planet was just a big
cesspool and the aliens could have it and welcome to it. For a long
while he sat there wet and shivering on the near wall of the bunker, which was constructed of bark-on logs he'd dragged from
a long ways out so as to cover his tracks if anyone should come
upon the stumps. And no, it wasn't anything like the forts he and
Cody and Billy Julian built when they were like ten years old, just
hammering anything together they could find, but the real deal,
straight out of the U.S. Army Field Manual, Chapter 20: "Survival Movement in Hostile Areas," most of which he could have
quoted verbatim if somebody asked him, but really all you had to
know was the acronym BLISS:

B—Blends in with the surroundings
L—Low in silhouette
I—Irregular in shape
S—Small in size
S—Secluded

Secluded, that was for sure, and you had to be secluded or
they'd find you with their car doors slamming and their barking worked-up irate old man's voices crowing, *What do you think
you're doing in there?* He never did get a chance to answer that day,
whenever it was, a long time ago or maybe not, but if he'd had the
chance he would have said, "I think I'm getting away from assholes like you." That's what he should have said and he was saying
it now to the dripping trees and thinking about starting a little
campfire to heat up a can of beef stew or just boil some water for
freeze-dried chicken cashew curry, hungry now, hungry all over
again since he'd just puked up a whole wad of nothing, not even
chunks, just mucus, and he went around doing that, gathering up
twigs that weren't too sodden and some scraps of newspaper and

then laying some of the bigger stuff he kept under his tarp across the top of it. He didn't like showing smoke in hostile territory—a thing Colter would never have done—but he wanted something hot. And besides, the war really hadn't started yet.

It was when he was dishing up the beef stew (blowing on it, actually; it was still too hot to eat) that an ugly thought occurred to him. It was the kind of thought a groundhog might have had studying his own burrow from outside in the hard light of day, a gnawing, paranoid kind of feeling that poisoned the smell of the beef stew and killed his mood dead. He shifted uneasily. His crotch was wet and it was going to start itching with the crotch fungus that made it feel as if your balls were on fire if he didn't change into something dry pretty soon—and what was he going to do, go to the drugstore every day? But here came that thought roaring into his head and he cursed himself again. *Fucker. Idiot. Moron. Shit for brains.* Here he'd been sitting around in hospital waiting rooms and fucking Sara in the dark and jawing away with a random old lady like some—it hurt to have to say it—like some *mental* case, and not a thought to the plantation, which he hadn't laid eyes on for two full days now.

He had to get a grip. There'd been a storm, rain falling in sheets and beating like a whole ship full of aliens on that old lady's split-shake roof, and what if it had damaged the plants? What if it had broken the stems supporting the pods that were only viable now, right now, because the growing cycle was something like ninety days and he'd been late receiving his seeds in the mail and then getting them in the dirt of his two hundred twenty-seven gopher-proof pots? Worse, what if the whole thing had washed away, the pots and plants and the brown balls of opium in the screw-top jar hidden in the secret recess behind the back wall of the bunker? What then?

The stew was hot, too hot to eat, but he ate it anyway, the wheel cranking round now as if it had no stop on it, as if it was going to break loose and tear right out of his head like a freak accident on the roller coaster. He didn't bother to scrape the can, just threw it down in the mud. The spoon too. And then he had his pack on, the rifle shouldered and the knife strapped to his thigh, and he was heading downhill, double time becoming triple time and then quadruple time till he was running full-out, running like Colter.

29.

SO MAYBE HE SLIPPED and fell a couple of times, the mud slick underfoot, the tread of his boots clogged with it till he might as well have had no tread at all, everything rushing downward and the rain starting in again. His pants were filthy, basted with mud and long filarial streaks of some green shit he didn't know what it was, and he'd managed to tear the sleeve of his shirt slamming into a tree to keep from pitching headlong into a ravine like some clumsy-ass motherfucker, but it was nothing more than what you would expect out here this time of year when the rain started in and just kept on coming, the kind of thing the average person didn't even know about or even suspect because the average person was sitting in front of a TV in a dry house with a remote in one hand and a bag of wasabi peas in the other. Plus he was on a mission here and whether he broke a leg or both legs or not really didn't enter into it—if he couldn't keep on his feet and hurtle every obstacle then he didn't deserve to have a plantation or live free or even think of calling himself a mountain man. So what he did was let his instincts take over and just go for it.

The plantation was a good four-mile trek from Camp 2 and it would normally take something like an hour to get there but he made it in record time, or at least that was what it felt like since he didn't have a watch or a cellphone because no mountain man ever carried a watch and cellphones hadn't been invented back then and plus in a state of nature you just knew the time the way the animals did, by the sun, by the shadows, by another sense altogether that wasn't a sixth sense—that was reserved for danger— but a seventh sense, that was what it was. He liked the idea of it, seventh sense, and he began wondering if there were more senses yet, like an eighth sense or a ninth, and what they would be. The eighth sense—that would allow you to get inside the hostiles' heads and know what they were thinking before they did, right when they got up in the morning and were taking their first steaming piss up against a tree, and the ninth, the ninth would not only allow you to know what they were thinking but change it like tuning a radio so you could make them skin themselves alive instead of you or Potts or any white men at all.

Of course, no matter how fast the wheel was spinning he hadn't lost all control or forgotten his tactics and so when he got close he put on the brakes and went low to the ground till he was mud all over, till he was indistinguishable from the mud, and crept up on his elbows and knees to take up a recon position and glass the plantation to be sure there were no aliens or hostiles snooping around or helping themselves to his crop. What he saw took the heart out of him. Half the pots, at least half, had been tipped over by the violence of the storm and another half of those had washed down a series of gullies that hadn't been there the last time he'd looked. That upset him, of course it did, and maybe it made him careless too, because he jumped to his feet and just burst right out into the clearing and started righting the pots and checking on the seedpods he'd painstakingly slit in six places with a razor blade so he could milk the sap out of them, backbreaking work. Boring work. Work he'd come to hate. Which was why he'd been two days away from it, distracting himself with little yellow pills and getting laid. Stupidly.

A lot of the stems had been bent out of shape or even snapped in two when the pots tipped over and the ones that had washed downhill were just a total loss, but what he could do was salvage as many seedpods as possible, dry them out and grind them up to make a sort of tea, tea that would get you high, or at least that was what he'd heard. But then he couldn't sell *that* and if he couldn't sell it then it just defeated the whole purpose of trying to raise some cash out of all this work and worry so he would have the wherewithal to do it again next year and the year after that because those little toast-brown balls of opium were his beaver hides, the modern-day equivalent of the plews that would make him independent and never have to say *Yessir, Cap'n, to no man.*

Truth be told, he was in a kind of frenzy, trying to put things right when he should have realized he'd just have to cut his losses, but every plant meant something to him because he'd grown them from the little black gnat-sized seeds he'd mixed with a handful of sand so they'd scatter nicely across the surface of the five-gallon plastic pots he and Cody had lifted from the back of a nursery one socked-in night when the only way you could see anything was with night-vision goggles. Some of the seeds never germinated. Others got chewed down to the stub by a mysterious nighttime presence he never was able to track down, whether it was bugs or rabbits or even deer. Or aliens. Could have been aliens. He wouldn't put it past them. But then why would they attack the half-grown plants instead of waiting for the flowers and the seedpods and the milky white drip of opium that made it all worthwhile?

What you had to do was score the pods late in the day so the sap wouldn't coagulate like blood but instead just drip in a nice wet flow all night long so you could collect it in the morning and set it aside to dry from milky white to golden brown for a couple of days and just store it up in your screw-top jar for personal use or sale on the street or maybe under the counter at the Big 5, and no, he had no interest in making heroin from it because that required boiling out the impurities and using chemicals and no mountain man wanted to go near chemicals. That wasn't natural. That wasn't *organic*. Dry it and smoke it, that was as far as he wanted to go, but he didn't even want to go there, not anymore, because really all he needed was 151 and pot and maybe, when the wheel was spinning out of control, a medicinal hit of acid to bring it back into line.

But here he was, in his frenzy, everything mud and half the

plants ruined, the beautiful tall stiff green stems he'd watched climbing higher day by day till they flowered and the petals dropped off and the seed pods started nodding under their own weight now just bent and broken and pretty much useless, the rain slacking off to a mist that climbed up the back of his neck like a slug and the beef stew sitting on his stomach like its own kind of death. Talk about miserable. He just wanted to raise his face to the sky and scream till his lungs gave out. And he might have, except that soldiers didn't complain or blame anybody for anything except themselves, and it was a good thing too because it was right then that he spotted movement at the far end of the plantation, in the treeline there, and just about jumped out of his skin. But he didn't do that either. He kept his cool and retreated, silent and swift, sluicing uphill through the mud till he slipped over the edge of the bunker and snatched up his binoculars, and he was bummed, of course he was, but there was something inside of him that kept swelling and swelling until it began to feel like joy. This was it. Finally. Definitively. The moment he'd been waiting for since the seeds arrived on his doorstep in a neat tan box with raised silver lettering you could run your fingers over again and again just for the sheer *transference* of it: *Russo & Ayers, Horticulturists.* And wasn't that a beautiful thing? The box? The seeds? The moment?

Had they seen him? No. They were there in the distance, bending over his plants, two of them, two aliens in olive-drab rain slickers and muddy boots and he was glassing them now, picking their faces out of the misting rain that hung over everything like poison gas and he was calm, utterly calm, as calm as Colter standing there naked while they decided his fate. But nobody was going to decide *his* fate. He was the one in charge here, he was the one in cover and he was no trespasser—they were. One of them he didn't recognize, or not right away, but the other one was turning his face to him now, looking up the hill toward the bunker, and that one turned out to be the Dog-Face himself, Chip Moody. He set down the binoculars and took up his rifle.

They moved across the field, making little discoveries as they went, gesturing to each other and conferring in low voices. One of them—the Dog-Face—bent down and pulled out a knife to cut through a section of black irrigation hose that had been left exposed by the rain. And now the other one did too. They kicked over a couple of the pots as if they didn't belong to anybody, as if they were just garbage, and that made him furious, all the work he'd put in, and for what? When they got close, close enough to hear what they were saying (*Mexicans? I don't think so, to tell you the truth, because they wouldn't bother with—*) he just couldn't hold it in any longer and before he knew what he was doing he came hurtling out of the bunker with his weapon in hand and shouting the first thing that came into his head, "FBI, FBI, you're under arrest!" And that was stupid, he could see that in retrospect, because what he wanted was to scare them off when he should have just dropped them both right then and there so they wouldn't go rat him out to the sheriff and all the aliens in his command and the helicopters too and the drones that were soulless metal and just kept after you till you were dead and wasted and giving up the maggots.

"What in hell?" the Dog-Face said. Or no, he barked. Just like a dog.

That was when the other one, his compadre, his backup, became very specific, his face constructing itself in a flash and never mind the hood of the slicker or the rain beads on his shoulders or the poison-gas mist drifting across the ground to conceal his person from view and his purposes too, he was the worst alien of them all, number one, pure poison himself. "Adam?" he said. "What are you—?" He didn't get to say anything more. There was no need. Just let the Norinco do the talking. Two bursts to spin him around and one to take him down. Smell it on the air. *Adios,* alien.

"Art!" the Dog-Face was barking and the Dog-Face was next, of course he was, another burst, clean as thrusters, clean as going to hyperspace, but the Dog-Face was taking cover and the Dog-Face was armed with a semi-automatic pistol that talked right back and there was nothing to do but take cover too and let the poison gas bring him down. Either that or outflank him and see how fast *he* could run.

PART X

Big River

30.

BIG RIVER WAS THE next watercourse down from the Noyo, and it drained an area of one hundred eighty-one square miles of timberland and spread wide to empty into the ocean just below the village of Mendocino. A sawmill had been built at the mouth of the river in 1852 and for a long while it had been the busiest mill in the county, but all that went defunct in the 1930s, and the mill was gone now, replaced by nothing, by sand, and though the watershed was still viable for timber, it was divided between four companies that milled their logs elsewhere and the Jackson Demonstration Forest, which was open to the public, as were the beaches. And the views. Gaze on the hills, as Sten was doing now, and all you saw from Fort Bragg to the north to Calpurnia in the south was a continuous forest that looked as pristine and untouched as it might have been when the Indians were in possession. The ferns dripped. Banana slugs longer than your hand oozed through the leaf litter. There were patches of ground up there that hadn't seen direct sunlight in a thousand years.

Sten was in the backyard sitting on the redwood picnic table, his forearms braced on the meat of his thighs and his feet resting on the bench, and he was gazing out on the hills so he wouldn't have to look into the faces of Rob Rankin and his deputy, Jason Ringwald, who'd played varsity football in high school and was a real little son of a bitch who'd been in the principal's office more times than Adam, but that was neither here nor there. What he was trying to avoid wasn't so much their faces—the looks on their faces, stony and cold and heartless—as what they were telling him. He was having trouble with that. He was denying it. Raising every objection he could think of.

"I want you to take a look at something," Rob was saying, and he was a little man, colorless as a transparency, and there it was in his hand, the thing—one of the things—Sten didn't want to see. It was a plastic Ziploc bag and inside it was a length of foil that had been molded into a kind of hollowed-out cigarette or pipe. One end was blackened where the match had touched it and the other featured a rounded aperture to draw in air—smoke—which would have been where the traces of DNA would collect. From lips, tongue, fingertips. "You ever see this before? Or anything like it?"

Sten came back to him now, but he had to drop his eyes because he couldn't let this man—or any man—look inside him and see what he was or how this whole business was twisting in his veins like rusted wire. Thank god Carolee wasn't here, that was all he could think. Thank god. "I don't know," he said.

A gull sailed overhead so that its shadow fell across the sheriff's face and then lifted again. "At school?" Rob prompted. "Surely you—or whoever—must have confiscated things like this at school." He paused. "It's what they call a blunt, for smoking marijuana?"

Sten nodded. He knew what it was. And he knew what was coming too.

"We found this at the Bachman crime scene. Actually, we found two of them. The other one, the second one, was up there where that bunker was?" The sheriff paused a moment to swell his cheeks and let out a long trailing breath, as if the whole thing was too much for him, traipsing from one crime scene to another, hauling things around in plastic bags to confront people with on a day like this, with the sun showing bright all the way up into the stratosphere and not even the faintest stir of a breeze. "And another thing," gesturing now to his deputy, who must have been all of twenty-two or -three, and if this kid smirked or even thought about it, Sten didn't know if he could hold himself back, not the way he was feeling now. This was the cue for the deputy, Jason, to hand him another plastic bag, inside of which were shell casings, dull silver in color, as if they'd been tarnished. "You recognize these?"

What could he say? They were shell casings. They could have come from anywhere, from anybody. He shrugged.

"Come on, Sten, I'm trying to tell you something here."

"All right, then tell me."

"These are casings from a Chinese assault rifle, not something you see every day around here. A Norinco—what was it, Jason?"

"SKS Sporter. Takes 7.62 millimeter rounds."

The sheriff was standing there on a patch of grass the rain had reinvigorated, the shoots gone green to replace the yellow that had prevailed for the past six months, new life springing up under the soles of the Belleville flight boots he preferred to standard issue. He had his hands on his hips. "I just wanted to ask," he said, and his eyes never left Sten's face, "—your son has a rifle, doesn't he? Adam?"

This was a cold question and Sten felt a chill all of a sudden though the sun was shining and the bay at the mouth of the river glittered like a heat lamp. Fatherhood. He'd never really wanted it, never sought it, and it had come on him late when Carolee, at the age of thirty-nine, had found herself miraculously pregnant. *We're blessed,* she'd told him, her face composed round the news, *truly blessed.*

"Yeah," he said, so softly he could scarcely hear himself.

"Chinese-made, isn't that right?"

"Yeah."

"What I'm saying is, Sten, and I know this is hard on you, it wasn't the Mexicans that shot Carey Bachman and they didn't shoot Art Tolleson either. You know that, don't you?"

What came next was a detailed account of what had occurred yesterday afternoon on Georgia Pacific property approximately three miles northeast of the house on the Noyo where Adam formerly lived with his grandmother—the house Adam had vandalized because he wasn't right in the head, because he was angry and upset and never had gotten over the death of Carolee's mother and the way the world kept letting him down.

"That's correct, isn't it?" the sheriff wanted to know. "He did live there, didn't he?" He drew a pair of drugstore reading glasses from his shirt pocket, shook them out and carefully fitted them over the bridge of his nose to consult the police report the deputy handed him. "At 3772 Forest Road?"

Sten nodded.

"You recall how long?"

"Something like six or seven years now, I guess," Sten said, his voice gone dead on him. He didn't want to hear this, but he was going to hear it whether he liked it or not.

The sheriff dropped his eyes to the report and continued, glancing up from time to time to make sure Sten was getting the full impact of it because this was a trial in progress, a prosecutorial marshaling of the facts and make no mistake about it. "It says that the victim, in the company of a local resident, Charles Moody, came across a growing operation at that location—opium poppies, the seedpods of which showed evidence of sap collection, which is illegal in the state of California and everywhere else in the United States as well. You can grow poppies all you want and let them go to seed and use those seeds to grow more poppies or sprinkle them on your bagel or do anything else you want with them, but when you cross the line and start scoring the pods to extract opium, that's a felony offense, that makes you a narcotics purveyor with intent to sell. You understand what I'm saying?"

"He's not in his right mind, Rob. He's not responsible. We've tried to get help for him, like that time at the Chinese consulate—"

But the sheriff wasn't paying any attention because mental states weren't the issue here. Murder was. Murder and felony drug violations. He went on, reading now: " 'As the victim and Mr. Moody made their way upslope in a light misting rain, they were unaware that the suspect was armed, concealed and lying in wait. It was their assumption that the operation had been abandoned, as it was late in the season and they saw no signs that anyone was in attendance. At some point, no more than ten minutes after they'd arrived, the suspect sprang from cover in a threatening manner and when the victim recognized him—called out his name, *Adam*—the suspect opened fire with his Chinese-made assault rifle, fatally wounding the victim, and then firing on Mr. Moody, who took cover and returned fire with a legally registered handgun he routinely carried for protection in the woods.

" 'The suspect subsequently retreated but began a flanking maneuver that caught Mr. Moody by surprise (he was at this juncture in full flight, in a heavily wooded area some two miles north of the river and the California Western Railroad tracks, or Skunk Railroad, as it is popularly known). Suddenly he came under fire again, and initially, using the trees for cover and returning fire to keep the suspect at bay, he couldn't determine from which direction the fire was coming. When he realized that the shooter was now in front of him, cutting off his retreat, he began evasive maneuvers, heading west in deep forest before again turning south, where he finally reached the railway tracks at mile marker six and was able to flag down the operator of a railway utility vehicle known as a speeder cart, who took him to safety where he subsequently placed a 911 call.' "

The sheriff glanced up, held him with his eyes, then slapped the report down on the table. "Just so you understand, Sten, Adam actively hunted this guy down, and if Moody wasn't armed and hadn't used his head, we'd be talking about three deaths here."

"He didn't kill Carey. That was the Mexicans. I saw them. We both saw them out there in their pickup—Carey even called 911 to report them." A glance at the deputy—and he *was* smirking. Or gloating. One or the other, take your pick. "What are you smirking about, you son of a bitch?"

And now the kid came to attention, all right, one hand instinctively going to his duty belt. "Who you calling a son of a bitch?"

"You. I'm calling you a son of a bitch."

"Back off, Jason." Rob straightened up with a sigh, put his hands on his hips. "In fact, why don't you go out to the car for me and I'll call you when I need you?"

There was a moment of hesitation, the deputy's face a field for the interplay of his emotions, and then they both watched as he turned his back on them and picked his way across the lawn to flip the latch on the gate and disappear round the corner of the house.

"Sten. Look. I know this is hard," Rob said, easing off the glasses and folding them away in his pocket. "But the evidence doesn't support that."

It *was* hard and it just got harder because he was trying to put Adam and Carey in the same equation, trying to picture the way his son would break with reality but always seemed to be able to come back to it, to right himself. Until now.

"I've got to ask you," Rob said, no trace of understanding or even consideration left in his voice, just calculation, "—you know where he is?"

Sten just shook his head.

"When did you last see him?"

"I don't know. It's been a while."

More gulls. The mountains. The ocean. Big River. And the sheriff, the sheriff calculating, because he was working on his own equation. "He was angry last time you saw him, isn't that right? He didn't want to leave that house. You had a fight, the two of you."

"That's right. But you've got to realize, Adam's not normal. He needs help. I've been on to social services about it, everybody, and all I get is privacy laws, all I get is it's none of my business."

"And when he left that night, he went where?"

He was trying to come up with an answer, trying to miti-gate, minimize, deny, but all he could do, even as Carolee came slamming through the back door with her hair in her face and her feet trying to run out from under her, was look toward the mountains. And point.

31.

THIS TIME HE DIDN'T wait for the reporters and the fluffed-up anchorwomen or the rest of the hyenas either. The minute the sheriff left he went in and disconnected the phone and then took his cell out of his right-front pocket and buried it in the top drawer of the bureau in the bedroom. And when Carolee's cell started ringing midway through dinner—a salad of cold chicken and avocado she'd numbly prepared at the kitchen counter with rigid hands and frozen arms, a salad neither of them could eat because food was the last thing they wanted—he got up from the table, dug the phone out of her purse and turned it off without bothering to find out who was calling or why. "What if it's news?" she said. "What if they—?" But they both knew it wasn't news and that they—the authorities, the cops, the SWAT teams Rob had already called in—hadn't found or done anything. He just shook his head. Her phone was like a bomb, like an IED, and it could go off any minute and bring the whole house down. Didn't she realize that? It was wrong. It was foul. It was dirty. So what he did was take it across the kitchen, down the hall and into the bedroom, where he buried it in the bureau right next to his own.

Neither of them slept that night. Every time he began to doze off he was aware of her there beside him, tense and alert, listening for sounds in the night. And he was listening too. Listening not for gunfire or the crackle of police radios or the rattling pulse of helicopters sweeping overhead, but for the furtive creaking of the back door, the sigh of bedsprings in the guest room, for Adam, come home to them. Because if he didn't come home, didn't get out of the way of everybody, didn't get treatment and meds and whatever else it was going to take—court-appointed

shrinks, the lockup—there was only one way this was going to
turn out. Adam might have known these hills, might have been a
mountain man—or boy, because that was what he was, a boy still
and always—but the sheriff had cordoned off the whole area on
both sides of Route 20 and banned entry to anyone for any purpose. They were carrying live ammunition out there. They had
dogs. They had heat sensors. If he didn't come in—and here was
a prayer, sent up to whoever might be listening—he was dead.

Then it was morning. Mist in the yard. Carolee asleep finally,
mercifully, and the whole world asleep with her. He was in the
kitchen making coffee and distractedly gazing out the window
when he saw something moving on the periphery of the yard and
his heart jumped. *Adam,* he was thinking, beyond all reason—
what were the chances, since he wouldn't even return to the old
house, the house he'd trashed, let alone this one?—and in the
next moment he was out the door, barefoot and dressed only in
the boxers and T-shirt he'd slept in. The grass was cold and wet
but he didn't feel it, didn't feel anything—not until the image of
his son vanished and rematerialized as some clown in oversized
shorts and high-tops with a video camera on one shoulder and a
microphone in his hand. "Mr. Stensen," he was saying, and he
didn't ask if he could have a word because he already knew the
answer and just plunged right in, "how do you feel about your
son being the target of the biggest manhunt this community has
ever seen?"

How did he feel? He felt about the way he had when he came
out of the jungle in Costa Rica and Warner Ayala had prodded him with the barrel of his weapon. What they wanted was
to provoke you, get you when you were staggered and confused
and ready to explode for the viewing pleasure of everybody out
there whose son wasn't psychologically impaired and crouching
in the woods like some kind of animal waiting for his brains to
be scorched out of him. He knew that. And he knew he had to
control himself if Adam was to have any chance at all, but it didn't

matter what he knew because there was no knowledge and no thought involved in what came next. It was just a kind of eruption, and he didn't hurt the guy, the reporter, whoever he was, and he didn't say a word to him either. All he did, once he'd got the parameters straight, was snatch the camera off his shoulder—a lightweight thing, half the size and heft of the ones they used in his day—and beat it methodically against the side of the house until there wasn't much more left of it than you could hold in the palm of your hand.

He didn't say a word about it to Carolee but by the time she got up all she had to do was look out the window to see for herself—a whole cordon of reporters lined the street with their cameras and microphones, cars and sound trucks were parked up and down the block like the grand opening of an auto show, and the helicopter that kept clattering overhead and buzzing back again had nothing to do with the police. That was a public street out there, he understood that, and he had no recourse unless they actually set foot on his property like the one who'd shoved the camera in his face before the sun had even cleared the horizon, but he'd called Rob Rankin nonetheless to tell him he'd better keep the vultures off or they'd be hunting him down too. Rob said he'd send a car by. And added, before he'd even asked, that there'd been no new developments, except for rumors and crank calls and the usual wave of sightings that turned out to be non-sightings. And he promised, as he'd promised yesterday, to do everything in his power to see that Adam came to no harm, but then—and here he'd paused so long Sten thought the connection had gone dead—that depended on Adam.

The day progressed, the first day, in a way that just didn't make any sense. They were both half-mad to get out and do something, anything—put up posters featuring Adam's face and a number to call as if he were a child gone missing, haunt the sheriff's substation in Fort Bragg in the hope of hearing even the least scrap of news, hike out into the woods and shout their son's name till he heard them and laid down his rifle and came back to them, but all they had to do was appear in the window and the cameras were trained on them as if the house was a cage and they were some rare form of wildlife never before seen in captivity. Step out the door and the shouts and cries came crackling across the lawn like verbal gunfire. It was frustrating, but above all it was humiliating, deeply humiliating—two men they both knew, knew and respected and liked, were dead, and they were complicit in it. Because their son, their crazy son, enacting whatever fantasy had invaded his head, had shot them dead, and who was responsible? Sten asked himself the question, over and over, through the long morning and into the interminable afternoon, but the answer never changed: they were. He was.

A week went by. There was no news. Or no, there was constant news, but none of it verifiable or relevant. Adam had been spotted wearing a hoodie at Kentucky Fried, he'd stolen a car in Gualala, climbed through a window on North Harold Street in Fort Bragg and raided the refrigerator, pried open the newspaper machine and taken all the copies of the *Advocate-News* with his mug shot on the front cover. People had heard gunfire down by Glass Beach. Somebody found a wadded-up sleeping bag and two shell casings behind the utility shed in his backyard. A goat disappeared under mysterious circumstances. It was ridiculous. Community hysteria. And it devastated Carolee, who wasn't able to sleep more than an hour or two a night and if she ate anything at all it was dry toast and coffee. He wasn't much better himself. They had the TV on constantly and the radio too, the electronic voices in contention, one squawking from the living room, the other the kitchen. And while he refused to plug the phone back in, after that first night he and Carolee had their cellphones pinned to their ears, calling anybody they could think of who might be even remotely connected to what was going on out there in the woods. The chatter only seemed to make things worse, but it wasn't the chatter that was killing them. It was the waiting.

Then one evening, past dark, when the reporters had given up and packed it in for the day, Rob pulled into the driveway in an unmarked car and just sat there a minute, as if gathering himself, then eased out the door and started up the walk. Sten had the door open by the time he reached it. Rob ducked his head, as if he were afraid of hitting it on the doorframe, but there was no danger there—he was a short man, short compared to Sten, anyway. "Mind if I come in for a minute?" he asked, and he wasn't bringing good news, you could see that from the set of his mouth, and yet it wasn't the worst either. Which meant that their son was still alive, still whole, still breathing.

Carolee was right there, her hands dropping helplessly to her sides. Her face was heavy, her shoulders slumped. There was no light in her eyes, nothing, just a sheenless dull glaze. What came into his head was that she looked as if she was drowning, but that was a cliché—no, she looked as if she'd already gone down. "Is it Adam?"

"Is there someplace we could sit for a minute?"

There was, of course there was, and in the next moment they were all three of them heading down the hall to the kitchen, to the oak table there, Carolee offering up everything she could think of—Coffee, did he want coffee? A sandwich? Cookies? She had some of those biscotti they made down at the bakery, or a drink, maybe he wanted a drink?—because the very request, *Is there someplace we could sit for a minute,* came hurtling at them with a force neither of them could bear.

Sten motioned to a chair and Rob pulled it out from under the table and sat heavily, Sten sliding into the chair beside him. "You know, on second thought"—Rob leaned back in the chair to call over his shoulder to Carolee, where she stood poised at the counter—"maybe a cup of coffee. If it's not too much trouble."

"So what's the news?"

"I just wanted to ask—did Adam ever have any military training?"

"Military training? Are you kidding? He was never in the service. I told you, he's unstable. And he's been getting worse. Why
do you ask?"

"Something happened out there today and I just can't explain
it—"

And now Carolee, who couldn't hold it in any longer: "What
do you mean—he's all right, isn't he? He isn't hurt—?"

Rob just shook his head, then turned to look in her direction.
"It's not that. It's just that I'm starting to have a bad feeling about
all this—not to mention these goddamned news conferences and
all the rest of the happy horseshit, because everybody, from the
governor down, is putting pressure on me like you can't believe.
But today? We had SWAT teams out there from Sacramento and
Fresno both—and more coming. Plus my men and the Alameda
County Special Response Unit too. With dogs and helicopters
and infrared. And these are professionals, believe me, and they'd
just got here, the Alameda team, just staging out on this logging
road near where the second crime scene is?"

The water Carolee had put on began to boil, a hiss and rattle
of the pot on the stove, steam rising, but she ignored it.

"We made contact with him." He held up a hand to forestall
them. "He's all right, for now. But I make no promises. Because
what happened, to my mind, was beyond belief—or in my experience, anyway. He fired on them, Sten, actually opened up from
cover. It was lucky nobody was hit. I mean, they were just standing around, getting their gear together, and suddenly they're taking fire."

Rob hadn't been there, hadn't witnessed it personally, but he'd
talked to the men who had and he'd taken the report. Apparently
Adam was moving around a lot—there'd been break-ins reported
at some of the outlying cabins as well as at the Boy Scout camp
and up and down the Skunk Line—and at two-thirty that after-

noon he'd been coming up a trail that intersected the road where the staging area was. One of the team, who'd barely had a chance to climb out of his vehicle, spotted him coming toward them and shouted for him to halt and put down his weapon. Adam didn't halt and he certainly didn't put down his weapon. Instead, he ducked into the cover of the trees and started firing and that got the whole team down in the dirt and lighting the woods up because whether they were highly trained and disciplined or not, they found themselves taken by surprise and maybe they were spooked. At least initially. But they soon regrouped and established a defensive formation while the K-9 handler set the dog on his scent.

Once the firing stopped, their expectation was that the suspect would have fled at that point and that running him down should have been routine, taking into account the unfamiliar terrain, of course, and the fact that cellphones were useless out there and they had to rely on the more limited range of their radios. That wasn't what happened. Adam outflanked them. And did it so quickly they were taken by surprise all over again, only now he was firing from their rear. Again, it was a miracle nobody was hurt. And when the firing subsided this time, the suspect did take off and the K-9 unit went after him.

Rob paused at this point. He had a cup of coffee before him now and he was staring down into it, slowly revolving the cup on its saucer. Sten found that he had a cup too, though he didn't need it and it would just keep him awake. Carolee was standing beside him, leaning into him, all her weight concentrated in one hip, and if he felt that weight as a burden, so be it. This was marriage. This was love. Two bound in one, in the flesh, for better, for worse. Rob looked up. "I don't know if you realize how good these dogs are," he said. "They always get their man, I mean, *always*. I've never seen them fail yet, except in the rare case where the suspect shoots the dog—"

Carolee let out a sharp breath. "Not Adam, no—"

He was shaking his head again, whether in wonder or disgust or some combination of the two, Sten couldn't say. "If he'd fired his weapon, that would have put us onto his location, so he didn't." A pause. "He was too smart for that."

But the dog *had* contacted him, that was for sure, because the dog came back with his backpack, or *a* backpack. Which contained Hershey's Kisses, a whole sixteen-ounce bag of them, a bottle of gin, ammunition for a .22 rifle (strange, because the recovered casings from the initial firefight were from the Norinco), and half a dozen packages of freeze-dried entrées—the imported ones, from Switzerland, that weren't exactly cheap. They'd sent the backpack to the lab for DNA testing, but really, there wasn't much point since it was ninety-nine percent certain it was Adam's. The SWAT team officer had seen him, positive ID, engaged him, and how he'd ever managed to get away from the K-9 unit was just a mystery.

Sten heard himself say, "What if I went out there?"

"You can't do that. Too risky."

"What if I, I don't know, went up the train tracks with a bullhorn or something, and called him to give himself up? Or the train. What if I took the train up there and just kept calling all the way up and back again—it's better than nothing. I'll tell you, sitting here is killing me. And Carolee too."

Carolee had an arm round his shoulder, bracing herself, and he felt her grip tighten now. "I could go too," she said. "He'd listen to me, I mean, more than—"

"Me? You mean more than me?" He could feel the anger coming up in him, anger at her, anger at Rob, but most of all at Adam, Adam with his thrusts and parries and the way he hid behind his debility, pulled it down like a screen to excuse anything, and so what if he was the principal's son? Was it really all that much of a burden? They'd tried to send him to another school, any school he wanted, but he wouldn't go, wouldn't behave or act normal or even try, wouldn't do anything anybody wanted except to please himself. "Because I'm shit for a father, right, is that what you mean? Because he hates me?"

"You'd have to wear body armor," Rob said, giving him a long cool look. "I wouldn't let you go out there without it."

Carolee pushed the hair away from her face and leaned in over the table, looking from him to Rob, her eyes fierce. "I'm going too."

"I can't allow that," Rob said.

"Can't allow it?"

"Too dangerous."

But she wouldn't have it. She stood there glaring at the sheriff, the cords of her throat drawn tight. "I can't believe you," she said, her voice rising till it broke. "You think my son would ever dream of hurting me? His own mother?"

32.

ON THE MORNING THE sheriff finally called to give his permission, Sten was still in bed. A long stripe of bleached-out sunlight painted the wall over the night table, where the clock radio showed half past ten. Carolee was nowhere to be seen, gone, he remembered, down to Calpurnia to work at the game reserve, *Just to get out of the house because I swear I'm going to start screaming any minute now.* He'd taken a sleeping pill in the middle of the night after something had awakened him—a random noise, a scurrying in the dark—and he'd lain there for what seemed like hours till he got up, made his way to the bathroom and swallowed an Ambien, dry, and then staggered back to bed. When his cellphone weaned him into consciousness, he didn't at first know where he was, his head fogged with the residue of his dreams, dreams that bucked and shifted and left his muscles kinked with anxiety till he felt as if he'd been crawling through a series of decreasingly narrow tubes all night long.

He was going to ignore the phone—he was trying to ignore it, two weeks more having dragged by since Rob had stopped by the house to quiz him on the subject of Adam's military background, the police presence in the hills inflated till there was a virtual army out there and still no news, no hope, no reason to do anything but lie flat out on your back like one of the living dead—but those two sharp bleats, followed by a pause and another pair of bleats and then another, were too much for him. He pushed the talk button and heard the sheriff's voice coming at him, a morning voice, caffeinated and urgent.

"Sten?"

"Yeah."

"Shit, I didn't wake you, did I?"

"No, I just—you know how it is." And now all his fears came to squat on his chest like a flock of carrion birds with their long naked claws. "What's the news? Tell me quick."

"No news. Nothing. Zip. No contact. But what I'm calling about is I think it's a good idea you going out there and see what you can do. We've arranged it with the railroad people."

The railroad people. Sure. Of course they'd be involved. Why not? They wanted this thing over with as much as anybody because they'd been shut down now since Adam started in—and that meant no income, no tourists being hauled up the hill by the hundreds and paying forty-nine bucks apiece for the privilege, which in turn meant that everybody who owned a motel or a restaurant or even a gas station was hurting too. The irony of it. But it was beyond irony—it was like some black-hearted joke the universe was playing on him. If before he couldn't step in the door of a restaurant or coffee shop for fear of some total stranger sending over martinis or picking up his tab, now he didn't dare show his face because of Adam, because of what Adam had done to Carey Bachman and Art Tolleson and what he was doing, single-handedly, to the local economy. The forests were closed, off-limits. And if the forests were closed, what was the attraction for the tourists—or anybody else, for that matter? Take Back Our Forests. Right. Take them back from Adam.

"Can you be ready today? For the afternoon run? That's at three-thirty?"

He said, "Yeah, I guess," but it came out as an airless rasp and he had to repeat himself.

"We're going to hook you up with a bullhorn, just like you wanted, because frankly we're all getting kind of desperate here. But you'll wear protection, I insist on that. And we're going to have a select group of agents on the train, a few females too, so it looks like the tourists are out again because we don't want to make the suspect—Adam, I mean—suspicious."

What could he say? The words were wadded in his throat. He needed water, needed breakfast, needed an aspirin. "So if he comes to me, you'll take him? Is that it? Is that the plan?"

"Listen, I don't want to risk any lives out there, and yes, that would be the ideal solution."

"If I can get him to come."

"Yeah, *if.*"

"And get him to put his gun down."

"It's a big if. But I tell you, at this point I'm willing to try anything."

There was a silence.

"And if he won't put it down, assuming he even comes to the sound of my voice?"

A sigh. The squawk of a radio in the background. "I wouldn't want to speculate."

The railroad was strictly a tourist thing now, though originally it had been used for bringing logs down to the mill at Fort Bragg, now defunct, like everything else, and he hadn't been on it more than three or four times in his life. The Skunk Train. With its cartoon skunk logo that made everything seem so innocuous and appealing, though the nickname had come about because the train had originally burned crude oil for heat in the passenger car and that left a sour odor hanging over the tracks. Half-day trips took you to Northspur from the coast or down from Willits up above. And you could see and document the redwoods without having to exert any more effort than it took to set down your wine glass and lift a camera off the seat. For his part, when he wanted to see redwoods, he used his legs. And what he smelled out there wasn't crude oil or diesel or even woodsmoke from the old steam engine they sometimes ran but just what nature offered up. Not that he was critical. Or complaining. Every town needed an industry, and now that the mills were gone, this was the next best thing.

Let the tourists go gaga over the big trees, let them grow fat and fatter. It was fine with him.

The first thing he did after he got off the phone with Rob was walk the three blocks into town for a big twenty-ounce caffe latte with a double shot of espresso, the air dense, the sea swallowed up in fog. There were tourists everywhere, though the season was petering out. Or should have been. But then the Boomers were enjoying their retirement and didn't have a season anymore—they just kept coming. He would have gone to the bakery or the breakfast place to put something on his stomach, if only for ballast, but he didn't really want to see anybody or have to make explanations or pretend to be grateful for the expressions of sympathy people kept laying on him, whether false or sincere or somewhere in between. Instead he went to the deli and had them fix him a couple of sandwiches, one for now, one for the train, then he went home to make his hundred daily phone calls in the frustrated hope of gleaning some bit of information that would provide the key here, the key he could turn in a lock that would open the door and make all this go away.

Just yesterday he'd heard from a source at the Fort Bragg police station (Freddy Aulin, who'd graduated from the high school in 1982) that a witness had positively identified Adam the night before. The witness—a man in his twenties, one of those free spirits who didn't worry much about grooming and slept rough and had a drug and/or drinking problem—was making his own camp off the railroad tracks up near the South Fork milepost, and while he wasn't oblivious to the sheriff's order he just didn't think it applied to him. It was unclear whether he knew Adam or not, but he was heading back from town along the tracks with a bottle of fortified wine and saw a figure coming toward him, moving fast, and recognized Adam. The thing was, Adam didn't seem jumpy or paranoid at all. In fact, he'd stopped and chatted with the man awhile, even going so far as to share a joint with him in a thicket not fifty feet off the tracks where transients were known to gather. Was the man afraid for his life? Well, no, he wasn't. For one thing, he was drunk, and for another he expressed nothing but admiration for what Adam was doing, *sticking it to them,* and they were brothers, that was how he saw it. Adam must have seen it that way too.

"You know," the man told him, "they're out here looking for you. Like a million cops."

Adam just shrugged. "Let them look," he said.

And how had this man come to let the police in on the encounter? Had he strolled in voluntarily to offer up information, maybe in the hope of scoring some reward money? No. He was arrested for urinating in public when he went back into town later that night for a second bottle, and as the arresting officer was handcuffing him, he happened to let it drop, whether out of civic duty or by way of extenuation wasn't clear. "I don't know if it means anything to you," he said, the words thick in his mouth, "but I just saw that dude you're after, Adam? Like two hours ago?"

So yes, Sten was making phone calls, and whether they led to anything other than frustration, more frustration, at least he was doing something. He spent the next two hours on the phone, learning nothing, then thought to call Carolee before he left for the train, just to let her know what was going on. She picked up on the first ring and right away he could tell something was wrong, just from the way she murmured hello as if it had to be pried from her lips.

"What is it?" he said. "You hear anything?"

It took her a minute. She was gathering herself, her breathing harsh and sodden, as if she were holding a washcloth over the receiver. "They shot the antelope."

"Who? What are you talking about?"

"Two of the sable. Corinna and Lulu. They're saying Adam did it."

"Adam? That's ridiculous. It's forty miles to get down there."

She didn't say anything to this, just breathed through the line.

"It's probably nothing. Some kid with a gun."

A pause. Her voice so reduced it was barely there. "Adam's a kid with a gun."

"Some other kid. Some apprentice yahoo. It's nothing, I'm sure of it."

"Uh-huh. Tell that to Cindy. And Gentian. They've got two dead animals on their hands, animals that might as well have been over in Africa, taking their chances there."

He didn't know what to say to this. Adam could easily have humped those forty miles in the last two days, but Sten was sure he hadn't. And even if he had, why would he shoot antelope? But then—and Sten's thoughts were racing ahead of him—why would he shoot Carey or Art or open fire on a SWAT team? The answer came rising to the surface like something buoyed on its own gases: because he was suicidal, that was why. Because he wanted to die. He wasn't going to come to the train, to the sound of his own name, to his father. That was fantasy. That was futility. That was the way to pain and more pain.

"I'm sorry," he said. "I am. Really. That's a terrible thing. But I'm sure it's not Adam, I'm sure there's some other explanation . . . but look, the reason I called is I heard from Rob and he wants me to go up the train line."

"When?"

"Today. This afternoon."

"I'm coming."

"You heard Rob, didn't you? Bullets are flying out there. And whether these cops are highly trained or not, you never can tell what's going to happen, so that's just not an option."

"And you really think he's going to listen to you, he's going to come to you? Because I'm the one. I'm the one he'll come to."

"Yeah," he said, "I know that," and here was the accusation again, the old thrust, why can't you be a better father, why can't you be home nights, why can't you get strict with him, lay down the law, make him stop this nonsense, why didn't you show up for the T-ball game, the sing-along, the cake sale, because what meeting is more important than your own son? "And if I didn't know it I'm sure you'd be there to tell me the next ten thousand times."

The train moved along at a walking pace, easing across the inter-section on Main with its whistle blowing for everybody to hear and take note of, whether they were stalled at the crossing in their cars and campers or hunkered in some ravine halfway up the mountainside ready to take on the world. Sten was dressed like a tourist, in shorts, running shoes and a woolen shirt that concealed the soft body armor Rob had insisted on, though it wasn't quite clear why since it wouldn't stop a round from an assault rifle. Slow it down, maybe, depending on how far it had to travel. Or a ricochet, it might stop a ricochet, which, of course, might not necessarily cooperate and strike you where you were protected. It could go anywhere, through your skull, the roof of your mouth, your groin. But he didn't want to think about that—or the last time he'd laid eyes on Adam, the fight they'd had, how Adam had shoved back with all the sick fury uncoiling inside him, and what had the Norse called their fiercest warriors? Berserkers. They didn't know fear. They were unhinged. And on the battlefield they went berserk. Adam Stensen. Sten's son. Son of Sten who was the son of Sten.

There was no one on the deck of the observation car— that would have been suicidal in Rob's estimation, Rob who'd declined to go on this little expedition because he had a command to oversee—and Sten wondered about that, about the imposture they were trying to pull off here. Various deputies were scat-tered throughout the two enclosed cars, men and women both, dressed casually, the men in loud shirts and reversed baseball caps, the women in big straw hats and pastels, but if they were really tourists, actual tourists, half of them would have been lounging

around the open car, beer bottles pressed to their lips and cameras
flashing. Would Adam notice? Would he care? Would he even be
anywhere near the rail line in broad daylight? And here, despite
himself, he felt a flush of pride: Adam *was* smart. He was elusive.
And he knew his terrain. He would have made a LURP in Vietnam, the ghost in the night who materialized amongst the enemy
to cut the throats of the unwary and scare the shit out of the rest.

The train rattled on, picking up speed but still going at half
the normal pace because it was a target and make no mistake
about it. A lure. A bait. But then why would Adam want to shoot
up a train or go anywhere near it? Sten had no answer to that,
except that Adam had a rage inside him and that rage had to come
up against something, just to rub it, feel it, let the world know
what it was to have a thing like that clawing to get out. He'd felt
it himself when he was in his teens and after too and he'd seen
it channeled through two generations of cynical slouching bull-
headed kids at the high school, of which Deputy Jason Ringwald,
seated two rows behind him and staring hard out the window,
was a prime example. Most of them suppressed it and went out
into the world to become cops and corporate raiders, army lifers,
mill hands, but some never could get loose of it and they wound
up in jail, crippled in motorcycle accidents or scattered across the
blacktop in pieces. Or shot. Shot dead.

"Any time now," a voice was saying and he looked up to see one
of the SWAT team honchos, a lieutenant, all eyebrows and a mouth
pursed round a set of small even teeth, hovering over the seat.

They were passing along Pudding Creek, which was tidal here,
and had been used to float logs during rainy seasons of the past
but was now a swampy stretch of nothing you could barely turn a
canoe around in. There were houses up on the hills. Roads. The
gleam of a parked automobile. "Here?" he said. "We're barely out
of town."

The man—he was in his late thirties, forties maybe, with flecks
of gray stubble along his jawline where he'd shaved hurriedly—

just gave him a look. This man didn't trust him. Didn't like him. None of them did. He was the father of the shooter and that made him damaged goods, and if he wasn't a suspect, in their eyes he should have been. "Might as well. You never know where he could be. Didn't they spot him along here night before last?"

"That's what I hear."

The cop held the look. "It's costing time and money. For the engineer up there, the two of them. And us. All of us." He gave it a beat. "We got families too, you know."

Sten shrugged and rose to his feet, the megaphone clutched in one hand. He was planning to go out there on the observation car no matter what anybody said, and if his son wanted to shoot him—Adam, if Adam wanted to shoot his own father—well let him go ahead. Anything would be better than this.

Until he stepped out on the deck, he hadn't realized how stifling it had been in the car. The air was in motion here, blowing cool on his face and drying the nervous sweat under his arms. He smelled bay, alder, pine, smelled mud and standing water, the dark funk of rot that underlay everything. The train swung round a curve, heading east now, heading uphill, and he caught a glimpse of a hidden glen thick with moss and fern, the light sifting through the trees in a luminous haze that made him forget for a moment just exactly what the purpose of all this was. He braced his hips instinctively against the sway of the platform and let the world open up around him, thinking how ungenerous he'd been to dismiss the tourists—who could blame them for wanting to come up here where it was silent and green and the trees had stood motionless since the time before Christ, at least the ones the loggers hadn't got to? The air rushed at him. The tracks sang. He found he'd gone outside himself for a minute there and it took the weight of the hard plastic butt of the bullhorn to bring him back, but then he raised the thing to his lips, feeling foolish and afraid and maybe a little fatalistic too because they were just wasting their time here, weren't they?

He called Adam's name, but nothing happened because he'd somehow neglected to switch the thing on. Behind him, a small army sat balanced over their weapons, watching him. He found the switch. Flicked it. And called his son's name, bellowed it, chanted it, threw it up against the changeless trunks of the trees till it came back to him riding on its own echo, and he kept on calling it all the way up the line and back down again, as the shadows deepened and his voice dried up to a hoarse reverberant rattle in the very deepest hollow of his throat.

PART XI

Route 20

33.

"You mind if we just eat in front of the woodstove tonight?" She was in the kitchen, cooking, calling over her shoulder to where Christabel sat in the rocker in the living room, the latest *Cosmo* spread open in her lap and a glass of the chardonnay she'd brought along dangling from one hand. "It's so much cozier in there, what with this rain and all, don't you think?"

Christabel was giving her a faraway look, half-looped already. She didn't answer.

"We don't have to stand on formality, do we?"

"No, no way," Christabel said, rousing herself. This would be one of the nights when Christa slept over, she could see that already. "Right here's fine with me. Better than fine: now I won't even have to move."

"You expect me to serve you?"

"Damn straight I do. I am the guest, after all, aren't I? I mean, I serve you at my house—"

They were teasing back and forth, bantering, and it was perfect, just what she needed, the fire going in the stove, rain at the windows, Kutya curled up asleep on the rug and dinner three shakes from being done. "Right," she called, pausing to take a sip of her own wine and then douse the fish with the rest of it, "and when was the last time that happened?"

She was cooking up the two dozen smelt one of her clients had given her—he was rich, in his sixties, and when he wasn't riding he was out on his boat, catching fish—and they were the simplest thing in the world: gut them, wash them, roll them in flour and sauté them whole with a little salt and pepper. High-protein, low-cal. She was serving a garden salad on the side and those Pillsbury dinner rolls that took fifteen minutes in the oven. After dinner they'd watch one of the DVDs she'd checked out of the library on her way back with the fish. Or maybe both of them, one a so-called comedy and the other horror, though she didn't feel much like horror tonight. Maybe they'd just turn in early. And if Adam had snuck out of the house yesterday morning before she even got up and took the bourbon with him too, she wasn't missing him, not with Christabel here and everything so slow and calm and easy. Or that was what she told herself, anyway. He'd show up when he was ready—and this was the kind of weather that made camping a pure misery, so most likely it wouldn't be long. But let him take his time—she wasn't tied to him. She had a whole life of her own. When he showed, he showed, why worry about it?

She tipped the fish onto a serving plate and set the plate on the table next to the salad, then pulled the rolls from the oven, letting the sweet warm wafting scent of them fill the kitchen even as the rain whispered on the roof and feathered the windows. "You want water?" she called.

"What would the French say?" This was one of their jokes, having once been suckered into watching a French movie on Netflix that had gotten good reviews but turned out to be all but incomprehensible despite the subtitles, because the French, they concluded, had different values.

"The French would say, '*Non.*' They'd say, 'Pour me some more wine.'"

"*Oui, oui,*" Christabel said, rising from the chair now, "more wine."

They pulled two chairs up to the stove, the door of which she'd left open so they could watch the fire crackling inside, and settled in, plates in laps. Kutya was interested suddenly and though she told herself she wouldn't have him begging she couldn't help feeding him a sliver or two of fish in between bites. He took it daintily, with the softest jaws in the world, bolted it down and looked up expectantly for the next morsel to come his way.

"This is good," Christabel said, as if she doubted herself. "Really good. I don't think I've ever . . . I mean the whole fish—"

"You don't think about it, though, do you? After the first one."

Christabel, chewing, staring into the stove, just nodded.

This was the kind of meal Sara loved, no chemicals, no BHT or food coloring or (the worst) *corn syrup,* just natural food, come by naturally. Except for the rolls, but she just didn't have the time or energy to make them from scratch, having worked outside in the rain half the day, but the fish were fresh-caught right down there on the coast and the butter lettuce, cherry tomatoes, cucumbers and radishes had come from her own garden. And the fish were free, which made it even better, free for the taking. Like mussels. She loved nothing better than to just pull over and make her way down a path to the sea at low tide, cut a bunch of mussels from the rocks (but not in summer, when they were quarantined because of the possibility of paralytic shellfish poisoning, which was fatal, thank you), and then steam them up and serve half as a starter with butter and garlic and homemade bread and then toss the rest into a pot of marinara at the last minute so you didn't have to worry about them getting overcooked and rubbery. And berries. Nothing better than gathering berries in late summer for pies and tarts, but then you had the calorie factor to worry about. Berries with a little half-and-half then. And the smallest sprinkle of sugar.

When they were done, Christabel insisted on washing the dishes but she told her no, just let them sit, because why spoil the evening with something so—what was the word?—*boring.* Or no, *tedious.* "Too tedious," she said, and she liked the sound of it and added, "Don't be tedious. Let's be the opposite—what is the opposite of tedious, anyway?"

Christabel let out a laugh. "I don't know, *untedious?*"

They talked about having an after-dinner drink—Bailey's, she had some Bailey's in the cabinet, but that stuff packed on the pounds like steroids. "They ought to give that to the cattle at the feedlots," she said. "That'd fatten them up. Pronto."

"Yeah," Christabel said, giving her a sloppy grin, "but what would the French say?"

"They'd say 'Make mine rare.'"

"Right. And then they'd say, 'Let's stick to wine.'"

So they stuck to wine, how many glasses neither of them could say, but the quantity turned out to be exactly the precise amount to make the so-called comedy funny—or, that is, to prime them to the point where they could get sarcastic and laugh *at* it, which, as it turned out, made it genuinely funny.

They were both laughing when they heard the sirens, and before they could even get up out of their chairs or pause the video or shut the stove so they wouldn't have to worry about sparks, the front door, which had been locked—she was pretty sure it had been locked—burst open as if it was made of cardboard and there were cops everywhere, shouting, "Your hands! Let me see your hands!"

She'd been a fool, that was her first thought, worse than a fool, because she of all people should have known they'd never let it go because once they got their claws into you, you had no more status than they did, and not packing up and moving to Nevada when she had the chance was just about the stupidest thing she'd ever done. What was wrong with her? What had she been thinking—that they'd forget about it? That if she stuck around, Adam would give up on the woods and come back to her? That it would be too hard, too much of an *effort,* to pull up her stakes here? She'd been lazy, that was what it was, living in fantasyland, and she was getting just what she deserved, because here they were with their boots and guns and bulletproof vests and there was no way out now.

She had her hands in the air. Christabel, who looked as if she'd been flash-frozen, had dropped the wine glass on the rug in the shock of the moment and she had her hands in the air too. And Kutya, Kutya was going bonkers. "Lady," one of the cops yelled at her, "will you control that animal?"

At first she couldn't understand what he was saying because they'd come to take Kutya away from her, hadn't they? Wasn't that what this was all about? That and maybe her no-show on the seatbelt thing. And the court date on the trumped-up DUI charge, to which she'd pleaded innocent, but that wasn't for two weeks yet, not that she had any intention of showing for it . . . or hadn't had. Until now. But wait—and here her blood froze—what about that little incident the other night with the police cruiser and the sugar water meant for innocent hummingbirds? They'd caught her on videotape, she was sure of it, because everything in the U.S.I.G.A. was on tape now, every breath you took, and what about the Fourth Amendment, what about that? Search and Seizure? Hello?

"Kutya," she called, "Kutya! Stop it now!" But when she tried to get up out of the chair and take him by the collar, the cop shoved her back down. "Hands!" he roared, and he had his gun trained right on her.

She was scared, had never been so scared in her life, but she couldn't help throwing it back at him nonetheless, "How am I supposed to control him if I can't even—"

"Shut the fuck up," that was what he said, or snarled, and then another cop had one of those muzzle things on a stick and seized hold of the dog's snout and the barking abruptly stopped.

It was right around then that she began to reconsider. There were cops everywhere, stalking through the kitchen, the bedrooms, their guns held out rigidly before them and laser lights poking red holes in everything—but why? Why would there be such a show of force over a woman who wasn't wearing her seatbelt? Even if she hadn't shown for her court date? Even if they knew she'd destroyed a police car, which, it became obvious to her in that moment, they didn't . . .

Another cop was there now, a bald-headed one, tailed by a deputy who looked all of twelve years old, and why did everybody have to shave their heads, was it some sort of cops and robbers sort of thing? He stood there a moment, just out of range of the one who'd pinned Kutya down with the muzzle-stick, staring at her. "Sara Hovarty Jennings?" he asked.

She couldn't do much more than just nod yes, her heart going like the StairMaster set on Alpine, but the words were on her lips—*Threat, Duress and Coercion*—and if he didn't back off she was going to start screaming and they could just go ahead and shoot her, but she surprised herself by finding her voice long enough to frame her own question in as nasty a voice as she could muster, "You got a search warrant?"

The cop ignored her. He swung his head in Christabel's direction, Christabel who was sitting right there beside her, her hands in the air still. "And what's your name?"

Poor Christa. She was so scared she could barely talk Or she couldn't, she couldn't talk at all.

"You can put your hands down," he said, softening his voice, "both of you." He was short, this cop, as nondescript as if he had his face on backwards, but he seemed to be in charge, and he had some sort of decoration or whatever it was sewed to the shoulder of his uniform. "Now, once again, *you*"—nodding at Christabel—"I asked your name."

"Christabel Walsh? I'm a teacher's aide?" She started to say where she worked, as if the name of the school would carry any weight, but her voice got choked in her throat and she couldn't go on.

And now one of the other cops, the one who'd been in the bedroom, going through her personal things, clomped into the room and announced, "All clear back there. Nobody here but these two."

"You go out there and check that yard, every blade of grass, hear me? Fence lines, all the fields around here. Get the dogs on it."

"Yes, sir." And that cop was gone, out the door and into

the yard where lights were at war and voices stalked around the corners.

It was then, just then, in the interval before the chief cop turned back to her, that she began to understand. "Is this about Adam?" she asked, and why she asked she didn't know—it was just some snaky intuition that made her heart hammer even faster and the fish go sour on her stomach.

At first the cop questioned them both together, but then, after he'd asked Christabel what sort of person Adam was and she'd said, "I don't know, regular, I guess, maybe a little weird—he's a nudist, I mean, sometimes, anyway," the cop called one of his men over and said, "Why don't you take her out in the kitchen and see what she knows. I'll take care of Sara here myself."

What he did then, with the lights flashing outside and cops all over the place as if this was some kind of war zone, was plunk himself down in the chair Christabel had just vacated, then scoot it over so that he was right there in her face, their knees practically touching. "You know, Sara—is it all right if I call you Sara? You know, I don't really think we have to get upset here or anything—or take this down to the station either. I just want to ask you a couple questions. About Adam."

"What did he do?"

"Why don't you just let me ask the questions, okay? This doesn't have to be hard. It's not going to be hard. As long as you cooperate, you understand me?"

What she felt then, under threat, duress and coercion like nobody could believe, was just the faintest breath of release: they hadn't come for her, they didn't care about her or her dog either. All they wanted was Adam. But why? What had he done? Sitting there knee-to-knee with the cop and the fire snapping and Christabel shunted away to the kitchen with another cop, she tried to picture him, and what she saw was his body greased with sweat, his arms, his bare arms, and the knife at his side. And the gun. The gun.

"You saw him last, when? Two nights ago, is that right? Wednesday?"

She just nodded. She flashed on that day in the car, the day she'd met him, when he'd gone ballistic over the sight of a cop car going in the opposite direction. But what had he done? They wouldn't bring a thousand cops around to swarm all over her if it wasn't the worst, but what was the worst? What was the worst thing you could do? She felt her scalp prickle. She could barely breathe.

"And he left Thursday morning, early, before you were up?"

"Yes."

"He say where he was going?"

"I don't know, the woods. I think he was, like, living out there."

"What about his rifle, did he take his rifle, did he have it here? With him, I mean?"

"He always had it."

The cop was silent a minute, as if mulling this over, Adam and his rifle. Then he leaned in nearer so that she could see his eyes up close, the little dance of his pupils. "You took him to the hospital, why was that?"

"He asked me to. He had the—the runs. Giardia." Kutya had been still, but now, in the far corner of the room, he began struggling again, though the cop there held him firmly down. "This isn't right," she said. "I don't have to talk to you. And I'm not going to say one more word until you tell me what this is all about."

Another silence, longer this time. The way he was watching her creeped her out, as if he was some kind of god looking down on the littlest thing in his creation, a bug or bacterium, when in fact he was just another tool of the system. "You want to get cute, I can arrest you right this minute."

She didn't want to push it, but she couldn't help herself,

because this was just sick, the whole slimy police-state Heil Hitler crap that had brought Jerry Kane down and was bringing her down too. "For what?"

"Oh, I don't know," he said, shrugging. "Accessory to murder. How does that sound?"

Everything seemed to stop right then, the stomping, the hollering, the banging of her heart and the whimpering of the dog, replaced by a long slither of white noise hissing in her ears. What the cop told her was that Adam had shot somebody while he was on his sojourn out there in the woods, shot him and left him for dead, and that everybody had thought the Mexicans had done it, but it wasn't the Mexicans at all. It was Adam. Proof positive. Adam had shot somebody and then he'd got sick and come to her, to her bed, and she'd washed his clothes for him and let him make love to her and he never even so much as mentioned it. As if people were nothing, as if you could just go around shooting and then drink bourbon and cook beef stew over a campfire as if it was the most ordinary thing in the world. She didn't know what to say. She was in shock.

"And don't pretend you don't know where he is—you had a relationship with him. For what, two, three months now?"

"I told you," she said, "he's in the woods."

"You getting smart with me? Because if you want to get smart, we can continue this down at the station."

"No," she said, "really. I don't know where he is, I mean, other than that. I told you, he left here yesterday morning, and I haven't seen him since. Or heard from him. Really."

"And yet you took him to the hospital for medication."

"Yes, but I didn't—"

"That makes you an accessory right there."

"I didn't *know*—"

"You didn't know he killed an unarmed man in cold blood?" She shook her head.

"Or today. What about today? You know he killed another

man today, right this afternoon? While you were what, *knitting*?"

It was all too much. She didn't have to listen to this—whoever said she had to listen to this? He was a liar. He was just trying to get to her because *he* was the criminal, not Adam. "I don't knit," she said. "And I have no contract with you—how many times do I have to tell you people?" Kutya squirmed. He let out a low growl and the lights flashed in the yard. She shot a furious glance round the room, the cops, the poor dog—Christabel, where was Christabel? "You know what you are?" she said.

He just sat there, his lips zipped tight, trying to burn his eyes right through her.

"You're just an actor, that's all. Somebody in a costume. Like you're dressed up for Halloween. And you know something else? I'm not into trick-or-treating."

34.

IN THE END, THEY must have believed her—and Christabel too, Christabel who by that point was scared sober and wearing a face like something she'd picked up off the floor—because eventually they took their muddy boots and clanking belts and double-barreled shotguns and faded back into the night, but not without taking two plastic bags of what they called evidence with them and leaving a patrol car just down the street with its lights off and two cops inside to see if she was going to run out into the woods, find her way to Adam and somehow warn him off. Which she would have, if she could. Because it was all lies and if you had to pick sides here she knew which one she was on. Adam never hurt anybody. And even if he did, even if it was true, whoever it was probably had it coming.

The cops left a vacuum behind them, whoosh, all the air sucked right out of the place. One minute the house was an armed camp and the next it was deserted. They'd also left a mess. Her clothes were scattered around the bedroom, drawers pulled out, closets yawning open. The kitchen floor was all tracked up and they'd left it that way because what did they care about freemen on the land and personal property or individual rights or anything else for that matter, but she didn't have the heart to take a mop to it before she went to bed and when she woke up from a night's worth of poisonous dreams, she didn't have the energy. Ditto for Christabel, who at least didn't have to go into work, thank god, because it was Saturday.

When she got up and came into the kitchen at something like half past six, Christabel was already sitting there at the table drinking black coffee and staring out the window. She was wearing a T-shirt she'd managed to put on backwards under a cardigan that hung loose over her butt and bare thighs, last night's makeup caking under her eyes and her hair looking as if she'd been fighting a windstorm all night long. Kutya lay curled up under the table, his dreadlocks filthy from the mud out in the yard—the mud on the floor, for that matter—and he never even lifted his head when she stepped into the room. Christabel didn't turn to look at her. She didn't say hi or good morning. All she said was, "Jesus, I don't think I've ever been through anything like that, not in my whole life. Not even that time I was in the accident."

"Me either."

"I was *so* scared."

All she could do was nod. She went to the counter and poured herself a cup of coffee, then lightened it with a splash of milk and stirred in two heaping teaspoons of sugar, real sugar and not that artificial crap. She'd worry about calories later. Calories were the least of her problems.

"You know, you can't say I didn't warn you," and here Christabel turned to look up at her out of bloodshot eyes, eyes that weren't even that pretty, really, but just a dull fixed brown.

She just shook her head, very slowly, the injustice of it all settling on her like a coat made out of lead, like one of those things they make you wear when they take X-rays of your chest. "Yeah, you warned me, all right, but since when do I have to listen?"

"Oh, Christ! You're not going to defend him, are you? He's a nut case. He killed two people. He could have killed *us*!"

"So the cops say. You believe the cops?"

She saw now that Christabel was holding something in her left hand, a slice of color, the sharp concentrated gleam of the Cloud sucked down to earth: her cellphone. "I believe this," she said.

And there it was, Adam's face staring out of the phone, Adam's face everywhere, on every site, proof run wild. He'd shot and killed two men, and here were their faces, their names and biographies, and she realized with a jolt that she knew one of them from the high school, and how strange it was to think he was dead—*slain*—and would never walk those corridors again or stand before a class of kids who might have loved him or hated him but had the same festering hormones and the same issues the class before them had had and the class after them would have and all the classes before and since. He was dead. Art Tolleson. He was dead and Adam had killed him.

She went into the living room and flicked on the TV and it was on every channel. The sheriff—and it was his face on the screen now, the poser with the grappling-hook eyes who'd sat right there in her own house and harassed her for the better part of an hour—was giving a press conference and telling everybody to stay calm even though he was cordoning off the entire forest range, from the middle fork of the Ten Mile in the north to Big River in the south, coast to mountains, and that no one was to be allowed in for any purpose whatever until the threat had been neutralized. And what about Route 20? Route 20 was a major artery, as was the Coast Highway, and they would remain open to traffic, but he cautioned people not to linger or get out of their cars—the suspect was armed and dangerous and if anyone encountered him or knew anything of his whereabouts they should call 911. Then up came the picture of Adam, full-screen—a picture, she realized, that must have been a mug shot from one of his past brushes with the system, but the thing was, he didn't look anything like Adam, not the Adam she knew. He looked like a thug, with his shaved head and one eye half-closed as a result of whatever struggle he must have put up when they were trying to take him into custody—and they must have gang-piled him because he was a rock and he could have taken on any three of them all by himself . . .

But then that was no way to think. The way to think was of how to cut him loose, all knowledge and memory of him, to forget him and move on. To Nevada. The sooner the better. "Okay," she said, nodding at Christabel, who'd joined her in front of the TV, "you were right, I admit it, and I should never have even thought about dating him—"

Christabel made a little noise of disapproval in her throat. "I've said it before"—she gave her a sharp glance out of those mud brown eyes with their dead eyeliner and faded mascara, Christabel the righteous, Christabel in the aftermath, picking through the wreckage—"I never could tell what you saw in him, anyway."

A week went by, then another. Her court date came up, and if she thought anything about it at all, it was just that she regretted the waste of ink it took to mark her calendar when she had no intention of going anywhere near the courthouse or the police station or anyplace else the pretenders pretended to conduct their so-called business. Still, though—and this nagged at her—she hadn't even taken step one as to getting herself out of Dodge and you had to chalk that up to inertia. That, and grief. She was grieving over Adam, over how she'd fallen so hard for him when clearly he was trouble—worse than trouble, a psychopath, a murderer, a cannon so loose he'd rolled right off the deck. But that was the problem: she *had* fallen for him and nothing could change that.

Adam. He was all anybody could talk about, on the news every night, national news now, at large for eighteen days and counting. People called her out of the blue, clients, friends she'd forgotten she had, reporters, and they all wanted to know what she knew, wanted details, gossip, dirt. What it all boiled down to, no surprise, was sex, though nobody came straight out and said it. How could she have had sex with a maniac, that was what they wanted to know. How could she have kissed him, invited him into her bed? And more, and juicier: What was it like? Was it good? Was it hot? Did he get rough? When she went out, she tried to keep a low profile, wearing bulky clothes and a hat, always a hat. But she did have to work, after all (no subbing, though, no way, not with all this notoriety), and when she went to her clients' houses just to see to their poor dumb horses that wouldn't have known or cared if she'd gone to bed with a hundred maniacs, with the Taliban or the whole U.S. Army, she couldn't have a moment's peace. Here were these people she'd known for years, women mostly, decent people, her *clients,* for Christ's sake, and they just draped themselves right over her while she manipulated her hoof pick and clinch cutters, sniffing and probing and working at her like paleontologists looking for the bones revealed in the dirt.

Then one day she went down to work at the Burnsides' because the Burnsides were marked on her calendar and she had to earn a living, no matter what the rest of the world was doing or thinking or saying. There were cops everywhere, as if it was some sort of convention, but she tried to ignore them because they weren't there for her, and when she came into Calpurnia, the fog, which had pretty well curtained everything in to this point, got denser suddenly, so dense she had to put her lights and wipers on. She almost went right on by the turnoff but caught herself at the last minute. There was nobody else on the road—even here, forty miles south, Adam had managed to cast a pall over things. Because they couldn't catch him. He was too smart for them. Too hard. They'd sent all those SWAT teams out there, helicopters with their infrared tracking devices, dogs—the very dogs Roger had told her about, *Good dog, Good dog*—and he'd outmaneuvered them all.

When she swung into Cindy's driveway, the gravel giving way under her wheels, she saw there was another car parked there in front of the barn, not Cindy's or Gentian's, but one that looked familiar somehow. Whose was it? The answer would come to her the minute she pulled up beside it, shut down her engine and climbed out of the car with her tool kit: it was Adam's mother's car, Carolee's. Because here came Carolee marching out of the mist with Cindy and Gentian flanking her, the two of them look- ing as if they were going to war while she looked like she'd just been punched in the gut. "Hi," Sara said, though Adam's mother was somebody she could definitely have done without seeing.

Gentian, a big man, once powerful, but now gone to seed around a face that drooped in folds right on down into the collar of his shirt, stopped in his tracks and the women pulled up then too. The look he was giving her was fierce, outraged. He spat out the words. "He shot Corinna and Lulu."

"Who? What are you talking about?"

Cindy answered for him: "Adam."

They all looked to Carolee, the mother, but Carolee had nothing to say, either in affirmation or denial. She was having enough trouble keeping her face composed. What she'd done—Sara could see this in a flash—was come down here to help out, to do something, anything, to get away from the terrible tension at home that must have been even worse for her than it was for herself. She'd given birth to him. Breast-fed him. Potty-trained him. Held his hand when he went to kindergarten and agonized over every inappropriate display and skewed adjustment through what must have been a chaotic childhood to a squirrelly adolescence and now this—they were hunting her son and he was their quarry, no different from the deer the sportsmen bungee-strapped to the hoods of their cars, and who hadn't seen the blood there striping the windshield and tarnishing the bright resistant strips of chrome? In that moment, Sara went outside herself and saw what this woman—her enemy, who'd rejected her right from the start—was going through. She said, "It wasn't Adam."

"How the hell would you know?" Gentian still hadn't moved, but she could see how furious he was, his fists clenched, the old splayed muscles tightening on their cords, something working beneath the skin at the corner of one eye. "Did you see him? Did you ask him?"

"It wasn't Adam."

Cindy said, "He's on foot, Gent. It's forty miles."

The picture of Corinna came into her head then, not the big-ribbed corpse she'd see bloodied in the field in due course, but Corinna after she'd had her first calf, proud and watchful and erect on her stiffened legs, her ears up and her nostrils to the wind. A dog had appeared at the periphery of the meadow one afternoon, a thousand yards away, a dog on a leash being walked along the street on the far side of the fence, no threat at all, not if she understood the situation. But Corinna didn't understand the situation. Corinna had perceived the danger in the way the light scissored between those four trotting legs and she charged halfway across the field, flinging up turf with her savage cutting hooves that could have decapitated that dog in a heartbeat and maybe his owner too. That was instinct. That was all she knew.

"Forty miles, shit," Gentian spat, turning bitterly on his wife. "You tell me who else is crazy enough to shoot defenseless animals like this? Who else is out there killing things with a rifle? Huh? Tell me that?"

No one answered him. The fog lifted and fell in beaded threads and tugged at the light in waves that seemed to pulsate across the yard. The gravel shone with wet. Gentian was red-faced. Cindy looked ashamed. And Carolee? Carolee looked as if she never expected her feelings to be spared again, looked like a pariah, mother of the murderer. And what did that say about *her* then? She was the girlfriend, no denying it, and that made her guilty too. As guilty, in their eyes, as if she'd pulled the trigger herself.

35.

IT WAS MIDWAY THROUGH the fifth week, Adam was still at large and the police were beyond crazy. They were stopping everybody on Route 20 just to look in their cars because in their feeble minds they imagined Adam squeezed under somebody's seat or packed into their trunk and they'd stopped her three times now but it was nothing more than a petty annoyance. They didn't ask for her papers and she didn't have to state her status. They didn't care if she was wearing a seatbelt or not and they didn't run her license plate or turn up the warrant out for her arrest on the grounds that she'd refused to play their idiot games or shuffle one more time through the charade of authority with the old hag of a judge in her courthouse presided over by the flag of the U.S.I.G.A. No. All they were interested in was Adam. It was all-out war now. They'd been made to look like the fools they were, big macho men with their big manly guns and all the resources of ten sheriff's departments and they still couldn't catch one twenty-five-year-old mountain man who was driving a stake through the heart of the local economy and scaring the bejesus out of the taxpayers so they couldn't even sleep at night.

She was at home, in the kitchen, listening to music and pushing two bone-in pork chops around a pan and sprinkling them with rosemary from her garden. She was tired of salad so she'd bought some fresh spinach at the farmers' market, rinsed it, tossed it with a little garlic salt and pepper, then splashed it with olive oil and balsamic and microwaved it for three minutes, easiest thing in the world. It had fallen dark now, the nights growing shorter—and colder—and Halloween just two days away. How would that play out? she wondered. What would parents tell their children? They'd have private parties, she supposed, because no one—absolutely no one—would be going house to house. Not with Adam out there. Would he consciously hurt a kid? Not the Adam she knew. But then he had driven his car onto the playground, hadn't he? And maybe he wasn't really the Adam she knew, not if he could shoot down Art Tolleson and the other one and just leave them there to rot.

Kutya stirred in the corner where he'd been lying asleep, laziest dog she'd ever seen and not getting any younger, and now he came clicking across the floor to her and the smell of the meat searing in the pan. "No," she told him, bending from the waist to look into his eyes, "you're just going to have to wait." Then she turned back to the pan and flipped the chops, everything in its place and everything quiet, but here she was in her warm kitchen with the smell of the meat rising around her and she couldn't help wondering what Adam was eating. He had a prodigious appetite and no matter how many freeze-dried entrées or cans of beef stew he'd squirreled away out there, how could it have lasted him all this time? He'd been breaking into cabins, they'd reported that, and he'd held that one old lady hostage back there at the beginning, but still. And that was another thing: no hot food. Even when it was raining, even when it was cold, and it had been getting down into the forties at night. Maybe he had a camp stove, the kind of thing you could risk cooking on in a deep secluded place, a cave or something, but even so he must have been pretty miserable. She tried to picture that a minute, him in a cave, with that rank wet smell caves always had and what, bats hanging overhead? He wouldn't dare travel in the daytime, not if he had any sense and he did, obviously, so he must have been roaming the woods in the dark—and if he was, he couldn't use a light. And if he couldn't use a light, how could he find his way? Plus, how could he keep from dying of boredom out there, even if he was putting everything he had into baiting the jerkoff cops and their killer dogs and no doubt enjoying it too? Adam. And why couldn't she stop thinking about him?

Maybe because nobody else could either. Anything went wrong within a hundred miles, even a flat tire, and Adam was to blame. Like with that whole debacle down at the Burnsides'. How quick they were to pin that on him, even with his mother—their friend, a woman who was just volunteering her time, for god's sake— standing right there beside them. *He shot the sable,* that was what Gentian had said, not someone shot the sable, but *he* shot them. The way it turned out, though, Adam had nothing to do with it.

Of course, the cops were there within five minutes of Gentian's putting in the call, swarming all over everything, their faces haggard and desperate because the system wasn't supporting them, the system was breaking down right in front of their eyes and there was nothing they could do about it. They searched the edge of the field and came up with some shell casings and they had one of their butchers slice open these beautiful four-hundred-pound animals and dig the slugs out of them and they tramped hell out of the place but didn't turn up Adam or anybody else. What they did discover, finally, and they took their sweet time about disclosing it too, was that two junior high kids had been fooling around with a deer rifle one of them found in his father's gun safe, which had been left unlocked. They found something in the liquor cabinet too. And thought it would be a great idea—or rad, wasn't that what they would say, a rad idea?—to go out and put holes in these beautiful animals that were fast disappearing from the earth.

She sat at the table to eat, idly paging through one of the magazines Christabel had left behind for her. Christa was a real hound for the gossip sheets—*Us Weekly, In Touch, People, The Star*—but basically they left her cold because it was just more of the same blindered attitude and slave mentality, as if whoever was dating whoever or buying what fabulous mansion had anything to do with the fact that the system was rotted all the way down to the stump. After dinner she went to her computer and read the latest about Adam, which was basically nothing piled on top of nothing, limiting herself to half an hour, and then she tried to read by the woodstove for a while, Kutya curled up at her feet, and finally turned on the idiot box to see if maybe there was an old movie on, one of the ones where people—Jimmy Stewart, Gary Cooper, take your pick—made all these stirring declarations about democracy and standing up for the little man while the heroine flashed across the screen in all these killer outfits. It was crap, but high-minded crap, crap in layers she could peel away till she found something there that took her back to a simpler time, a time before the corporations had taken over and made a mockery of everything everybody said on the screen. A movie. It was just a movie. A way to pass the time in an empty house on a night when there was nothing going on and the world had been reduced to these four walls and this gently ticking woodstove and the dog, in his dreadlocks, on the rug at her feet.

The funny thing—or odd, *odd* was a better word—was that it was just like the last time, nothing moving, nothing shaking, but there was a feeling coming over her that she wasn't alone. She looked over her shoulder. There was no one there. The doors were locked, she was sure of it, and if anyone should try to get in, Kutya, old as he was, would be up and barking his head off. She turned back to the movie, someone sitting by a deathbed on a ship, flimsy walls that were just a stage set and another movie playing through the porthole to give the illusion that the ship was moving and this was all real, and then the feeling stole over her again and she turned around and there he was.

He didn't say hello or help me or I love you, but just stood there, like Adam, exactly like, only different because of what he'd done and where he'd been and how he'd been putting it to the cops for all these weeks now. Kutya didn't stir until he spoke and even then he didn't bark because he must have remembered him, without preju- dice, because he was only a dog. Adam said, "Turn out the lights."

She said his name, but she didn't get up from the chair, though the dog had crossed the room to him, sniffing.

"Do it," he said.

She got up then, but she didn't go to him, instead working her way from lamp to lamp till the room was lit only by the TV. He looked older somehow, thinner, a lot thinner, and his clothes were ragged. She could smell the woods on him, the rot, as if he *had* been living in a cave. With the bats. And the lice. And the giardia parasites.

"Kill the TV too."

"We'd be totally in the dark," she said. "No, no way." And then, standing poised there in front of the lamp over the desk even as the glow of it faded away, she said, "What are you doing here, anyway? Are you crazy? The cops are watching this place, don't you realize that?"

He shrugged, dark in his dark clothes. There was a slash across his face, a welt there, fresh and livid, and the first thing she thought was that he'd been grazed by a bullet, but she saw that it wasn't that at all, more likely a mishap in the dark as he was creeping up on the place. He just stood there, his hands hanging at his sides. And where was his gun, his rifle? There, propped against the wall in the hallway that led to the back room. He looked exhausted, looked beat—beaten, beaten down.

She began to fear for herself then—not out of fear of him because she didn't care what he'd done, he would never hurt her, she was sure of it, but of the cops. If they found him here, if they found even the minutest scrap of evidence that he'd been here, then she *was* an accomplice and all the shit they'd brought down on her already was nothing compared to what was coming. "What do you want?" she demanded.

"I'm hungry."

"I can't give you food, I can't give you anything—they'll put me in jail."

"Who?" he said, his voice thick with contempt. "The hostiles? The aliens?" And then he laughed, but it wasn't a happy laugh. "Not while I'm here they won't."

"You've got to get out of here," she said. "They'll kill you."

He laughed again.

"I'm not kidding, Adam—they've been here. They tore the whole place apart. You've got to go. Right now. *Now,* hear me?"

"You won't give me food?"

"No."

"Colter would have got food," he said. "Colter would have—"

She cut him off. "Enough with Colter. Colter has nothing to do with this. Colter's dead. He's been dead for like two hundred years and the world isn't like that anymore, you know it, you of all people—"

"I want to sleep with you."

They were ten feet apart and he didn't come to her and she didn't go to him. They were like statues, talking statues. That moment? That was the moment that tested her more than any other. And if she saw herself packing in a frenzy and sneaking him and Kutya into the car and making a run for Stateline or wherever—Canada—it was because her heart was breaking. She was his mother too. His mother and his lover. And they were going to kill him. "No," she said. "You have to get out. Get out and never come back."

The light of the TV flickered across his face, black and white, somebody dying on a ship and everything as false and artificial and make-believe as it could be.

"Get out," she said, fighting to control her voice. "If you don't get out I'm going to call the police."

"Really?" he said, and still he hadn't moved. "You'd really do that? Even to Colter?"

"Yes," she said. "Yes. Even to Colter."

PART XII

The Dead Zone

36.

THE COTTONWOOD TREES ALONG the river waved like flags, their leaves struck yellow and flapping in the breeze that came down out of the north, not much to look at really, but to Colter, running, it was the most beautiful sight he'd ever seen. He was bloodied, his feet were like pincushions and his legs were growing heavier, and yet with each stride he was closer to making it out of this alive. He was within sight of the river now and the Indians were somewhere behind him. Hooting. Cursing. Running as fast as their legs could carry them, reinvigorated by hate and the thirst for revenge. If before this was all a kind of game to them, now it had gotten personal.

Colter never broke stride, the dried-out scrub giving way to the denser vegetation of the riverbank, to dogwood, sumac, wild grape and the shining coppery leaves of poison ivy, then to the weeds and sedges taking root in the sandbars, then to damp earth, then to mud, and in the next moment he was launching himself into the water in a knifing fluid dive. It was a shock. The water, snowmelt from the big blunt mountains above, was like liquid ice, but Colter was generating his own kind of heat, beating across the river to an island that had been pushed up out of the current in a time of flood. There was a huge raft of uprooted trees there, hundreds of them, the whole interlarded with smaller debris, and that was what he was making for. And what was he thinking, his brain fueled by the adrenaline of the chase that was like cocaine running through his veins? He was thinking that if he could get to that heap of debris before the Indians appeared on the bank, he could find a place somewhere in the water beneath it to hide himself. Of course, that was a big if, because he could hear them shrieking now, pounding closer, sure they would find him floundering in some backwater where he'd be as easy to spear as a buffalo fish.

He was almost there, the thatch of logs taking on color and dimension, the bark slick and black, branches splintered and trailing in the water and the water dark and swift where it fought to pull the whole mess back out into the river. Snatching a breath, he plunged under, gliding like a beaver, but this was no beaver lodge and he couldn't find a place to surface and breathe. Desperate, his lungs burning, he had no choice but to back out and thrust his head up again even as his eyes raked the shore: if they saw him, he was doomed. No one there yet. But here they came, hooting, hooting. He took the deepest breath he could hold and went back down again, feeling along the bottom of the pile for a gap, a hole, a crevice, and still nothing. Were his lungs bursting? Yes, yes, they were, but he kept on, his hands frantically digging at the debris, ready to drown rather than give himself up, but he was Colter and he was legendary and to be legendary you had to be lucky too. And he was. At the last possible moment, when he was about to give up and fill his lungs with another medium altogether, the medium only fish could make use of, not humans, he found an air pocket and surfaced.

He was too worked up to feel the terrible life-sucking chill of that water yet and because he was Colter and because he'd escaped, at least for the moment, he couldn't help smiling to himself there in that dark hole where the water-run thatch filtered the light and held him in tenuous suspension. Their voices came to him then, the war whoops giving way to a querulous snarl of disbelief as they came to the deserted bank and saw that their quarry had eluded them, and though he couldn't fully understand what they were saying, there was a lot of blame being thrown around, a lot of contention. Some of the braves, judging from the direction of their voices, had already started down the bank, poking through the reeds, searching the shallows, straining their eyes to see the glistening ball of his head bobbing with the current so they could draw a bead on it and put an arrow through one ear and out the other. Let them go. That was fine with him. He smiled wider.

But then he froze. There was a noise above him, a heavy footfall, voices. Two, three, four of them had apparently swum across to the island and they were probing the raft, tearing at branches now, thrusting their spears into the gaps and all the while jabbering and arguing with each other, probably along the lines of *You shithead* and *I told you so*. That was a hard moment. Colter never made a sound, even when a spear thrust came within a foot of him. He barely even breathed. What he was thinking was that one of them would get in the water and start searching the underside of the pile, same as he had, and his mind started playing tricks with him, the water itself, the very branches, feeling like the skin of an enemy come to discover him. But no enemy discovered him and a good thing too because that brave, though he might have sent up the alarm, would have been throttled and drowned in a heartbeat.

All right. But Colter was shivering now and they didn't seem to be moving on. They kept jabbering and arguing and tugging at one log or another, and that was when a new thought entered his head: What if they set fire to the raft? Wasn't that the way to flush out a rat? He'd die of smoke inhalation before the flames even got to him because he wasn't going to move no matter what—he'd rather go that way, rather burn if it came to it, than give them the satisfaction of flushing him out so they could spear him like a muskrat. That water was cold. Cold enough to induce hyperventilation. Cold enough to kill. And they weren't going away. On the positive side, though, they didn't seem inclined to come into the water and get underneath the thing—and they didn't seem to want to bother setting fire to the whole business. Or maybe they just didn't think of it, maybe that was it.

Three hours. That was how long Colter stayed under that raft.

Eventually the braves treading overhead moved on to search the rest of the island and probe both banks going upstream and down, looking for the place where he would have left the water. They didn't find that place, of course, because he hadn't left the water and now night was coming on. How did Colter survive? Once they'd moved on and he calculated it was safe, he began to widen the crevice he'd found so that eventually he was able to raise his torso out of the water, though it took a feat of strength and determination to hold himself there till his muscles must have locked on him. Plus, he was still naked and still shivering and he had no sustenance of any kind or any way to get it.

When it was fully dark and he hadn't heard a voice for as long as he could remember, Colter slipped out from beneath the debris—and what fortitude it must have taken to get *back* in that water, what toughness, what balls—and started downstream, careful to keep his hands beneath the surface so as to make as little noise as possible, to make no noise, to let the river carry him through a long looping mile till finally he could make his way out of the water and up the bank and hide himself in the bushes. Could he rest? Could he pluck the cactus spines out of his feet and wrap his feet in bark? Eat? Sleep? No, of course not. He had to run and keep running because they would be on his trail at first light.

37.

HE LAUGHED TOO, SAME as Colter, because they might have squeezed him into a tight spot but he outwitted them and one-upped them royally—piss on them, really, just piss on them—because for all their swagger and body armor and big-time SWAT-team training they were just bloated Dorito-sucking Boy Scouts who sat around on their couches all day long with a remote in their hand while he double-timed it up the ravines and climbed sheer cliffs with only his boots and his fingernails just to show himself he could do it. And he could. And he did. All the time. So maybe they had the element of surprise when he was coming up that trail that cut across the logging road all the way down there where he'd tried to set up Camp 2 before the alien came slamming out of his car and lost his life for it and maybe he wasn't as alert as he should have been because he was listening to a raven at that moment and having a real breakthrough like Doctor Dolittle because he could understand what it was saying and what it was saying was *Meat here, meat, but it's mine, mine, mine.* Okay. So if he wasn't exactly taken by surprise, he had to admit he was *surprised* to see the two cop vans there and the cops themselves hauling their crap out of the back and restraining their dog on a leash because the hostiles were massing and they might as well have been Blackfeet warriors for all it mattered to him.

One of them saw him, eye-to-eye, right there where the path cut across the road, not two hundred feet away. "Halt!" the alien shouted. "Drop your weapon!" And here were all the other aliens another hundred feet beyond that, clustered by the vans without even the most basic regard for tactical advantage or even protecting their rear, and they all swung their heads like elongated lizards in his direction. The raven fell silent. And a good thing too, because in the next instant the Norinco was doing the talking, and if he missed the alien that was his failure and he might have cursed himself for it but the alien missed him too, *chukka chukka,* the bark just flying off the trees.

Now it got good. Because he was gone like smoke, and not running from them the way they would have expected, but driving through the undergrowth on silent feet, hurtling really, almost flying as if he'd gotten inside the raven and mastered its spirit, and while they were all down on their bellies in the dirt of the road and training their weapons on the place he'd already vacated, he was moving into position behind them, and it was only the weird angle of the shot and the sun in his eyes that prevented another alien from biting the dust. It was *that* close. The initial burst must have passed right between two of them because he saw it slam into the van—pepper it, peppered van, peppered Potts—and the next burst chew up the dirt while they scrambled mad to cover their sorry asses. Okay. Okay. Time to suck it up and run like Colter. Which he did before they set the dog on him because he knew enough to understand how important it was to put distance between him and them before the dog got into the act.

He ran. And if he was wearing the smaller pack, the daypack, which didn't really have all that much vital matériel in it—a bottle of gin he'd liberated from a cabin just that morning before dawn though he didn't even like gin, plus some Hershey's Kisses and .22 shells and whatnot—that was all to the good. It just meant he could go faster. It just meant that the full pack, the one with all his essentials, the lion's share of his ammo, his razor, the packets of food and his two Colter paperbacks, was safe back at Camp 2, the real and actual Camp 2, not the aborted one, the camp they'd never find even if they had a whole pack of dogs. Which they didn't. Anyway, he was running, and he'd probably gone a mile, more than a mile, before the dog came for him.

He was in a ravine, a cut sharp as a knife blade, the creek there shifting and shimmering and a whole lot of water-run debris scattered along its length like pick-up sticks, when here came the dog, humping fast and absolutely silent but maybe having trouble with the debris, with getting over and under and around the logs and the quick-grabbing branches, but a quadruped for all that and everybody knew that four legs were better than two. The fastest human alive, the Olympic champion, ran the hundred-meter sprint in just under ten seconds and a dog could do it in half that. Nobody could outrun a dog. Not even Colter. But what the aliens didn't figure on here is that a human being is a whole lot smarter than a dog, even a big-shouldered fur-fanned thing like this Malinois coming up the ravine, and that a human being, if he's trained and resourceful enough and can keep his head in a tight situation, can slam that dog in the face with his backpack and let the dog with his three-hundred-pound bite force take hold of that while the human being, with nothing other than his boots and fingernails, scales the cliff right here in front of him. And let's see the dog do that. Let's see him grow wings. Let's see him race on back to the aliens with a back-pack clenched in his jaws and find out whether they're going to feed him his kibble for being such a good dog or just take him out and shoot him because he failed in his mission. Because he's stupid. Because he's a dog.

That was one day. The day the war started in true and earnest. And the next day, the very next day, he was fifteen miles to the south, on the other side of the Noyo, raiding cabins to get whatever he wanted, whether it was booze (no more gin, gin was shit) or canned peaches or toilet paper to wipe his ass with. The cops were nothing to him. They were clowns, fools, amateurs. And if one of those cabins had a security camera videotaping everything coming in and out the front door he didn't rip it off its support and smash it with the butt of the Norinco, which he could easily have done and thought about doing too. Instead, he just brought

his face right up to it and gave the camera a big shit-eating grin.
Then he backed off a couple of feet, just to get things in propor-
tion, and gave them the finger, two fingers, one on each hand,
jabbing at the air in a long withering *Fuck you!*

Some nights passed. Days too. It might have rained. He kept
going, every day, all day, and half the nights, and every time he
circled back to Camp 2, the only camp left to him now since
Art Tolleson and the Dog-Face had blown his cover at Camp 1,
which was its own kind of disaster because he'd been weak and
stupid and unprepared and had let the Dog-Face get away so it
was absolutely one hundred percent certain the pigs had tramped
in to confiscate his plants and his supplies and everything else he
had there, he settled in beneath the camo tarp over his new and
improved bunker and ate his meals cold and slept with real satisfaction. He could have used more drugs, though he had found
and liberated a fat prescription bottle of medical marijuana (Pink
Kush) from one of the cabins he'd broken into, so he was all right
there, at least for the time being.

But what was it like? What was it like now, finally, to be
running—or more to the point, what was it like in the dark, the
dark absolute, in the nights that were getting longer and colder
too and no recourse but to lie there huddled in the Boy Scout
sleeping bag and see his grandmother hovering over him, see Sara
with her big tits, see faces come out of the rain, people are strange,
see Colter, see the Blackfeet in their paint, see his own self lift out
of his body to drift over the whole continuous redwood forest and
watch the hostiles scramble below in their vans and body armor
with their dogs at their side and their weapons laid out like an
armory? It was like peace. Like a kind of peace.

In a way it was like the scene at the Chinese consulate, or the
scene he'd hoped for, anyway. He'd been suing for peace, that was
what he'd been doing, but the Chinese were aliens and the aliens

were the new hostiles and they saw it as an act of war. Unfortunately. Because when you're fired upon, you fire back, don't you?
That was a no-brainer. Fight fire with fire, come out swinging
and may the best man win. What he'd done was drive across the
Golden Gate Bridge and into San Francisco where he'd been all
those times with Cody and some of his other buds when they
were still his buds, cruising North Beach, scoring drugs, watching totally nude women on a little stage shaking their big tits and
not-so-big tits, eating what, pot stickers, *Chinese* dumplings, and
washing it down with Tsingtao and that weird Chinese liquor
that smelled like dirty underwear. This time he was alone. And it
must have been before the playground thing because he still had
his car then.

The idea he had was to make peace with them, the Chinese,
so he could get them to divulge their secrets, which must have
involved some kind of portal (okay, maybe he wasn't thinking
absolutely as clearly as the shrink with his meds would have
wanted him to, and maybe it was kind of sci-fi, but then the
whole slithering browned-out world was sci-fi, wasn't it?). Plus,
they were ninjas and he had a ninja suit he'd got as a kid for Halloween one year and he figured he'd return that to them, along
with the Chinese Communist stars he'd made out of cardboard
with red foil stretched over it, as a gesture. As a peace offering.
If they took it, there was no need to go to war, no need to run
naked across the plain. Save your spears. Save your war whoops.
Lock up the pigs.

So what he did, late, very late, was drive around till he found
a parking spot, which had to be in somebody's driveway because
that city goes to bed early and every parking spot on every street
is gone and done by eleven o'clock and how anybody could live
with that, with the crowding and shitting and the noise, was
beyond anything he could imagine. He was dressed in black.
He was wearing a black watchcap too and he'd used greasepaint
under his eyes. The wall was a wall. And no, he wasn't going to

scale it, though he could have gone right up and over it as if it wasn't even there at all. No need for that—and he was thinking clearly at that point—because who knew how they would take it. You didn't just blow into a Blackfoot village and expect them to like it, especially if you weren't an alien but just somebody interested in what, *communication*? He tossed the ninja suit (pajamas, really) and the stars over the wall, the stars in several places, all the way around, and that would have been it except they had their cameras going and before he knew it the pigs were there with their patrol cars and their guns drawn and *Down on the ground* and *Show me your hands*. So it wasn't peaceful. And that, right there, went a long way to explaining how things had come to this pass, to war, all-out war. Take no prisoners. Or if you did, make sure you skinned them alive.

And then there was a day after a night when he'd seen and heard things he didn't really like and the tarp over the bunker kept changing shape on him and it rained again and he woke up feeling sick, not giardia sick, but with something like what they called a general malaise, and wasn't he an officer in the Union Army, General Malaise? That was what he used to joke to Cody when he was reading about the Union troops after the war who went out to take on the hostiles a whole lifetime after Colter was gone—*Hey,* he'd say, *I'm General Malaise, who are you?* It was a whole routine, something you could act out when you were stoned. And they were always stoned. At least in high school. After that, he was on his own, because Cody was away in college and he was living with his grandmother because his father was a pain in the ass and his mother was his mother.

He woke up sick. Time had gone by, days and days of it. There was rain and then there wasn't rain. He'd run short of food and put himself on half rations, so maybe that was part of it, but sick or not, there was a war on and so he got up and had some cold hot cocoa and a pouch of some shit mixed with water, shouldered his pack and his rifle, and went out to reconnoiter.

What he wanted to do was get a little farther afield and find another cabin to break into, like that day with the old lady, but the hostiles were everywhere now—you couldn't go over a ridge and not hear their helicopters and walkie-talkies and sometimes even the barking of their dogs—and it was too dangerous, not strategic, not strategic at all. A voice told him to hump north, hump all night, every night, till he was fifty or even a hundred miles up the coast in a place where there were pristine cabins, cabins untouched since the part-timers and gray goats and summer people had left, where he could sleep and eat and shower to his heart's content, but another voice told him that that was running and you couldn't run forever. Even Colter, the greatest runner of them all, couldn't run forever.

Colter came out of that river shivering so hard he thought he was going to fracture his ribs, but the way to conquer the cold was to run and so he ran. All that night he ran, knowing they'd be on his trail in the morning. They'd look for him along the river, obviously, but that wasn't where they were going to find him. He made straight for the mountains, guided only by the stars that whitewashed the sky overhead till it got milky and gave way to dawn. How many miles he'd put between himself and his pursuers he couldn't say, but he must have lain down then and slept in fits, expecting at any moment to hear their footfalls on the shingle that lay scattered over the slope like cast-off teeth. He was chilled through to the bone and so he found a place protected from the wind where he could hunker against a slab of rock and let the sun warm him, but of course this was problematic too, not only because every moment of delay was a moment they were potentially gaining on him, but because he had to add sunburn to all his other issues. His face and hands were like leather, but the rest of him had never seen the light of day, save on those rare occasions when he went into one creek or another for a wash. Colter gave himself fifteen minutes maybe, then pushed himself on, not yet realizing that the Blackfeet had never found his trail, which was a mercy because the more he drove himself, the sooner he got back to civilization and the better his chances of survival.

Which were slim. And for any other man, anybody other than Colter—or maybe Glass—wouldn't have added up to anything more than zero. At any rate, Colter kept on, just as he had after he'd been wounded and left for dead by his so-called comrades, only this time he didn't have his rifle or his knife or any means to make fire. Or even clothes. Clothes to protect him from the sun in the day and the cold at night. It was three hundred miles to Fort Lisa on the Big Horn. You could probably drive it in five hours today. But on foot, shoeless, facing into the wind, it took Colter eleven days of nearly continuous walking—and he paused only to dig up the roots of the plant known as prairie turnip or peel bark from a tree just to have something on his stomach—before he saw the palisades of the fort rising out of the plain like an assertion of might and right and well-being.

On this day, though, the present-time Colter was hungry, though maybe nowhere near in the same ballpark as what the original must have experienced on that second trek back out of the wilderness, and he went off to see what he could find. He'd put out snares for rabbits, but for some reason he'd been unsuccessful in nailing any, and then he became paranoid about the traps themselves, thinking that maybe the hostiles had found them and were waiting there for him, turning a trap into a trap. Striking out in a new direction, away from town, away from where the cabins and regular houses too sprouted up along the back roads, he went east, paralleling Route 20 but giving it a good wide berth. He wasn't thinking of Sara, or not especially—it would be suicidal to try to get to her house—but just of seeing what was what out there, like maybe running across a daytime house on the outskirts of Willits where there was nobody home because they were at work or something like that. A place where they didn't have any dogs. Or neighbors. Or alarms. A place where maybe they'd left a window open or a door unlocked. A garage even.

A lot of people kept second refrigerators in their garages. Tools. Sometimes even guns, not that he needed another weapon, but if one came to hand—and a few rounds with it—why not?

He was beyond the noise now, beyond the helicopters and the squawk and squelch, legging uphill, up and up, nothing but trees around him and once in a while a meadow where there'd once been a clear-cut, but he skirted the meadows for tactical reasons. No sense in taking chances when all he was doing was taking chances because you had to be smart if you were going to be a one-man army. Like Colter. But these trees with the slivers of light caught up there in the tops of them like shining silver blades, they were the real thing, the thing that endures, and they'd been here long before Colter had gone into Yellowstone and if the aliens didn't get to them they'd be here long after everybody alive now was dead. His father. His mother. Sara, with her big tits. He saw those trees—maybe he'd been in this spot before, maybe not—and just stopped and looked up into them for so long he began to go outside of himself again so that the wheel slowed and there was no hurry and hassle and paranoia, no state of war, only wonder at how they could be and how they could pull down deep and hold all these mountains together, because they were the beginning of it all, weren't they? Or close enough.

What snapped him out of it wasn't a noise, but something else, and not his sixth sense either because there were no hostiles anywhere near him. It was the kind of thing that happens when you're dreaming awake and then come awake again, two textures, two worlds, slipping against each other like the plates that were one day going to slide this whole mountain range back into the ocean. Whatever it was, it made him feel refreshed suddenly, as if he'd been humping up a mountain peak in the Andes and been lifted off the snowfield and set down on the beach under a full warm tilting sun. He shook his head, tugged at the strap of his pack, and started off again.

It might have been another hour (again, time didn't matter,

not out here) and he figured he'd covered at least half the distance to Sara's, not that he was seriously considering showing up there, but just by way of figuring. That was when he came across what at first looked to be a natural clearing where maybe a couple of the giants had fallen and the understory had taken over, but which turned out to be something entirely different. It was a clearing, all right, but it had been made by humans—and not loggers, but growers. Suddenly all his senses were on alert. He'd been playing cat and mouse with the hostiles and their dogs and here he was just about to blunder into some cartel's plantation. They were outlaws too but they weren't mountain men. Not even close. They were campesinos maybe, farmers, or maybe just punks recruited to suffer a little downtime in the wild. They didn't like the hills or the trees or anything that scampered or swam or walked and breathed out here. They were scum. Booby-trappers. And they'd shoot you as soon as look at you, a whole new kind of hostile and they were worse than the Blackfeet because they didn't know the land and only wanted to rape it. For profit. Profit only.

The voice again, the one deep inside: *Skirt it. Get out.* But the wheel was spinning and the other voice was saying, *Fuck them. Because they can die too.* For a long while, he drifted from cover to cover on the fringes of the clearing, glassing the place, looking for movement. There was none. Not so much as a bird or squirrel. In fact, as he was coming to realize, this was an abandoned operation, already harvested, the land poisoned and the garbage piled high, an irregular plot that was just dead now, a dead zone, and it wasn't ever going to come back.

How did he feel about that? He felt that life was shit and more shit. He felt that aliens were aliens, no matter where you found them. He just wished he'd found them earlier, right in the act, so the Norinco could have had something to say about it.

38.

THE COPS MIGHT HAVE been thick as locusts—or cock-roaches, thick as cockroaches—but their ranks thinned out con-siderably the higher he climbed. He came up out of the dead zone shaking his head in disgust, all that crap, all that waste, poisons and pesticides and every can and wrapper of every bite they'd taken just screaming there where they'd dropped it and not even burned up in a fire ring, which even the Boy Scouts would have employed, a new tribe of hostiles up here and what were the cops and the fly fishermen and the Sierra Club nerds going to do about *them*? It was getting dark, dark below already, but the light lingering here toward the crest. Double time, hut one, hut two. He moved like a spirit, moved like Colter, and the only thing that worried him now was the drones because you had no defense against drones. They were up there, way up there, alien spacecraft, *Made in China,* and before you suspected anything you were just meat. But still, you had to look on the bright side, and the bright side was this: it was a whole lot easier to use drones on ragheads out in the treeless desert than it was here, where the BIGGEST LIVING THINGS ON EARTH threw up their branches to shelter everything beneath. Everything that wasn't already dead and poisoned, that is.

It was full dark by the time he reached the field across from her house because that was where he was going whether he wanted to admit it or not and he spent a whole lot of time there on his belly, glassing everything, and it was just like that night when they'd come to get her personal things because the aliens wouldn't let them come in daylight. He felt sick still, but he chalked that up to the fact that he was hungry, starving really, just like Colter coming up naked and filthy and sore-footed on Fort Lisa. She'd make him pasta, that was what he was thinking, and then he'd fuck her in the dark and sleep in her bed and have a shower and be gone before the sun came up. The problem was the aliens. They might have thinned out their ranks way up here on the outskirts of Willits, but there was that patrol car parked up on the shoulder of the road under cover of a big flat-topped bush, and who did they think they were fooling? Willits Police. The County Sheriff. SWAT and swat again. He could have picked them off without even trying, putting two neat holes in the windshield, one on each side, just over the dash, two rounds and done with it. But he didn't want that. He wanted Sara.

So what he did was wait while everything alive spoke to him from the deep grass and the bushes and the hollows in the dirt. Crickets. And scorpions too, rustling around in their hard shiny shells, looking for something to paralyze with that big stinger so they could have some food to put in their stomachs, same as anything else. After a while, and they were talking their many languages, he could begin to understand them, to hear them clearly, and what were they saying? They were saying *Make War, Not Love*. Because they were at war down there too, war that began the minute they hatched from their eggs or crawled out of their mother's body, eat or be eaten and then go ahead and sing about it. Spiders there too, the big quick wolf spiders that made their meal of anything they could catch and overpower. And what if one of them climbed up the inside of his pantleg and bit him? What if a scorpion lanced him with that wicked stinger? He'd enjoy it. He'd welcome it. At least it would wake him up because he'd been here now, flat out on his belly, for the whole of his life.

And then some alien shut the lights out in the house up the hill from hers and the dark rushed in to fill the void and he was crawling, his weapon at the ready, crawling all the way across that field like he was in ambush training, like he was his father in Vietnam, inch by inch and nothing for anybody to see because he was invisible. Even from the drones. He had to rise to a running crouch when he crossed the road because he couldn't risk lingering there where some car might come along with its lights and tires and three thousand pounds of steel and glass and plastic that no thing made out of flesh could resist. A car. People drove cars. He used to drive a car. But now he was in the fringe of bushes that separated her house from the house of the aliens on the hill, back to the belly, back to the crawl, and of course there was a window open in the bedroom, coolish night or not, because she liked to feel the fresh air on her face when she went to bed.

She was sitting in front of the TV. The TV flickered like gunfire. The dog, Rasta dog, cool dog, just lay wrapped up in dog oblivion, hear no evil, smell none either. "Turn out the lights," he said.

"Adam," she said.

"Do it," he said.

And then there was a whole lot of discussion, but he didn't want discussion, he wanted spaghetti and meatballs, he wanted 151, he wanted her, her big tits, her wet cunt, wanted a shower, wanted bed, wanted surcease. Or a treaty. At least for tonight. "I want to sleep with you," he said. She said no. She said she was going to call the police if he didn't get out. All that made him feel very weary, weary and depressed, and where was the person he used to be, the one who humped planting soil and good rich guano out to his plantation with nothing more than a good strong back, who had a grandmother and a life and built walls and one-upped the hostiles everywhere he went?

"You're not going to call the police," he said.

"I am. I swear I am."

"I don't believe you."

"Just try me."

He tried her.

She didn't call.

What she did was give him a look that brought out all the

lines in her face because she was old, never forget that, and then she got up and flicked off the sound on the TV, though the images still jumped and shifted there on the screen till he had a moment when he couldn't really tell what was the TV and what was the room. With her in it. And the stove. And the dog. Then she came over and took his hand, her touch there, softest thing, and led him into the kitchen. What she said was, "Right after you eat, you promise me, you're out of here."

This was funny, because that wasn't what was going to happen and they both knew it, and so he started laughing then, or sniggering, actually. Through his nose.

"What?" she said. "What's so funny?" And she was smiling for the first time since he'd walked into the room, her big soft lips spreading open across her teeth that were like polished stones in the weak light dropping out of the fixture recessed in the hood of the stove.

"First things first."

"First things?"

"Or second things. First we eat, then we go into the bedroom."

He might have fallen asleep. He did. He definitely did. Because she was there, shaking him awake, her voice drawn down to a whisper. "It's quarter past four," she said.

Black dark. Dog on the floor. Light from the clock.

"I washed your clothes."

He didn't say anything. And he didn't want to get up out of that bed but he had to. First thing he did, after he got dressed and laced up his boots, was check the Norinco, eject the magazine and shove it home again. Then he shouldered the pack that had crackers in it, a loaf of bread, canned tuna, Campbell's Chunky Chicken Corn Chowder, a bottle of red wine with a yellow fish on the label he'd go through in an hour. It was very still. The dog never stirred. And she was there, giving him a look in the gray ghosted light that was like a look of sorrow, as if she knew what was coming. He knew what was coming too. But he was a soldier. He was Colter. And when he went out the door he never looked back.

Yes. And this time he just humped across that road and that field on his two windmilling legs, no more belly-crawling for him, and if the aliens in that cruiser were awake and watching, he was ready, more than ready, *to engage the enemy.* But they weren't awake and they weren't watching. Maybe they weren't even there. So what he had was freedom, back down into the cleft of that canyon, the light opening up around him and nobody and nothing to say where he could or couldn't go. Maybe he would head north. Or maybe just go back to camp and wait them out. They were pussies, they were amateurs. Once winter came on, really came on, when it rained like the deluge, the original deluge that came after the original Adam, the somebody Adam, the legendary Adam, they'd forget all about him and go back to their TV remotes and their fat wives and their fat kids and, what, fat dogs too.

But the thing was, even Colter turned soft, and that was something he could never figure. Or stomach. The whole idea of it was like a sharp stick dipped in the bitterest thing there was and jabbed right through him. He just couldn't understand how Colter, after all his feats, after his *run,* could just give it all up and go back to civilization, to a woman named Sallie who probably wasn't even that good-looking, and live on a farm busting sod like anybody. And just die there, in bed, of jaundice, on a morning that lit the hills, May 7, 1812, when the Blackfeet and the Crows and all the rest of the hostiles were out after the buffalo where the buffalo grazed the spring grass and no white man dared tread.

That was how it turned out. That was how it always turned out. For everybody on this planet. You could be made out of wood and they'd set you on fire. You could be made of steel and they'd hose you down till the rust got you. You could be Colter and give up and die in bed. There was no way out and it didn't really matter. You just had to be as hard as hard and make your own legend and let the chips fall where they may. That was what he was thinking and then he wasn't thinking anymore, just letting the wheel spin and his legs conquer the ground, faster and faster, hut one, hut two, and if he didn't see the two snipers camouflaged in the big mottled arms of a sycamore climbing up out of the streambed in a thick pale grove of them, that didn't matter either.

His feet hit the dirt, his elbows pumped, double time, triple time, hostiles on the loose, hut one, hut two, got to go, got to go, the wheel churning faster and faster, and he was running now, running like Colter . . . and then, abruptly, it stopped. The wheel stopped. And it was never going to start again.

PART XIII

Little River

39.

THE WINTER RAINS CAME and buried everything. They swelled the streams, scoured the ravines, drove deep to refresh the roots of the big sentinel trees that stood watch over the forest and climbed steadily up into the greening hills. Botanists put on their slickers and went out to take core samples and hoist themselves three hundred feet up into the canopy to measure the new season's growth and biologists set up bait stations to collect hair samples of fox and marten for DNA analysis. Fishermen fished. Drinkers drank. It wasn't the tourist season, but a few people ventured up the coast from the Bay Area, mainly on weekends and mainly to stroll arm-in-arm up and down the six streets of Mendocino village, and the Skunk Train started hauling tourists up the Noyo Valley again, though on the usual limited winter schedule.

After the funeral back in the fall, Carolee went to stay with her sister in Newbury Park for a few days, and when she returned, looking haggard, looking unrested and every bit as tragic as when she'd left, she kept harping on the theme of traveling, of getting out and seeing the world. Just a trip. Anywhere. If only to get out of town for a while because she couldn't take the way people looked at her wherever she went, whether it was the library or the post office or just picking up the dry cleaning, and Sten felt as burdened as she did and gave in without much of a fight. They wound up driving down to Death Valley for the wildflower bloom at the end of February and then continued on to Las Vegas to throw money away and watch some overpriced idiotic revue he could have done without, once and forever. What he said to her was, "This is just like the cruise ship, except it's floating on dirt instead of water."

And she said, "Without the world-class indulgence," smiling when she said it, because she was beginning to climb up out of the pit Adam had dug, the steps and handholds shaky at first but firming up as the days passed. They came home to an empty house, but then the house had been empty of Adam for years now, and if Carolee had ever harbored any dreams of grandchildren, whether produced by Sara Hovarty Jennings or some other woman unstable enough to hook up with their son, those dreams were buried now too. It was for the better, it really was, and he told her that, though he meant it to be comforting and not just purely cold-blooded. The truth was, he couldn't imagine going through this all over again and couldn't even begin to guess at what a child of that union, of Sara and Adam, would have had to cope with. Or no, he could. And that was why, all things considered, Adam's death had been a kind of blessing, the true blessing, and not his odds-defying birth or the sweetness of his early childhood or the sense of completeness this kicking perfect blue-eyed baby lying there in his cradle had given them. He was their son, evidence in the flesh of the interlocking of the genes they'd separately inherited, genes their parents and parents' parents had held on to through all the generations there ever were. More biology. *Reproductio ad absurdum*. Adam, the product of an older mother. An old mother.

He could adapt. Carolee could adapt too. But the thing that lingered longer than the sorrow, the thing he just couldn't shake, was the shame. It was like a dream you can't wake from, the vision of himself up there on the stage in the high school auditorium, urging everyone to remain calm and not rush off on some sort of witch hunt. Or chasing down those Mexicans with Carey, dead Carey, posturing beside him. Sitting there at the picnic table and trying to deny the evidence Rob Rankin presented in his little plastic bags. Living with the guilt. He wasn't used to hanging his head or ducking away from anybody, all his life one of the big men in town, from his years on the football field in high school to his return as a decorated veteran and then a college grad working his way up from history teacher to assistant principal and finally principal and master of all he surveyed. He tried to be bigger than the shame, tried to get on with his life, but he found he couldn't really face people anymore, couldn't look anybody in the eye, even strangers, without wondering if they knew and how much they knew—it got to the point where he began to think there was no other solution but to pack up and move. Sun City, in Arizona, wasn't that where old people went? Or Florida. What was wrong with Florida?

He came in from a walk one afternoon, his mind churning over the possibilities, and sat Carolee down and told her there was no other way, they were just going to have to move.

"Move?" she'd said. "Where? I mean, we practically just moved in here, didn't we?"

"What about Florida?"

"Florida? Are you crazy? The tropics? You really want to go to the tropics?"

He shrugged, let her see his open palms. He was just thinking out loud, that was all, exploring the possibilities. "I don't know. Up the coast, maybe. Eureka. What's wrong with Eureka?"

"Another broken-down mill town? We don't know anybody there, not a soul."

"Right," he said. "That's what I mean."

Well, they'd put that on hold, because in a time of crisis, a time like this, it was ill-advised to make rash decisions, everybody said that. So they did the little things that make up a life, anybody's life, cooking, eating, running the dishwasher, sitting by the window with a book, knocking the mud from the soles of your boots, building a fire at night and staring into it with a cocktail clenched in your fist. Going to bed. Getting up. Watching the rain. Watching the sun. Watching the flies crawl up the windowpane.

She couldn't go back to volunteering at the preserve, not after the way the Burnsides had turned on her, and he couldn't very well go out patrolling timber company property anymore, for obvious reasons. He wouldn't have wanted to, in any case. In fact, he looked up into those mountains from the back window and saw nothing there that was even remotely attractive to him, not anymore. If he hiked, he hiked the beach. And if he wanted exercise—and he did, because he wasn't dead yet—he went out on the golf course. The golf course. He never thought he'd sink so low, but he did, like every other old duffer across the land. And what was golf but a way to fight off the desperation?

On this particular day, a day in the first week of April when the sun broke through early along the coast and Carolee was sleeping late, which was a mercy in itself, he tossed his clubs in the trunk and drove the two miles south to Little River and the course there, which was only nine holes, but nine holes were plenty as far as he was concerned. Until the past month, he hadn't touched a club since he was a teenager and back then he'd never got much past the thrill of whacking the hell out of the ball, whether it was on the first tee or at a driving range. He remembered that, the driving range, how he and his buddies—R.J. Call, Rick Wiley, Mark Stowhouse—would down a couple of beers and compete to see who could send that little white sphere the farthest, over the nets even and into the field beyond. Hit it hard, that was all that mattered to them, and as far as the subtleties of strategy and making par, the irons, putting—playing the game to win—they could perfect all that later. When they were old.

Well, now he was old. Now he was an old white man with sunburned kneecaps lifting a golf bag out of the trunk of his car and trudging across the parking lot to the first tee, and if he didn't have a partner it was because he didn't want one. He didn't need chatter, he didn't need companionship, or not yet, anyway. What he needed was to get out of the house and that was what he was doing on this bright early morning when there was no one stirring but him and maybe the odd squirrel. The course looked out to sea, where the mouth of Little River opened up on the waves, and there were always seabirds here, pelicans gliding overhead as if they were being drawn on a string, gulls fixed to the roof of the Little River Inn like replicas or perched atop the flag at one hole or another and messing the green with the long trailing white stripes of their guano.

For a long while he sat on the bench behind the first hole, sipping the coffee he'd brought along in a thermos, crossing and uncrossing his legs, reaching back to adjust his hair in the grip of the rubber band he used to bind it up in back. The clubs, a cheap set they'd bought for Adam one Christmas when he was eleven or twelve, thinking to interest him in something beyond video games, sat propped against the bench. It was chilly, with a light breeze coming in off the water, something he'd have to account for when he was driving the ball. When he got to it. He turned up the collar of his jacket and stared out across the fairways and the greens that were so bright they seemed lit from within, all the way out to sea, where a pair of fishing boats stood like signposts at the place where sea and sky came together.

He was thinking about a day not too much different from this one, a week or so ago (he couldn't really say because there wasn't much to distinguish one day from another, light in the morning, dark at night, and whatever went on in between). Carolee had wanted to do some shopping up in Willits—or not shopping, really, but just cruising the various junk shops in the hope of finding treasure there, whether it be in the form of somebody's dead grandmother's crocheted doilies or salt and pepper shakers molded in the shape of Scottie dogs—and he'd agreed to come along just to do something and maybe take her out to lunch someplace.

He dropped her off and drove around a while, seeing things he'd never had time to see before, mostly signs of decay, empty storefronts, ruptured sidewalks, graffiti scrawled on the cornerstones of the buildings along the main drag, the big hopeful welcome-to-the-world banner that loomed over the road in promise and challenge both: *Willits, Gateway to the Redwoods.* He

went to the hardware store, though he really didn't need anything, and poked around there for a while, then he sat on a chair
outside one of the antique shops and tried to read a paperback
book he'd brought along to ease the tedium because he was determined to give Carolee as much time as she wanted to sift through
whatever the tourists and the newly dead had left behind. Finally,
he just wandered up and down the street, peering in store windows, watching the traffic gather at the lights, thinking, as old
people do, of lunch.

Carolee wasn't answering her cellphone. An hour of his life
had marched on into oblivion. His stomach began to act up on
him—acid stomach, exacerbated by the coffee and booze that
seemed to round out his life, morning and evening, like prayers—
and he told himself he was hungry, that was all. It was one o'clock.
He'd planned on taking Carolee to the Mexican restaurant, the
nice one, but he found himself getting back in the car and running over to the fast-food place at the top of Route 20, just to get
something to hold him, a burger, chicken sandwich, anything.
Whopper. Maybe he'd get a Whopper.

The place was crowded, a fact that normally would have
driven him up a wall. He'd spent his whole life being impatient,
expecting everybody to clear out of his way, the slow drivers to
pull over and the crowds, wherever they were—the movies, the
ballpark, the airport—to gather some other time, some other day
and hour when he wasn't there to share the planet with them.
He was always cursing under his breath, always wound up, but
not now, not today. Today he had all the time in the world. Of
course, the dropouts behind the counter moved as if their feet
had been nailed to the floor, but finally the line in front of him
dwindled down to just him and he put in his order and went over
to the fountain to pour himself a small drink, eyeing a table by
the window where somebody had left a newspaper. He was just
making his way toward it when he glanced down the row and saw
Sara there, sitting at a table by herself, a half-eaten sandwich at her

elbow. She was dressed in her work clothes—jeans, boots and a long-sleeved shirt, and her apron, her leather apron—and she had her head down, absorbed in some sort of pamphlet. She seemed to have gained weight. Or maybe not. He couldn't really remember.

It was an awkward moment. He didn't want to see her, didn't want to talk to her, didn't want anything to do with her, but there he was, going down the very aisle of disarranged plastic tables where she was sitting, and he thought about swinging around and just walking right out of the place, getting in the car and forgetting about the whole thing—Whopper, did he really need a Whopper?—but he didn't. He just continued on down the aisle, trying to slip past her, but at the last moment she lifted her face to him. "Sara?" he heard himself say.

Her eyes were adrift, soft and unfocused, and he watched them narrow to take him in. "Oh, hi," she said, her voice so throaty and soft it was barely present.

"You all right?"

She shrugged. "Not really. You?"

"Day to day. Carolee's still not over it, if she's ever going to be. Which I doubt. But life goes on, right?"

She didn't answer. Just dipped her head to take a bite of her sandwich as if she'd suddenly remembered what she was doing there. The door opened and closed. People drifted in, drifted out. "You want to know the truth, I've had it," she said, glancing up at him again. "Soon as I can manage it I'm out of here."

He was standing awkwardly in the middle of the room, nothing more to say, really, but something he couldn't name held him there. He shifted his weight. Watched her chew.

"I'm thinking Nevada or maybe Wyoming? Someplace where you can live free without all this Big Brother crap. I've had it. Really, I've just had it."

He didn't know what to say to this and if he nodded his head it wasn't in agreement or sympathy but only just to work the muscles at the back of his neck. Things came toppling down on you, whole mountainsides, and there was nothing anybody could do about it. If you were lucky—very, very lucky—you got to step out of the way. "Yeah," he said finally, his breath released in a drawn-out sigh, and he opened his palm and closed it again, bye-bye. "You have a nice day now."

"You too," she said, and he was already moving down the aisle.

It was nothing, just a moment cookie-cuttered out of his day, but it was enough to see the look of hurt and incomprehension on her face and to brush it off too. How long had she known Adam? A couple of months. What was a couple of months? Nothing. A memory, a whisper, pages flapping in the breeze. He settled in at the table in back and picked up the discarded paper. When he looked up again, she was gone.

He was the one who'd had to identify Adam's body, never any question that it was up to him and him alone because he wasn't going to expose Carolee to that. It was there in a drawer at the morgue—*he* was there, Adam—looking as if he was asleep. There wasn't a mark on his face but for a thin welt that might have been a rope burn, and what Sten was feeling in that moment was hard to contain. He'd seen corpses before, laid out on the ground, their lifeless faces turned to the sky, awaiting body bags and a chopper and then a flight back to the States, but they hadn't prepared him for this. He didn't break down, but it was close. Standing there alone in that room with its unnatural cold and the smell of chlorine bleach so harsh and pervasive it was like a public urinal, he fought to contain himself, because there was another odor beneath it and it wasn't of the flesh or of its fluids, but of fear. Fear and regret. And what did that smell like? Like the body's essence.

What he was remembering was Adam's first day at the high school, freshman year, the teachers just back from summer vacation, everybody trying to settle in, the students decked out in their new skirts and jeans and oversized T-shirts, electric with excitement. First day. The whole year to look forward to, the ritual starting over again in a stew of hormones, timeless and immemorial. Math, history, the ballgame, senior prom, elections, lunch, gym class. There were never any fights the first day, never any discipline problems—everything was too new and everybody on their best behavior. Except for Adam. Within the first hour he was in the office, hauled in by Joe Buteo, the assistant principal, the enforcer. Adam had been in a fight. The other kid—a stranger to him as far as anybody knew—hadn't done anything to provoke him. They were in the hallway between classes and Adam had seen something he didn't like, something he couldn't tolerate, some vision, some hallucination, and it was the other kid's misfortune to have been part of it. It had taken two teachers to restrain Adam. The other kid—his victim, a junior twice his size who'd never caused anybody any trouble—had lost a tooth in front and his shirt was like a bloody flag.

Sten didn't say anything, not then—this was the assistant principal's job and he certainly didn't want to give any impression of favoritism when it came to his own son—but when he got home you can be sure he laid into him. First thing. He came through the front door and stalked down the hall to his son's room and he didn't pause to knock either.

Adam was wearing a look that was to become habitual with him, his eyes hooded, his mouth drawn tight. He was in his dreadlock phase then, his hair matted and looped and hanging like brush in his face. He had a magazine in his lap. He didn't even bother to look up.

Sten had never been violent with his son—violence didn't work because it just provoked resentment and resentment led to more violence, a whole downward spiral of it—but he was on the verge of it that night. The principal's son. First day of school. "What were you thinking?" he demanded. "You don't just go and attack people—what did he do, anyway? I'd like to hear that. I really would."

"That kid?" Adam said, and he hadn't moved. "He's an alien."

Nobody shouted out to him from that tree. Nobody said, "Throw down your weapon," or read him his rights. Shoot to kill, that was the order Rob gave because Rob was left with no other choice. Adam was armed and dangerous. He had his finger on the trigger. He'd come after them, stalked and fired on them—and worst of all, the unforgivable sin, he'd made them look bad. They'd fired twelve rounds, the two officers in the tree and their team member stretched out flat in the dirt with his rifle trained on the trail that wound down along the streambed there. Seven rounds went home, all in the torso, crack shots, these SWAT team studs, with hundreds of hours on the shooting range and a squeeze as gentle as held breath: Adam must have been dead before he hit the ground. He hadn't suffered. Hadn't even known what was coming. At least there was that.

But Sara was gone, pulling out of the lot now in her battered blue car, the fuzzy dog sticking its snout out the window, and they called his number and he went to the counter to pick up his order, everything too loud and too bright, people everywhere. His first thought was to go back to the table, but then the cell started buzzing in his pocket—Carolee—and he decided to detour out the door and go get her and take her to the nice place. He didn't want the burger anymore. He wasn't even hungry, not really.

"Hello?" he said, pinning the phone to his ear so he could hear over the noise as he pushed through the door and out into the lot.

His wife's voice, small and satisfied: "I'm ready."

"Where are you?"

"On Main? That place with the redwood carvings out front?"

"I'll be right there."

"Wait till you see what I found—just what I've been looking for."

"Really?"

"Uh-huh. Two of those yellow Bakelite bracelets to go with that amber pin you bought me?"

"That I bought you?" He loved to joke that he was always buying her things but never actually realized he'd done it till he saw them around her neck or dangling from her wrist.

"And these Art Deco linens with a tatted edge—in perfect condition—from like the thirties—"

He was going to say something like *Isn't that a little old for you—I mean, you didn't come along till the next decade, did you?*, but the glare of the lot hit him in the face and he lost the thread of it.

"Sten? Sten, are you there?"

"I'll be there in five," he said. "You be out front, okay?"

He was just strolling across the lot minding his own business, tangled up maybe over seeing Sara there and all that entailed, memories, tricks of memory, and when the pickup lurched back out of the space in front of him, it took him by surprise. He stepped awkwardly out of the way, his feet colliding and the bag, the Whopper, dropping to the pavement—he very nearly went down himself. It was just a moment, a random moment, but the truck's engine roared in neutral, stick shift, and here was the face of the driver, a punk with a shaved head and the tattoos every kid had to have now climbing up the back of his neck, and a stud, a silver stud, punched through one nostril. "Why don't you watch where you're going," the kid snarled. And then, gratuitously, as if that wasn't enough, he added, "Grandpa."

And here it came again—*boom!*—gasoline on the coals. He was five feet from him, from this kid who couldn't have been more than eighteen or nineteen, the apprentice tough guy, the clown in the truck with the big-dick tires. He should have just let it go but he couldn't. "Fuck you," he rasped, his voice clenched in his throat.

And now the kid, throwing it back at him—"Fuck you too!"—and what else could he say, pro forma, call and response, the same text, the old text, oldest there was?

He couldn't say "fuck you" one more time, couldn't stand

here under this sun, in this lot, at his age, and play this game, so
he just turned his back and listened to the hot squeal of the tires as
the victor shot triumphantly across the lot and lost himself in the
traffic heading down the hill to the coast.

Something awakened the gulls on the roof of the inn and they
rose in a sudden flap of wings to sail out across the parking lot
and the road beyond, fracturing the light. He pushed himself up,
hoisted the clubs and ambled over to the first tee, glad there was
no one around to observe him in his ineptitude. He was going to
whack a little white ball and then he was going to follow it around
for an hour or two and then he was going to go home and do
something else. He'd watched a couple of golf videos and he was
trying to improve his swing along the lines they laid out—head
still, feet apart, focus on the ball and not where it's going—but he
hadn't really made any gains and maybe didn't expect to. It was
enough just to be here, in the morning light, thumbing the tee
into the turf and balancing the ball atop it like an egg in a miniature cup.

He swiveled his hips. Arched his back. Took a practice swing
to loosen up. And then he tightened his grip, raised the club over
his shoulder and came down with everything he had. There was
the flat head of the club, there the ball, and he saw it so clearly it
was as if it had been caught in stop-time. He hit it. Hit it squarely,
hit it hard, and it wasn't a great shot or even a good one, but there
it was, looping up into the great vast ocean of the sky, and it kept
on going and kept on going.

About the Author

T. C. BOYLE is the *New York Times* bestselling author of ten collections of stories and fourteen novels, most recently, *San Miguel*, followed by the second volume of his collected stories, *T. C. Boyle Stories II*. His work has been translated into twenty-five languages and won a PEN/Faulkner Award for Fiction. He is a member of the Academy of Arts and Letters and lives in California.